# The Wreck Emerged

## JOSEPH V. WEBERS

MYRTLEWOOD PRESS

Published by: Myrtlewood Press, PO Box 978, Murfreesboro, TN 37133

First printing, August 2021

ISBN: 978-1-7371764-2-8 (paperback), 978-1-7371764-5-9 (ebook)

Printed in the United States of America

PUBLISHER'S NOTES

This is a work of fiction. Names, characters, places, incidents, and IP addresses either are the product of the author's imagination or are used fictitiously, and any resemblance to actual persons, living or dead, is entirely coincidental and beyond the intent of either the author or the publisher. Any resemblance in this work to actual FBI, CIA, or other government agency operation, source, or method is entirely coincidental and is purely the product of the author's imagination.

The publisher does not have any control over and does not assume any responsibility for author or third-party websites or their content.

Cover design: Dissect Designs
Author photograph: Carolyn Webster
https://josephvwebers.com

*To all who have taken the journey with Maggie, may you find a life of peace, joy, and supernatural fulfillment.*

# ACKNOWLEDGMENTS

Many thanks to Caterina Novelliere and the rest of the Williamsburg Writers for their valuable help with the storyline and editing, to Paula Williamson for her wonderful insights into all sorts of things, to Dr. Carolyn M. Webster for her help with obstetrics questions and Dave Hamrick for his help with aviation questions, and to George Karahalios for his excellent advice and encouragement in getting this book published. I'd like to recognize all my associates in the US Marine Corps who demonstrated the embodiment of their warrior ethos. A special thanks to John Allison who kept me from going off the deep end. K.C. Lin did a wonderful job helping me set up the score for Matt's Wedding Song.

# GLOSSARY OF ACRONYMS, ABBREVIATIONS, AND OTHER TERMINOLOGY

| | |
|---|---|
| 6-30 | 30mm machine gun used on MiG aircraft, short for GSh-6-30 |
| 53K | MH-53K, US Marine Corps heavy lift helicopter |
| A-10 | US Air Force fighter plane |
| ABIN | Agência Brasileira de Inteligência (Brazilian Intelligence Agency) |
| ANC | Airport code for Ted Stevens Anchorage International Airport |
| ATC | Air Traffic Control |
| AW, AWA | Air World Airlines |
| BA | Britannia Airlines |
| C-130 | US military fixed-wing cargo plane |
| CG | US Coast Guard |
| DHS | US Department of Homeland Security |
| DTG | Date-Time Group |
| EOD | Explosive Ordnance Disposal |
| EPA | US Environmental Protection Agency |
| F-18 | US Air Force fighter-bomber plane |
| FIS | Federation of Indian Scientists |
| GAH | An incomplete word starting with a "g", caused by a break in radio transmission |
| GAU-8 | 30mm machine gun used in an Air Force A-10 |
| GSM | Good Ship Myrtlewood |
| IAF | Indian Air Force |
| IBC | International Bread Consortium |
| JATO | Jet Assist Take-Off |
| JFK | Airport code for John F Kennedy International Airport, New York City |
| JLTV | Joint Light Tactical Vehicle (US Marine Corps) |
| K103 | Designator for a decommissioned oil platform in the Gulf of Mexico |
| LAX | Airport code for Los Angeles International Airport |
| LHR | Airport code for London Heathrow Airport |
| MH-53K | Military designation of Marine Corps heavy-lift helicopter "King Stallion" |
| MI-5 | UK Security Service |
| MI-6 | UK Secret Intelligence Service |
| MiG | Russian fighter aircraft designed by Mikoyan and Gurevich |
| MRE | Meal, Ready-to-Eat |

| | |
|---|---|
| MSP | Airport code for Minneapolis Saint Paul International Airport |
| NCO | Noncommissioned Officer |
| NOAA | US National Oceanic and Atmospheric Administration |
| ORD | Airport code for O'Hare International Airport, Chicago |
| P wave | Primary (or pressure) compression wave (earthquake detection) |
| psi | Pounds per square inch |
| Roger | Yes, or, I understand |
| S wave | Secondary (or shear) transverse wave (earthquake detection) |
| SDS | Sand and Dust Storm |
| STRATCOM | Strategic Command (US Department of Defense) |
| T-1 | Local code name for Top Secret-capable phone line |
| USAF | US Air Force |
| UTC | Coordinated Universal Time |
| VTC | Video Teleconference |
| WMD | Weapons of Mass Destruction |
| Z, Zulu | Greenwich Mean Time or Coordinated Universal Time (four hours ahead of Eastern Daylight Time) |

# THE WRECK EMERGED

He saw her the moment he stopped. The aisle in front of him was blocked; the line going back to economy had stopped at 18D as passengers were stowing luggage in overhead bins. Her shoulder-length brown hair swept across her face and hid her eyes, which were, at the moment, turned down toward a wiggling pink bundle on her lap. She cooed softly, seemingly oblivious to the passengers trudging past her.

He stared, as if remembering something from the distant past. No identity came to mind, but it seemed to him he should know her, even though he had seen only a small part of her face. The line backed up briefly, then surged forward a step. She was now a row and a half in front of him.

She looked up and their eyes locked briefly. No, he had no idea who she was, but she looked like someone he had seen before, perhaps on the silver screen? Her face was rather plain, but he found her soft features, clear complexion, and scarcity of makeup attractive. However, her identity was still elusive. Her expression turned from one of idle looking-around to a puzzled pensiveness, and her eyebrows puckered almost imperceptibly, but he noticed.

She followed his eyes as he turned to the bundle and smiled. A deep, satisfied smile; the pink blanket brought back a flood of memories. He looked at her again, but she was looking down, and, subconsciously perhaps, moving the blanket back to give him a better look. She was dressed in jeans, as he was, and wore a dark blue long-sleeve tee shirt with a light-colored open front vest embroidered with dark flowers. A preppy look, he thought. Early thirties, maybe, the same age Rachel would have been. He stifled a tear and looked away.

He felt a slight jab in his back and glanced up. Realizing the line was moving, he readjusted his grip on his leather carry-on and exited the business class rows toward his seat in 21E.

Seat 21D, the seat on the aisle he had come down, was unoccupied and he settled his six-foot, two-hundred-pound frame into the seat beside it. He was in his early sixties, although most people would have guessed late forties or early fifties. He was glad he was somewhat fit; the walking habit he had acquired over the last several months meant he wasn't as squished as he would have been during his sedentary working years. Power-walking, they had said. Power-distracting, he had countered.

Although the business class cabin was already completely occupied, he could tell he was one of the first ones on. There had been plenty of room in the overhead bin, and 21H, the seat next to his, was still empty. Maybe this flight from Chicago to London would be sparsely filled and he could stretch out across all three seats.

A moment later, his hopes were dashed as an elderly man and woman, wearing identical brand-new Virgin Islands sweatshirts, flopped down into 21H and, in the row across the other aisle, 21K, still arguing about which grandson was cuter when he was two. Everything had gone into the overhead except *Field and Stream* and *Good Housekeeping*. He could tell by the wrappers that they had just come from the magazine shop next to their exit gate. Following immediately after were the two grandsons in question, looking to be in their early teens. They took the seats on either side of their grandmother, while their grandfather stayed in 21H.

The flight attendant, Adela, strolled by, checking seats. The exit door was due to close in a few minutes. He was hoping 21D would stay empty, so he stopped her and asked. "Perhaps," she said.

She consulted her list again. It was a list of all the empty seats, based on who had already checked in. "They haven't checked in yet. This is supposed to be a completely full flight. In fact, there are eight people not checked in yet, and interestingly enough, they are registered from several different cities in Russia. I can't show you the list, though. However, the seats are scattered all throughout economy. I just think it's a little odd. But maybe they all were coming together and got delayed. I hope they get here soon. We can't wait for them."

A minute later, the welcome announcement was issued from the cockpit in both English and French and he settled back to wait for takeoff. The Virgin Islanders had made up and were settling in as well.

But the plane didn't move. There were thuds and noises from the baggage compartment below his feet, and he presumed that they were removing the baggage of the missing passengers. A moment's silence, then more activity underneath. Adela came by to let him know that 21D would be vacant for the duration of the flight. "We got their baggage just about out," she said, "when the ground crew found out they had taken an earlier flight. Their baggage didn't make it on that flight, so they reloaded it back onto this flight."

The look on his face told Adela he had a question, which she attempted to answer. "They were traveling together from Los Angeles. Their flight was delayed and they had a close connection, so to be on the safe side, they got booked on this flight in case they were late for their scheduled flight."

"Yes, I figured that, but I would have thought your computer systems would have caught that and taken care of those notifications?"

Adela realized she was giving too much information, so she simply said, "I don't know. But we're about to depart, and I have to finish my preps."

As her skirt twirled around and swished down the aisle, all the individual screens, commandeered by the on-board master, began showing how to buckle your safety belt, and what to do if you come down in the water.

In the cockpit, Captain Chuck Merkel and First Officer Joel Barth were puzzled by the baggage glitch. Joel was the first to offer a possibility. "I saw this once before, where the lists weren't updated and it turned out it had something to do with foreign passports. But that was several years ago, and I thought they had fixed that."

"Yes, I remember that, too. It was also an overseas flight, to Israel that time. And yes, they did fix it. It's odd these are all Russians." He consulted a different list. "Even odder—two originated in MSP, four from LAX, and the other two from ANC. That's three identical glitches!"

"Three separate flights into ORD?"

"No, it looks like the Anchorage flight connected at Minneapolis, so just two arriving flights, from Los Angeles and Minneapolis. Maybe just two glitches."

"I have a friend here in Chicago," the first officer said, "who might be interested and might be able to shed some light on this. We were in the Air Force and flew on numerous missions together. He was in intelligence and I flew the plane. We became close friends. Sometimes I got the impression he was just wearing the Air Force uniform but was really part of some three-letter outfit. He would never talk about it. However, we retired together and he was wearing the uniform then."

"Okay, Joel, go for it." Chuck was busy preparing the big jumbo-jet, a Boeing 787-9 Dreamliner, for being backed out of the gate by the mule. The flight safety messages had ended and control of the individual screens was now dutifully returned to the passengers. Joel quickly encrypted an email to his Chicago contact and resumed his checklist items.

"Chuck, I've flown this route several times before, and this doesn't seem like the normal flight route. Did you notice that? It seems rather odd to me."

"Yes, we are flying somewhat southeast instead of the normal route. You'll notice the beacon list has us flying just north of Philly and just south of JFK, before we head out over the ocean. Our normal route was compromised. When they rerouted us, they wanted us south of the New York-to-London corridor, as that will be quite saturated this morning until about 1900 Zulu."

"What did you mean, the normal route was compromised? Are there weather issues? I imagine we could simply fly above the weather." He pulled up the weather report. "Besides, the weather looks fine."

"Not weather. Human activities. Did you read the security summary?"

"No, not yet."

"You always need to read those. Look on page three."

Joel looked on page three, and read, " 'Aircraft lasing activity reported in Lewisporte, Newfoundland. Several different locations. Green lasers.' Then it goes on to list the flights impacted. Wow, one flight at thirty thousand feet. Looks like they're purposely targeting the aircraft."

"It appears they are located at different spots on the island, not just Lewisporte. They can't pinpoint the locations. I got an update just before I came on board. Until they can get a handle on this rogue lasing, they are keeping us out of the area."

"They can't lase us."

The captain glanced over at his first officer. "Oh?"

"We're in the cockpit on the top side of the aircraft."

"Yes, if they were directly below us. You can see the ground in front of us, right? So the ground can see us. Besides, we have two hundred eighty-five, correction, two hundred seventy-seven passengers, and it would scare the living daylights out of anyone seeing bright green flashes coming through their windows."

"Plus an infant."

"Anyway, we'll be flying over the North American Basin, the mid-Atlantic Ridge, the West European Basin, then on into Heathrow. We would probably be safe with the see-and-avoid rules, but for the little extra time it would take us, normal traffic doesn't have to watch out for us. And we will have plenty of fuel."

Joel did a quick calculation. "That will take us about five hundred miles out of our way. With all the built-in time allowances, we'll get into London about on time. Do we need to let the passengers know?"

"No, they don't know the original flight route, and the map they can follow on their consoles is vague enough they won't see any differences. Besides, the rerouting takes us right into the middle of the jet stream, so that will increase our speed a good deal."

At the National Oceanic and Atmospheric Administration observatory base K103 at a remote location in the Gulf of Mexico, an alarm had wakened Jacob Strauss and alerted him to an abnormal seismic event. Checking the seismogram trace, he had found the P and S sound waves from the event each lasted less than four seconds, and their time separation put the distance to the epicenter at twenty-five hundred miles away, plus or minus fifty miles. It was the amplitude of the trace which had him puzzled, however.

In his training for this gig, he had never seen such a strong signal. The pens had reached their physical limits and bounced back before settling back to zero. It was not likely to have been an earthquake; if it had, the leading and trailing sound waves would have lasted for several minutes. No earthquake meant no tsunami, so Jacob had gone back to bed.

K103 was an early oil platform which had reached the end of its useful life, one of over six hundred decommissioned drilling platforms slated for demolition. One federal government organization had used the Sustainable Fisheries Act to gain control of the platform to be a monitoring station. It was being used by NOAA, EPA, and two other government organizations for storm and weather, current, tsunami, seismic, water conditions, and petroleum leakage monitoring. As well as other things nobody talked about.

Most of the NOAA monitoring sites were unmanned; Jacob was there primarily for training and equipment troubleshooting, and secondarily for monitoring. The main purpose for the monitoring was to answer the question, will there be a tsunami and if so, where?

After breakfast, his morning workout, and completing reports on yesterday's activities, Jacob turned his attention to the seismograph output. The device itself was functioning properly, and his query to the station watch on duty at two o'clock that morning revealed the platform had not been bumped or otherwise experienced anything that might be the source of the vibrations.

Intrigued, he logged into the NOAA library of worldwide seismograph recordings. The library was relatively new, but recordings had been added, so far, all the way back to the mid-sixties. Jacob downloaded the digitized trace from the seismograph and fed it into the library's search engine. About twenty minutes later, the search ended, producing five exact matches. He noted that the early morning event had not yet been added.

Each record showed the trace and the name of a metadata text file. These files showed the date and time of the seismogram, epicenter, and a comments section, among other data. Two were from this year; the other three were from 2011. Same exact spot, 35.177 degrees north latitude and 52.204 degrees west longitude. Identical traces. He checked the dates of the earlier activity and the dates of the other two recent events. Eight days to the minute between first and second, second and third.

There were three events in both cases, and eight years to the day between the series of events. The comment on the event of June 20, 2011, was that a recommendation was sent up the chain to examine the sea floor at that location, but there was no further annotation indicating if this had yielded any data. However, the metadata for the June 28, 2011, trace had the following comment: "Audio file 20110628A201 declassified upon decommissioning of submarine USS Houston, SSN-713, 26 August 2016."

Following the devastating Indian Ocean tsunami in December 2004, the National Tsunami Warning Center expanded its scope to the North Atlantic from Canada to the Gulf of Mexico. Since there were no recordings matching this trace prior to that, who knows how long these events may have been occurring?

Jacob guessed that if the USS Houston had detected the results of a disturbance in the ocean floor, NOAA would have already known about it.

He downloaded the traces, the metadata, and the audio file.

He put in a call to the tsunami warning center, located in Palmer, Alaska. His friend Naquita Phillips answered the phone. "My, you're up early!" Jacob said.

"Actually, I get off in about a half hour. Are you still at Pearl?"

"No, I left Hawaii about eight weeks ago, did the NOAA training, and now I'm at K103 in the Gulf." They caught up briefly, then Jacob asked her about the seismograph readings.

"Over a hundred monitoring stations reported the disturbance, including yours. Since there was no reason to suspect a tsunami, we didn't pursue any more details. But I can give you the triangulated location if you're interested."

"Yes, that's all I really need." She gave it to him and they said their good-byes.

Wow, he thought, another match!

After listening to the audio file, he decided he needed a second opinion.

Jacob stuck his head into the office next door. All Jacob knew about his friend's job was that he was monitoring various activities which he never talked about, for a government agency located somewhere in Virginia. However, in the short time Jacob had been on K103, they discovered common interests of trout fishing, elk hunting, motocross, and redheads. Both had served in the military. One lived in northern Minnesota and the other in northern Wisconsin. "Hey, Jimmy!"

"Hey, Jake, what's up? Are you out of beer already?" They both laughed; beer, along with all other alcoholic beverages, was not authorized on the platform.

"Not yet. I want you to listen to an audio and tell me what you think it is."

They traipsed back to the Seismology Lab and Jacob cued up the audio. Jimmy put on the headphones and Jacob pressed Play. The audio lasted less than five seconds.

Jimmy knew exactly what it was. "It's the crack-boom of ice breaking on a frozen lake. There's no other sound like it! I remember the first time I heard it. I was ice fishing with my dad. I was scared out of my wits! I thought the ice was going to split apart right where we were. Where was this, and when?"

"That's exactly what I thought too. The cracking of lake ice. It happened in the middle of the North Atlantic, about 35 degrees north and 52 degrees west, about two this morning. I watched the seismograph long enough to realize it wasn't an earthquake, so I looked into it when I got up this morning."

Jimmy was always on the lookout for more information-gathering techniques. "How did you get this audio so quickly?"

"The audio is eight years old. In fact, it is exactly eight years old, being dated June 28, 2011." Jacob went on to tell Jimmy of his research that morning. "I've been here only a week, so I missed the events of the twelfth and twentieth."

Jimmy was coming up with a theory. "How deep is the ocean at that location?" They checked the ocean charts together. "What were the coordinates they gave you?"

"Within one hundred miles of 35.177 degrees north latitude and 52.204 degrees west longitude."

"Wow! The ocean is over five thousand meters deep there. Over three miles!"

"It's interesting, Jimmy, that the audio was so clear. The USS Houston couldn't go down more than two thousand feet, and I assume this audio was generated on the seafloor, well over fifteen thousand feet below the surface."

I wonder, Jimmy thought, if the sound wasn't the seafloor cracking like the ice. It sounded outlandish, so he kept it to himself. "Maybe that's the difference between the travel of sound in water versus in air."

"It seems like it's been cracking for years. And on a regular schedule."

In less than four hours, Jimmy would see those exact coordinates again.

At seat 21E, flight preparations were ongoing. He stood up, removed the sport jacket he had brought in case he got cold on the plane, and deposited it in the overhead bin. He emptied his pockets into the briefcase at his feet, and sat down in 21D. His long-sleeved white polo shirt with the terrier embroidered on the front should be sufficient for warmth. Although it was the end of June, the Chicago Airport had been cold, like he remembered it from his years of flying for an international food company.

He relaxed, rubbed the graying hair of his temples, and closed his eyes. Immediately the young woman in seat 4A came into his mind, and he remembered exactly where he had seen her. It was in last night's dream! It was a good thing the rear jet bridge had malfunctioned, he reasoned, causing him and all the other economy passengers to enter through the front of the plane; otherwise he wouldn't have seen her. So he would see her again, he concluded.

His thoughts returned as they did almost continually for the last two weeks to the words, "I have a job for you." Then to the past year, and the grief threatened to swallow him up again, as it had for nine months following the first tragedy.

Rachel, his thirty-two-year-old daughter, her husband Mike, five-and-a-half-year-old granddaughter Amy, and two-year-old grandson Jack, had been on a mission trip to Costa Rica. They had gone with a group from their church to a poor area outside one of the larger cities on the Pacific side. The idea had been to live among some poorer families, help them to improve their dwellings, and share the gospel, with translators of course.

It had worked well until the Wednesday of their stay, when unusually heavy rains inland caused major flash flooding in the area where they were staying, wiping out dozens of homes and killing fifty-seven people. Three of the mission families had been among the deaths. Nine of the ten bodies were recovered, including Mike, Rachel, and their kids, but one little boy was never found. He blamed himself for not warning them of the danger, and was inconsolable for exactly four weeks, when the next tragedy struck. Then about a month after the second tragedy, Helene, his wife of forty years, died of a burst brain aneurysm.

His whole family gone, he had become listless. Purposeless. Merely going through the motions, barely managing. Trying to write haiku for therapy. Grieving. Hanging on to God for dear life, knowing that God hadn't abandoned him. He needed to change the subject, so he pulled the airline flight magazine out of the seat pocket in front of him. He read the pictorial article about Rio de Janeiro, the mini-bio success story of the Britannia Airlines Systems Analyst, the article about food preparation for international flights, and the information for the best wine-tasting tours. Nothing seemed to help much.

In the cockpit, Chuck revisited the conversation about Joel's Air Force Intelligence friend. "I flew Air Force too," he said. "Bombers. Mostly F-18s."

"No, that would be a cargo plane."

"Don't be a jerk! That joke is so old, I've forgotten it twice already." Every military pilot knows Air Force Two is the Vice President's plane, a Boeing C-32 cargo plane.

"Sorry, I couldn't resist!"

"Yes, well, I set myself up for that," Chuck said. "My dad was also a bomber pilot. Vietnam in the late sixties. I flew in Afghanistan after 9/11. My dad and I have this in common, that we were both shot at by MiGs. Neither of us were hit, but he got a lot closer to it than I did. We both lived to tell about it. My brother was a pilot for the Marine Corps. Flew helicopters. He's retired now, too."

"I started off in fighters, then switched to recon. Never got shot at. I met JC, my friend in Chicago, early in my career, shortly after I started flying reconnaissance. I carried him and his team all over the world. They were the ones actually doing the recon, I just flew the plane."

"That's one nice thing about flying commercial for Air World," Chuck said.

"What's that?"

"Ever since I started flying for Air World, and their partners like today's Britannia Airlines, I've never been shot at."

Yet.

Julius Caesar Smalley had just finished breakfast when his phone alerted him to a new email. He got hundreds daily, it seemed, but the alert ringtone identified the sender as one of those in his contact list. He opened the phone and tapped the Mail icon. It was from his friend Joel Barth, but the body of the email was just gibberish. Why did Joel send him an encrypted email?

He opened his laptop, downloaded the message, and sent it through the decoder. The decoder asked for the key code. What would Joel have used as a key code? He thought back to their days flying to various parts of the world on intelligence-gathering missions. Joel had been his favorite pilot and they logged many hours together. Air Force pilots all had nicknames; Joel's was "Dolphin" but he had never told him why.

He tried Dolphin and the decryption algorithm converted the message to more gibberish. Nope. He didn't call Joel, Dolphin; they had grown close enough they had their own private nicknames for each other. Joel was Ace and he was Spook. He tried Ace. Nope. If Spook didn't work then he'd have to send a plain-text reply asking for help.

Spook rewarded him with words in plain English. He chuckled at the first three, "Third try, right?"

Then he read, "Need help. In air on AW flight 94 to LHR. Eight passengers AWOL, all Russians. Double-booked, but all made earlier flight. No problem with that. Their baggage is all on board, but change not reported by system. Four arrived from MSP; four from LAX. Identical glitches? Seems strange, don't have a good feeling about this. Let me know what you find out. Joel. PS. Use the same PW."

Using the same password would eliminate the guesswork for Joel, who would have enough on his mind already.

He reread the message, felt the adrenaline rush, grabbed his phone and started dialing. "Please be there," he muttered to himself.

"FAA Regional Field Office, Smith here. How may I help you?"

"Jack, JC Smalley here. Your office has a new name?"

"We have caller ID so I knew it was you. No, we're still the External Security folks. What's up?"

JC briefly outlined what he knew and asked for an administrative password to Air World's data system.

"Are you freelancing, or is this official business? Can someone vouch for you? Do you have a time constraint?"

"The first officer on that flight sent me an urgent message. Joel Barth. They're already in the air."

"Okay, I'll check on that. Are you still at the same email address as last time?"

"Yes."

"We have new rules now. I can't give you a password lasting more than two hours. If you need more time you'll have to call me back."

"Roger."

Jack Smith checked a spreadsheet he had pulled up while they were talking. "It'll be encrypted. Use the last four of your social."

"Thanks."

Since the flight was already in progress, Jack was able to pull up the flight data and confirm the first officer's name. That was good enough. He called the security office at Air World Airlines.

Two minutes later, JC received the email he was hoping for. Thirty seconds after that, he had logged into Air World's Flight Information System. He pulled up the flight data for flight AW94 and quickly confirmed the Russian passengers. It wasn't hard; their names gave them away: Egorkin (Vaughn and Misha), Lebedev (Sasha and Anichka), Nikolevski (Nikola and Sasha), Petrov (Mikhail and Katrina). The status column for each of the names confirmed the reservations were made, then cancelled with a "PP" in the remarks column. JC right-clicked the column heading and found out that "PP" indicated that their baggage was still loaded on this flight.

"How do I get to the baggage?" He didn't mean to say that out loud, and at that moment, Nicki appeared in the doorway with a cup of coffee for each of them.

"What, honey?" She saw the look of pure concentration on his face, and fifteen years of marriage told her his question was quite irrelevant. Both "It's work, isn't it?" and "How soon do you leave?" occurred to her at the same time. She asked neither.

By this time, he had found the Flight Information button, and the submenu presented him with a Baggage Info selection. He clicked it and was rewarded with another database consisting of information on about six hundred pieces of baggage. Already sorted by last name.

Odd, he thought. Normally, it would not be sorted, but would be listed in the order the data was entered. Someone's already been in this list, he concluded.

"Oh, nothing. And thanks for the coffee."

JC wasn't fooling his wife. "Not nothing, Julius. I know that look!"

"My old Air Force friend Joel needs some help. You remember Joel Barth?"

"Yes, he was at your retirement."

"He retired at the same time. Now he's flying for Air World, and he's in the air with suspicions of something he can't quite put a finger on. We spent enough time together that I trust his suspicions a lot. But so far, I'm not seeing anything."

He scrolled down the list to the first entry for Egorkin and clicked on it. The whole row lit up. Good, he thought, I'll just copy the entries into my own spreadsheet. Holding down the control key, he clicked on the rest of the Egorkin entries, and found the other three couples and highlighted them the same way.

He right-clicked to prepare for the copying, and was astonished to see the message pop up, "Selected baggage on hold. Delete at this time? Yes/No." He quickly clicked No and found a different way to copy.

JC Smalley, USAF Retired, with thirteen citations for his intelligence work while on active duty, was now a freelancer. A thin, wiry man with a bushy moustache on a boyish face, he had moved back to the north side of Chicago after his retirement to be near his aging parents. He mostly did research and analysis work for an old colleague who was fairly high up in a three-letter organization in the DC area. Occasionally, JC would be deputized for actual field duty where his personal risks would be rather low, but those were few and far between. However, there was enough office work for JC to keep his intelligence skills sharp.

Which is why, when he saw the popup "Selected baggage on hold. Delete at this time?", he immediately realized why the glitch occurred with the baggage as flight AW94 was being loaded. Someone else had put the selected baggage on hold.

On a hunch, he clicked the System button at the top of the screen. Mining through the different selections, he found one allowing him to see what other computers had recently logged into this particular data sheet. It merely showed the computer's IP address and time stamp. There was only one entry. IP address 191.6.118.145 at 8:45 that morning.

There's a rat in the woodpile, he thought, I can see its tail.

He was able to trace where else that IP address had accessed the airline's info. The previous flight, where the passengers actually flew. Baggage Info on both flights, and flight routes, including a change due to some laser activity in Newfoundland. A double whammy, he wondered, for flight 94? Could the lasing be related to this baggage issue? He finished his search, wrote down the pertinent information, and logged out.

Next, he googled the IP address. Brazil? Macapá, Brazil? Really? This has suddenly gotten too much for just me. Time to call the big guns!

JC quickly encrypted an email back to Joel, and picked up the phone.

In seat 4A, it was time to feed the infant, who was starting to fuss. Just a little, her little girl was such an angel! Rummaging through the carry-on sprinkled with brightly-colored jungle birds, she found the empty bottle, all the paraphernalia that allowed the liquid to actually exit the bottle, the can of formula, no water. Not allowed through security. She would have kicked herself if she had had her foot free, for not bringing along an empty water bottle to refill at one of the many hydration kiosks.

She found the call-the-flight-attendant button and soon had enough warm water for this feeding and spares for the next one or two. A burp and a half later, a smiling face rewarded her with a gurgle. She held the baby close and closed her eyes.

Immediately, she felt in her belly the same feeling she had when the man had smiled at her and Jenny, while he was waiting for the passengers in front of him to move. It was a tingling that went up and down her spine, coupled with a heightened sense of anticipation, similar to the anticipation one would feel as Door Number Three was about to be opened.

But there was no Door Number Three, just a stranger who had an unknown draw on her. Who was he? She drew his image back out of her memory, but couldn't make any connection. She took some comfort in his not recognizing her either. The image seemed to be calling to her, however, beckoning her. She did not feel annoyed or threatened, only puzzled.

She reflected on her last two weeks. The visit was fun, as she had anticipated, but disappointing in a way. There had been a growing dissatisfaction with the direction her life was taking. The hope that this trip might point her in a new direction was slowly dwindling. She had no problem with her job; her students were the age that represented the happiest times of her life. It was all the other little things that were not providing the fulfillment, or even the promise of fulfillment, that she had been expecting.

In spite of the difficulties surrounding her birth, Jenny was her one and only bright spot, and she loved her with all that was within her. She recognized that much of the disappointment had been self-inflicted, and was starting to realize she had no idea how to find a way out.

She looked back down at her little girl as if to force herself back to reality. Their eyes locked on to each other's, and a contentment beyond words enveloped them: a delicate little face so reliant on the tender face above. All four eyes closed together; one pair of eyes to sleep and dream, probably of milk, the other pair to shut out the world and wonder.

Up in the air, checklists finally completed, Joel checked his email. The encrypted email from his friend was scarce of details, but promised more news as available. Joel read between the lines. "Chuck?" He was somewhat hesitant to draw the obvious conclusion. "We may have a problem. JC, my Chicago bud, is saying there is more to look into concerning the missing passengers."

Captain Charles M. Merkel, USAF, retired bomber pilot, was immediately and momentarily back in the F-18 Hornet he flew until the day he retired. Then he realized he had no afterburners, no flares, no chaff, no speed, and no hope of outrunning any Russian military interceptor. "What does that mean, Joel?" A moment later, "Does that mean we should fly below the radar? You can't chase what you can't see."

"Whoa! All he said was there was more to check on." A quick scan of the instruments indicated unmitigated normalcy. "He's pretty quick, at least he used to be, but I imagine we'll be on the ground before I hear back from him. He did mention it was actually eight separate glitches."

First Officer Joel Barth had no idea how quickly he would hear back from his old friend.

JC Smalley heard the phone ring twice, then pick up. "Henry," said the voice at the other end.

"Phil, this is JC Smalley. Do you have a few minutes?"

Phillip Henry worked in an office within the FBI which monitored domestic issues. Because of budget constraints, the department was always understaffed, and the pace was hectic. Everyone in his office had more than they could handle. At his level, Phil worked on the cases which had the farthest-reaching implications. "We're really busy. Are you freelancing?"

"No. Well, almost no."

"Okay. You have three minutes to get me interested. We're working a few really hot issues, but I know you wouldn't have called on this secure line if it weren't urgent."

"Thanks, Phil." It took JC ninety seconds to brief Joel's email and the findings in the Air World data system. "The odd thing, and the reason I called, is there was someone else nosing around in the database. He had a foreign IP address, as far as I can tell."

"It might have been spoofed. Read it to me."

JC heard some papers shuffling on the other end. "Okay. 191."

"191."

"6."

"Hold on. Is the next one 118?"

This took JC completely by surprise. "Yes! How did you—"

"I need you to come see me. Pronto. Bring what you have. You've just become hot." Phil conversed briefly with someone on his end. "Wait. You have a plane in the air. I'll have my driver pick you up. Plan for about a week. Afterwards we'll go hunting at my cottage behind the Outer Banks."

"Roger."

"Be downstairs in about fifteen minutes. And give Nicki a hug for me." Click.

JC took a moment to decipher the codes. Fishing would have meant pure office work—research and analysis. Hunting meant there was fieldwork involved, possibly armed. It also meant being deputized, sworn in, with hold-harmless and other forms to fill out and sign. He was used to all those. A hug instead of a kiss good-bye meant in Phil's opinion, it would not be terribly dangerous. Fifteen minutes meant fifteen minutes, so he'd better get busy.

JC Smalley still hadn't figured out "hot" when he reached the foyer of his apartment building. He had packed a duffel bag and a small suitcase with what he considered would last indefinitely if he had access to a laundry. Included was a pair of holsters JC had grown particularly fond of. If this trip involved packing, he didn't want the government-issued holsters that were always stiff, ill-fitting, and obvious.

As he exited the elevator, a young man he had never seen before approached him. "Mr. Smalley, I'm Luke. Please come with me. You keep your briefcase and I'll take the other luggage."

JC eyed him with suspicion. There were plenty of others in the foyer just then. "Luke, how do you know who I am, and why should I go with you?"

Luke grinned at him. "One, you look just like your picture. And two, Phil said to ask if you hugged Nicki. Shall we go?"

"Lead the way!"

"The way" led to a compact American-made car double-parked in front of the apartment. Luke put the luggage in the back seat. "Ready?"

"I know a shortcut to the airport if that would help."

"Sure." Luke handed him a large soft-pack envelope coated with a metallic film. The writing on the front told him to put his phone, laptop, and other electronic devices in the envelope and fold the flap over. When he had complied, Luke had him put the envelope in his briefcase.

"We're not going to the airport," JC said. It was more a statement than a question.

Luke pointed to a small device plugged into the cigarette lighter. There was a green light in the corner. JC had noticed the device when he got in the car, and the light was red then.

"We're secure now. When your devices get vetted, they'll be added to the list on board this scanner. No, we're not going to the airport. Chicago will be your home for a little while longer. We have a stop to make before we get there. It won't be long. I don't have any more I can tell you. I'm just an escort."

After another block, they came to a parking garage for city visitors going to the shopping district. The lighted sign said the garage was completely full. Luke pulled in anyway, and when they got to the sixth floor, a car was just backing out of a space. Luke pulled into it.

"Grab your briefcase and the scanner, and I'll get the other stuff." Luke got out, fished around in his pocket for keys, and opened the doors of the car in the parking space next to them. The transfer was made in about twenty seconds, and as they drove away, JC saw Luke give a brief nod to a man lounging near the elevator. JC checked his watch; it was less than ninety minutes since he had gotten the email from his friend Joel Barth.

Luke drove for about fifteen minutes before pulling into the entry drive of a modest-looking office building. "Go meet Penny," he said. "I'll bring your stuff."

A tall, athletic-looking woman with dishwater blonde hair, appearing to be in her mid-thirties, was just emerging from the elevator. "I'm Penny. Please come with me."

As they shook hands, JC glanced at her badge. Penelope Hasid. Her picture. And a logo he couldn't identify. Her voice sounded vaguely familiar, but he couldn't quite place it. He should have, he thought, he was usually better than that.

She noticed his glance. "Don't try to figure out the logo. It doesn't mean anything."

She was carrying a clipboard with various forms and papers, which she gave him on their way to the ninth floor. "Once we get there, you'll have about five minutes to sign these before the meeting starts. Phil is already there."

Surprised, he was about to say something, but then it occurred to him this would be a video teleconference of some sort, a VTC. Then he remembered the voice.

"Penelope."

"Nobody calls me that!"

"Is that because your name is Wanda?"

"I was wondering if you'd recognize me. I've lost forty-five pounds and changed my hair color back. It's been what, eight years?"

"At least. You look good. You know, I heard your real voice only once back then, and after that it was strictly by phone."

"You were so helpful to me. I owe you. You talked them into giving me a shot, and so I volunteered to do this. Anyway, please call me Penny while you're here, and here we are."

JC glanced over the papers, standard issue he had seen several times before, while working for Phil. One caught his eye; a permit to carry several different government-issue side arms. "Nice!"

He quickly signed them all. He gave them back to Penny along with the envelope containing his electronics.

"We still have about two minutes, so let me fill you in on something that may put your mind at ease. I'm in training to be an agent! After the first phase, we came here. I guess we impressed them that we would make it, so they gave us new names, which we would use as agents. There are three of us. You met Lucas. There is also Harper. We'd been here about a week when all this started. The training has temporarily stopped and we've turned into assistants. So it's still sort of training. We're not clerical though. When we found out you were coming, we were told you would need help, and I volunteered. We all have other tasks, too."

"This? What is 'this', how long has 'this' been going on, and how long have you known I was coming? I still don't really know why I'm here."

"Oh? We were told you were already somewhat deeply involved, you know, with the airplane, but that everything else would be new to you. 'This' has been going on for a little over a week, and we've known you'd be here for about forty-five minutes. We found out when Luke got orders to go pick you up."

They were at the conference room door. "Here we are," she said. "I'll be with you for a few minutes to help get you situated. Press the On button on the headset and that will alert Phil, who will be at the other end, that you're here."

She opened the door and they went in. As he entered, JC couldn't tell which was stronger in him, the sense of excitement and expectancy, or the sense of doom.

What was she doing, going from business class to economy, to visit a man she had never met, who was old enough to be her father? This wasn't like her. Ever since she was twelve, it had been her habit to shy away from the opposite sex. Relationships with men were difficult, and she avoided them when possible. The bundle on her lap showed that there had been at least one, however.

She couldn't justify it in her mind, but right then she wasn't listening to her mind so much. She looked for an excuse; he had smiled at Jenny, and that was good enough. "I have to walk the baby," she told the flight attendant who wanted to know if anything was wrong. In other words, why are you leaving your assigned area?

In 21D, he had turned to the crossword puzzle and tried to focus. A fishing net, nine letters. Nothing came to mind; maybe some of the down words would help. He drew a blank on the first six. The seventh, four letters, cake decorator. He printed in I-C-E-R, then tried to fit the I into the fishing net. Frustrated, he had put the magazine back into the seat pocket and was facing forward with a thousand-meter stare when he saw a wiggling in the curtains separating them from the rich folks. He hoped it was Adela to update him on anything in particular; maybe she would know the fishing net.

The curtains parted and it was not Adela; it was the young woman in 4A. The memory of her delighted him in a way he didn't quite understand. The baby perhaps. Maybe how her eyes had reminded him of his daughter's, pensive but not brooding. Most likely that she had been in the dream.

She paused and looked around. She continued to look around as she slowly made her way down the narrow aisle, as if searching for a particular familiar face. She got to row seventeen before she saw him. After that, she never took her eyes off him, smiling shyly, with a little uncertainty, slowing down and finally stopping even with row twenty.

"Hullo, I'm Maggie."

Her thick British accent surprised him. He was expecting she would be from California or Ohio. She was also a little shorter than he anticipated; again, perhaps because of Rachel, who was five foot seven.

She waited, putting on her most darling face. Well, this is rather forward, he thought, but how else was this supposed to happen? Smiling, he moved back over to 21E and welcomed her to his aisle seat. "Hi. I'm Matt."

If she had been expecting anything but a Midwestern accent, she would have been disappointed. When she stopped twisting around and they both had buckled their seat belts, he asked, "Who have we here?"

The pink blanket was still. Maggie had been holding it close to her chest, but lowered it to her lap. She opened up the blanket to reveal a plump face with a pudgy little nose and wispy light-brown hair held in place by tiny barrettes. "This is Jenny," she said, beaming. "She's a few days more than three months old."

"She's beautiful," he said. "Absolutely gorgeous! So perfectly formed. Aren't babies wonderful? I remember mine." He swallowed hard at the memory, his throat suddenly tight.

It was rather small for a conference room, JC thought, as he made his way to the table that was obviously for him. He could see the door through which they entered with the EXIT sign above. Straight ahead, the opposite wall had an array of forty-six-inch monitors, four wide by three high. Eight of the twelve were lit up; people were sitting at tables similar to his.

The other four monitors were on, he could tell, by the zoom and volume control icons in the lower left corners. There was an additional monitor, a huge one, off to the side, which also appeared to be on, but the screen was blank. In front of him were two notepads and a pen, a microphone with the mute button lit, a blue mouse, a red mouse, a phone, and the headset Penny had mentioned. All were plugged into a control box. He donned the headset and pressed the On button on the control box.

In about five seconds, Phil came on the line. "Good morning, JC, and welcome back on the government payroll. I imagine you're still pretty much in the dark about this, because Penny just hasn't had time to brief you properly. You were right about Penny, by the way, more than you could have known. She catches on quick, fits in well, is perfectly loyal, and has the right background.

"You're here for two reasons. First, you will be our go-between with the flight Joel Barth is on. The field office there in Chicago is finding the secure radio for that. There may be trouble or not—their flight should be landing in about six hours. Hopefully, all will be well.

"The second reason is the same reason all the other folks are on this VTC, which is to look into a chemical warfare agent threat with ties to the same IP address you started to give me on the phone. This meeting will last about an hour, after which Penny will give you as complete a briefing as she can, and introduce you around the office. The meeting will reconvene throughout the day as needed, as tasks are completed and more information or questions arise.

"The headset connects only to me. The mic in front connects you to the meeting. I will now break into the meeting and introduce you. Use the blue mouse to adjust all their volumes. As soon as you unmute, your camera will be on."

Penny was still there. "Who are all these people?" JC asked. "Can you get me their pictures and a large-font label with their names, offices, and what they do?"

"Sure. We anticipated that, so we have some of them, but the folks keep changing. I'll try to get the principals, though."

When JC pressed the unmute button, the light went out, and one of the dark monitors lit up with his picture at the table. He noticed interruptions in the other eight monitors as they realized there was a new face in the meeting. JC noticed them all turning toward the newly lit monitor at their locations. He waggled the blue mouse, and found it controlled all twelve monitors. When he unmuted all the different locations, a green monitor border would indicate who was speaking.

A quick look around revealed the meeting was made up of mostly civilians, but JC noticed a US Navy uniform in one of the monitors. He took a closer look. An Italian-looking man with thinning dark hair had a chestful of medals and was wearing the rank of a navy captain.

Phil waited for a break in the conversations. "Excuse me, everyone. I'd like to introduce a new team member. Mr. JC Smalley works for me out of the Chicago office at present. He may be moving around as needs be."

JC hadn't recognized Phil in any of the monitors; he hadn't seen him since he started growing his beard. He quickly drew a map of the monitors on the pad, and started filling in names.

Phil went on, "JC has joined us because he was investigating some abnormalities in Air World Airlines flight 94 from Chicago to London, which took off at 9:15 this morning. In checking the Air World flight database, he discovered someone hacked into it earlier from a location in Macapá, Brazil, using the IP address we are already familiar with. It may be a spoof, but JC will be in constant contact with the flight until it lands at LHR. He will be in a separate VTC room from the Chicago office, because if something happens with the flight, we will immediately stop the internal chatter to focus on what is happening in the air."

Phil paused a moment to let everyone focus on the newcomer.

"Now then, JC, the rest of the task force. Say Hi as I introduce you, so JC will see who you are. Titus 'Ty' Harris, State Department, representing their Bureau of Counterterrorism and Countering Violent Extremism. Did I get that right?"

"Yes. Hi, JC, and welcome."

JC noted it on his map.

"Next is Jonathan Whitaker, everyone calls him Jon, of the FBI Weapons of Mass Destruction Directorate. Kirby Drinkard, DHS National Counterterrorism Center, and right now the center is sorting out the right personnel for this task force, so you may see different folks in her monitor as we go along.

"Captain Louis Palova, US Navy Special Operations, will be representing the entire Department of Defense if needed. Pedro Santos, assistant to the US Ambassador to Brazil. Barry Mantile, Treasury Department, Under Secretary for Terrorism and Financial Intelligence. Dusty Mae Watt, special agent in charge of the FBI Field Office in Chicago. And of course, I'm Phil Henry of the FBI National Security Branch."

Wow, he thought, what a crew! JC decided he'd better say a few words, to settle himself as much as anything else. "Hello everyone. Thanks for the welcome. I'm JC Smalley, retired Air Force Intelligence and friend of the first officer on flight 94. At this point, we have no idea if there is a threat to the aircraft. We have no idea who hacked in or what their interest is. I will be contacting the flight, and we will also get a line to Air Traffic Control to give them communication priority. Hopefully, I will not have much to contribute. When they land safely at LHR, I will butt in and let you know. Thanks."

Penny came over and whispered in his ear, "As soon as I back away, smile at the camera and press the Freeze button."

He did so. A woman approached from a side door.

"Hi, I'm Jackie. I'm running the video teleconference for you, and it looks like Penny has gotten you the radio setup you need. I'd like to suggest that while you are busy on the radio, that the conversation be displayed as text on your VTC monitor. The complete radio traffic will be recorded and converted to text anyway, and if anything crucial happens, I can unfreeze you. They can all still watch you and listen to the audio."

"Okay. Is there some way I can tell you to turn it off or on? Or can I do that myself? Everything might not be appropriate for display."

"Yes, we'll work something out."

Penny had been busy setting up the bundle of equipment she had brought in, with the help of a technician. "There is a secure channel on every large aircraft that the pilots must verify as part of their run-up checklist. It rarely gets used, even in emergencies. It was initiated after 9/11 for just this sort of situation. To you, it will be just another radio, which scrambles and descrambles your traffic. The pilots know this channel is secure. We will not be using the silent mode, but the system will announce us so the pilots won't be startled when you start talking to them.

"Once the channel is opened, you will hear the audio in the cockpit even when they are not speaking on your channel. ATC has given us the code for flight 94 and we have entered all the protocol streams. When you flip this toggle, you will be talking to the pilots. These two switches on top allow you to talk to both simultaneously or just one of them."

Jackie came over and hooked several wires to various ports on the radio. "Here's the headset. Before you flip the On switch, I need you to do a communications check with me to ensure the recording and reporting is working right." While JC donned the headset, she went back to her station and programmed the rolling display to show the Zulu time stamp, the source of the radio transmission, and the message.

He gave a slow count to Jackie. After she gave him a thumbs-up, he said to Penny, "I have two headsets, one for Phil and one for the aircraft. You'll have to be my link to Phil."

"Okay." She sat down next to him and put on the headset. "Phil, this is Penny. JC is on the call with the aircraft. ... Yes. ... Roger."

She wrote him a quick note. "He said you did well on the intro. He'll let you know if he needs to talk to you, and if there's anything you should listen to, in the other part of the VTC."

JC looked over to where Jackie was sitting in the doorway. He gave her a thumbs-down and she nodded. He flipped the On switch to talk to the aircraft, then glanced down at his watch. It was 1105 hours.

The cockpit was relatively quiet and the flight was progressing smoothly. They had not been flying over the North Atlantic very long, when a sound like a goose honking alerted them to the secure channel, which was now blinking red. Neither Chuck nor Joel had ever seen or heard this except when completing their pre-flight checklists. Joel reached up to the secure console and pressed the blinking button. The honking stopped and the red light was steady.

A voice came through their headsets, without them having to change any channels. "This is JC Smalley. Who am I speaking with?"

"Captain Chuck Merkel."

"First Officer Joel Barth."

"Good, I had to verify I had the right flight, flight AW94 heading to LHR. I need to speak to Joel first, then both of you. I am not quite familiar with this radio, so I might not get it right on the first try."

The first officer heard an electronic click, followed by the voice of his friend. "Is that you, Chuck?"

"No, this is Joel. I don't think Chuck heard you."

"Good. I'd like to chat, but that will have to wait. I need you to answer just yes or no. Understand?"

"Yes."

"Good. Have you known Chuck Merkel a while?"

"Yes."

"Does he seem like his head is screwed on right?"

"Yes."

"Have either of you been drinking, or impaired by drugs or medications, or crew rest issues?"

"No."

"Do you have a third pilot with you?"

"No."

"I know you well enough to be able to answer this about you, but do you have any reason to doubt his ideologies or loyalty to our country?"

"No."

"That's what I was hoping for. I'm going to turn you both on now."

Another click. "Chuck, I'm back. In response to Joel's email, I did some checking in Air World's flight data. Someone had hacked in and put a temporary hold on the luggage for some reason. I could see his IP address, and it was from a foreign country. I have no idea what he wanted, so I called up my FBI contact in DC. I told him the IP address and it turns out there's already an international issue connected with that."

Chuck and Joel looked at each other, a little concerned by the issue but relieved they were getting some helpful attention.

"I was immediately deputized and brought onto a team that has all kinds of resources to help if need be. Of course, everything you hear on this channel is highly classified. I will be listening to everything going on there, your voices and all the radio traffic. This won't interfere with normal radio transmissions, and you won't hear me unless I speak. If there is anything, anything at all, out of the ordinary, tell me. I'll be listening until you land at LHR."

"Thanks. I assume you'll hear either Joel or myself?"

"Yes. And if anything does happen, follow the normal ATC protocols. I will glean what I can from those first, but I'll be with you the whole time."

Then silence.

After the call to the pilots, JC gave Jackie a thumbs-up, and since the radio was quiet, he tuned back in to the briefing in progress. Ty Harris, State Department, was talking about a shadow regime of some sort and the tracking of their agents. "There's quite an international flavor to this, and it would benefit us if the organization responsible for foreign intelligence were brought on board."

JC waved at Jackie. He pointed at his mic to let her know he wanted to speak to the group. "And since we have this flight heading to London, we ought to call the Brits and let them know about it. Maybe they can have someone meet this flight or even the one carrying the Russian passengers. At least, they ought to be aware."

Phil answered both. "Good suggestions. Ty, I have a contact there. They may already be tracking, and if not, would certainly be highly interested in getting involved. JC, we'll get right on that."

Jackie turned him off, and JC's monitor went dark once more.

Chuck Merkel saw the plane first. "Joel, did you see that?"

"Yes, what was it?"

"It looked like a MiG. Couldn't tell if it's a twenty-three or twenty-seven."

"They look identical from a distance. Look, there's another one! They're too close! They seem to be tracking us specifically!"

"Joel, I need to concentrate on flying this, and can't deal with them in the sky here. Let someone know what's going on."

"Affirmative." He switched to the ATC channel. "Boston Tower, Air World flight 94."

They began to notice a little static in their radios. There was no response from Boston Tower. Joel tried again, again with no response. His Air Force training started to kick in. He tried Kennedy Tower, then Newark Tower. There was no response at all.

"Try Halifax. It's Canadian and on a different frequency set, but they are actually closest to us."

Halifax Tower did not answer either. Joel switched back to the Boston ATC frequency.

"JC, are you there?"

"Yes, I've been following you. Two MiGs, and no contact with ATC. Can you describe the planes? Do they appear threatening?"

"Black on top, light blue underneath, both of them. No other markings. They just appear to be stalking us. Wait — they're flying off, toward our ten o'clock and slightly below us."

Abruptly, Boston, Kennedy, and Newark Towers were calling them.

"Chuck, they were jamming us!"

"MiG twenty-sevens have jamming capability. Next time we'll just transmit in the blind, and maybe the message will get through."

Joel called the anxious control towers and explained about the MiGs and the jamming. "Did you track them?"

Boston Tower responded for them all. "When we heard you calling, we answered, and when you didn't hear us, we homed in on your location. We couldn't see them until they left you, then we saw them heading north."

"Thanks, Boston Tower. They may be back. We'll keep you posted."

In Chicago, JC suddenly heard voices in his headset at the same time it was being flashed across his monitor and started scrolling.

TIME 16:15:24Z. SOURCE AWA94. "JOEL, DID YOU SEE THAT?"

TIME 16:15:30Z. SOURCE AWA94. "YES, WHAT WAS IT?"

TIME 16:15:34Z. SOURCE AWA94. "IT LOOKED LIKE A MIG. COULDN'T TELL IF IT'S A TWENTY THREE OR TWENTY SEVEN."

JC noted the six-digit, down-to-the-second, time stamp in Zulu time, five hours ahead of Chicago's Central Daylight Time.

Phil was watching at the same time he was speaking to his counterpart, Bob McGee, at the CIA. He motioned to his VTC operator, and the meeting was filled with the audio from JC's radio. He gave the code for the VTC to Bob. When he hung up, he dialed his contact in MI-6 in London.

JC signaled Jackie, then addressed the group. "This is JC. Can we get the passenger list checked to see if there is a significant person on board, including the Russians, as a possible target? Captain Palova, or anyone, might there be military aircraft in the area which could provide cover or escort? Thanks."

At CIA headquarters, Bob McGee spat out his gum, drained his can of diet soda, grabbed his sweater, and headed to the VTC room. On his way out the door, he glanced at the thirty-year service certificate on his wall, affectionately dubbed his "marriage license" by his co-workers and subordinates. I love this job, he said to himself.

A minute later, the tenth monitor lit up in Phil's meeting.

"JC, this is Chuck. Those MiGs don't have radar, but they found us, so I assume they are talking to some station that is tracking us. My gut was telling me earlier to fly below the radar, but I have a lot of passengers and we need to know the best course of action if those guys come back. 'Below the radar' is thirty thousand feet below us."

"I have a US Navy captain here," JC said, "and he has really been scrambling since we started tracking you. He just let me know there is a carrier somewhere in the North Atlantic on an exercise, and he will get me the location. If they're close, they might be able to provide you cover or an escort. You might have to descend for them to protect you. He is also getting with his flight experts to advise you on your best maneuver courses."

Chuck's gut was talking to him again. "Sounds like starting a descent now might get us a head start on whatever course of action we come up with. We can reestablish our altitude later."

He explained the situation to Boston Tower. "At your discretion, descend to five thousand feet," they replied.

JC came back on. "The Air Force has two armed F-18 fighters in the air already, but they are about an hour away from where you'll be in an hour, assuming your current speed and heading. They have been directed your way."

The captain was on the intercom with the passengers, letting them know they would be descending as a precaution, and all services would be suspended until afterwards.

"Thanks, JC. Chuck is getting the passengers ready. Any word from the Navy?"

"Matter of fact, the office just got a call on the location of the aircraft carrier. Hold on a sec … How close are you to, it looks like, 35.3 north and 52.4 west?"

Joel consulted the flight map to plot the latitude and longitude. "That's just east of us, maybe twenty or twenty-five minutes. Good. Let them know we're coming."

A minute later, JC had some advice from the task force. "The consensus here is to descend below five thousand feet, pick up the escort, then ascend back to your original altitude."

Chuck did a quick calculation. "We've started our descent rather shallow, but we'll steepen it out to over eight hundred feet per minute. The passengers won't feel it, and we'll be below five thousand feet about the same time we reach the carrier. About thirty minutes. Let the Air Force know about the change."

Joel contacted Boston Tower and received authorization for the change in altitude.

"JC, why were you not jammed when all the towers were?"

"I think because this secure channel is digital and sends in bursts, like text messages. Because it's digital, it burns right through the analog signal the jammer is using."

Nothing to do now but wait.

"Say, Maggie, do you know a nine-letter word for a fishing net?"

Maggie laughed. "I saw that, too. I love crosswords. I saw the crosswords when I first got on and decided to save them for later. Did you already finish the easy one? The fishing net was in the hard one."

"You mean there are two?"

"Yes. I like doing the American ones because they are harder than the British ones. I spend most Sundays online doing American crosswords. Evan Birnholz is my favorite puzzle author. He's very clever. Plus, I get to learn American words and slang."

Matt didn't realize they put those kinds of words in crossword puzzles.

"Not all slang is vulgar, you know," she replied. "When my cousin Clarice said 'y'all' I knew what that meant. And when her five-year-old daughter Clara asked for a Moon Pie, I knew we were in for a treat and said I wanted one too."

"What was the clue for Moon Pie?"

"There've been several. I've seen it more than once. RC-Cola go-with, and s'more cousin. That's how I found out what a s'more is. And do you know where to get an RC-Cola? Eight letters. Fourth letter N."

"Um, I give up."

"Drinkbox. At least that's the way it's spelled. Clarice told me it's really pronounced drankbox."

They both chuckled at her attempt at speaking Southern.

"You came to visit me from first class. From luxury to not-enough-room. From five-course meals to bag lunches. From royalty to the commoner." He threw that last one in because of her accent.

"Haha! Yes, first class is very nice," she replied, not knowing she would never see that business class seat again. "I wish I could afford it!" She saw his quizzical look and went on. "I won a prize. I'm a primary school teacher in Bristol, and the city held a raffle to raise funds for all the primary schools there."

"We do that in some parts of the States."

"Yes, we learned that from our sister city in Tennessee."

"What city is that?"

"Bristol, of course! Not an official sister city, though. Anyway, the sponsors got Britannia Airlines to provide the tickets. From London rather than from Bristol because the Bristol flights are so much more expensive. First place was round-trip in first class for a family of four to anywhere they flew. Second place was first class for one person. Third place was an all-expenses-paid tour of the Royal Castle in Edinburgh, Scotland.

"I got the third-place prize, but the second-place winner was afraid to fly and offered to swap with me, because she had always wanted to see the castle, she said. My cousin Clarice lives in Macon, Georgia, and was thrilled I wanted to come see her. Second cousin, actually."

"To me, this is an Air World Airlines flight."

"BA is a partner with Air World. This flight has a BA flight number and a different AW number."

"It was nice of your husband to let you go."

"Oh. I'm not married. I was, but I'm not now."

"I'm sorry. I really am." He looked at Jenny. "I made a bad assumption."

"It's okay. It's really complicated, but I don't mind you knowing. My husband, John, couldn't get me pregnant. We both had tests done and it was him, not me. His best friend and best man at our wedding, Edward, offered to help. We both told him no. Not too long after that, we tried again and I got pregnant. Then we, my mum and I, found out that John and Edward were more than just best friends. They had had a lover's quarrel, and long story short, they got in a fight and killed each other. After they died, I grieved for a while, but was over it by the time Jenny was born."

Something didn't ring true. Matt thought she was a little too glib, a little too eager to tell the story. But he was enjoying Maggie's company and didn't say anything. Time would tell, he thought.

"How long had you been married?"

"About a year and a half. He was really kind of strange. Rather cold toward me. Pleasant enough but no warmth. Looking back, I think he wanted to put on a respectable front while he was sorting out his sexuality."

Matt was ready to move on past this unfortunate story. "Well, may he rest in peace."

"You mentioned you had children. Tell me about them. Are they grown now? Are you a grandpa?"

"Yes and no. I was,"—he choked back a tear—"but they are all gone now. And my wife, Helene." He looked away, off in the distance.

"Oh, no! I am so sorry! Can you talk about it?"

Matt took a minute. "I had a son and daughter. Todd and Rachel. They were both married to wonderful spouses and had five children between them. Both families died in separate accidents within a month of each other. Then a month after that, Helene had a brain aneurysm that burst, and she died of a massive hemorrhage before the ambulance could even get there.

"That all started about nine months ago. I was a mess for quite a while after that. I couldn't think. I couldn't plan. Life seemed to have lost its meaning. It was all I could do just to hang onto God. It would have been impossible except I knew he was hanging onto me. Does the term 'basket case' mean anything in England?"

Maggie had never heard words like that before, about hanging onto God. She knew there must be a God, but that was about all. And she had heard a little about Jesus, whom people mentioned when talking about God.

"Then," he continued, "about a week ago, I realized my self-pity was dragging me under. When I quit feeling sorry for myself, God spoke to me and told me he had a job for me."

She had never heard of such a thing. "God spoke to you?"

Matt was about to speak when the pilot came over the intercom. "I am turning the fasten-seat-belt lights back on as a precaution. We will be descending below ten thousand feet and you will be advised to turn off your electronics at that time. You will be further advised when the precaution is over, but until then, it will be necessary to remain in your seats, including the flight attendants." The intercom clicked off, and the movies and games resumed.

"Did you hear that?" he asked. When she nodded, he continued, "Well, it wasn't like that at all. It was more like just knowing. It's kind of hard to explain. The words just came into my consciousness, and way down deep in my spirit it was like, 'These are my words—listen to them.' I didn't hear that; but I knew it like I know my own name."

"I'm not following that very well."

"Okay. I'll try to find a better explanation. It might take me awhile though. Anyway, it looks like you and Jenny are stuck here until we pass through the shadow of death."

Maggie had heard of the shadow of death before but couldn't recall where. "We'll be fine. I just fed Jenny and she'll sleep for about an hour. At least, that's what happened on the flight over. She was a little fussy on the hop from Atlanta, but she settled down once we were on the ground. When you got on the plane, we had been on for about fifteen minutes and she was starting to get hungry. I fed her a little, but she didn't want much. They brought us dinner, and then I fed her again. I hope we are able to move around soon. All my stuff is up front. The only things I brought back here with me are our passports."

"May I hold Jenny?"

"Sure, but first I want to show you something, so it won't take you by surprise." She moved Jenny forward onto her lap and removed the pin holding everything in place. "It's much easier trying to keep her together on the plane—aren't big safety pins wonderful?"

As she undid the blanket at her feet, her left foot appeared, covered by a dainty white bootie with pink laces. Her right foot seemed to be hiding in the folds of the blanket. Maggie gently tugged on her right leg. There was no foot. Just part of a heel, then a stump.

"When I was about twelve weeks pregnant, I went in for my ultrasound. They said the heart was beating okay, head looked good, but it took them a long time to look over the rest of her. They took pictures and several doctors came in. Then they showed me. Both legs had formed normally, but something had caused my amniotic sac to form extra bands of tissue, one of which wrapped around her right ankle and kept squeezing it until it stopped the blood supply. Without a flow of blood to it, it stopped developing. What they showed me was that her foot was already gone. They said there was nothing they could do.

"When I got my twenty-week ultrasound, they confirmed the findings. Before I left the clinic after the ultrasound, a new doctor spoke to me about it. He said with amniotic band syndrome, these bands may strike again, wrapping around another limb, the umbilical cord, even the head. He said Jenny would not be normal, and there also may be other maladies or a still-birth.

"He told me it was not genetic, and they don't really know what causes it or how to prevent it. He did tell me if I got pregnant again, I would have less than a one-in-twenty-five-thousand chance of it happening again. He paused, and recommended I abort the baby. It was the best thing to do, he said, and I should think about it.

"I thought about it for as long as it took me to get my mouth open, and I told him I would never abort her! I will love her whatever happens to her. Period. I went home and cried. Not for me but for Jenny. By that time, we knew she would be a girl."

She rewrapped Jenny in the blanket, redid the pin, and Matt gently took her in his arms. She was so light, so little!

He now got a good look at Maggie without the babe-in-arms. She had a slender frame, but her body looked too thin, almost emaciated, in the dark shirt that looked one size too large. Her face was normal enough, though, with a glow of good health. And the flowers on her vest! "Those are my favorite colors," he said.

"Well, these are my favorite flowers. Petunias."

"Yes, I recognized them. I had a dream about them last night."

"You did? What about?"

He didn't want to sound morbid or weird. "Oh, not much. Tell me, what do you teach in Bristol? A grade level or a particular subject?"

She would ask about the petunia dream later. "Year fives, nine and ten-year-olds. I had twenty-two children last school year, and I'll have twenty-three kids when school starts up again in a couple of months. The numbers hold pretty steady, but the students are different every year. Last year was a good year, but the year-four class I'll get seems pretty lively."

She felt like it was his turn. She turned toward the lean, broad-shouldered man, noting his clean-shaven face. The hint of age lines gave his clear and engaging eyes an air of decency and openness. "If you want to, Matt, would you tell me why you're going to London?"

"I'm not sure where I'm going. My first step is to get to England. I'm taking it one step at a time now, which is quite an improvement." He stopped briefly. "I may get emotional. Maybe you should take Jenny back."

He wasn't worried for the infant, but he thought it would be easier to control his emotions if he could use both hands.

Maggie took Jenny and rocked her as well as she could. It was easier in first class, but she wouldn't go back there right now for the world.

"Are you sure you want to hear this?"

She could sense his pain, but gamely said, "Yes, definitely, if you want to tell me. Will you need tissues? I have some up front." Maggie always needed tissues when emotions were involved.

"I have some." He told her of the Costa Rica deaths of his daughter and her family. "Rachel was about your age, thirty-two."

"I'm twenty-eight," she quickly interjected.

"Oh. Sorry, I'm not too good with ages. Anyway, I completely blamed myself."

"How could you do that? You weren't even there!"

"Several weeks before they left, I had a dream."

Another dream. "About petunias?"

Soon. Not yet, Matt decided. "God gives me dreams sometimes, that's one of the ways he speaks to me. In this one, there was a big red circle with a red slash through it. You've seen them. Sometimes they have pictures in them. No parking. No cigarettes. No pets. No guns."

She giggled. "I've never seen that one anywhere in England."

"The 'do not' symbol was just kind of sitting there. Then the word 'precario' floated into the scene, and floated into and out of and through the symbol. This happened three times, then I woke up. I had no idea what it meant. I thought maybe it was 'precarious' misspelled, but how could that be from God if there's a word misspelled? So I forgot about it. Then a week later, I had the same dream again. I still made no connection with Rachel's mission trip so I dismissed it again. I just prayed and hoped God would take care of them. When the church called us to tell us what had happened, they told us where Rachel and her family had been staying."

Dealing with suspense wasn't one of Maggie's strong suits. "Where was it?"

"They were staying in a place called the Precario. When I heard that, I just went to pieces."

They both had tears streaming down their cheeks. Matt reached into his briefcase and pulled out two tissues. Maggie put her hand on Matt's forearm. "I'm so sorry. It must have been terrible for you. What could you have done,

Matt? What should you have done?"

"If the dream came from God then I could have, should have, asked him what it meant."

They were both quiet for several minutes before Maggie broke the silence. "What does that have to do with your trip to England?"

"Ah, yes. After Helene died, I was completely broken. It was torture just to wake up in the morning, to eat, to try to put one foot in front of the other. I had some good friends who appointed themselves to be my guardians. If not for them, I don't know how I would have made it. They kept me company all day, every day for months.

"I went for long walks. Long aimless walks, with friends at my side. I actually got some tone in my body after many years of a desk job. At some point several weeks ago, I realized how much I was feeling sorry for myself. I pulled myself out of that by writing poems about what had happened. It's poison, you know, feeling sorry for yourself."

"Poem therapy?"

"I tried different forms. Regular four-liners. Limericks, but those are supposed to be funny. I finally settled on haikus. They are three-line, seventeen-syllable poems originally done in Japan. Rhyming not required. For example, 'My children are dead. Does it really hurt so bad? Unquestionably!'"

"I've heard of those."

"After several days, I looked back over what I had done and found that every haiku had the words 'pain' or 'misery' or 'anguish', words of that sort. I decided this was helping, so I continued. Each line had to be either five or seven syllables, and I would say the lines out loud to make sure they sounded right. It seemed like good therapy, so I continued. Don't ask me what they were, because I threw them all away. I was starting to work on a new one. I forget what the line was I had made up, but when I went to say it, what came out of my mouth was, 'I have a job for you.'

"I thought that was crazy—it was six syllables. I tried another one. I wrote it down and counted the syllables. There were seven. Perfect! I said them out loud. 'I have a job for you' again. Those weren't even the words I had written. Suddenly, I realized those weren't my words at all. Just as suddenly, I knew whose words they were. And like a major shot of adrenaline, I was filled with energy and a feeling of purpose."

He stopped to catch his breath. "This time I asked God. And I heard, deep down in my spirit where words aren't even audible, yes, yes, yes, that I should go to England—I think I saw a map—and there I would find out what the job would be. 'That was odd,' I thought. But, why not? I booked the first flight that was available, and here I am. And, I might add, here you are."

Matt had perked up when he got to the part of his having purpose for his life again.

"That's incredible," was all she could muster, but she was still curious. "How did you know it was God?"

He said simply, "Because I know his voice."

Adela came up the aisle with snacks. Sometimes flight attendants forget to obey the pilot. They both had a soft drink. Matt got a little bag containing exactly eleven mini-pretzels and Maggie got a little bag of exactly eight peanut M&Ms.

A good time to change the subject. "Maggie, why did you come to visit me?"

She was expecting the question to come eventually, but at that point hadn't developed a plausible explanation. "Well, I noticed how you looked at Jenny and wanted to show her off."

"A wonderful reason." Then, after the perfectly timed pause, "but I'm not buying it!"

"Well, okay. I just wanted to hear about your petunia dream."

That deflection didn't work either. "I'll get to that soon enough."

She looked down shyly, fussing a little with Jenny's blanket. Then resolutely, she turned and looked him straight in the eye. "I don't know."

She was surprised at his response. "Now that's an explanation I can accept."

"Jenny and I were loving on each other when you came through the exit door. You said hello to the steward and your voice sent a tingling up and down my back. It was almost weird, that's never happened to me before. I didn't recognize your voice and as soon as you came into first class, I looked back down to Jenny. Then you stopped in front of me, almost like you had an appointment, and I was afraid to look up. But then I couldn't not look at you. I don't understand it.

"We looked at each other, and, um, I guess I was inspecting you. Who was this? The tingling came back. I got confused and excited at the same time. It was a big relief when you looked at Jenny." It came blurting out all at once. "After we took off and I fed Jenny, curiosity got the better of me and I just had to find out. Your looking at Jenny gave me the excuse I was looking for, and that's the reason I gave myself to come here."

"Actually, I knew you were coming. Didn't know exactly when, though."

Maggie's eyebrows furrowed. "What?! How could you know that?"

"Let me tell you the petunia dream first. I was seated in the center of what appeared to be a tribal circle, with people all around the edge watching intently. I seemed to be the center of attention, but I didn't know why. A woman came to me, a big woman. Taller than me. Bulky. Not obese or like a sumo wrestler, but she had a thick belly, thick chest, thick arms and legs. Perhaps Polynesian. Strong facial features, but no facial expression. Short dark hair.

"She was wearing a pale green muumuu with all kinds of fish all over it, from minnows to whales. She was carrying a dead baby and was giving it to me. The baby was little and had jet-black skin and pale yellow hair. I couldn't tell why the baby was dead. It didn't seem to be her baby, but she was somehow responsible for it. I took it and she stepped back. I held the baby up in the air as if to give it back to her.

"All of a sudden, flowers started falling out of the sky on top of the baby and her. I could tell they were petunias. When the ground was covered, we were all deluged by more petunias. She and I and the baby. Then she took the baby and raised it over her head. As soon as she did that, the baby came to life and started waving its arms and kicking its feet. She set the child on the ground and it started dancing around, all the way to the edge of the circle of people. I watched as it got there, and I noticed there was one face I recognized on the front edge of the circle."

"Wow, that is fascinating! Whose face was it?"

"Maggie, it was yours!"

She was quite taken aback. "How did you know it was mine? You'd never seen me before, as far as I know."

"I didn't last night. When I saw you this morning, I thought you looked vaguely familiar but couldn't place you. I thought maybe I'd seen you in a movie. It wasn't until I got to my seat and settled down that I made the connection. I guess it *was* sort of like a movie."

Maggie didn't know what to say, or even what to think. Was he making it all up? If so, where did the feeling come from that seemed to draw her here? She felt comfortable with him, but decided to see where this led before allowing herself any emotional involvement.

"As soon as I realized the face in the dream was yours," Matt said, "in that calm and quiet voice God uses with me sometimes, he said to me, 'I want you to tell her a secret from me.' So I knew you'd be coming to see me. But I have to tell you, I have no earthly idea what this is all about. I seem to be just as in the dark as you."

"I wish I could hear God speak like that. You're the first person I have ever heard speak of God that way."

"I'll tell you what the message is, but I feel like I need to do it quietly."

Matt lightly cupped his hand around her right ear, and in a low but distinct voice, said, "God will prove himself strong on your behalf during the next twenty-four hours."

Maggie was baffled. "I don't know what all that means. Did he give you any explanation?"

"No, like I said, I have no idea what it might mean, and I don't know if I have any part in it."

"When I was at the university, a friend invited me to go with her to a campus Bible group. I went a few times, but nothing ever seemed to make much sense."

Matt and Maggie finished their snacks and chatted for the next fifteen or twenty minutes, about where they lived, where they were born, their college experiences. Maggie mentioned her dad had passed away when she was fifteen, in an accident at the tin mine where he was a team leader. Her mum was still living in their home in Cheltenham, a town not far from Bristol. Matt mentioned the international food company he retired from after Helene died.

Maggie had gone to the University of Bristol in Clifton and received her Bachelor's of Education with an interest in childhood studies, and was hoping to go back sometime for her Master's in Education. He had gone to Ohio University and gotten a Bachelor's and Master's in Business Administration.

They both liked classical music and American bluegrass; she liked British pop and he liked Dixieland jazz. Maggie mentioned her brother Charles, about four years older, married with a boy and two girls. Matt told her about his sister Martha, a few years younger, with six children and fifteen grandchildren.

During this time, a ding sounded, indicating they were below ten thousand feet. Followed by the inevitable directive to turn off the electronics listed on page fifty-seven of the flight magazine.

As soon as it had become obvious that AW94 was being jammed, JC Smalley had addressed the group again. "JC here. Is one of us in touch with Boston Tower? We're getting their audio, but contact with them might be helpful for their radar feeds and any other actions they are aware of. Also, when does the previous flight arrive at Heathrow, the flight the Russians actually boarded? Should they be alerted?"

Silence. Then Dusty Mae Watt, Chicago special agent in charge, spoke up. "We'll handle that here in Chicago. We'll also have them contact the other flight if they haven't landed yet, and they'll be able to tell us about that flight."

"Thanks. If AW94 meets up with the carrier, will we need the Air Force sorties?"

Captain Palova answered, "The F-18s are armed, whereas the carrier aircraft are strictly in training mode. It would take them too long to switch to combat mode, and the escort to London would take them away from their current mission. They would do the escort, though, if the F-18s didn't show. As of right now, we don't know if any protection will be needed."

He did not seem too eager to commit military assets, JC thought.

Everyone in the VTC was transfixed by the events unfolding. Only three had military experience, and only one had seen combat. The actual dangers to the flight were unknown, although the jamming of their radio transmissions seemed to signal hostile intent. To those there, the dangers were very real and the suspense excruciating.

Bob McGee, Central Intelligence Agency and the newest member in the VTC, took the time to introduce himself while flight AW94 was performing its descent. "You may be wondering what department I'm representing. Just let it be CIA at present. Based on the little I heard from Phil, we may have some pertinent information for you, and as I listen to this meeting, I will know which folks to task. At any rate, I will be getting a brief together to share what we have."

TIME 16:40:19Z. SOURCE AWA94. "JC, WE'RE AT FIVE THOUSAND FEET. NO EVIDENCE OF A CARRIER. ASK THE NAVY IF IT COULD BE STILL IN THE

WATER."

Where else would it be, JC wondered.

Captain Palova, hearing the audio, answered before JC had a chance to respond. "Tell him it is probably moving so slowly you won't see a wake until you're closer. It needs a little movement for stability, so it is probably not still. The ship knows they're coming and when it finds them on radar, it will contact them directly. What is their current location?"

It scrolled on his monitor as JC passed the information and request to Joel.

TIME 16:42:04Z. SOURCE AWA94. "THIRTY FIVE POINT THREE ZERO NORTH, FIFTY TWO POINT FOUR FIVE WEST. NO SIGHT OF OTHER AIRCRAFT."

Something didn't look right to Captain Palova. With an urgency in his voice, he said, "JC, please scroll up to the coordinates you gave the aircraft."

Jackie scrolled up.

TIME 16:20:30Z. SOURCE JC SMALLEY. "MATTER OF FACT, THE OFFICE JUST GOT A CALL ON THE LOCATION OF THE AIRCRAFT CARRIER. HOLD ON A SEC. HOW CLOSE ARE YOU TO, IT LOOKS LIKE, THIRTY FIVE POINT THREE NORTH AND FIFTY TWO POINT FOUR WEST?"

Everyone could see on his monitor that Captain Palova blanched. "That's what I gave you. That's what I was given. I just called the ship to verify, and evidently, the numbers are backwards. The carrier is at 52.4 North and 35.3 West. That's almost fourteen hundred miles away. I'm sorry."

Jackie pressed the End button and the latest audio appeared.

TIME 16:43:53Z. SOURCE AWA94. "BELOW TWO THOUSAND FEET. ALL QUIET."

TIME 16:44:07Z. SOURCE JC SMALLEY. "CHUCK, JOEL, WE WERE GIVEN THE WRONG COORDINATES FOR THE CARRIER. IT IS NOT CLOSE TO YOU."

TIME 16:44:33Z. SOURCE AWA94. "AFFIRMATIVE. WE'LL COPE. THE AIR FORCE WILL BE ALONG IN WHAT, TEN MINUTES? DO THEY HAVE OUR FREQUENCY?"

TIME 16:45:02Z. SOURCE JC SMALLEY. "WAIT."

"Captain Palova?"

"Hold on. I'm talking to STRATCOM direct. ... Yes, have them use this." He gave JC the frequency, which JC recognized as the standard for Air Force combat emergencies.

JC passed the information to Joel.

TIME 16:45:58Z. SOURCE AWA94. "CHUCK THE MIGS ARE BACK. NINE O'CLOCK. TWO."

TIME 16:46:07Z. SOURCE AWA94. "BOSTON TOWER, AIR WORLD FLIGHT NINETY FOUR."

There was no response.

TIME 16:46:21Z. SOURCE AWA94. "BOSTON TOWER, AIR WORLD FLIGHT NINETY FOUR. IN THE BLIND. TWO MIGS, NINE O'CLOCK, TWO OR THREE KILOMETERS, CLOSING FAST."

TIME 16:46:35Z. SOURCE AWA94. "JC, THEY'RE SPLITTING UP. ODD UNDERBELLIES. CAN'T TELL. CHUCK IS TELLING THE PASSENGERS TO BRACE."

"That reminds me," Maggie said, "you never told me about what happened to your son ..."

"Todd. Todd and Gretchen. They were both thirty-seven. Rachel was five. She was named after her aunt, my daughter. The twins, Timmy and Ryan, were three."

The intercom came back on. "We are about to experience major turbulence. The ride might get extremely rough, but please stay relaxed. Flight attendants, do a walk-through check and assume in-flight precaution positions. This shouldn't last more than about five minutes."

Matt guessed "in-flight precaution" was code for something much more serious.

"I'll finish the story later. Do you think you could make a run for your seat up front?"

Maggie was scared. "No, I'd like to stay back here with you."

Matt nodded. "Okay. Here, give me your hand."

He took her free hand in his left and laid his right hand on Jenny's head. Then he asked God to protect the crew and passengers, and especially Maggie, Jenny, and himself.

The pilot was right. It didn't last more than five minutes. But everyone who heard him would have wished that it had.

TIME 16:46:43Z. SOURCE AWA94. "WE ARE ABOUT TO EXPERIENCE MAJOR TURBULENCE. THE RIDE MIGHT GET EXTREMELY ROUGH, BUT PLEASE STAY RELAXED. FLIGHT ATTENDANTS, DO A WALK THROUGH CHECK AND ASSUME IN FLIGHT PRECAUTION POSITIONS. THIS SHOULDN'T LAST MORE THAN ABOUT FIVE MINUTES."

TIME 16:48:00Z. SOURCE AWA94. JOEL, LET'S HOPE THIS IS MERELY HARASSMENT."

There was a thundering noise in the audio not captured by the scrolling text. The scrolling text also could not capture the excited alarm in Chuck's voice.

TIME 16:48:14Z. SOURCE AWA94. "THAT'S NOT A SIX THIRTY, THAT'S A GAH–."

The audio stopped and the red light went out on JC's radio at the same time.

It didn't take JC two seconds to understand what just occurred. "Gentlemen, we have lost contact with Air World flight 94. Ladies, too— sorry. I'm afraid if we want more information, we will have to find the black box."

Matt looked around, but couldn't see more than a few faces. Those he saw showed concern and a little fear, but no panic. The flight attendants had disappeared out of his field of view. His seatmate in 21H was asleep. He checked the man's seat belt; his seatmate was a good traveler and was still wearing it. The traveler in 21A pressed the button to lighten her window, affording a view of the outside world. Sunshine, blue sky, and a slight haze was all that was visible above them. Only 21A was able to see what was below them, and she promptly fainted.

Matt turned to Maggie and offered the most comforting words he could think of. "Remember God's promises, to you and to me."

Suddenly they heard a high-pitched b-r-r-r-pt coming from outside the plane. Before their brains could interpret the sounds as a rapid-fire machine gun, the front of the aircraft was rocked by a series of loud explosions. More explosions seemed to be coming from underneath and behind them. 21H woke up, and three quarters of economy went into panic mode. The entertainment systems all went dark. Adela grabbed the intercom mic from her seat in the front of economy, but the whole communication system was dead. The machine-gun sounds stopped; they had lasted only about ten seconds.

The on-board air sensor system immediately dropped down the oxygen tubes and masks to each seat. Most of the passengers grabbed the masks as lifelines, and a few managed to don them properly. Maggie's hands were occupied holding Jenny, so Matt made sure hers was on securely, then took his own and put it over Jenny's face.

"Switch places with me," he shouted over the screaming of the passengers. "I'll go find one in another seat."

They undid their seat belts, and Matt got into the aisle and started toward the front. The plane was dipping slightly to the right. Maggie had moved into 21E, but changed her mind, thinking she'd probably have more freedom of movement in the aisle seat, especially holding an infant. She glanced out the window as she started to sit, and saw flames and billowing black smoke blowing past. It's the engine, she thought.

The plane abruptly lurched hard as the right wing dipped into the water, then leveled off as it lost much of its speed. Matt was thrown face down onto the floor. Maggie, still holding Jenny, was pitched out of the seat into the aisle. She too was heading to the floor face first, but caught an armrest on the way down. She ended up on her back with Jenny on her belly.

The explosions started happening again. Matt managed to turn himself around with his head facing toward the rear. He turned to look toward the front, and saw daylight in front of the business class section. He guessed the entire front of the plane was missing. A fire had broken out in business class; plastic was burning, especially near the oxygen masks. The passengers were mostly motionless, as if the air rushing in from the front had incapacitated them. Matt could see blood, and the back of an unoccupied seat had been blown off. He could tell that many in the first five or six rows were already dead from the shrapnel and debris.

Maggie had her arms around Jenny, who was crying loudly. She heard and felt the explosions happening in the cargo hold. It seemed there were a lot of explosions in the rear of the plane. Smoke was blowing strongly past her.

Suddenly the plane bounced, with a rapid deceleration. The front section of the plane had been torn loose by the explosions. It was still connected, but only at the bottom. The metal and cabling acted like a hinge; the whole nose was simply hanging down. The cargo section underneath was shredded. There were big gaping holes in the front, and the metal skin covering the rear half of the underbelly was completely gone. When the nose section made contact with the water, it jerked the whole plane and broke off.

Inside the plane, everyone still seat-belted snapped forward, either breaking their necks or knocking them out on the seatback in front of them or on the bulkheads. Matt felt his knees buckle against the bulkhead in the front of economy, and Maggie, with her legs caught in the aisle between the 20C and 20D seat supports, was held fast.

The bounce caused the rear end of the plane to flip into the air. The tail flaps forced the plane back into a level attitude, but it over-rotated, slapped the water, and bounced again. It soared straight up into the air, nosed over, and came crashing straight down into the water.

On the second bounce, Matt and Maggie were tossed into the air like rag dolls. As the Boeing Dreamliner dove down into the ocean, the water came hurtling through the cabin with the force of a firehose. It blew past Maggie, carrying her with it out through the missing tail section. The water drove through faster than the plane sank. It shot her into the air and she landed in the ocean. It all happened so fast she didn't lose consciousness.

The water was cold, but the bigger shock was that she noticed her arms were empty. Where is Jenny? She screamed, and in a panic, started thrashing the water with her hands and arms. "Jenny! JENNY!" With much effort, she swiveled completely around. There was a small fire on the water a short distance away where the plane had gone in, and aside from some debris which looked like it was about to sink, Maggie was all alone.

There was a stunned silence as the rest of the VTC struggled to make sense of JC Smalley's pronouncement. Only a few knew what had just happened. Kirby Drinkard, DHS, was not one of them. The last text from AW94 was frozen on the screen. "What do you mean? What was their last statement, about six-thirty? Was that a time?" she asked.

JC hesitated, then spoke carefully. "A combat-loaded MiG-23 or MiG-27 could have, as standard armament, a flex-mounted six-barrel thirty-millimeter machine gun known as a six-thirty. Did you hear the thunder in the background right at the end? The six-thirty could make that sound. It can fire up to one hundred rounds per second. But Chuck thought it was something different. It could have been an air-to-air missile or a different machine gun or something else. Evidently, he recognized it, but the radio was killed before he got the words out. Hopefully, the cable leading back to the black box was intact long enough."

There were questions and exclamations from all the other monitors at once, then a pause, allowing Dusty Mae an opportunity to report her contact with Boston Tower. "Radar shows nothing in the area where they were reported to be, meaning any activity there had to happen within about five hundred feet of the surface. They showed AW94 suddenly disappearing a few minutes ago as it descended below radar detection. The only other aircraft they show are the two Air Force planes coming in from the northwest."

Phil broke in, "Can we get a video and/or audio feed from these planes? Can we talk to them directly? Do they have the radio system JC is using?"

Captain Palova responded, "The military planes don't have the same secure system. I can get a radio here to talk to them, so that should provide the audio feed. I'll see if we can patch them in to the VTC. At worst, you'll hear their transmissions through my monitor, and I might have to forward any of your questions to them, since continuous radio traffic with the VTC would keep them from other channels."

The meeting had come to a standstill. No one had anything appropriate to contribute, and no one wanted to leave, to miss anything. A sense of morbid curiosity pervaded the assembly, like they were watching a boat going over Niagara Falls.

The water bypassed Matt at first, but coming around the bulkhead to the right, it pushed him into the stream behind Maggie and out through the tail section. As he was passing from the darkness of the cabin into the light of day, he became aware of an unnaturally dark purple strip preceding him through the hole. Extremely bright flashes on this strip resolved themselves into letters, then into words. Four words. He found himself in the ocean, about four feet underwater, before he figured out which way was up. By the time he broke the surface, the plane was gone.

Matt didn't have any trouble finding Maggie; her voice gave away her location. "Jenny! JENNY! Where are you?! God, you should have taken me and not her! Jenny! I'll find you! Come back!" Screaming, panic stricken, unable to keep her head completely out of the water, she was swallowing too much salty brine, and coughing.

Matt swam to her quickly. "It's Matt!" he shouted. He could tell she was nearly exhausted. The salt water was providing some extra buoyancy, but not enough for the condition she was in. "Maggie! I'm with you! Give me your hand!"

"Matt!" she screamed, "I can't swim! I lost Jenny! I was holding her and all of a sudden she was gone! I can't find her!"

Treading water, he reached out his hand. She grabbed his right arm with her left, then grabbed his shoulder with her free hand and tried to climb up on top of him to get a better look. They both went under. Maggie instinctively let go. Matt turned her around and grabbed the collar of her vest. He brought them both up to the surface, but Maggie, still in a panic and suddenly feeling her movements restricted, broke free by swinging her arms wildly. He grabbed her collar again and she was quiet for a moment, breathing heavily.

A sudden frenzy in the water below got their attention. A large silvery object was hurtling upwards toward them. Shark!

She screamed again and tried to get out of its path. Before she could move, it broke the surface about six feet away.

It was the tail cone section. Because of its aerodynamic shape, it was being driven upwards with great speed by a large bubble of air below it. It exited the water and flipped over. They could see it was about four feet in diameter and about two feet of its height was above the surface of the water. The metal rim of the tail cone, where it had been ripped from the plane, had sharp, jagged edges interspersed with holes from the exploding bullets. The end of the cone, which was submerged, had a hole in it which was causing the cone to fill with water.

In her panic, Maggie looked at the object as a platform to get a better look at her surroundings. "Let me go! I want to climb on that to see if I can see Jenny."

"No! It's very sharp and it's sinking! You'll cut your hand to shreds and it will suck you under when it goes down!"

She fought him, but he held on. The tail cone was very close to them. Suddenly, just for an instant, Maggie felt a calm and a peace that all would be well. Then panic took over again and she broke free of Matt, to try to climb on the tail cone. Instead, she sank again, swallowing more water and choking. The tail cone section sank with her. Matt pulled her up again by the collar of her vest.

"Maggie, relax! Trust me! I've got you!"

"How? I can't relax! I have to find Jenny!" She screamed again. Her wild movements were doing nothing to keep her above water, but Matt, from behind, was at least keeping her head in the air.

"I'm going to keep you from sinking! Trust me! I'm helping you!" He was shouting at her. "Trust me!"

Her ears heard the words but her mind was slow to respond. She knew it was Matt's voice and she was already beginning to get comfortable with him on the plane. But this? Then she forced herself to remember the fleeting calm and peace from about fifteen seconds earlier. She took a deep breath and relaxed.

The sudden stillness took Matt by surprise. Her face went under even though he still had the back of her vest, and he went under with her. He kicked twice and they were able to breathe again. He checked her to see if she had passed out.

"I can't swim," she screamed, "and I can't see Jenny! I lost her!" She broke into loud sobbing.

Matt was concerned she might go into shock. He was also concerned that he himself might go into shock. But he had more bulk about him, keeping him somewhat warmer and somewhat more able to float. "Maggie, listen to me!"

She nodded, and he realized she would be able to cooperate and wouldn't pull him under again. He relaxed his grip and grabbed her arm, allowing her to turn and face him. He was kicking hard, treading water for them both.

"There's something over there we can hold onto." He nodded toward it. "I'm going to swim us to it. I'm going to try to keep your head above water the whole time, but you need to take good breaths when your mouth is out of the water in case you go under a little."

She nodded again. His Boy Scout days were about fifty years behind him, but he thought he remembered the salient points from his Lifesaving Merit Badge. "I'm going to turn you around and crook my arm around your neck.

Then with your back on my hip, you'll be face-up and level. Put both hands on my arm, and pull on it if I start to choke you. That will give your neck more room."

Maggie could tell he was starting to get tired. "Okay. I'm ready."

The object was about twenty-five yards away. His arms and legs burned well before they got there, and his chest was heaving terribly when they finally reached it.

Maggie felt him quit moving, and when she didn't sink, she pulled herself from beneath his arm and grabbed what Matt had found to hang onto. It was a coffin handle.

Panting heavily, the two survivors were holding onto the only other thing left floating from the drowned aircraft. It was a coffin, but as they relaxed and became vertical in the water, they bumped into an object underneath the coffin. They discovered the coffin was strapped onto this object, which turned out to be a shipping pallet slightly larger than the coffin. On a hunch, Matt pulled himself to the end of the coffin and around it, and saw two more coffins attached to the same pallet. "Maggie," he yelled, "we might be able to climb up on this!"

Maggie joined him. "Boost me up, I'll be able to see better. Quick!"

This was easier said than done. Although they had been in the water just a short time, they had gotten used to the buoyancy the salt water provided and she felt like a ton as she used the pallet as a step to climb onto the coffin. She finally made it up and stood on top looking all around. "There's another one up here," she called down. The coffins swayed as she shifted her weight. Her hysteria was starting to subside.

"I'm coming up. Do you see any sign of Jenny?"

He was anxious for her, but he already knew what the answer would be. Just then, a wave passed through their little floating island, and the sudden lifting of the end where Maggie was standing pitched her back into the ocean. She grabbed a lungful of air before she hit the water, then closed her eyes and waited for Matt to find her and bring her back on board.

Matt pushed off after her and soon they were climbing onto the nearest coffin. On her way up, Maggie had thrown up most of the seawater she had swallowed. She was weeping, and Matt surmised her scan of the water around them was unfruitful.

Directly overhead, the sun bore down on them in full strength. There was not a cloud in the sky. That's why it was a puzzle when they heard thunder. They didn't pay too much attention to it, since at that moment, a haze began to form over the water. With it, a supernatural calmness came over the pair. Matt recognized it; he had experienced it before. All Maggie noticed was that the shock, both physical and emotional, was replaced by peace in her body and clarity in her mind.

In any disaster, the first thing to do after you catch your breath is a damage assessment. Matt put himself in charge of that. "Maggie, are you hurt at all, anywhere? Are you bleeding?" He saw her hair all over the place. "Turn around and let me see the back of your head!"

He turned his head to show her the back of it. "I'm okay as far as I know, but take a look here."

"I'm okay too," she said. "Your head looks fine. I'm kind of sore from all the water gymnastics, and I must have banged my shin sometime since the last time I was dry." She rolled up her pant leg to find a lump on the inside of her left shin. "But it's not bleeding. The skin's not even broken."

That was a good sign, Matt thought, complete sentences, and a little bit of humor. "Okay, let's do an inventory. I see we both have our sneakers, you still have your petunia vest, and I have my watch."

He looked at his watch. The crystal had broken, and judging by the black spot on what was left of it, the seawater had caused a short and the battery had burned out the works inside. "Check your pockets."

"I have our passports held together with two broccoli rubber bands and a penny. Clara gave me the penny at the airport, and said, 'Keep this and you'll never go broke!' I always keep our passports in my back pocket; everything else is replaceable. 'Everything else' is what I left up front when I came to visit you."

"And I have my passport in my pocket for the same reason as you. Let's see what else we have."

"I don't understand about the penny. Is this like a good luck thing in the States, to give someone a penny when they go on a trip?"

Matt grinned, in spite of their situation. "No. How can you be broke if you still have a penny?"

They turned their attention to their lifeboat. As Maggie had noticed, there was a fourth coffin sitting loose at an odd angle on top of the three, which were strapped to the pallet with thick plastic strapping belts. They straightened it, and tipped it over slightly between two of the bottom coffins. Matt noticed all the coffins were held closed with wing nuts rather than the coffin bolts they use at funerals to lock the coffins. He opened the front end of the coffin on top, where the head would be, and was relieved that there was no head there, just a pillow. He closed the cover.

The shipping label said the pallet would have gone on to Charles De Gaulle International Airport after the transfer at Heathrow. "These are all made of myrtle wood," he told her. "I guess they don't see much myrtle wood in Paris."

"How do you know? Are you a wood expert?"

He grinned at her again. "No, there's a sign on the end here!" He read it. " '100% myrtle wood. Myrtle trees are found in only two places on earth: Oregon and Israel. This wood possesses a variety of different colors and is sought for its great beauty. Hardwood Casket Co, Redmond Oregon.' And there's a shipping address in Paris."

"It doesn't look very beautiful now. Look at the burn marks all over them. Little charred spots, like cigarette burns you'd find on the tables in a cheap pub. On the sides, though, the finish they covered them with looks like it will keep all the water out."

"Hmm. I would have thought the explosions I heard would result in splintered wood. I wonder if they were shooting a special kind of ammunition. But," he added, "it sure did a number on the nose and tail."

"I heard them too, and it seemed like little sparks were shooting through the floor whenever there was an explosion." She checked her clothes. "I was lying on the floor part of the time, but it doesn't look like those got me!"

"It didn't seem like they were trying to get us passengers, but they sure shot up the cargo section. Maybe they just assumed everyone would be killed."

"Matt, that was the tail of the plane I wanted to climb on. I'm glad I didn't, but I wonder why they went to such trouble to shoot it off."

Matt thought a moment. "I'll bet they didn't want the plane to ever be found, and they were trying to destroy the black box."

"What is that?"

"It's the voice and data recorder that investigators can use to tell why a plane crashed, or had an emergency. It also sends out a signal so searchers can find it when they get close enough. They probably weren't trying to cause the tail to come off the plane—that was God's work. If the tail were still on the plane, then we'd still be on the plane too!"

The thunder got a little louder. They looked around, but couldn't find its source. All they saw, was that the fire on the surface, which seemed to be fed by fuel leaking from the sinking plane, was moving away from them. Maggie stood up again to look for Jenny, holding Matt's outstretched arm for support. Nothing. The sea was fairly calm, and there was a slight breeze. Matt pulled Maggie down to him, and hugged her tightly. "I think Jenny must have gone down in the plane. I'm so sorry!"

She turned around, buried her face in his chest, and sobbed. "I'll never see her again!"

Presently, Captain Palova's monitor showed him making a communications check with one of the Air Force planes, whose call sign was Hotel Romeo Seven Three. JC couldn't tell if Captain Palova's call sign, Papa Mike Zero Six, was his real call sign or one made up for the occasion. Evidently, Hotel Romeo 7-3 had been briefed about whom he would be talking to.

After a few minutes, the Air Force called. "Papa Mike 0-6, this is Hotel Romeo 7-3. We are approaching the way point. There is black smoke in the distance."

JC interjected, "Black smoke may indicate burning jet fuel."

"This is Hotel Romeo 7-3. There are two aircraft in the area of the smoke. We should be on-scene in twenty seconds."

"Hotel Romeo 7-3, this is Papa Mike 0-6. Roger."

Matt and Maggie were startled by a loud screaming noise accompanying the thunder, which was now deafening. Through the haze they could see what appeared to be two military fighter jets coming directly at them! They passed overhead, and began firing at the blaze in the water and all over the place in that general area. They heard a loud explosion and a plume of black smoke rose from a spot a bit farther away from them than the surface fire. They circled around and came back, firing again, and there was another explosion. And a third.

Suddenly a different screaming. Two more aircraft appeared and gave chase. Matt recognized them. "That's our Air Force!" he exclaimed, pointing. All four aircraft quickly disappeared out of sight, and it was eerily quiet.

"This is Hotel Romeo 7-3. Aircraft appear to be MiGs. Perhaps twenty-threes. They have departed, approximate heading one-eight-zero. We are pursuing with intention to engage upon authorization."

Another voice broke in. "Raptor Base. Negative, do not engage. I say again, do not engage. Pursue at a distance to ascertain exact direction. Do not overtake. What is your fuel level?"

"Roger, base. Approximately one hour forty-five minutes. Scheduled refuel in one hour. Papa Mike 0-6, location of fire is 35.177, negative 52.204."

Raptor Base came back on about five minutes later. "Hotel Romeo 7-3, this is base. Discontinue pursuit, return to fire location for assessment, report info to Papa Mike 0-6, then proceed to refuel. Provide video if available."

"Roger. Video not available. Hotel Romeo 7-3 clear."

Five minutes later. "Papa Mike 0-6, this is Hotel Romeo 7-3. Direction at break pursuit was due south, one-eight-zero. We are at fire location. Fire still burning, very little smoke. There is a slight ground haze not affecting visibility, and we and Hotel Papa Five Seven observe no debris using standard search protocol. Sorry we weren't there sooner. Is there anything else we can do for you?"

"This is Papa Mike 0-6. Negative and thank you." They ended communications.

Maggie and Matt were both motionless on the little craft, stunned.

"Matt, they didn't shoot at us! How could they have not seen us? We were sitting ducks!"

"They didn't see us. Perhaps it was the haze and they couldn't see through it. I don't think they were shooting at the fire. I think they were shooting at something else."

"But what? There's nothing else out here."

"I don't know," he said slowly. Then he continued in a different vein.

"Maggie, think back to when you were blown out of the plane through the tail. Did you lose consciousness? Tell me what you remember."

"Well, the plane bounced and I was thrown onto the ceiling. I think I still had Jenny at that point. Then the plane pitched over and I was in mid-air. I may have lost her then, because I was wildly trying to grab onto something. Then the water hit me and I was just squirted out into empty space, like water coming from a garden hose. No, I never lost consciousness. I came down in the water and my first thoughts were for Jenny. How about you?"

"I remember all the explosions underneath us. I had gone forward to find an oxygen mask and saw daylight where the front of the plane should be." He wondered if he should tell her what he saw. No, maybe later. "I was thrown down at the bulkhead between coach and first class. The plane lurched this way and that, and I found myself in mid-air just like you. It was surreal. I should have been knocked out or at least overcome by the events to a point of witlessness, but I was completely at peace.

"It was like slow-motion. Then the plane bounced, and I could see everyone's head snap forward. Except yours and mine, because we weren't belted in. Then the water grabbed me and spewed me out right behind you. I'm surprised I didn't land on you. As I was going out, from the darkness into the brightness, my eyes caught sight of something very bright, even brighter than the daylight."

"Was it a reflection of the sun off something?"

"No. It was words. Bright, golden words made of letters that seemed to be on fire. They seemed to be attached to a long, dark purple banner. It was spectacular!"

"Could you tell what the words were? What did they mean?"

"Yes, I could read them. And I know what they mean in general. But I don't know what they mean in particular. In fact, I've seen them ever since I first saw them. I can still see them. But now they are darkish blue letters on a pale yellow background."

What Matt was now seeing was like a negative, like when you look out a window into the daylight; the window frame looks dark and the window bright. When you close your eyes, the scene is still there, but the frame is white and the window is just a black square.

"Tell me! Please?" She felt like one of her year fives. She caught something out of the corner of her eye. "Oh, no!" she wailed, "It's a real shark this time!"

Phil had resumed control of his meeting, addressing the members of the VTC. "First of all, a word to our military. Thank you for your support in this. Captain Palova, do not think of this as a failure. It seems they, whoever 'they' are, were determined to kill AW94. If the pilots knew the real location of the carrier, the flight would have been killed at thirty thousand feet instead of at the surface, since it would have taken what, over two hours to reach their actual location?

"If you think about it, there is a benefit to the crash taking place near the surface, and that is we know exactly where to look for it, and the black box will have a greater chance for survival, and may even still be connected to the plane.

"Secondly, I noticed there are new faces at this meeting. Let me give you a quick synopsis of what else we know, especially for Bob's sake, so he can brief us on what the CIA knows. A week and a half or so ago, we became aware of a group operating in this country. We have no firm idea of the group's identity, personnel, agenda, or resources. That's why we're calling it a shadow regime. We've been operating mostly on rumors and speculation, although these have come from fairly reliable sources.

"A week ago, Barry Mantile from Treasury let our office know of strange money transfers into and immediately out of a bank account in California, an account Barry's folks had been monitoring. As soon as the transfer-out occurred, the account disappeared completely. This all was accomplished out of Macapá, Brazil, using the same IP address JC said was hacking the Air World flight data. The same sources are hinting at some new form of chemical agent already somewhere on the West Coast.

"Bob, does this give you enough to go on? We are taking this very seriously. This is the first VTC where we think we have most of the right players involved. Captain Palova's participation was just a guess to keep him in the loop, just in case. Louis, now I'm glad you're with us."

"Phil, Bob here. I'll see what I can find out. Give me a couple hours."

"Thanks. Lastly, we need to pause and regroup. The world will know about AW94 shortly. We know more than anyone else, and our organizations will be flooded with questions and rumors. Let's quash what rumors we can, without divulging what we know. Let's meet again at 4 p.m. Eastern, if everyone can make it. I know it's a Friday, but we might have to meet through the weekend based on what we hear from Bob."

Matt looked in the direction Maggie was pointing. "Oh, not to worry!"

"What?!"

"Those are dolphins. They have just one dorsal fin and their tails are flat in the water."

There were two of them. They watched as the dolphins reached their craft and chattered, showing off. When they started playing around their boat, Matt remembered the banner. "I'll tell you the words, but there's something else to tell you first." He looked at the water beside their little raft and pointed. "What do you see?"

"Um, it looks like a jellyfish. Just floating there, not trying to swim. But it's moving past us, like the current is pulling it."

"Yeah, do you feel the breeze?"

"Oh, I see. Maybe the breeze is blowing it."

"Then why isn't the breeze blowing us too? No, something is pulling us, against the breeze, and against the current. And, I might add, away from the fire and whatever those planes were shooting at."

As if on cue, the US Air Force returned. The pair of jets circled the area at different altitudes. One flew directly overhead.

"They're looking for survivors!" Maggie and Matt shouted simultaneously, and they both began waving their arms, trying to signal their existence. The two planes circled once more, however, then took off together. Soon they were lost to sight. Their arms dropped, their shoulders sagged, and there was disappointment written across both faces.

"They didn't see us any more than the first planes. If they had, they would have acknowledged us somehow." Matt was getting this from old war movies. "One of them would have flown as low and slow as he could, circle us, and dip his wings or something. If he could get close enough, we might have seen him waving!"

"Well, that was quite a let-down! I hope they send a salvage ship to get the plane off the bottom. They came straight back to us, so they must have GPS'd the location of the fire." Then she added, "I wonder where we are."

Matt could see that Maggie, in spite of the pain of losing her daughter, was in survival mode and was moving on from the lost rescue opportunity.

She was actually trying to process the breeze and the jellyfish. "It seems that everything but us is standing still and we are being pulled into the breeze instead of being pushed by it. Like we had a trolling motor attached."

Matt was astonished. "Maggie knows trolling motors?"

"Of course! Eight letters for 'trolling motor manufacturer.' I had no idea what a trolling motor was, so I had to look it up. Then I knew what that was, but I had to get all the crossing words to find out that it was Minnkota that made them. An American crossword, of course. But I'm dying to know what the words are!"

"I can still see them. Maggie, I still don't understand their particular meaning, but I get the distinct impression that the words are for you and that you will know. But I know who they're from. God has spoken to me before this way, and his words never come unless there is also a deep-down conviction that they are from him and they are trustworthy. It's just four words, and here they are: 'Rachel will suckle Jennimoore.' "

Her expression changed abruptly and Matt found it impossible to decipher it. But all she said was, "What do you think it could mean?"

"Well, I started thinking perhaps Jenny could be short for Jennimoore, but I've never heard of that name. I thought it would be just Jenny, or maybe Jennifer or even Jenalyn. Then I thought maybe my Rachel was in heaven taking care of your Jenny, but that wouldn't work. It should have been 'is suckling' rather than 'will suckle.' And Jenny shouldn't need suckling in heaven. I'm totally at sea about this, so to speak. Let me know what it means to you."

"You can still see the words?"

"Yes."

"How is Jennimoore spelled?"

"J-e-n-n-i-m-o-o-r-e."

For a moment, Maggie couldn't move. Tears were streaming down her face, and she made no attempt to stop them. Her lips quivered; she was trying to speak but no words were coming. She reached into her back pocket and pulled out two passports held together by two thick green rubber bands. She looked at one and handed the other one to Matt. "Look inside," she whispered hoarsely.

Matt opened it to the page with her picture and read, "TRILLBEY,

RACHEL MARGARET."

"I am Rachel! My parents felt obliged to name me that in memory of his grandmother, who died two days before I was born. But they never called me that. I've been Maggie ever since I could remember. You couldn't have known, because I only called myself Maggie. And I know you couldn't have figured that out by looking at the passports, because Jenny's passport proves you haven't seen them." She handed the other passport to Matt.

He opened it. "TRILLBEY, JENNIMORE LOUISA. I don't understand—I didn't spell it right."

"No! You did spell it right. That's just it! As soon as I got her passport, I took it right down to the passport office and explained they misspelled her name. She needed to have a corrected passport. They told me no one I showed it to would know the difference, and if I wanted it corrected, I should wait until I get back. They could send in the correction, but I wouldn't get it back before we were due to leave. Those idiots! If you had seen the passports, you would have misspelled Jenny's name just now."

Matt had a different take on the idiots. Oh, how God makes all things work for good.

As soon as the VTC was over, Penny brought JC his cleared electronics and showed him around the office, introducing him to everyone there. She was not able to add anything to what Phil Henry had briefed the group. After a quick meal at the cafeteria, she brought him to a small suite where his luggage was waiting. "I'll be back in a half hour. There's a secure phone here, but if you want to make personal calls you'll have to use your cell. There's one more area here I want to show you, then it seems like there will be plenty for you to do on this case. I'll be around if you need help, but I'll be pretty busy myself."

JC called Nicki first. He had explained what Phil had meant when he told him to give her a hug, then had given her the obligatory hug. Then a real hug. He missed her already, but kept that to himself. They chatted briefly; he would miss their lunch date tomorrow and probably wouldn't be home for the service on Sunday.

"I'll miss you, but this gives me some time to spend shopping with Cassie." Cassie was her adult daughter from her previous marriage, JC's step-daughter. They professed their undying love for each other and hung up.

"So, Maggie, what is your conclusion about the message?" Matt asked.

"That you couldn't be making it up. It would be impossible for you to make it up. My first thought was that you were just trying to make me feel better. It would have been cruel when I found out it was made up and not real. Then I realized I had already trusted you, twice, with my very life, and you haven't let me down yet. I believe you wouldn't do that to me."

"You're right. I wouldn't. So, where do you think the message came from?"

Maggie trembled inside. Who was she that God would have regard for her humble state? How could she ever think she deserved to have such a good thing happen to her? Jenny was gone…

"I dare not hope," was all she could muster. "Besides, I wouldn't be able to suckle Jenny."

"Do dare! God can do anything! Things we think are impossible, are possible with God. Can't you see how he has been working on your behalf? Oh, and I owe you an apology. What I whispered in your ear earlier wasn't the complete quote. I left out the word 'all' by accident. It should have been, 'God will prove himself strong on your behalf all during the next twenty-four hours.' "

"I don't understand how that is different."

"Well, without the 'all', God could have done just one thing for you. With the 'all', it will be continuous."

They were sitting on top of the exposed bottom coffin and leaning against the one on top. It was not very comfortable and they kept shifting their weight. Maggie thought it must be easier for her because she could cross her legs, but it didn't look like Matt was quite so flexible.

It was warm. Matt checked his watch again. It was still broken. The breeze had stopped, and the sea was like glass, except where the surface was broken by the dolphins frolicking nearby. The haze was still hanging in the sky above them; had it not been for that, they both would have been as red as the proverbial beet.

"Well, Matt, I hope he starts soon."

"Huh? … Let me review things that have happened to you since I said that in your ear and you tell me if you think it qualifies as God watching out for you and caring for you."

"All right, go ahead."

Maggie suddenly realized she was about to lose this game big-time.

"You weren't wearing your seat belt when the plane bounced, and therefore didn't have your head snap forward, breaking your neck or at least knocking you out."

She thought briefly. "Yes."

"You got thrown out of the plane alive."

"Yes."

"You were conscious the whole time."

"Yes."

"You didn't get caught on anything in the plane or come in the slightest contact with any of the jagged, twisted metal on your way out, so that you aren't bleeding, and have no broken bones or other injuries."

"Yes."

"Our plane was shot down and destroyed."

"No!"

"Right. That was a trick question. That happened, but it's hard to see how that was God watching out for you. However, I'm going to ask you again tomorrow, to see if you change your answer. How about, that all those same things happened to me?"

"Yes. Without you, I'd be dead right now. I'm starting to feel miserable about not answering your question."

"But there's more! We weren't even detected when those planes came and shot up everything floating on the water."

"Yes."

"God moved us away from the center of action so we wouldn't be hit by mistake. Then he gave us a breeze and jellyfish, to show he was the one pulling us."

She was beginning to marvel. "Yes."

"He gave me a message for you, and proved to you he was the author of the message."

"Yes!"

"What question?"

"That one. 'Where did the message come from?' How could it not be God? But it is completely beyond my comprehension, why he would do this for just me. So I will say it, Matt. Yes, I believe God was the author of that message. You said you understood it in general, even though you didn't know who the Rachel and Jennimoore were. What did you mean?"

"Well, I knew instantly those were God's words. Just as instantly, I knew I would be all right, otherwise, why the message? Somehow, the word 'suckle' told me that I wasn't by myself, since he had already given me one message for you, and the petunia dream. Therefore, we would both be safe.

"By the way, Maggie, now that Jenny is gone, I think perhaps you are the big woman in that dream, bringing me the baby. And do you know, if they hadn't misspelled Jenny's name, you would have no reason to believe it was God's message? Anyway, as soon as I hit the water, I started looking for you."

"Two seconds delay, and you wouldn't have found me. I'd have been completely under and going down."

They watched the dolphins at play for a few minutes. Matt was about to remind Maggie of something she had said, but she spoke first.

"Matt," she started, somewhat bashfully, somewhat contritely, "you apologized just now for leaving out a single word. I feel I need to apologize to you for something a whole lot worse, something I said to you. It was a complete lie, an utter fabrication."

"Oh?"

"Yes. Jenny's father. It didn't happen that way at all. I thought at the time that you didn't really believe me, and you were right. Did God tell you?"

"No. I don't know any of your secrets, other than what you tell me yourself. I did think it a bit odd, though. I had just met you, and I thought you were a little too willing to tell that story."

"I've never been married. I've been a real wreck for the last couple of years. I was disappointed with life. I made bad choices. Sometimes I hated myself. I wasn't happy being single, but I thought I'd be much more miserable married. I'm fairly gregarious, but sometimes I wonder if that's just learned behavior, rather than being naturally me. I get along well with my fellow teachers, and I love all my little year fives. They're the perfect age!

"Anyway, I met a fellow at our fifth college reunion. He worked near London and was visiting Bristol for a few weeks. He decided to come to the reunion. He was charming. I had too much to drink, and we had a one-night stand. I guess I was looking for something. Eight weeks later, I found out I was pregnant. He told me it wasn't his. I told him it couldn't be anyone else's.

All this over the phone."

She paused, anxiously searching Matt's face for support or acceptance, she didn't know which. His eyes gave her both.

She went on, "He called back about a week later, and told me he had thought it over and decided he should do the right thing. Could I come to London? The alarm bells should have been going off, but weren't. I told him I would be busy for two or three weeks and I'd come after that. I wanted to show him Jenny's first ultrasound, but I didn't know about her foot yet.

"I brought the pictures with me to London and showed him right off when I got to his place. Looking back, I think he was just going to use me, then dump me when I got too pregnant. Jenny's foot took him by surprise, and it didn't take him three minutes to tell me he didn't think he could ever be her father. Or words to that effect. I cried all the way back to Bristol that evening."

"Maggie, is that really the way it happened? What about everything else you told me?"

He believed she was telling the truth, but he wanted to hear her say it.

She passed up the opportunity to feel wounded at his questions, knowing she brought it on herself, and not denying his right to express it. "Oh, Matt, it is. I'm sorry, and I promise I will never lie to you again."

Matt was curious. "Why did you lie to me, anyhow?"

Maggie was coming face-to-face with her carefully constructed persona and she was finding it rather distasteful. Maybe Matt … "I wanted it to look like I had it together," she started. "Also, it would keep people from judging me for getting pregnant." Then, with tears, "And it would keep people from judging me for not aborting Jenny. That would have been the worst. It would be a complete rejection of me as a person."

"Maggie, I appreciate how willingly you have bared your soul to me, how you have owned up to the truth. And I don't judge you at all."

He noted her bewildered look, so he said, "I was about to ask you about something you said in the water, when you started telling me about Jenny's dad."

"Wait, before you do, let me say one last thing about that. Even though he was out of my life forever, he is, in fact, Jenny's biological father. I wanted to give her something to remember him by, if she wanted to. His name was Louis Moore. She is half him, so her name is half his. Jennimoore Louisa Trillbey."

"It's a beautiful name! My compliments on making lemons into lemonade, as they say."

"Thanks! What were you going to tell me?"

"You had just landed in the water. You were hysterical, and you called out to God, saying, 'It should have been me, and not her.' Or words like that. While we were watching the dolphins, that was playing over and over in my mind. Then I believe I heard two questions God has for you."

"Yes, I was frantic, beside myself, hysterical. I couldn't find Jenny. She trusted me and I let her down." The thought of her daughter brought fresh tears. "I wasn't thinking about it, I just said those words to God, the first thing that came into my mind, without even thinking. I don't even know anything about God. Jenny was part of me. It was like losing an arm, but much, much worse."

She got a little nervous. "What are the questions?"

"When God asks the questions, sometimes he already knows the answers. So when you hear the questions, think about them and answer them as truthfully as you know how, both from your mind and from your emotions. You can ask me about it, and I'll help if I can, but the answers will be entirely yours. Are you ready for the first question?"

"You're scaring me a little, but yes."

Matt held her hands in his and looked her straight in the eye. "Are you really willing to die, so that Jenny might live?"

Maggie withdrew her hands from Matt's and pulled them firmly to her chest. She squinched her face and squirmed.

It looked to Matt like she had just bitten into a lemon. He knew this would be a very painful question for her to answer honestly, but so much was riding on her answer. He also knew that God's response to her answer would, when she heard it, reveal whether her answer was the truth.

He wondered how he would have answered, if he had had that choice for his wife, for his son, for his daughter.

She closed her eyes tightly. Jenny flowed into her consciousness. The near-tragedy of the breech delivery, the first sight of her truncated leg, the memory of her first real smile. An overwhelming ache was forming in the pit of her being, along with an insatiable longing. But Jenny was dead …

Something within her was shouting, "No, this can't be." Her mind knew better, however. She opened her eyes.

She saw Matt, staring, concentrating on something a thousand miles away. Although the rest of his face was calm, even peaceful, his eyes exhibited a pain she felt she might never be privy to. He caught the slight movement of her eyes opening. She saw him turn toward her, his eyes now filled with comfort and understanding.

"What does this mean, Matt? I'm in agony about this," she finally asked. "Is this what you meant about my baring my soul?"

"Yes, it is. I dearly want to help you, and I'll do anything I can to help you find what's in that soul. Remember this is God's question, not mine. I believe what he means is that you would be dead, and your death would mean you would never see her again in this life. He would watch over her, protect her, and raise her. Not himself, but someone who loves him, whom he can trust."

Maggie closed her eyes again, and images of Jenny came back. So did the longing. Abruptly, the image of Jenny evaporated, as if pushed out of the way by an unseen hand. Jenny came back, arms outstretched, reaching for her. The unseen hand swirled her away again. Something else wanted her attention. She struggled, wrestling against the unseen, desperate to understand. The only thing she treasured, now gone. No, a thought whispered, the only thing you controlled, now gone. She felt pinned to the mat, and longed for a way out. The dull ache was showing no signs of leaving as she opened her eyes.

"Matt, I know I've been self-seeking. I see there is no time for that anymore. I know I was wrong when I got pregnant, and now she is in heaven where she will be safe and whole forever. But it wasn't her fault she died, it wasn't her fault she's missing a foot, and anyway she never had a shot at living. I had my shot at it, and I blew it completely. I want her to live, and maybe I could just go take my lumps and be done."

Matt wanted to make sure she understood the options. "Maggie, if you choose to live, God would give you a fresh start. He does that, you know."

She was still wrestling, searching out all the possibilities. "Yes, but Jenny would never have a fresh start, or any start at all. Isn't there a way we both could live?"

"That wasn't the question."

She was anxious for her daughter. "If I chose heaven now, would I be able to watch Jenny from there?"

"I don't know what we'll do in heaven, or if that's even possible. If you cannot watch Jenny from heaven, it's because God has something more wonderful for you. But why do you assume you will go to heaven, if your choice is to die so Jenny can live?"

"Is there another place to go? I thought everyone went to heaven when they died?"

"There is another place, and some do go there. And you do know of that place, way down deep, although you may have thought of it as a myth. Our societies don't talk very much of hell anymore, yours and mine, but it is a very real place."

"Do you think I'd go to heaven?"

"Do you think you would? Think about your life, and tell me what would qualify you. One of the things about being a human is that every single one of us knows deep down that the standards are very high, and that we don't measure up."

Maggie thought about it, putting aside the wrestling for a moment. "No, I don't," she said, then she brightened. "If I said yes, so Jenny could live, do you think I might go to heaven, you know, as a reward?"

"No. God won't negotiate on that. It's his heaven, and he sets the standards."

"Would it be possible for me to live for a while, and then give a yes answer sometime in the future?"

"No. You would always come back to this, and never say yes. And it wouldn't take you long at all to forget all about Jenny."

Eventually Maggie ran out of possible scenarios and questions. She looked pleadingly at Matt, who was patiently and lovingly waiting for her to decide.

Behind his comforting façade, however, Matt understood the dilemma she found herself in. Her daughter was alive in heaven. If Jenny were to come back to live on earth because of her mother's sacrifice, Maggie wouldn't end up in heaven, and he knew she was now aware of that. He knew there would be no solace until she decided, and maybe not even then.

She paused, agonizing, comprehending the dilemma just as clearly as Matt. "I don't know what to say."

She closed her eyes again, as if to seek the comfort of her daughter's presence once more. However, there was no Jenny, just a dark black void. *Why, then, did he promise me I would suckle Jenny? And why is he asking me this?* This last question reverberated, echoing louder and louder. And somewhere, way deep down inside her, where the scream had come from, the faintest flicker of a light began to glow.

A moment passed. She snapped her eyes open, and resolutely said, "Wait, yes, I do. I say, yes, I am willing to die so that Jenny might live."

"Are you sure? Is that your final answer?"

She thought again. "Yes."

Matt waited a moment for her to change her mind. "God says, 'Yes, so it shall be done.' "

Maggie breathed a deep sigh, then gave a slight smile. "I don't know what will happen next, but I know I've made the right choice."

She noticed the ache was gone, and so was the desperate longing. She looked down at the burnt coffin top and began to cry.

"Maggie!"

She looked up. Matt was beaming! Her mouth said "Huh?" but there was no voice with it.

"Maggie, that was so much the right answer. All of heaven was waiting for you to decide, and when you said yes, they all shouted for joy, because they knew God was pleased with your answer."

"I don't understand. Why was it such a big deal to them?"

"Here are the words God impressed on me to tell you. 'Tell her I did the same for her, and she is totally worth it.' "

"He did, for me? What do you mean?"

"He died so that you might live."

"But he's God! How could he die?"

"In order to die, he had to become a human being, one like he created, like you and me. Once he lived in a human body, then he could die. So he did. That human being that was God was named Jesus, and God called him his son. He died so you could live. He also died so I could live, and Helene, and Jenny, and Louis Moore."

"I just said I would die so Jenny could live. How will that work for me?"

"That depends, Maggie, on your answer to the second question."

She had forgotten about the second question. "Oh, no!" she groaned.

"Do you want to take a breather?"

"No. Whew! That was an easy one."

Matt grinned at her. "That wasn't the question."

"Yes, I knew that. That was just my breather."

"Here it is. Are you willing to live so that Jenny might live?"

"Huh? ... Yes!"

"I know that sounds contradictory, and so it is. First God asks you if you would die so Jenny can live, and when you say yes, he asks if you would live so she can live. Let's rest a few minutes, and then I'll explain. By the way, the real test was not so much that you said yes to the first question. While that certainly was important, it was much more telling how you responded when he said, 'Yes, let it be so.' You submitted to his sovereignty, not knowing what would happen, instead of reacting against him."

They changed places and rested. Maggie noticed the burn marks on the covers to the coffins kept them from slipping on the otherwise slick and polished surfaces. She would have said something about it, but found she didn't have any words left. That would soon change.

The dolphins, which had been lazily playing all around their little craft since they arrived, suddenly became very active. In perfect unison, they were bounding out of the water and back in, circling the pair of humans as if in anxious curiosity, as if to form a barrier against an as-yet-unseen foe. Maggie saw it first—a great triangle rising up out of the water with a greater triangle about ten feet behind. "Look! Shark!"

Matt looked. She had said that about the dolphins, but this time she was right.

JC Smalley was on the phone with Jack Smith at the FAA, who had gotten him the entry into Air World's flight data. "Jack, I need you to call Air World back, if you don't mind. Someone hacked into their database using what appears to be their real IP address. It seems odd to me they wouldn't try to hide inside a virtual private network or a spoofed IP address. Can you ask them about that?"

"Is this about flight 94? We're starting to hear that there's some issue with that flight."

"Yes. There's no easy way to say this, but flight 94 has ceased to exist. Please don't quote me. You'll be hearing officially soon enough, and the whole world will know shortly. Please find out soon. Air World's security folks will have their hands full, maybe already."

"Okay. I can't see your number. All I see is you're calling on a secure line. I'll call your cell and you can call me back."

While he waited, he washed up, unpacked his luggage, and thought about

Penny. She owed him, she said. He wondered what other area she wanted to show him. He thought he had detected some excitement in her voice when she had said that. He almost wished he had gotten the male assistant, Luke, for Nicki's sake. It gave him some reassurance, though, that Penny was acting in a thoroughly professional manner. In the end, he decided to trust his judgment of eight years ago, when he had recommended her for a promotion based on his observation of her loyalty and professionalism. Still, he would be careful.

His cell phone rang. It was Jack, and when he returned Jack's call on the secure line, he thought he sensed some emotion in his voice.

"You were right, JC. Their security was getting the call right before we hung up. Lost at sea, they said. I didn't let on I knew something different. Two hundred seventy-eight passengers, plus a crew of fourteen and two pilots. They're trying to figure out what happened. Anyway, their flight data system can detect if a user is using a virtual private network, and won't let them log in. It also sends a query to the IP address the user claims, so it can detect a spoofed IP. It's possible to reroute your traffic through a legitimate IP address, but that would be iffy and time-consuming. I also let them know to change their password."

When they hung up, JC took a moment to think this through. Both the California bank and Air World would be using sophisticated security systems. Yet, both were hacked using the same IP address. Could it be a coincidence? One hacker used a faked IP address which happened to match the real IP address hacking into Air World's secure website? And a coincidence that the flight whose data was hacked was just shot down? No, he was certain there were connections between the three events. But what were they, by whom, and why?

The shark and the dolphins dove simultaneously. Matt grabbed Maggie and they held each other, watching the scene unfold, hoping the much smaller dolphins would somehow scare off the shark. The dolphins surfaced in seeming triumph, chattering wildly. Matt and Maggie cheered! If they had understood dolphinspeak, however, they would have known it wasn't victory the dolphins were proclaiming.

Halfway between their floating wood boxes and the dolphins, there was a roiling of the waters. A head shot out of the sea, followed by fifteen feet of fish. The mouth was unmistakable—a great white shark!

Maggie saw Matt abruptly relax as the shark disappeared. The dolphins were gone too; the surface was undisturbed. What was up? He didn't seem the least bit concerned with their predicament. On the other hand, her whole fight-or-flight instinct was on high alert. She felt like she might be safer inside the coffin. "Are they gone?"

"Heavens no! But all three are exactly where they need to be."

He beckoned her to move up as high as she could comfortably get, by leaning against the top coffin, to see what he knew was about to happen. He turned to her as she cried out, shaking with fear and uncertainty. "Maggie, God didn't make those promises to you so he could let you down. Relax, and know that he is God!"

Maggie had yet to see one of the promises fulfilled. "Is this where I die, so Jenny can live?"

She heard her travel companion of less than four hours, full of confidence, tell her, "He will not fail you or abandon you! Don't be afraid! Watch carefully," as he turned around to face the sea.

The shark broke the surface about five feet from their craft—mouth wide open—rising in the water until about eight feet of it was showing. Maggie gasped. The giant fish was twice as big as their lifeboat!

She saw Matt stand on the coffin and point at the shark. He declared in a loud voice, "Shark, in Jesus's name, give it up!"

The shark started to sink forward toward them. She hadn't expected to see the dolphins again, but they simultaneously appeared from either side of their boat, crashing with great energy into the belly of the shark, level with its dorsal fin, knocking it back. Their work done, they swam away.

What happened next was forever burned into Maggie's memory. Hit by the dolphins and commanded by Matt, the shark did indeed give it up. The shark vomited. It was a tremendous stream of small, identical, silvery fish, about four or five five-gallon buckets worth, which sank immediately. Followed by thirty-one unopened and eight partially filled water bottles, which Matt fished out and threw in the space between two bottom coffins. Then a lot of various-sized fish in various states of digestion, a squid, half of a life preserver that said Y USS OKL on one side and CG 5 on the other, lots of seaweed, other plastic debris, a small harbor seal, and finally, a lot of white and green and brown opaque digestive fluid.

"The shark must have mistaken those water bottles for fish," Matt said, pulling the half life preserver out of the water. He glanced at the water bottles, meaning to put them in the top coffin when they had cleaned them off. "Some of those are really old. They don't make caps like that anymore."

The shark disappeared. The digestive fluid was slowly dissipating. Matt gasped. "Maggie, come quick and look!"

She was already there and was already seeing what Matt saw. There, about a foot below the surface, was a little pink blob. "JENNY!" She screamed it again. "JENNY!"

She took a deep breath and jumped in. She grabbed the pink blanket and Jenny's outfit with one hand, then found she couldn't swim any better than she could before. She opened her eyes to see where the lifeboat was, and immediately slammed them shut because of the burning. But Matt was watching from above. He grabbed her arm and pulled her onto the coffin. She was still clutching Jenny tightly.

She couldn't open her eyes. "My eyes are burning!"

The triage didn't take Matt two seconds. He took one look at Jenny, and realizing she was dead, immediately moved to help Maggie. He opened a water bottle. "Lie on your back here." She complied, with his help. He knelt on the coffin at her head, to keep his feet out of the shark's stomach fluid. "I'm going to pour water over your eyes one at a time. No, I can get them both together. When you feel the water, blink, blink, blink until I quit."

He doused the bridge of her nose, spreading the water from the whole bottle evenly to her eyes. And another bottle. "Keep blinking a little longer."

"Aah," she replied.

"I noticed your wrist was real slippery when I pulled you out. I think you got digestive juice all over you. Is your skin starting to itch or burn?"

It was, but that was not her main concern. "Jenny?"

"I'm sorry."

"Yes, I was afraid to look, but I just knew she was gone." She was remarkably peaceful about it. "While there was a chance she was still alive, I was frantic with worry. But now she is dead, and I cannot bring her back. When it sinks in, I will grieve deeply, I know, but until then we are still alive in the middle of the ocean, and my skin is starting to feel like it's on fire!"

Matt considered the options. "Quick, take off your sneakers and socks and your vest. That end of our raft looks to be clear of the fish fluid. Get in the water, take everything off, and rinse them and yourself thoroughly. Rub your skin and rinse your hair to get off any slickness. The bottom of the pallet is underwater. I'll loop my belt through it and fasten it. You can hook your arm through the loop, so you won't sink."

They jumped in together, Maggie holding onto the bottom of the pallet which they had used as a step when they first embarked. The water was already starting to soothe. Matt fastened his belt, then got out. "Don't drop anything or you'll never see it again. After you put your pants back on, let me know and I'll do your back."

A few minutes later, she called him. "Just lean forward and away from me," he said. "I'll grab the front of your neck for leverage, so don't think I'm trying to choke you." He descended off the pallet, took care of business, and climbed out. "When you're dressed, let me know, but don't get out yet."

She called again. He brought the pink bundle and handed it down to her. He joined her in the water. "We need to do this quickly. The water is still cold, and I imagine it's our adrenaline that is keeping us warm. You bathe Jenny's body like you did yours, and I'll take care of the blanket and her outfit."

"I don't think we need to keep this nappy. It looks rather, um, used. Can I just let it go?"

"No, Maggie. Did you see how much plastic the shark threw up? Let's not add any more. I'll rinse it out and we'll keep it with us until."

"Until what? Oh."

"Yes. Most of the untils are not mentionable or even to be considered. When we get rescued, we'll take it with us."

They finished their chores, but Jenny needed one more thing. Matt outlined a plan to Maggie, and she agreed. He put the clothes and blanket on the coffin. "If fish fluid comes out, just wave it away from us."

With Jenny's mouth and face below the surface, Matt applied pressure to the chest and stomach area. He felt the whole area compress, and some opaque fluid came out. Maggie swirled it away with her hand. Then he relaxed, allowing clean seawater to reenter. He did this several times until the water came out clean.

Back on their craft, they realized they were both shivering. "We still need to rinse out your vest and footwear. Drink some water while I take care of that."

The shock to her psyche of seeing Jenny was quickly turning into numbness. "Thanks, Matt. You are being very kind to me. I'm, uh," she remembered their earlier conversation, "a real basket case right now."

Penny Hasid was back. She led JC Smalley to a thick steel door located between the accommodations and the business area. Inside, she flipped on the lights. JC's mouth dropped open. A fully functional twenty-five-meter indoor firing range greeted him, equipped with soundproof and bulletproof walls, paper and mannequin targets, and bullet traps behind the targets. A shooter's dream!

JC felt a little ashamed of his earlier thoughts. "Wow, I'd no idea. This is great!"

"You can fire any pistol or shotgun, and rifles up to 7.62 millimeter. No hot loads though, those are too powerful for the bullet traps, and the bullets will ricochet."

Penny opened a cabinet and pulled out an ammunition can with JC's name on it. Inside were two holstered pistols: a Ruger nine-millimeter and an old service .45 caliber. She handed him another box. "Here are a hundred rounds of each. If you need more let me know. Cleaning kits are on that wooden table. You can shoot any time the range is free."

She showed him his spot in the cabinet, and he noticed a lot of other ammunition cans and ammunition. "In the cabinet, you can find ear and eye protection, which are both mandatory here." She pointed out the switch by the door. "Up is a blinking red light outside the door and it means you're here. Down means you're shooting, and the light is steady. When you leave, put it back in the center. Down turns the ventilation on, and let the air clear before you turn it off."

"Great. Thanks!"

"Just one last thing, now that you have your phone back. We need to trade numbers, so we can get ahold of each other."

Together, Maggie and Matt examined Jenny. They saw no visible damage— no teeth marks, her bones and joints all seemed intact, and rigor mortis had not set in. The pin holding her blanket together had also held her body together, but the flap over her face had not protected it very well from the shark's digestive fluids. Matt held her by her ankles to let any water drain from her stomach and lungs. They redressed her body and wrapped it in the blanket.

Matt was still thinking about the shark. "Most of those water bottles looked new, like they were from our plane. Some looked really old. The labels were gone, and they had really thick caps like back in the eighties. I was wondering why the dolphins decided to help us out, because God showed me what to say right before the shark came up the last time. I think the dolphins kept the shark from emptying out her entire stomach. The water bottles must have come floating up through the tail of the plane, and the shark got them at the same time she got Jenny."

"How do you know it was a she?"

Matt discarded three humorous answers, then said simply, "That one was huge. We didn't even see the whole thing. The males are a lot smaller than the females."

The shark was gone, and Maggie didn't care to think about it anymore. "Jenny's body is intact."

"Yes. I think it would have been terrible for you to see her crushed and broken."

"She wasn't trapped in the plane. She wasn't tossed around violently like everything else was, including us. She wasn't cut apart by the broken metal while exiting the plane. The shark swallowed her whole." She started to cry. "I think God was letting me see her whole one last time, maybe to protect my memory of her."

"Thank you," she added, to Matt or God, or both.

"Maggie, let me piece together all the messages God gave me for you. Are you ready?"

"Yes. You told me lots of wonderful things, but all I have to go on is my experience. And my experience is telling me Jenny is dead."

"You are about to have a new experience. Everything I heard from him for you, says that Jenny will live."

"Why isn't God telling me himself?"

"Because you don't have ears to hear, or eyes to see, yet. He will give you those in due time. In the meantime, he gave you me. For the time being, I am your ears and eyes."

"So, I am to die for Jenny to live, and I am to live for Jenny to live." She was trying to process this, and not finding much success. "When is the due time, when he will give me eyes and ears to see and hear?"

"When you die ... Wait, Maggie, stay with me! I told you I would explain, and this is my start of it. When you go into your garden and plant a petunia seed, what happens?"

"The seed germinates, and a petunia plant comes up."

"No, the seed dies first, then it germinates. If you dug up the seed right before it germinated, you'd just have a dead seed."

"Yes, I know. I've actually done that, when I was little and couldn't wait."

"Right now, you're like the seed. Do you know about Adam and Eve?"

"Yes, in the garden of Eden. God made them first, and we're their descendants."

"Good. God made them perfect, Maggie, without any predisposition to do wrong things. But they were tempted."

"The serpent."

"Right. The serpent told them a lie, and they believed it and acted on it, without asking God about it first. Now, God had the same standard for them as he does for us. When they ate that fruit, their act of disobedience caused their nature to change, and now they were prone to bad behavior. It got into their DNA, so to speak, because now their children *did* have the predisposition to be selfish, to lie, steal, murder, and the like."

"Sins."

"Yes. It broke God's heart, but he had a plan. People by their very nature commit all these sins, and so disqualify themselves from heaven. God loves the people he created, like you loved Jenny, but infinitely more. God could have decided to relax his standard, but he had promised death to Adam and Eve if they ate the fruit, so he bound himself to keep that promise. It wouldn't have been fair to let Adam and Eve start the whole human race, and then have them be the only ones in hell, would it?"

Maggie was beginning to have a glimmer of hope; perhaps the plan would apply to her. "What was his plan?"

"His plan was to get people back their original nature, the nature Adam and Eve lost by eating the fruit. That would requalify them for heaven. The problem is, there is a price for that, and it is so steep that people can't pay it. They are already condemned to death, so they have nothing to offer. But his love for us is so great, that he decided to pay it himself."

Maggie unpinned Jenny's blanket, rearranged it, and repinned it. "You said God did come as Jesus and died as a person. How could he have paid the price then?"

"God arranged that Jesus, as a man, should have the same nature as Adam and Eve before they ate the fruit. You might think that would make it easy for Jesus, not having Adam's new sinful nature. But he was tempted like no other person on earth. Jesus faced any temptation you can think of, and resisted it every time. And because of that, as a human, he was qualified for heaven without having to pay the price for himself. And so he could pay the price for us."

"Adam and Eve fell for it on their very first temptation."

"The hardest temptation he faced was seeing the cruel and humiliating death that awaited him. He was tempted to chicken out and avoid it. Do you know how I think he succeeded?"

She was taking in his words with rapt attention, and her face clearly said she had no clue. So he went on.

"I believe, in his mind he looked forward about two thousand years, saw a certain Maggie Trillbey, and said to himself, 'She is so worth it, to go through all this just for her!' "

"Just me?"

"Maybe. No, me too for sure, and lots of others. But it brought him such joy that he willingly endured that death. Then after they killed him, they put him in a tomb, hiding his body behind a big rock. But his death satisfied God's standards, and by raising him from the dead, God declared his death would pay the price for all humanity. Since he paid the price for all people, God made him the owner and ultimate authority over every person. That's what we mean when we call him 'Lord'."

"So the price has been paid?"

"Yes, but it doesn't guarantee you the nature Adam was created with. To you, that would be a new nature, one that for you didn't exist before. Let me tell you, that new nature is absolutely wonderful! It is what will allow you to hear from God directly. God will put his spirit in you, and you will have a new relationship with him. But sadly, not all want that new relationship, because entering into that new relationship means that we recognize his complete authority over us and our accountability to him."

"As you've been talking, I find I have a stronger and stronger desire to have that new nature. It seems to be the same drawing I was trying to describe to you when you first came on the plane, but even stronger."

A sudden thought occurred to her. "Matt, isn't God already the boss, and aren't we already accountable to him?"

"Yes, but some refuse to acknowledge that. They have various reasons, but in the end it all comes down to them wanting to be their own god and not accountable to anyone."

"Well, when I was my own god and not accountable to anyone, I did some really dumb things, and just made a mess out of my life. I thought I was being smart and mature, but I see that I would just continue to be like that unless I get this new nature. How do I do that?"

"It would be a secret transaction, just between you and God. You would have to die. You are just the seed, as I mentioned, because the petunia has not yet sprouted. Don't worry about the death part though. You will not even notice it. I didn't. But you will surely notice the coming alive part. He will change your life. Forever!"

"I think I'm ready. What do I do?"

41

JC had asked Penny to get him some supplies, explaining the use of each item. After she left, he spent the next hour at the firing range, getting acquainted with the pistols he was issued. He wasn't as good a shot as he remembered; the mind plays funny tricks sometimes. He used up all the ammunition, and spent the rest of the time disassembling and cleaning the weapons before putting everything away.

Dusty Mae came by his suite after he returned, and asked him to stop by her office after the VTC. He asked her if there were an unused office he could use; he didn't feel comfortable conducting business in his living quarters.

"Yes," she said, "it's a small conference room we don't use much. There's plenty of table space. We also have a small drafting room if that would suit better."

JC looked at them both and chose the conference room. It was located off the main hallway, and had a window in the door to allow those in the room to check for hall traffic before opening the door.

Penny came back with a globe, undersea maps of the North Atlantic, a cloth measuring tape graduated in millimeters, and his ID card for access to the building and the offices. "We had the globe and maps here, but I had to go to JoAnn's around the corner in Norridge to get the tape. I'll be right back. I have to get the credit card back to Walter."

"I'll be in the conference room, room 926. Dusty Mae set me up an office there."

When she got back, JC had moved what he needed to room 926, and had set up a spreadsheet table on his laptop to record distances in millimeters and convert them to ground miles.

"Okay, Penny, the reason I'm doing this is that a MiG can fly only about thirteen hundred miles on a full tank."

He measured the circumference of the globe and recorded it in the spreadsheet, 1,014 millimeters. Then he googled the circumference of the earth, 24,901 miles. "Now we just measure on the globe, do the math, and we can figure out distances on the earth."

JC measured carefully and put a dot on the Atlantic Ocean to mark the spot of the fire reported by the Air Force jets. "Wherever the MiGs came from, they had to get there and back on whatever fuel they left with. They don't have in-flight refuel capability, so let's see what is within six hundred and fifty miles of the dot."

"They flew around for at least a half hour in the middle of that, right?"

"Good, Penny. Yes. And I'll need another table to convert miles on the surface to millimeters on the globe."

"May I do that? I'm fairly familiar with spreadsheets."

"Sure."

She finished the new table as he was measuring the distance to Halifax, Nova Scotia, the closest land capable of having a runway.

"Twenty-seven millimeters to Halifax. Plug that in, Penny."

"That makes six hundred sixty-three miles. Six hundred fifty miles is only twenty-six millimeters."

"So they must have extra fuel pods, external fuel tanks. Question is, who would have those: the MiGs, fuel tanks, machine guns that may not be standard, or some other weapon system, ammunition, and the ground support system for all that?"

On the seafloor map, he found the depth of the ocean at the spot of the fire to be fifty-four hundred meters, well over three miles.

JC put another dot on the globe at twenty-six millimeters from the spot of the fire. Using a compass he found in the drafting room, he scribed a circle on the globe representing the maximum distance round-trip the MiG could fly without extra fuel. All that was in the circle was ocean.

"Are you doing all this for Jenny's sake?"

Maggie thought a moment. "I was at first. Now I realize there is more at stake, much more. Ever since you started telling me about this, I haven't been thinking of Jenny."

The numbness in her psyche was starting to dissipate as she looked down at the lifeless body of her daughter. She started to become puzzled at her lack of sadness for Jenny, until she became aware of a stronger emotion pushing that out of the way—hope. Hope for herself as well as for Jenny.

"Matt, if there hadn't been a Jenny, my desire to belong to God would have been just as strong!"

Where did those words come from, she wondered, about desiring to belong to God?

"I'll tell you what to do, but first you need to know your part of the transaction. You must believe, in the innermost core of your being, that God raised Jesus from the dead, since that is evidence that the price is paid. This is not the same as believing it in your mind, since then you would have to have proof of some sort. This is believing with no proof. God himself, by his spirit, will provide the proof as you say the words. So you won't be saying it because I said so, but because God said so. And you must receive him, Jesus, as the master and ruler of your life, since God made him to be that."

Matt was almost finished. "This is about trusting God for what he has said. This transaction between you and God will result in you having the authority to call him a new name. God considers this his most important attribute in his dealings with people. That new name is 'Father'."

"God the Father. Yes. I've noticed when people use God's name to curse and swear with, they never use the word father to refer to him."

"Yes, God the Father. He so wants people to trust him, that he demonstrates it by this intimate relationship. When we are little, we trust our fathers …"

Matt had been watching her closely, and his voice trailed off as he saw her face take on a look of horror, changing swiftly to shame, revulsion, and fear. Then tears.

"I'm sorry." He thought briefly. "Do you remember, when you first landed in the water, how panicky you were? How you were beside yourself with fear, for you as well as Jenny? How you fought me in the water, even though you couldn't swim? I kept on telling you to trust me, that I would keep you safe. And all of a sudden you did. You trusted me with your life. The way you relaxed took me by surprise, and we both went under. You continued to trust me, to believe I would do what I said, even when the evidence said otherwise. That's the kind of trust I'm talking about with God."

"I hardly knew you. But you had a kind of authority about you. Deep down, finally, I believed you would keep me safe."

"Okay. If you understand your part and are still willing, then you are ready."

"Yes, I am," she said eagerly.

"I said the transaction was secret, but it starts out in public, with your words. Really, you are just responding to God. He has been calling to you, exciting you, getting you ready for this exact moment. So talk to God now. Don't worry too much about what to say, he will help you. As eager as you are, he is much more eager. I can just see him waiting with a bill with your name on it in one hand, and a stamp in the other that says, 'Paid in Full'!"

"God, I believe with all that is in me that you raised Jesus from the dead," Maggie said. "And … Wow, I really do believe! And Jesus, I receive you as the master and ruler of me and my life, my Lord. I need you. I messed it all up, but now I want to belong to you."

And there was more. Matt was watching in sheer wonder. As she talked to God, she said things that he had never told her about. And that she had never told him about. Turning from her own ways and choosing to follow his.

She was silent for a long time. He knew what was happening by watching the changes in her facial expressions. He thought about the misery of the months since Helene died. He realized he was watching a process that far made up for any distress he had experienced.

Maggie opened her eyes, finally, and started giggling. Soon it turned to laughter. A deep, contented laughter that Matt recognized from his own past. And the joy! Her face was as radiant as the sun.

"I saw Jesus! He hugged me. He grabbed me and threw me up in the air. He was laughing, gleeful. And oh, the music! It was coming out of him. We were like a bride and groom at their reception. Then he said 'Look!' and showed me his hands, and I knew that I had done that to him. I started to weep convulsively. He said, 'Don't weep. I chose to do this for you, because you're my friend. I heard all the words coming from your heart, and I forgive you and receive you. You belong to me now, and I also belong to you.'

"He breathed on me, and said he would live in me and through me by his spirit, and he would show me the Father. He was so warm and lively. He called me his sister! It seemed to last a lot longer than my telling it to you right now. Just before the scene changed back to here, he told me I would see wonderful things as long as I kept my eyes on him."

No, Matt thought, she wasn't on cloud nine. She was on cloud nine hundred!

"Oh," she said suddenly.

"What?"

"I completely forgot about Jenny! I was with the one who could make anything and everything happen, and I forgot to ask!"

"Maggie, remember I said it would be just you and God? He was drawing you to himself and making you his. He wanted you all to himself just then. Don't worry, he hasn't forgotten about her!"

"By the way," he added, "you are so gloriously radiant right now, that if they don't find us by nightfall, they would just have to send a plane out to find out where the glow is coming from!"

Without warning, Maggie stood up and started jumping up and down on the lower coffin lid. Screaming, laughing, shouting, crying, all at once, it seemed. Grinning, Matt grabbed Jenny's body to keep it on board as the little craft swayed precipitously up and down. Maggie grabbed the top coffin handle to keep from losing her balance, and that coffin came perilously close to ending up in the water. Then, spent, she sat down, looked at Matt, and burst out laughing.

"Wow!" he said, excited for her. "That was wild!"

But Maggie was too breathless to respond.

After the excitement of the plane, and Jenny, the shark, Jenny again, and her spirit coming alive, Maggie needed a rest. They both needed a rest. Time for their bodies to rejuvenate, now that the adrenaline had quit flowing. They both leaned back against the top coffin, and found that their combined weight didn't push it off into the ocean. Maggie pushed her hair back so she could see. A slight breeze caused very few ripples in the sea around them.

They could tell the sun was way past its zenith and was coming back down. It had been over an hour, it seemed, since the Air Force had headed to parts unknown. They never saw the other aircraft again.

Matt looked over at Maggie, resting quietly about two feet away on the other side of Jenny's pink cotton pall. Her eyes were closed and although the excitement had waned, the joy on her face remained in full force. Her regular breathing told him she was at peace. He began to sing, softly at first.

But Maggie wasn't asleep. She was reliving her visit with Jesus. She heard Matt start to sing. It sounded vaguely familiar, but she couldn't quite place it. It sounded like he didn't know it very well, and knew only one verse. But he had a nice singing voice so she didn't want to interrupt.

The words told her it was a worship song, and the way he was singing it made her think he expected the object of that worship to be listening. He was singing directly to God. She opened her eyes to watch. Then it seemed like he switched to a foreign language, and sang with much more confidence, like he had learned the song in the foreign language and had to translate into English each time.

What struck her was not the words, per se, but the intensity and passion in those words. The melody was slowly changing, too. The song became quick and light, joyful, and as she described it later, dancing. She got goosebumps all over her arms, neck, and scalp. The song morphed into a rich and full, pulsating, rhythmic theme. It was calling her! She felt the tingling in her spine again. Then it was triumphant; he seemed to be singing of a great victory that had just taken place. All at once it was over. He relaxed and opened his eyes. The entire song had taken only a few minutes.

He smiled at her. "I thought you were asleep. I didn't mean to wake you."

"I was resting. The quietness was good for me. You have a wonderful voice. I've actually been awake the whole time. The song was absolutely beautiful!"

"Thanks. It really wasn't me, though."

"It sounded like it was you, but I couldn't tell what language it was. And what were the words, in English?"

"I hope this doesn't sound weird to you, but I have no idea what the words were or what they meant. It was a song, it was a prayer, it was the spirit of God, the Holy Spirit, singing through me. Jesus breathed his spirit into you, too. It's the same spirit. Sometimes I can get the drift of what the song is saying, like one time it was a long and continuous battle cry, another time

I felt like I was in a swordfight."

"Did you win the fight?"

Matt laughed. "The fight just sort of ended and the song moved on to something else."

"What do you call it?"

"The song? I just call it singing in the spirit. It's actually a gift from Jesus. At another point in the song, I felt like the words and melody were awakening something in you, a deep calling to deep. The Holy Spirit calling to your new spirit."

"I hope so. You're much deeper than I. I have so much to learn."

"When you entered this new relationship with our heavenly father, you became fully alive, and as deep as you'll ever be. We're as deep as each other right now. But this new life will be a life of discovery. The old Maggie has died and a new Maggie has come, but there may be things in your past that need to be healed, released, and restored."

"It was beautiful. I want you to tell me more about this later, but right now can we talk about Jenny?"

"You took the words right out of my mouth. While you were with Jesus, God showed me what we need to do to get ready for Jenny to come back. You still believe she's going to live, don't you, now that you've met your end of the bargain and died?"

"Oh, yes."

Matt changed his mind. "There's one more thing we need to do before that, which is really part of the preparation."

"Right, what's that?"

Matt proceeded carefully and tenderly. "I saw how your expression changed when I started talking about your own father. I saw great pain and anguish. I saw your impossibility to trust him, so I used your trusting me instead, to show how trustworthy our father in heaven really is. Is there something you'd like to tell me about that? I don't mean to pry, but our heavenly father gave us natural fathers to show us how our relationship to him is supposed to work, and I don't want anything to hinder your relationship with him. You don't have to tell me, or give me any details, or even remember anything you don't want to remember."

Maggie was still for a few moments. She felt like there was a closed door, that if she opened it, memories that had long been buried would come flooding out. Matt's talk of trusting her father had brought her to the door, and she had involuntarily reacted to get away from that door, as she always had. "I don't want to remember. Not right now, I feel too wonderful!"

But there were words written on the door, a quiet and calming summary to allow her to acknowledge the door without opening it. She added, as if reading the words, "I was afraid to be near him. And I always thought he would rather have had another son instead of me."

How crushing, Matt thought, to suffer parental rejection. "God can and will heal you in your memories," he said. "It may take some time. I believe that even now our father is beginning to prepare you for that day. Let's move on to Jenny. The Lord showed me that Jenny would get her life back through you. He showed me that both you and she need to wash with water, the areas where there would be skin-to-skin contact in nursing. He said it would symbolize the free flow of the spirit of life. Here, let's start with Jenny. Are you ready?"

She was considering her role in this, and started getting a little nervous. She got out a water bottle. "Will this be enough?"

"Oh, yes. Enough for both of you. I'll hold Jenny with her mouth open. You fill her mouth with water and swish it around, cleaning off her tongue, inside her mouth, and her throat. Then wash off her face and lips the same way."

It didn't take long, and Matt turned the body over and let the water drain out. Overhead, the sun was still beaming down on them, and the ever-present haze protected them from its wrath.

At Terminal 3 of London's Heathrow Airport, a man and woman approached the line of passengers exiting Britannia Airlines flight 1539.

"Hullo, Mr. Petrov? Mr. Mikhail Petrov?"

"Yes, I am Petrov."

"My name is Andy Nelson. I am a translator for Mrs. Jane Cooper from Britannia Airlines. This is Mrs. Cooper."

Mrs. Cooper smiled at Mr. Petrov and said a few words to her translator. They had gone over the script a few minutes earlier, so Andy was aware of where Jane was going, and could phrase the questions more in line with that, if there were difficulties.

"Mr. Petrov, is that your wife with you?"

"Yes, this is my wife Katrina."

Andy signaled to one of seven other pairs of BA representatives and translators, who joined them and introduced themselves. Tom Barbary from BA and his translator, John Whitfield.

"Mr. and Mrs. Petrov, there has been a problem with your baggage. You made it in time for this flight, but your baggage did not. It was delayed until the next flight."

"That is okay, sir. We have a fairly long layover until our flight to Saint Petersburg. It will probably catch up to us. How long was the delay in Chicago before the next flight here?"

"That's not the issue, Mrs. Petrov. Your baggage will not be arriving at all. We would like you both to accompany us to one of the Britannia Airlines offices, to go over the contents of your baggage, and to ask you a few questions about it."

Jane Cooper, who wasn't really from Britannia Airlines at all, but part of a security organization high in the British government, read their faces as they received the news of their lost baggage. A fairly normal response to the announcement, she thought. She was glad BA had enough spare uniforms that each of the eight team members got one that fit well. A glance and nearly imperceptible nod to the other teams indicated her evaluation that the Petrovs didn't seem to be hiding anything.

The other six teams were called, one or two at a time, as the other six Russian travelers were identified when they cleared the hastily-erected checkpoint just outside their arrival gate.

Jane and Andy, the other team, and the Petrovs headed to a bank of twelve identical offices, each about ten feet square, with tables and chairs, a whiteboard, set of maps of the whole world, and unobtrusively placed cameras and microphones. The cameras and mics automatically started recording as soon as the door was shut, and the recordings were generally deleted when the interview was over and no issues had developed.

Today was different, however. Eight other agents were watching the proceedings; they had encrypted communications back to their headquarters, as well as radio feeds to the earpieces worn by Jane and the rest of the security team.

Jane, through Andy, explained they needed to speak to Mr. and Mrs. Petrov separately. If questioned, they would explain that when insurance companies are faced with claims like this, they would want to ensure there was an honest accounting for all the baggage. Therefore, it was BA policy to get good descriptions of the contents from each traveler separately, then afterwards to resolve any differences. But this wasn't necessary for Jane and Tom; it seemed to them that the Petrovs were used to this kind of treatment.

The whole world would know in a matter of hours that something disastrous had happened to the plane carrying the Petrovs' baggage, so Jane with Mr. Petrov, and Tom with Mrs. Petrov, started out with that announcement.

"Mr. Petrov, please call me Jane. May I call you Mikhail?" It sounded strange to Andy to say that.

"Yes, Jane. Is something serious the matter? We will help in any way we can."

"The plane carrying your baggage has been lost at sea, over the middle of the Atlantic Ocean. As far as we know, the only survivors are those who didn't make the flight, namely you and your traveling companions. Are you all travelling together? There are eight Russians who have connecting flights here at Heathrow."

"No, we met the Nikolevskis on the flight to the US two weeks ago. Nikola had recently retired, as I have. Over a beer we talked of traveling together on our US tour, but we both knew that would take a change in plans for one of us or the other. They were going to Los Angeles, and we were traveling north to Minneapolis-Saint Paul, to see Minnesota."

"I see on the manifest that you and your wife had three pieces of checked baggage." She showed him a baggage chart. "Could you show me which pictures correspond to your baggage? The check-in record shows one weighed 22 kilos, one was 21 kilos, and one was 10 kilos. The first two were close to the weight limit. Show me those first."

Mikhail carefully looked the chart over, then pointed. "They were two identical number twenty-twos right here, except for color. Mine was dark green, Katrina's was brown. The spare was a black number two."

A voice in Jane's earpiece confirmed the information about the Nikolevskis. And later, about the baggage.

"What do you mean, 'the spare'?"

"All we had in the black suitcase was some warm clothes—two sweatshirts and long underwear—in case it got cold while we were in Minnesota. That was all."

"For the fee for the extra baggage," Jane observed, "you probably could have bought that in Minnesota and discarded it before you came back, and been money ahead."

"That wasn't the only purpose for that suitcase. We had planned to fill it with souvenirs for our children and grandchildren. However, when we went to the gift shops and saw something typically American that they might be interested in, all the items were labeled 'Made in China.' So we never bought anything. We don't have anything against China, like some of our comrades, but we wanted to impress them with something made in the USA."

"Did you pack your own suitcases before the flight back? Were you in control of them from the time you packed them until you brought them to the airport security station?"

"Oh, yes! We inventoried the contents often, like we were advised before we left. We had heard stories that hotels do not guarantee the security of baggage, so we were constantly checking. Come to think of it, we never needed the clothes in the spare suitcase, so we never opened it the whole trip. Do you need a list of the contents?"

"Yes, I was just getting to that. Here are some inventory sheets. Please list everything as detailed as you can remember. Take your time. Accuracy is more important to us than speed right now. Wait, dictate to Andy and he will write it in English."

Mikhail took about twenty minutes to remember everything, including the sizes of his wife's clothing and the color of her shoes. "I was an accountant during my career," he explained. "I can tell you the number of buttons, if that would help."

Jane smiled. "Not necessary, but thanks. Let's move on to where you have been since you left your home in…"—she consulted the printout again—"Sertolovo. Aside from all your connecting flights, did you visit another country besides the US?"

"Yes, we drove up to International Falls. We wanted to see the coldest spot in the continental US, and how it compares to Sertolovo. Of course, it's not winter there. It's the beginning of summer, but we could tell how they prepared for the cold just by looking around. Then we drove across the Rainy River to Fort Frances in Canada. We went to the McDonald's to compare Canadian McDonald's to American, British, and Russian McDonald's. After that, we drove across the street to the Dairy Queen to make the same comparisons. Then we drove back across the Rainy River to Minnesota."

"So you drove? Did you rent a car, or did you have friends you met who brought you places?"

"No, we were by ourselves. My wife speaks English very well, so I have been little more than a passenger the whole time. It was great!"

"Right, let's start out in Sertolovo. Try to remember every detail from getting in your car at home, to when you claimed your baggage at the Minneapolis Airport and picked up the rental car. What you saw and who you talked to. Where you went in the US besides your trip to Canada. Your sequence of events from the time you woke up yesterday morning until you were seated on the plane. I am going to record this, and we will get what we need of it transcribed later. I will try not to interrupt, but I may ask for some clarifications along the way."

She unlocked her phone and tapped the voice recorder app. She knew it was unnecessary; it was just for show; the microphone in the background was picking up both the Russian and the English translation. At the other end, the voice recognition and translation programs were producing English documents as fast as Mikhail, Jane, and Andy were speaking. The security handler for Jane and Andy marveled at how accurately Andy was translating in both directions.

It took Mikhail about an hour, going to great lengths to itemize every step. Jane didn't want to miss any of it; there was no telling what little detail might be important later on. After about five minutes, her earpiece told her that Katrina was finished, and five minutes after that, she found out the other six had finished also.

After all the questions were complete, Mikhail had a question of his own. "It seems to me based on all your questions, that our baggage was not merely 'lost at sea,' but something much more serious has happened. Tell me, are we suspects?"

"We don't know what happened. We know we lost communication with them as well as radar tracking. Until we find out, then yes, everyone is a suspect. What intrigues me is the suitcase you never opened. Are you sure you never opened it, even for a short time?"

"Yes. We kept it locked in the boot of the rental car, and we put the other baggage in the back seat for easier access. We did not take it out until we got back to the airport."

Jane just remembered the airline baggage glitch. "Did you have anything abnormal happen when you checked in?"

"No. Well, at first they couldn't find our reservations in their system, but that happens a lot, so I did not think anything of it. Katrina told me about that later."

"Thank you for your cooperation. The British authorities have asked us to turn you and Katrina and the others over to them for a few days, while they sort things out. I hope you can understand. I don't mean to scare you, but this will be for your protection as well."

Those authorities met them at the door and escorted Mikhail to join his wife. The eight teams made their way to a door marked "Britannia Airlines Personnel Only" to change out of the BA uniforms into something more in keeping with their security mission.

As the door closed, there was an announcement over the airport loudspeaker system that anyone at the airport here to meet the Britannia Airlines flight from Chicago due to arrive at 10:45 p.m., should make their way to Gate Eleven or Zone F for some important information concerning the flight.

The cleansing of Jenny's face, mouth, and throat now complete, Matt tenderly replaced the pink blanket over her wispy strands of freshly cleaned hair, leaving her increasingly bloated face exposed, and gently laid the body in a crevice to Maggie's left, between the coffins that were their lifeboat. "Now it's your turn," he whispered, not wanting to disturb the solemnity of the moment. "You need cleansing too, to get you ready."

Matt looked at Maggie. She was struggling, her brown eyes suddenly filled with trepidation and a desperate pleading. "I can't bear this," they seemed to be saying. He started to say something, then closed his mouth. He opened it again to speak, but closed it a second time. And a third. Silently imploring God to give him understanding, he could see pain wracking her soul.

Then in a moment, in the twinkling of an eye, he saw, as real and vivid as if he were there watching. She was twelve...

Then he understood. He saw no details, but perceived horror. He heard her crying, then screaming. He saw blood, a lot of blood, hers. Doctors scurried about. Suddenly a large plank was thrown upon the scene and a great iron hammer nailed the plank in place. The hammering and the plank faded away, and she was still there, her eyes still imploring as if no time at all had passed.

He stared purposefully at her chest. "Maggie," he started slowly, "did you vow a vow?"

She burst into tears as he shifted his gaze to her face. Compassion for her, both in her present being and as a child, rolled over him, swirled around them both, and settled in his eyes. She didn't see what he had seen; all she saw was God's love for her streaming from his whole being. Through his eyes. Through his tears.

It was her eyes that gave her away. Yes, they whispered. The memory of it presented itself to her for inspection. Yes, they said. The horror he had perceived settled itself over her like a shroud. Yes! they shouted. Through her tears, she saw Matt lean forward and open his arms toward her. She grabbed at him like she had grabbed at him in the water.

He held her briefly, then she swung around with her back in his chest. He leaned against the upper coffin and they both relaxed. He wrapped her tightly in his arms. Next to them both, on their right side, Jenny's lifeless body, still swaddled in her pink blanket, twitched and gurgled in a random fashion, as the decay processes were eager to return this little one back to the dust from which she came.

"Tell me," he said softly, and waited. Maggie stiffened up, then relaxed. Sobbed some. Tried to move her arms, but he was holding her. He couldn't see it, but her eyes were closed. It seemed to Matt that she was reliving the horror. "You're safe," he said. "I'm holding you."

He could feel he was being a comfort to her. He rocked her, ever so slightly and ever so slowly.

As she told her story, she broke down at times. Sometimes she paused, to regain her composure and strength, to remember more of the details. "I was twelve. It was my birthday. I was reaching puberty earlier than my friends, and was starting to develop. My brother Charles and I were at home by ourselves. He was sixteen at the time. Shortly after lunch, a couple of his friends came over, Billy and Ted. I was in the living room reading a Nancy Drew when they came in. Charles said, 'It's time for your birthday spankings.'

"I had never heard of birthday spankings, and said so. Billy, or maybe it was Ted, said, 'We'll show you.' At that, Ted, or maybe it was Billy, grabbed both my hands. I tried to get loose, to get away. I told him to leave me alone, but he just laughed. I got real scared. I struggled, but all I was doing was wearing myself out. They grabbed me by my belt, and I was on the floor.

They pulled my shorts down to my ankles. I was petrified. Then they took turns sitting on a chair, and I was draped over their laps with my bum in the air.

"They got a ruler out of the desk and each one gave me twelve hard slaps with it. My underpants didn't soften the slaps at all. It hurt, it really stung, and I cried. After the first or second slap, I begged them to stop. I knew threatening them with telling on them would be to no avail, but I did it anyway. They just laughed at me, a kind of cruel laugh, like when Ted had crushed a frog in his hands, and laughed about it. After the first one finished, the one holding my hands had his turn. Charles took over for him, so he must have been first.

"Since I was still struggling, Charles decided to make his turn easier, so before the other boy let go, Charles pulled my shirt over my head and wrapped it around my arms, around my elbows and forearms. After the last one finished, they joked about how hot my bum was. 'Feel it,' they said, 'you'll burn your hand!' I tried to get off his lap, but he held me there. Suddenly, the last boy gave me a very hard slap with his hand. It was such a surprise that I peed on myself and screamed.

"At that point I just thought this was a cruel way to do birthday spankings. I didn't know. I was only twelve. But then they put me back on the floor, on my back, with Charles still keeping the shirt wrapped around my arms. One of them knelt down over my legs, and sat back on his heels. I couldn't move. I was pinned to the floor. One said, 'So you think it was funny to pee on me? We'll teach you what funny is!'

"Then they started to tickle me. I was very ticklish. I thought I would throw up. I laughed so hard. I couldn't help myself, of course. I wiggled and squirmed and thrashed about on the floor. Then I couldn't get any air. So they'd ease up till I caught my breath and start again. I almost passed out several times. Sometime during the tickling, my bra came loose, so they started pinching me. They would say things like, 'Laugh if you want me to pinch you.' Then they would tickle me and I would laugh. I couldn't help it, so they would pinch me. Hard.

"This went on until my laughs turned to screams. Everything ached so badly: my bum, my breasts, my tummy. Then they said, 'Okay. Now the birthday spankings are almost done. Just one last step.' I tried to throw up but couldn't. I retched but nothing came out. I was still trapped on the floor. They got the ruler out again. 'The grand finale, a pink-belly!' Thirty-six more hard slaps, this time to my tummy. Me screaming the whole time. Then they all three jumped up and ran out the door to Ted's car and off they went, leaving me still on the floor."

Maggie paused in the story. Matt held her firmly but tenderly. As she told the story, Maggie grew more and more determined to tell it all, nothing held back, no matter how much the memory hurt. Her bum hurt again; her tummy hurt again; everything came back into sharp focus.

Matt marveled at her lack of reluctance to omit anything, and knew she wasn't done. "When you're ready, tell me about the vow."

Maggie nodded, and a glance at the little still body beside them gave her renewed purpose. "I feel like I'm dying inside, but I have to tell it. I've never told anyone before, not even my parents. But you're different. I'm feeling your tears for me.

"I finally was able to get up, and I ran to my bedroom. I had run out of tears. I looked at myself in the mirror. My bum was striped every which way, and there were welts on there and my tummy. My breasts hurt like hell and I was bleeding. My parents got home about that time. I could hear them moving around downstairs. My breasts started to swell and they became numb. I touched them and couldn't feel anything."

Maggie paused again and Matt waited. After a while, she went on. "I knew what I was going to do. I put on a shirt and went downstairs to my dad's toolbox and got his utility knife. Nobody saw me. I came back up and took off my shirt again. My breasts were still numb. I touched them but it was like touching a stone." She paused. "I was twelve. Happy birthday to me."

"Then," she choked up and had to breathe deeply for several moments. "Then, I looked in the mirror and said aloud to myself in the mirror… I wasn't thinking clearly, you see."

Another pause, another choked up spell, another glance at Jenny. "Then I said, 'No one will ever enjoy these breasts again, FOREVER!'

"And I took the knife and cut myself across my chest, from one side all the way to the other."

She shuddered convulsively at the memory. "I thought because my breasts were numb that I wouldn't feel any pain. And that was true, but just for an instant. Then the pain came like a tidal wave. I screamed, dropped the knife, and fainted. Next thing I knew, I was in the hospital with wires and tubes and stitches and a crowd of people wearing masks and gloves.

"I was so emotionally spent that I was like a zombie. The doctors were able to fix my skin, but I have no feeling there to this day. My breast development died, and what was already there dried up. At least a half-dozen people asked me what happened, and I gave them all the same story. I said I couldn't remember a thing. That the last thing I remember was eating breakfast that morning. But it was a lie.

"The doctor who sewed me up told me he was able to reattach everything. I didn't want to kill myself. I had adjusted the knife blade so not much was sticking out. I don't understand why there's nothing there."

"It wasn't the knife, Maggie, it was the words of your vow that dried everything up. It was a curse you put yourself under."

Exhausted, Maggie leaned back and promptly fell into a deep sleep. Matt began to sing softly, starting where he always started, with his favorite worship song. "Holy, holy, holy," he began. Although it was his favorite, he knew only the first verse. "Are you Lord God Almighty!" He felt the vibrations from his chest coming through her body into his arms. "The whole earth is full of your glory!"

Then, as before, he launched into a language known only to God. The melody and tempo morphed and became a long, drawn-out, almost dirge-like funeral hymn. Something was dying. The words were heavy, guttural, hard to pronounce. Words he could feel in his arms. Words that were going through her, penetrating, cleansing, purifying, liberating. They woke her up. A breeze played with them, warm and cool at the same time, refreshing. Only a few minutes had passed.

"Okay, I think I'm ready now. What do I need to do?" She reached for the water bottle Matt had used for Jenny, and swung around to face him again.

"No. Not yet. We have a big chore ahead of us. Do you remember what God said?"

They both looked at Jenny, whose whitish skin was beginning to look mottled. Only her lips looked intact. "She is ready," Matt said, "and will stay ready. But you are not. Definitely not."

She attempted some playfulness. "Well, make up your mind!" Then she perceived the gravity of the situation. "I'm sorry. I shouldn't have said that. What is it?"

"Do you know the Bible story about Jesus raising the little girl from the dead?"

"No. I don't know much about the Bible at all. I don't know much about Jesus at all. I do know, though, that he has come to me and has received me. All I really know about Jesus is what you have told me over the last few hours. That, and, as you know, how he personally revealed himself to me."

"One day, Jesus was asked to heal a man's daughter who was very sick, near death. He went, but when he got there, she had already died. He raised her from death, just like he will do with Jenny, and what do you think was the first thing he said to the parents after that?"

"I don't know. What is her name? Don't let her get sick again?"

He shouldn't have played this guessing game. "No. Jesus said, 'Get her something to eat!' The poor girl would be hungry. So it will be with Jenny. But you have nothing to feed her. The vow you made is making it completely impossible to provide her any nourishment."

He could see the anguish rising up, so he softened his tone. Or at least tried to. "Don't you know that generally both the mom and baby both find the nursing to be quite pleasurable? But you have, by your words, negated that, and not only that, eliminated the possibility of keeping her alive."

Matt's words were harsh, and Maggie knew that every word was true. Although the delivery was full of compassion and love, she was nearly inconsolable. Glancing around as if looking for a way out, Maggie grabbed his left hand in both of hers, and looked up into his face. "What are we going to do?" her eyes seemed to be asking, desperate to the point of despair. His countenance softened, and it appeared to Maggie that he knew a secret he was about to share with her.

"You have to break your vow, cancel it, make it null and void. Without doing this, God will be bound to honor your words that you spoke many years ago."

"I thought God could do anything. You told me that, and you were talking about Jenny."

"Yes. He *can* do anything, but there are things he *won't* do. God gave us the freedom to choose, to make moral choices. In other words, he gave us free will. But there are always consequences to our choices. If there weren't, then it wouldn't matter what we chose. God bound himself to never do anything to make us do something or not do it. He can lead us, he can show us the consequences, he can arrange circumstances, he can get us information to help us, but in the end, the choice is ours. We can choose the good or the evil. Why do you think he did that?"

"Why do I think he gave us free will?"

"Yes."

"I don't know, Matt. Sometimes I wish other people were prevented from choosing evil, though."

"God is looking for a specific choice you make in your life, and he will not make it for you."

"Does that choice have to do with him?"

"Yes, exactly! He has given you complete freedom to choose him. Or to not choose him. He has an infinite desire for you to choose him, but he will not make you, because then that choosing of him would be meaningless."

"I think I get it. I can accept him or reject him. I'm glad I chose to accept him."

"Let's go back to your vow, Maggie. You have been suffering the consequences of that for over sixteen years. God is allowing the consequences because it was your choice. The bad news is that it is impossible to break the vow in our own strength. The good news is that God has provided a way out. It is not easy, and it is very costly. But in your case, the reward is very great. It is Jenny and more. I saw you on the plane, how you love and cherish her. I made a vow once and I learned there are steps to take to break the vow."

"You made a vow too?"

"Maggie, I'm not an angel. I'm not God. I'm just like you in my humanity. Maybe that's why God picked me to help you. ... Yes, when I was nine or ten, I realized one of my parents' ways of punishing me was to take away things I had fun with. So my vow was, 'I will never have fun again!' And I didn't, not for a long, long time. Oh, I pretended sometimes, but it just wasn't there.

"After a while, I forgot about the vow, but could never understand why life was so boring, why nothing was ever satisfying, why nothing was ever fun. After I received Jesus as my Lord and gave my life to him, he came in and started making changes in me by his Holy Spirit. He reminded me of the vow I had made, and yes, I sure wanted to cancel it. There was obviously not as much riding on mine as yours, but still I was pretty intensely eager to break that thing."

Maggie interrupted. "Oh, I remember another vow, and maybe it's part of the same one. Or maybe it's not even a vow. I blamed those three boys, my brother and his friends. I blamed them for disfiguring me. I hated them!

I hated them with a furious hatred. Every time I saw my scars in the mirror, I would plot my revenge. When the other girls were getting nice figures, I would cry myself to sleep sometimes, thinking about how I would get even. I always thought I'd get back at them through their children."

"What happened to them? How did they turn out? Do they have children?"

"Charles started out in the tin mines, like my father. Then he went to school to become an administrator, and went back to the mines to work in management. Ted became a sports announcer, and Billy is a schoolteacher like me. I've never seen Ted or Billy again. I ask Charles sometimes, so I'll know when they have their children.

"To this day, Charles doesn't know I remember the whole thing, or even parts of it. I don't think Billy is married. Charles and Ted have children, and they are all older than Jenny. After she was born, I realized, how could I ever do that to their mothers? I love Jenny so much, and I'm sure the boys' wives do too. It makes me sick, thinking about what I was planning to do to their kids."

Matt thought a moment. "Yes, it's all part of the same vow. At least, dealing with it will be a package deal. Let me tell you how I was able to break my vow, with the Lord's help. Without the Lord's help, it will be impossible, as I mentioned.

"The first step you've already done, and so had I. That is, I had to become a new creature, a new being. The old being, my old self, your old self, had no desire to break the vow, only to wallow in it. But the old self was dead.

"The second step is a toughie. It involves forgiveness. You must forgive Charles. You must forgive Ted. You must forgive Billy. That's why I said it was a package deal. Finally, you must forgive yourself. Did you ever blame your parents for not being there for you, for not protecting you?"

"No. I blamed them for a lot, but not for that. I realized they were incapable of wanting to help me, anyway. I don't know if I could ever feel any forgiveness for the boys. They were so mean, and I was so unable to protect myself. They deliberately wanted to hurt me, to humiliate me."

"Maggie, that is what forgiveness is all about. They don't deserve it and would probably throw it back in your face if you told them. But forgiving them will break the hold they have over you. Not forgiving them will eat at you your whole life. Anyway, forgiveness is an action, not a feeling."

She looked up, surprised. "Oh. … I don't know if I could do the action. What is it?"

"You have to say the words. By an effort of your own will, you have to say the words. Either address them personally, or to God. Either 'Charles, I forgive you for…' or 'Jesus, I forgive Ted for…' then fill in the blank with what you forgive them for. I've had to forgive people, and I usually finish by asking God not to hold it against them, either. That's what forgiveness is all about, not holding that thing against them any longer. Just let it go and don't worry about fairness. I say that to God so that I know I mean it, but really, if you can say the words out loud, then you mean it. Just like the vow itself."

She looked out over the ocean, overwhelmed by its enormity and the frailty of their lifeboat. "They were young and stupid. They didn't know what they were doing. Their oats were just starting to kick in."

She would have added more, but Matt interrupted her. "Maggie, stop! That's not helping. You're just making excuses for them. They hurt you. They molested you. If you just make excuses, you'll never forgive them and will just hold onto the hurt, maybe forever. Forgiveness is harder, a lot harder. But it's only when you do forgive, that the hurt is able to be healed."

"Oh … yes, I can see that."

Maggie gave Jenny's remains a long look, then said the words. Ted first, then Billy. She saved Charles for last; there was a lot more to forgive him for. Matt didn't interrupt to tell her it was just for his part in her vow, because he knew she would be forgiving Charles for the other things she mentioned before too long, anyway. As soon as she asked God not to hold any of those things against Charles, she leaned over the side and vomited into the ocean. A long, slimy, green-and-yellow mass came out of her mouth, and quickly sank into the depths of the sea. A swig of water cleaned out her mouth.

"Wow!" she said. "At first it was really hard, especially saying their names, but then it got really easy. And I did mean it. I don't know what I threw up, because my stomach is really empty, but now that it's gone I realize it's been in there for a long, long time." She looked over the side where she had vomited. "God forgave me, too, when I came to him." Her eyes glistened and her mouth began to quiver. "Thank you."

"Yes, he did. Now you must forgive yourself." Matt handed her the half-empty water bottle. "We still have plenty left after this. It looks like you're running out of tears, and I suspect you'll have some more before you finish this step."

He was right. And even though he knew all the details now, all its nuances and all her failings, she felt that this was something she wanted to do in private.

"But where would I go?" He looked around. Their entire world consisted of three coffins bound together on a pallet with a fourth piled on top.

"Here, maybe this will make it a little easier." He moved closer to her, put the lifeless body of her daughter in her lap, sat beside her, and put his arm around her shoulder. "I'm for you," he said quietly, "not against you. And God is about to do something wonderful!"

Whether what he said helped or not, she needed no more prompting. "Father, I forgive myself," she started, then continued slowly, as precisely as she could, outlining every aspect and result of the vows she had made. Slowly was necessary, for the tears were a necessary cathartic, and there were a lot of them. But she got through it, and gave Matt a big hug.

Matt was ready to move on. "One step left."

"But I can't step left or I'll end up in the ocean!" The levity felt good; they both needed a break after the heaviness of the last hour and a half.

"The last step is to renounce the vow," Matt said. "But before we talk about that, I have a question. You said people asked you what happened, and you told them you couldn't remember anything. Just now you said you really could remember everything, but I saw the agony you went through as those memories were coming back. Please explain this to me."

"I would look at the scars, and I would blame those boys for what they did to me. I hated them for doing it, and soon my part in cutting myself faded. I saw the scars, they did it, and they must pay. But what they did to me didn't leave any lasting marks. Only the cutting did. When we began to get Jenny ready, I started to get nervous, because I was next. I began to realize that perhaps I had played a part, but couldn't remember what it was.

"As soon as you told me it was my turn, I came face to face with what I had done to myself. When you asked about a vow, the memories started flooding back. As I recounted the trauma the boys did to me, in my mind I couldn't get past the vow I'd made. I could see that I was the one responsible. I was horrified at myself. I'm glad it's over."

"God is showing you things a little at a time," Matt said. "There may be more. Are you ready for that?"

"Oh, yes! This cleaning out felt really good at the end. If there's more, I want to get it over with."

"Okay, let's renounce the vow. In order to do that, we have to realize that vows which need to be broken are based on a lie. Not a lie that you told, but a lie that you believed. Maybe more than one. Jesus said that the truth will make you free. We, or you, need to examine the circumstances to figure out what that lie was. Then we, or you, need to replace the lie with truth, and then the vow will become of no effect.

"In my case, the lie I believed was that my parents didn't love me and looked for excuses to abandon me. I believed their discipline had nothing to do with making me a better young lad. And finally, I believed that I had a right to be in control of my own life, especially at that age."

Maggie thought for a few minutes. Matt took that time to look around. The sun was slowly getting lower; it would be dark in another two hours, he guessed. He stood up, steadying himself on the top coffin, looking over the quiet sea toward the place he thought the plane went down. There was still nothing. The dolphins had never come back.

He looked on the other side of the top coffin from where they had been sitting, and to his amazement he saw, stuck among the remains of cargo netting, sitting low in the water, a stainless-steel cabinet like the ones food service contractors use to load the meals on planes. The door was facing up, and he hoped the door seals would have kept water out. It looked like the cabinet was stuck well enough that it wouldn't go anywhere. He sat back down as Maggie finished her recollections.

"Okay," she said finally, "You know my story pretty well and can let me know if I'm on the right track, or if I missed anything. I believed, like you, that I had a right to be in control of my life. I believed I had the right to deny anybody and everybody, including myself, and especially Jenny, pleasure from my breasts because someone took advantage of me, or for any other reason. I believed that mutilating myself was justifiable and an acceptable expression of my hurt. Finally, I believed that by mutilating myself, people, especially my parents, would pay attention to me and love me."

"Yes, I think you nailed it. Let's replace the lies with truths. Who has the right to be in control of your life?"

Maggie was starting to get excited. "God!"

"Yes, that's what you acknowledged when you made him your Lord. The next one is kind of tricky. Obviously, not everybody has the right to receive pleasure from your breasts. How would you replace that lie with the truth?"

"Um, I'm not sure. I could make a list?"

"Who would be on the list? More importantly, what do they all have in common? And, of course, there are different ways to enjoy your breasts."

"Maybe we could make it a more general truth?"

"Let's go back to the list. Would a husband be on the list?"

"Yes, of course."

"How about you? Would you be on the list?"

"Yes."

"How about Jenny, and perhaps other children?"

"Yes. Yes."

"How about me?"

She didn't answer right away, but she was thinking about it. "Well…" she said slowly.

Matt interrupted. "No, I would not be on the list. But I will say this: I intend to take great pleasure in watching Jenny chow down the first two times."

She was missing something. "Two times?"

"Of course. Both breasts will need to have a reset, and Jenny will do them both. Anyone else?"

"Maybe. But it would have to be for the right reasons, and at the right time."

"Yes, good. So go back to the lie you believed, take out the lie and insert a truth. What would the new statement be?"

"Okay. But first I'm going to rephrase the lie. God, please help me. You know I just want your truth." She stopped for a moment and listened. She drew in her breath. "I believed I could use my body for revenge. Now I believe I have no right to use my body in any way displeasing to God."

She went on and moved ahead. "I believe mutilating myself is an act of destroying something God made beautiful. I believe forgiveness is an acceptable response to being hurt, and I believe that I can't make people love me, but that shouldn't stop me from loving them."

"Bravo! Beautiful! Now you've eliminated all the lies enabling the vow, so go on and renounce the vow or vows, however you want to put it into your own words."

"By God's power and love, I renounce any intention I ever had of revenge on Charles, Ted, or Billy. By God's power and love, I renounce trying to manipulate my parents or any other person. And by God's power and love, I renounce my words, that no one will ever enjoy these breasts again!"

And it was done.

The VTC started promptly at 3 p.m., since all the participants were already logged on. Penny Hasid had brought photos annotated with the agencies of all the different participants. JC Smalley arranged them in the holders just out of sight of the camera he was facing. Phil Henry started the meeting, and immediately turned it over to Bob McGee, who had two other CIA reps with him.

"Jeff Peterson and Harvey Hostetler work for me. Jeff will start off talking about a chemical threat and Harvey will follow with a discussion of the Brazil connection."

"Hi, I'm Jeff Peterson. We checked the credentials of those in the monitors, but we have no way of knowing who else might be listening in. If you have less than a Secret clearance, please excuse yourselves. I'm looking for you all to tell me when that is done."

After all locations had verified the security clearances, Jeff started his briefing. "This briefing is classified Secret. Please don't ask about our methods or sources. We found out not too long ago that a Russian engineer had disappeared from his work location. He was one of the more senior chemists working in their chemical warfare program. His name is Luka Stanković.

"Originally from Serbia, he attended college in Moscow and attracted the attention of Russian military recruiters for their research programs. He was known to be working on a new generation of nerve agents, similar in effect to the nerve agents used by both the US and Russia, but much simpler and safer to manufacture. It is not known why he disappeared, where he might have ended up, or if he took any samples, formulas, or production methods with him.

"It is rumored that he might have found his way to the States, on the West Coast somewhere. We have no customs record of entry anywhere using that name, Luka Stanković. We are currently looking for a photo or other identifying information.

"The reason I am telling you all this, is that the only things we know about Stanković is that our information about him meets the timeframe of the airplane event, and he is the sort of person for whom shooting down a fully-loaded passenger aircraft is no big deal. When we sorted through the different scenarios worldwide, we eliminated all of them but this one. We don't see an immediate connection, but since things sometimes move very fast in this business, we thought it necessary for you to be made aware."

Kirby Drinkard, DHS, had a question. "Could this be a binary nerve agent, where two or more harmless chemicals are combined to form the agent?"

"Yes, that's very probable. The US developed a binary nerve agent for artillery shells years ago. The technology exists, so it is logical to assume that 'simpler and safer' would indicate a binary. ... If there are no more questions I'll be followed by Harvey."

There weren't.

"Hostetler here." Bob's monitor displayed a map of the north part of Brazil. "Here is Macapá." His cursor appeared on the map circling a small section of the Atlantic coast and Amazon River. "We have been tracking the IP address Mr. Smalley found, 191.6.118.145, for a while. That router is being used by a known hacker. There are actually three there, rotating on and off: a white male, a Latino, and a white female.

"We found their physical location easily enough. We have had them under surveillance for the last ten days. We have seen that at least one of them has hacking skills that are rather advanced. They usually use various spoofed IP addresses in the Great Lakes area, so it surprises us when they occasionally use their actual IP address.

"Our surveillance revealed that they were in radio contact with an entity with whom they were communicating via encrypted messages. They were using word substitutions, which meant we couldn't decipher them without the word list. Three days ago, we obtained a copy of the word list.

"We were also able to use directional antennas to get the approximate location of the entity's base, which is located over one hundred miles southwest on a tributary of the Amazon, the Rio Jari. Our intel does not indicate any civilized activities in the area, and the satellite imagery is also inconclusive. Not too far away, to the west, is the town of Munguba.

"What we got from the encrypted messages seems to indicate some kind of a clandestine aircraft retrofit facility. Barges move the cloaked and partially disassembled aircraft to and from that location. The messages mostly are schedules for the barge movements and requests for supplies, food and water, and insect repellent.

"Mr. Santos, it is good you are here. We are in contact ourselves with the US Ambassador to Brazil, as well as the Brazilian Ambassador, to apprise them of the situation in Macapá. Does anyone have any questions?"

Pedro Santos suspected that they knew more than they were saying, as he had worked with them before, on drug and counterfeiting investigations. "Yes, we are aware of your contact," he said, "and we will pass along this latest information to the Ambassador."

"JC Smalley here, at the Chicago FBI Field Office. Dusty Mae Watt, our Field Office Chief, is also on. I may be able to shed some light on the hacker's use of his real IP address. He or she hacked into the Air World flight database using that because the security system for the database required a real IP address."

He explained what he had learned from Jack Smith, and continued, "MiGs can fly only about thirteen hundred miles on their internal fuel tank. That's about six-hundred and fifty miles each way, plus they were on-station for a good half hour between the time they were first spotted until we lost contact with the plane. I'm not sure where they were flying from, but I can tell you they do not have in-flight refuel capability. The aircraft retrofit facility may be connected with this event."

"Thanks, Mr. Smalley," Harvey said. "The MiGs can carry external fuel tanks. Do you know the capacity of those, or how much added range they give? If you don't know off the top of your head, we can get the information internally."

JC had thought of that, but didn't have time before the meeting to look it up and do the calculations. "No, I don't."

"Barry Mantile, Treasury. Were you aware of the bank transfers in Bakersfield traced to that IP address?"

"No, sir, not until we heard it from Mr. McGee a couple hours ago. Perhaps the bank had the same security system as Air World."

Phil came back on. "Does anyone else have anything to report? I suspect we were all trying to put out fires since the last meeting. If there's no new or old business, I'm going to let everyone get back to their other jobs. Please stay near your phones. I won't call you this weekend unless it's urgent. There won't be much to do in reference to the flight until the National Transportation Safety Board, or whoever, can get a salvage ship to that area. Do we know how deep it is there?"

JC knew. "Somewhat over three miles."

"Thanks, JC. Please give me a call in a half hour. For the rest of the group, we need to meet again as soon as we hear something about the Brazilian meeting. Bob or Pedro, do you know when that might be?"

Neither knew. "I'll call Phil no later than 1400 hours on Monday," Bob said, "and the group can call his office after that."

One by one, the monitors went dark.

Matt was weeping softly. "I am so proud of you!"

He held his hand up between the sun and the horizon. Then the other hand on top. "It will be dark soon, maybe a little more than an hour. About eight fingers of daylight left.

"Now it really is your turn. Just like we got Jenny ready, we need to get you ready."

Matt wondered if this would be awkward. Maggie answered that for him. She took off her vest, which had dried by then. Then she pulled off her still-damp shirt. As he suspected, there was just skin underneath.

"I haven't worn a bra since my twelfth birthday," she said. "I was covered with bandages, and by the time they came off, there was nothing to support."

She lifted her arms over her head to give him the full display. "There it is. It doesn't hurt. And see, I have full range of motion."

The scar was ugly. It was grotesque. It was hard to look at, and at the same time, it was hard to avoid looking at. At twelve, it was a straight line. At twenty-eight, her body's growth had caused the line to zig and zag, curved in places, and the skin was slightly puckered where her breasts would have been. There were stitch marks the entire length. Where the skin had been cut through, the discolorations made it seem like her insides were showing. He wondered if the surgeon were trying to teach her a lesson. He stared, the horror of it all showing on his face.

"I'm so sorry..." There were really no words.

Suddenly, reality kicked back in. Fetching a new water bottle, he cracked the top for her and passed it over.

She splashed her chest with water, gently massaging the places where there would be mouth-to-skin contact, and rinsed herself off. She donned her vest.

"Do they feel any different? Not trying to be nosy, just curious."

She didn't mind. "No … Yes! They're warm now. They've always been like ice to me before."

"Then let's … Here, let's put Jenny here and we'll ask together."

Matt had a thought. "Wait, let me get something."

He opened the lid to the coffin on top and ripped out the pink-and-gold lining from the side closest to him, about six feet in length. "We have to dress her right for the occasion."

Maggie removed the pink blanket and Jenny's outfit and wrapped her in the lining. "It's velvet. It's soft. It's perfect!"

"I saw that earlier when I was checking to see if there were any occupants. I expected it to be stiff plastic cloth, but I guess people want their loved ones to be comfortable in their final resting places."

Maggie knew Matt was just joking; she knew now, beyond the shadow of a doubt, there was no such thing as a "final resting place." She put Jenny's stiff, grayish-blue, lifeless body between them and they both moved forward, as if to provide a sanctuary for the little one. They joined hands.

Matt started. "Father in heaven, please let it please you to send Jenny back to us, to Maggie. Her body is dead, lifeless, full of decay. Every part in it needs to be restored to life. We rely on your promises. We have nothing else to hold onto, except your love for Maggie, and your ability to do what is impossible for us. We ask in Jesus's name that you make this body a fit vessel for her to spend her life in while here, that you restore her foot, and that you breathe back into her, the life that was so recently sucked out."

Maggie added, "Thank you, Father, thank you. We receive Jenny back now, in Jesus's name."

They both looked at Jenny for several minutes, but there was no movement, no change. Then Matt reminded Maggie, "God's message said you would suckle her. Do that. Her mouth is already open; just put it up to your chest."

Maggie had never had any reason in her life to learn anything about nursing an infant. Nevertheless, she picked her up and forced the little mouth on her right breast. Maggie gasped as the pressure in her breast began to increase; she felt something flowing into it from all over her body. She felt Jenny's lips contract just a little; then her tongue reached out and touched her. She looked down; from Jenny's upturned nose to her wiggling ears, all were flushed a beautiful pink. Jenny closed her eyes and clamped down, feeding voraciously. Maggie didn't know whether to scream or shout or cry.

103

"Thank you," was all she said, her eyes cast heavenward.

Both sides needed healing; the other side was still dead. "Don't let her get full! Switch her to the other side."

Milk sprayed all over Jenny's face as Maggie pulled her away. Jenny waved her arms and kicked her feet in delight as the other side became fully operational. Maggie noticed. "Matt, check her feet!"

"I can't tell which one it was," he replied. "They're both perfect. Well, her right one needs to have the nails trimmed. It looks like there's about three month's growth on them. ... No! Just kidding about the nails. But they are both the same, both perfect."

"How does it feel, Maggie?"

"Amazing! But after what I did to Jenny all those years ago, I have no right to feel this good nursing her."

Matt watched the nursing briefly and wondered. "Oh, Jenny, Jenny, Jenny. What did you see? What did you hear?"

It was supposed to be a rhetorical question, but just then Jenny unlatched, turned directly toward him, waved her arms, and said, "Da-da-da-da-da! Da-da, da-da-da!" Loudly, it seemed, with great conviction.

Maggie laughed. "She's calling you Daddy."

Matt shook his head. "No. I was curious if this might happen. I believe she was in heaven, waiting to come back. That she was not an infant while there. And that she was with Jesus from the time she drowned until the time she started nursing. That's just a guess on my part. My next guess is that her memory of heaven will fade very rapidly, maybe even already."

Maggie was frantically joyful; she was beside herself with wonder and delight. Matt was not far behind her. Jenny was the anchor holding them both on the earth.

At K103 in the Gulf of Mexico, Jimmy Branson did a double-take when he read the incoming message. It was the report from headquarters about an Air World Airlines flight being shot down over the North Atlantic Ocean. What got him was not the approximately three hundred deaths, or the audacity of some entity to shoot down a loaded passenger plane, it was the location. He checked with Jacob next door to confirm his memory. Sure enough, the latitude and longitude matched exactly.

He hoped that the lack of excitement here in the remoteness of the Gulf of Mexico wasn't what was driving him to immediately sit down and send a response back up through the chain of command. He hoped too, that the excitement at the other end wouldn't cause his response to be buried for the next five months. However, he had no idea how the seafloor noise might relate to the airplane attack.

Matt finally caught his breath. "Maggie, there were actually three miracles that happened just now."

"Well, one of course, was God raising Jenny from death. Another was I was healed. That makes me wonder, will my scars fade away as part of my healing?"

"You could ask God for that, but I don't think completely. Look at those scars as a gift from God. For years those scars reminded you of the revenge you were going to exact, and of the death you wrought on yourself. You know, the lies you believed. Now those scars will remind you that the revenge has turned to forgiveness, and the death has turned to new life. I do hope they fade somewhat. Now, do you know the third miracle?"

Maggie didn't know the third miracle.

"I'll give you an analogy for it. Do you know the story about when Jesus healed the man born blind?"

"I think so. That was one of the lessons at the college group I went to. A man was born blind through no fault of his own. Jesus healed him, and he lived happily ever after." Maggie was rather proud of this recollection.

"That's the best synopsis of that story I ever heard in my life!" Matt said. "There were two miracles there. One, the man could see. The other is that his brain could take what his eyes were sending it, and know exactly what he was seeing. God had to create a whole lifetime of images in his brain in order for him to tell the difference between a horse and a cow, between a house and a tent, and between an angry face and a happy face.

"In your case, as I watched, you and Jenny were the perfect pros at nursing, even though neither of you had done it before. From the start, you had milk and not colostrum. And I'll bet you never have the soreness that happens when you start to nurse. Helene was sore for a week with both our kids. That, girl, is the miracle."

Maggie was grateful for that miracle too. "As soon as I picked her up, I felt like I knew what to do. Connecting her to me and switching sides just felt so natural, like there was no other way to do it."

Jenny was finished, and she rewarded them with a loud belch. Minutes later, she gave testimony that her entire alimentary canal was functioning perfectly.

"Yikes!" Maggie, startled, almost dropped Jenny into the ocean in her attempt to put some distance between herself and the rapidly discoloring coffin liner. Matt jumped up, causing their little craft to sway ominously, and ripped another section of liner from the top coffin.

"Look what I just found!" He held aloft a stout plastic zipper bag. "A coffin tool kit. I'll bet there's one in each coffin." He surveyed the contents: several of different size safety pins, some zip ties, a small sewing scissors, needle nose pliers, a two-meter measuring tape, a coffin key and eight coffin bolts, straight and curved needles with different colored thread, nail clippers, a whole assortment of makeup including powders and fake nails, a tube of silicon glue, instructions in English and French, and a small piece of paper inscribed, "INSP BY STEVE S".

He gave a large safety pin to Maggie. With a slight bow, he pointed to the top of her vest. "For your royal modesty."

She joined him in his silliness, as he fashioned the cloth into a diaper, and showed her how to fasten it with just one safety pin. "We need to name our little rescue ship."

"Oh? Why?"

"Because they will need a name for the movie they will make of our adventure." They both laughed heartily.

Matt emptied the tool kit contents from the zipper bag into a small pouch he made of coffin-liner material, then cut holes in the front of it with the sewing scissors. "Plastic pants!"

Maggie pulled it up around Jenny's legs, made some adjustments with the scissors, and pinned it at the waist so it wouldn't slip down. "Perfect!"

Matt had a thought. "How about the Good Ship Myrtlewood? But we'd have to spell it the British way."

Maggie wasn't aware of alternate spellings of good and ship. "How is that?"

"G-o-o-d-e and s-h-i-p-p-e."

"Oh, you!" She gave him a playful slap on the knee. "I never heard of those spellings, and I'm a teacher."

"No, I'm serious. That's just the point. I've never seen those in a crossword either. After the movie, the GSM will be famous. Goode blank Myrtlewood, a six-letter word, fifth letter 'p'."

"Okay, goody shippy it is then!"

They eventually eliminated the extraneous embellishments; it became simply the Good Ship Myrtlewood.

Maggie was still holding Jenny, who had developed decided drowsiness and drifted into dreamland. "I will never let you go. Once I did, and God gave you back. I love you to the ends of the earth and heaven." It was a brand-new song with just one verse, which she sang several times. Then an idea struck her. "Jenny, what did you see and hear when you were in heaven?"

Jenny, hearing her name, opened her eyes, then closed them again and went back to sleep. Matt and Maggie exchanged knowing glances, and the matter was never mentioned again.

"Maggie, let me have that dirty liner. I think I remember the difference between milk poo and formula poo. That poo just seemed to come out too quick."

He carefully unrolled Jenny's arrival outfit. "Formula came out first, then milk at the end." He laughed at his own joke. "But look at what's in-between."

He showed her the black goo. Embedded in it was what appeared to be a segmented sea worm, some small broken pieces of shell, small pieces of plastic, and a ring with some different stones attached. "It must have been forced down her throat while she was rolling around in the shark's belly. That first shot of milk must have acted like a powerful flush."

He examined the milk poo closer and concluded the cleansing was sufficient. He rinsed the velvet in the sea, shaking it vigorously underwater before laying it on the top coffin to dry. Looking at it closely, he hoped they could get more than two uses out of it before it disintegrated completely. He rinsed off the ring and put it in his pocket.

JC stopped in to Dusty Mae's office before calling Phil. "Hi! Thanks for the conference room. It's working out perfectly."

Dusty Mae Watt got right to the point. "Please tell me who y'all are and why you're here. I know y'all work for Phil and you're here at his bidding, but that's about all."

JC sensed some defensiveness on the part of the Chicago Field Office special agent in charge. He chose his words carefully. "I was in Air Force Intelligence for over twenty-three years. Fairly early in my career, I started being flown around by Joel Barth, the first officer on the Air World flight. We became pretty tight. He was the best recon pilot I knew and I chose him for every mission I could. We retired together.

"I also served with Phil on some missions. We didn't become all that close, but we had great respect for each other's abilities and achievements. After I retired, I heard that Phil had joined the FBI, so I looked him up. I've done some work for him over the past five years, and he keeps calling me back.

"I'm here because I discovered the connection between the Air World flight and the hacker in Brazil. I called Phil, who wanted me to join the task force, as it turns out. He wanted me to come to DC, but when he realized the plane was already in the air, he had me brought here to take part in the VTC already in progress.

"I have no experience in FBI matters. The work I've done for Phil was generally done as piecework or one-on-one with an agent. I'm not surprised at the competence and professionalism I've seen here, and I appreciate the help I've gotten from Luke and Penny. The field office seems to be running very smoothly from the little I've seen of it. How long have you been here?"

Dusty Mae relaxed and remembered her manners. "I'm sorry. Please don't let me get your feathers ruffled. I should be a better host. Would y'all like some coffee? We have an endless pot here."

"Yes, that would be great. I've been on the go since breakfast, when I got the message from Joel."

Over coffee, after some brief chit-chat, she told him what was on her mind. "I've been special agent in charge here a little over five months. I applied for the job after getting excellent reviews as a field agent, profiler, and intelligence analyst. But y'all know what rumors are like. The rumor said I was picked in order to fill a quota. My probation period is over. I'm still here, but I'm not getting any feedback about my job performance. I thought when you suddenly appeared, that perhaps my job was at stake. Is that true?"

"I don't know anything about that. I'm not here to spy on you or take your job." He was looking her straight in the eyes as he spoke, and he realized she was watching his hands rather closely. Her question had come out of the blue, and perhaps his hands would have given him away if he were lying.

"Do you get along well with your staff?" he asked. "Any undercurrents? Hostilities? Resentments about working for someone your age, gender, skin color, training, or anything else? Are you fairly good at reading people?"

"I have a wonderful staff. Enthusiastic as all get-out about the mission and supportive of me personally. And I feel like I reciprocate. By the way, when Penny found out you were coming, she came to me to volunteer to be your assistant. She told me about you. She seems to be in awe of you. She'll make a good agent one day, and she gives y'all the credit for giving her the break she needed to get started. Now, you'd better go and call Phil before I get in trouble!"

"Maggie, you've seen wonderful things, and God's not done yet," Matt said. "You're just getting started in this new life God has for you. I want to tell you about your part in this new life, and there is a lot to tell you. You will grow in wisdom about the things of God, especially as you continue to be in awe of him.

"As you mature spiritually, you will understand more and more the necessity and promise of wisdom, of preparation, of determination to follow the Lord's will for your life. There will be sacrifices as we recognize that the kingdom of God, and His glory, is what we give ourselves to, willingly, because He is our maker. When you get back, you will have a wonderful story to tell. It will be a story of God's wonderfulness and love for us. And for your listeners. We have a lot to talk about."

"I'm trying to catch my breath," Maggie said. "I'm in total awe of everything that's happened. How he has used you, and you have refused to accept any of the credit. He has given me a wonderful example to follow. I hope I can do what he calls me to do."

"It's getting dark," he said a little later, "about four more fingers of daylight."

They looked around. The only ripples in the water were caused by them moving around on their lifeboat. Matt was not used to spending hours sitting on a hard surface, and he was getting a little sore. A lawn chair would be nice, he thought. A glance at Maggie confirmed she was suffering the same discomfort. She had the added burden of holding Jenny, since there was nothing to lay the baby on. Matt took Jenny to give Maggie a break from time to time.

He got the coffin pillow and gave it to her for Jenny. "Do you remember the dream I told you about, where the woman brought me her dead baby?"

Maggie took the pillow and sat on it instead. "Yes. The petunia dream. The woman wasn't me and it was me. The baby wasn't Jenny and it was Jenny."

Matt wished he could get the other three pillows for her. "Well, yes, it was that dream. Actually, the woman wasn't you and it was you and it wasn't you. Same for Jenny. I had another dream just after Helene died that interpreted the third part, where it wasn't you again. I remembered it as soon as we got on board the GSM, but I knew in my spirit God was going to give us back Jenny, uh, give you back Jenny, and so I waited until now to tell it."

As curious as Maggie was to know the dream, there was a more important issue to settle. "Don't think of Jenny as being just mine. I hereby pronounce Jennimoore Louisa Trillbey as being part yours, also."

Jenny stirred again briefly.

Matt wasn't exactly sure what his ultimate relationship to Maggie would be. "Thank you," he said solemnly. "I receive her, at least for the time being, as my niece. Or my granddaughter. Or whatever. I will always love her and cherish her. I am already quite fond of her as I am of you. When God brings us back to civilization, you and I may go our separate ways, but Jenny will always have a connection to me. By the way, I can't imagine that ring not belonging to her."

Maggie was sad when he mentioned going separate ways; she had grown quite fond of him also. But the sadness had no foothold in her; it left quickly as her joy returned in full strength. "Yes, it's getting late. And now please tell me your dream."

"Maggie, are you enjoying these dreams? Are you realizing they are gifts from God? Yet, in all my dreams, I've never been the beneficiary of God's blessing or activity. Someone else always was."

"I'm really new to all this. It's really thrilling. I get goose bumps listening and thinking about what God has shown you in dreams and messages."

"As I said, I had this dream shortly after Helene died. I had opened an *Acts & Facts* magazine to an article about the ocean and how it talked about God's wonderfulness in what we see in it. My eyes were just kind of staring at the pages, but I wasn't focusing on a thing. I put the magazine down and went to bed.

"I dreamt I was hovering over a very deep part of the ocean, maybe in a hot-air balloon, not very high up. I couldn't see land in any direction. I felt something like electricity flowing all through me, and I called up an island from the bottom of the sea. It was a big island. It had a river and forest and a small city. The island was full of life. I remember I specified all kinds of details, but I can't remember them except for what I just told you."

"And?"

"Oh, don't you see? The petunia woman is the sea, great and broad, in which are swarms of fish without number, small and large. The little boy is the island. While on the seafloor he or it is dead, but as soon as it is raised above the sea, it becomes full of life and activity. And the best part?" He paused. "You, Maggie, were there watching the whole thing."

"Wow, a little jet-black towhead! You know, though, it was the sea that brought Jenny to us, the shark. Was there a shark on the woman's dress?"

"Yes, there sure was. Maggie, you're brilliant!"

"It's the dream that's brilliant. I wonder what will happen next."

"I don't know. We'll have to see."

JC made the call on the secure line in his quarters. Phil was waiting and answered immediately. "JC, the situation is changing direction somewhat. I need you to tell me if you're all in or if I need to find someone else. I can't tell you what it will entail at this point, or for how long. All I can tell you is national security may be at stake."

"You know me well enough to know I'll do what I can. Yes, I'm all in. Nicki already knows what indefinite means. What do you want me to do? Is my clearance what it needs to be?"

"Yes, I believe so. Find Dusty Mae and have her give you access to the T-1 line. She can give you my number here. Tell her I appreciate her participation this afternoon."

"You should tell her yourself. It would mean more coming from you. You have to give her the approval for me to use the T-1 line, right?"

"Yes. Okay, I'll tell her."

A few minutes later, there was a Top Secret conference call on the encrypted T-1 line among JC, Phil, and Bob McGee.

Bob started off. "As I was telling Phil, we get intel through various means. Surveillance, espionage, diplomatic means, and military intelligence to name a few. Sometimes we want our enemies to know things that they can't find out any other way, so we leak it to them. They do the same for us. Now I'm speaking specifically of Russia. There are different reasons we do this, but the bottom line is it's good for both of us.

"Let me give you an example. Remember the soldier who was taken prisoner in Afghanistan several weeks ago? We had no idea he was even missing, but our quote 'reliable source' let us know not only that he was captured, but where they were holding him. When we sent in the troops and rescued him, we gave our own intelligence folks great credit for it. Of course, they knew better, and the Taliban didn't know it was their allies who spilled the beans.

"It was a nice deal that didn't cost them anything. Now we're obligated to return the favor. Actually, in that case, they were the ones returning the favor.

"Now to the nerve gas threat. I'm going to call our reliable source 'Rudy' for convenience. That's not how we know him and we don't even know—or care—what his real name is. Anyway, all the information Jeff Peterson gave this afternoon came from Rudy over the last several days. It doesn't fit his usual pattern of information. Normally, he just gives us tidbits—a fact or event here, a name there—and lets us figure out the significance of it. This is how we generally do it, too.

"There was more, too, tying Stanković to the bank job that Treasury asked us if we knew about. He even told us what bank it was. We alerted Treasury, and Barry's folks are the ones who found out the IP address from the bank. Harvey didn't know about this because he was strictly working the Brazil angle.

"It would seem that if a madman were on the loose in the US with a weapon of mass destruction, they would keep quiet about it. It almost seems like they lost him, can't find him or the WMD, and want us to do that for them, including bearing all the risks. Bottom line, we are going to operate based on the assumption Rudy is telling the truth, while trying to figure out what their motive is in this.

"One of the first steps is to see what's going on down in Brazil. We have a team in Macapá to take the hacker crew—there's three of them—but we don't have enough agents there to get the jungle group, which we need to do simultaneously with the Macapá operation. I'm presenting this to the US Ambassador for his talks with his Brazilian counterpart. I hope we can get Brazilian security forces involved, either their military or the ABIN, the Brazilian Intelligence Agency."

Phil offered to help. "We are forbidden by statute to provide personnel to help. However, I have been in contact separately with Captain Palova, anticipating a need for help from his elite warriors. Not to fight, per se, but to act as advisors, a role they've done before. Armed for self-defense, of course, to work with the Brazilians.

"He has to go up two levels in his chain of command, but he thinks he can make it work. He will give me the contact information of that decision-making authority. Maybe you can call him and help explain the situation. Also, JC, I am going to send you there as soon as the appropriate diplomatic arrangements are confirmed."

JC was quick to respond. "You know I'll do what I need to do, but I'm curious as to why I'm even involved at all. I understand about the airplane, but that's over now. Others from different agencies will do a much more thorough job than I can do, investigating this whole thing. I'm not trained in field agent operations or methods. What could I possibly be bringing to the table?"

He was hoping the answer didn't imply the word "expendable", as in, "You're expendable."

Phil didn't have that in mind at all. "I've seen your file, JC. You're an expert in what I would call strategic intelligence. Those conducting the operations on the ground have tactical intelligence, you know, what information they need to get the immediate job done. You're right, the airplane is finished, at least for you. It seems to me, that airplane was merely a window into a much bigger picture. No, I'm not intending to get you into harm's way. You are far too valuable in doing what you do best."

JC took the compliment humbly. "Thanks."

Bob added, "We will establish an operations cell—a command post, if you will—at a location amenable to the Brazilians. You'll stage there initially, and operate out of there. I expect it may be the middle of next week before all the diplomatic maneuverings are complete. I don't think we'll have anything to report by Monday's 2 p.m. check-in time."

Phil changed the subject. "Just heard from our contact in London. They questioned all the Russian passengers who owned the luggage on AW94. They are sending transcripts soon. I will send you both a copy, and we'll examine them here, too."

Phil started tying up loose ends in preparation for ending the call. "Bob, please get a single point of contact on your end for JC. I believe you already have his contact information? JC, take the next couple of days to get ready. Wait a day to let the shock hit the whole world, then stand down if you want to, until you hear from Bob's folks. Go home if you want. Don't worry about the transcripts for the time being. You can look at them later. I'm really sorry about your friend. I understand you were closer than you let on during the VTC."

JC found a large window overlooking the city. Life goes on, he thought. Joel Barth had a wife and two school-age children. He stared out the window for a long time.

"Maggie, I just remembered. Let me show you what I found earlier."

Matt quickly took off his sneakers and socks. Maggie picked herself up by holding onto Jenny with one arm and grabbing the coffin handle with her other hand. She saw Matt go over the coffin and disappear. "Hey!" She peered over the top. "All I see is the top of your head."

"Oh. Okay. I'm going to slide this coffin off the edge a little so you can see. Hold onto it so you don't lose your balance." Carefully, he pushed it part way off the bottom stack. As soon as it cleared her, she saw Matt standing on the pallet in the water, holding onto a badly damaged cargo net, and proudly exhibiting … a stainless-steel cabinet!

Her mind flashed back to the *Castaway* movie, where if Chuck Noland had just opened that last package, he would have found the radio, matches, poncho, and packet of seeds. "Open it!"

It was empty.

"Well, maybe we can use it for something." They were both disappointed. It had been a long time since they had eaten eleven mini pretzels and eight peanut M&Ms.

Presently, Jenny awoke. Hungry, she broke into a little bleating cry. In an instant, Maggie experienced what mothers all over the world experience when they hear that cry—she felt milk rushing into her breasts, the pressure building, and finally milk oozing out from both sides, such was the abundance. She felt a glee and a giddiness she had never felt before.

This was a new experience for Matt, too. He had never heard Jenny cry. Seeing Maggie with the front of her vest all wet thrilled him to jubilation. "The healing is complete!" he exclaimed triumphantly.

Maggie grinned. Jenny latched on, and all was good.

Matt tore the rest of the lining out of the top coffin. There was more than he expected; the bottom was especially well-lined, and padded to accommodate thinner bodies during the viewings. He made a pile of diaper-sized pieces, as well as some larger pieces to use as coverings for Maggie and him to take the chill off the night air, if necessary. They both were coming down off their adrenaline highs and found themselves quite exhausted. The thick pad would make the best mattress Maggie could hope for, and extra velvet would help ensure the baby would be warm enough. If it got too cold, there was enough cloth, pinned together, to allow the three of them to wrap themselves into one big cocoon for warmth.

They tried to figure out arrangements so they both could sleep. They couldn't both lie down safely without jettisoning the top coffin, and they couldn't lie side-by-side next to the coffin without one being in danger of falling into the drink. In the end, Maggie made a sling out of a length of velvet lining and tied Jenny to herself. She and Matt sat side-by-side on the padding and leaned back against the coffin.

The sun was going down. High in the sky, the moon was little more than a sliver. It would shed scant light on the pair as they chatted.

The sea was at a dead calm as it had been the last several hours; not a breeze, not a ripple. It was pleasantly warm but starting to cool off. Maggie had redonned her shirt when all of their clothing had dried. They had taken off their shoes to let their socks dry, and Matt had taken off his polo shirt and dried it on the coffin. His undershirt dried as he wore it. The smoke from the fuel fire had disappeared along with the slight breezes they had enjoyed earlier. There was no longer anything to mark their location. They were completely alone.

"Maggie?"

"Yes?"

"Maggie, are you there?"

She was actually close enough to touch him on the padding. She didn't know where he was going with this. "Yes, Matt. We are both here."

He turned his face toward hers, and could see her face was still glowing with the joy which hadn't diminished since she had met Jesus. "Maggie, are you dreaming right now?"

"It is like a dream, and yet nothing has felt so real in my whole life. It's hard to believe all the amazing things that have happened to Jenny and me since we first saw you on the plane."

"Yes, in many ways it is like a dream, but I tell you right now that you will never forget a single detail of what has happened. Every fact, every feeling, every word God has spoken to you, every word you yourself have spoken, you will remember in the exact sequence and with the exact intensity. Father, I ask this for Maggie in Jesus's name."

"Thank you. Yes, Father, let it be so! But why did you say it that way? It was great, but it sounded so formal."

"It was a blessing. I spoke what I believed I heard the Father saying. It was a prayer, and it came from the same spirit of God who gives me the words for the songs I sing, and the same spirit of God who was calling to you through that song earlier. It is the spirit of Jesus he promised you. The Holy Spirit, we call him."

"That singing you did was really beautiful. But more than that, things were happening when you sang, and it felt like you had a connection to God as you were worshipping him. How did you ever start doing that?"

Matt fished around in the open coffin and found an empty bottle. He dipped it in the ocean and filled it with seawater, and replaced the cap. "It's called the baptism of the Holy Spirit. A total immersion in God's spirit. See this bottle? Let's say it represents you. When Jesus breathed on you, he filled you with his spirit, the Holy Spirit."

"Yes, that's exactly what he said when he breathed on me."

"You're filled; you can't hold any more. Which is okay, because you have all of him. And he will live the life of Jesus through you, and your life will be more fulfilling than you can possibly imagine. So the water represents the Holy Spirit. You carry him around with you wherever you go. Are you good this far?"

"Yes, I think I got it."

"Look around. What do you see?"

"The ocean forever in all directions. Even down as far as I can see into the water."

"Yes, exactly. That's the real extent of the Holy Spirit. And that's where he wants you to live." Matt dropped the bottle into the water. "Total immersion," he said, "the baptism of the Holy Spirit."

"I've heard of baptism. That's where your body gets dunked. But here, your whole spirit, your whole being, gets dunked. Is that right?"

Matt marveled at her perception and understanding. "Yes. With regular baptism, a person goes under the water to symbolize joining Jesus in his death, and coming up out of the water to symbolize the new life of Jesus in him. That baptism also is a picture of the baptism of the Holy Spirit. First the natural, then the spiritual."

"Is that how you are able to sing in the spirit?"

Just then Maggie noticed the bottle in the water had moved out of reach. "Uh-oh," she said, pointing.

Matt hadn't dropped the bottle straight down, but had given it a little momentum away from the side. "Where is it going?"

"I don't know. I suppose the current will take it wherever it wants to."

Matt reached toward the bottle and pulled the water to the side of their little craft. The bottle followed the water flow and Matt pulled it on board. "Yes, exactly! That's the whole point. I don't know where it's going either. I'm glad you saw that when you did. I had forgotten about it."

"What's the whole point?"

"Remember I said when you, the bottle, are filled with the water, you carry him around with you wherever you go? When the bottle is in the middle of the water, the water carries you around wherever it wants you to go. The water is now in control. That is, the spirit of Jesus, of God."

"So he sings through you?"

He knew where she was heading. "Yes, but wait. I have to tell you first, that this could be a little scary. Jesus promised he would perform this baptism of the Holy Spirit on those who asked him. It's not automatic like the filling is. Those who ask him for it have to realize they are giving up control, and many people are not willing to do that. Actually, when you think about it, when they make Jesus their Lord they are already giving up control, and the baptism of the Holy Spirit should just be a normal part of living their new life in him. But sadly, it's not.

"However, for those that do ask, the Holy Spirit may use them to do wonderful things, like using them to heal people, speak messages from God, give divine wisdom, know things they couldn't possibly have found out naturally, and cause miraculous things to happen."

"Like you did with Jenny. And those messages and dreams for me."

"Yes, I'm thrilled that God picked me to do that for you. There is an extra benefit, too. When Jesus baptizes you, he gives you the ability to allow the Holy Spirit to speak through you. A language not your own, but all your own nonetheless. You can pray it, you can speak it, you can sing it, you can even think it. One thing you can't do, though, is understand it.

"It is yours to use whenever you choose. He will never force you or embarrass you or take you by surprise. The language may change often or sometimes or never. It is not your language but his, although in singing, he lets you set the melody, tempo, volume, and duration and other things like that."

Maggie stood up and briefly contemplated the vastness of the ocean, suddenly feeling quite small. As she started to get to her feet, Matt volunteered to hold Jenny. So little, so frail, so alive! He wanted to give Maggie a break, as well as to let her have her hands and arms free for what he felt would be coming next.

Maggie sat back down, cross-legged on the coffin. "I want that, all of what God has for me. I want the wonderfulness I see in you. The confidence you have with God, and the peace. I'd say the joy, too, but I don't know if I would survive if I had any more than I already have."

"You already know the benefits and ramifications. Think about it, and when you're ready, you just need to ask Jesus for it."

She wasted no time. "Jesus, please baptize me in your Holy Spirit."

She closed her eyes and opened her mouth, but no words came out, not a sound. She waited a couple minutes, but still nothing.

"Did Jesus baptize you?" Matt asked.

"I believe he did. I felt a strange and wonderful warmth come all over me. My face still feels a little flushed. But I didn't say anything. Did I do something wrong?"

"No. Your experience just now was exactly the same as mine. The language is a little tricky to get started. You actually have to start speaking, but you don't know what to say. There seems to be this void spot in your mind. There's a syllable or two there, but you don't recognize it. Some people can start right off, others don't. It took me a few days. Just relax, though, your bottle is now adrift in the ocean, and God who loves you more than you can ever know, will do wonderful things as long as you keep your eyes on him."

"He told me that too."

"Yes, I was quoting you from before." Matt's grin told her everything would be all right.

"Okay, I'll be patient. For a little while!" They both laughed.

Jenny was awake, and she couldn't take her eyes off her mother's face, a face of great delight and love, of compassion and gratefulness.

Maggie stole a sideways glance at Matt, as he was trying to get the nail clippers to cut through a strap securing one of the three bottom coffins to the pallet. Nope, didn't work. He looked up suddenly, and she quickly looked away, but not before they made eye contact.

Matt had seen that look before, a long time ago, a lifetime it seemed.

The coffin padding was almost as long as the coffin. They had doubled it over to make it more comfortable to sit on, but now they opened it back up, to give themselves some distance between them, to be somewhat alone, to ponder, to be quiet, perhaps to pray.

Matt glanced over at Maggie, who was busy getting reacquainted with her daughter. "Lord," he said silently, "I'm know I'm getting old, but I—"

He didn't get a chance to go on. He heard very distinct, unmistakable, and commanding words. "Stop! I will bring glory to myself however I will."

Matt's mouth dropped open, but receiving this humbling reproof, he understood. He remembered God has a plan for his whole kingdom, not just for him. "Yes, I'm sorry, and thank you." He thought a moment, then continued his silent conversation with God. "She is like a sponge, Lord. She is so eager to learn, and it is delightfully easy to teach her."

"Yes, she is. A sponge I don't have to squeeze anything out of first. I kept her that way. It is one of my gifts to her. She has given herself totally to me. She may think she did that to get Jenny back. I know her heart, and she would have given herself to me the same way, even if I had kept Jenny."

"I don't want that sponge to have any wrong thing go into it on my account. It would grieve me knowing I did that." Matt knew that God's spirit was the real teacher, and that eventually Maggie would go directly to him for having that sponge indulged to the full.

"That's why I picked you. You are also my gift to her, but not in the way you were thinking just now. And you will like my choice for her. Let me show you something else."

God opened the eyes of his spirit, and Matt got a tiny peek into Maggie's future. "Wow, books!" He felt a little bold. "May I ask then, why you did give Jenny back to Maggie?"

"Because I promised. Because I have chosen them to work together for me. And because you asked. You have some more asking to do, tonight."

Matt tingled for a few minutes after that, his eyes moist, but his spirit bright. He dozed.

Maggie cooed softly with Jenny for a few minutes, letting her eyes, then her attention, drift over to Matt, who had his eyes closed peacefully. How he loves me, she thought. We were strangers until this morning, how he has taken care of me since then. Even before, while we were still on the plane, how he sacrificed his own oxygen for Jenny. He would do anything for us. How he has shared God's love. How he has been God's love! Then some more thinking: How I love him.

Then more thinking, and this time her thoughts were more directed. "Oh, Father," she began, becoming quite comfortable and delighted calling him Father, "I belong to you. I didn't know how wonderful that could be, or would be. All the great miracles you did for Jenny and me. And Matt belongs to you. We both belong to you. I'm wondering if you would do a miracle for Matt, too? I know he's a lot older than me, but I don't think thirty years is impossible for you. It could work. I can see that he loves me and his life has been so hard since his family all died…" She wasn't sure how to continue, and she hoped God didn't think she was being selfish.

She needn't have worried about how to continue. She became aware, in her mind, of a voice other than Matt's. "Maggie! Dear one!" She immediately recognized the voice. "My love and care for Matt is more than you can ever imagine. He has been my gift to you for this time and place, but he is not the right one for you for forever. I have been preparing the right one for you since before the universe began. You and he will be a perfect fit as you both follow me without reservation. He will love me. He will love you and Jenny. There may be others for you both to love, cherish, and nurture. Do not be afraid, Matt already understands this."

The voice, his voice, went on, "I am showing you great things because I have a great work for you, and you need to understand my abilities and my compassion. But you are not ready yet. My spirit will make you ready, but there will be lessons along the way. I have given you a heart to learn and a mind to retain. Matt will be your teacher for a little longer. Learn from him."

Maggie didn't know whether to feel sad or relieved, but was glad to note that the heartache she was beginning to feel had disappeared. She thought about the wonderful things God had promised her, and decided to enjoy Matt's company and tutelage, loving him however she could, within God's new guidelines. Her joy undiminished, she made sure her charge was secure for the night, leaned back on the coffin, and joined her daughter in dreamland.

The little craft was turning slowly, and the setting sun lit upon Matt's face and woke him. He checked his charges; both were slumbering rather fitfully. He noticed Maggie's long brown hair scattered across her face—it had been doing that often since she first landed in the water. He stood up, reached into the top coffin, and pulled a strip of velvet loose, a long ribbon of pink and gold.

Maggie woke from the jostling of their lifeboat and the sound of tearing cloth. Seeing her awake, Matt brought his offering down to her. "For your hair," he said. "I'll help you tie it back."

"No thank you," she said quickly. "I don't need it."

She saw Matt open his mouth to respond, but then he closed it again. She could see she had hurt his feelings. How could I have done that, she wondered. Why was I so testy just then? She watched as he sat back down on the padding, knees drawn up. She felt quite rotten about it, but didn't want to open her mouth again for fear of what might come out. She watched as he slowly wadded the cloth strip into a ball and flipped it into the water, where it straightened out and floated limply a few feet away. Neither of them moved. Neither said a word, and soon the last edge of the sun slipped beneath the horizon.

On the other side of the world, Rishaan Chabra was wakened by a jangly ringtone.

"Rishaan, the mission has been completed. There was nothing left on the surface, except a small fire. They were chased away by the US Air Force, so the site has probably been GPS'd."

"Thank you, Maria. How far away is that from the nearest land, and how deep is the ocean there?"

"The sea map I have is from the sixties, but it should still be good. Looks like over eleven hundred kilometers from Canada, and five to five-and-a-half kilometers deep. I was in constant contact with Jackson. She's pretty good."

They hung up, and Rishaan hummed a happy tune as he made himself breakfast.

Matt was the first to break the silence. "Maggie, I saw how you looked at me earlier."

Maggie didn't have to ask what look he was talking about. She hung her head, a little sheepish and more than a little embarrassed. He noticed, she realized, and now everything has changed. Jenny was still sleeping peacefully. Maggie rearranged her blanket and waited for the axe to fall.

"I have to confess," he went on, "I was starting to feel that way too. I received your look, and thoroughly enjoyed it, savored it, delighted in it. In spite of our ages. So I asked the Lord about it. He told me, in no uncertain terms, 'No!' Knowing his will made it easy for me to turn off those feelings, to put them away forever. What I want you to know is that I don't love you any less right now, and I can guarantee you it is one-hundred percent God's kind of love."

Maggie felt like a fool, like she had botched it. It was just a hair tie. Then she realized that wasn't what he was talking about. "I am so sorry. The truth is, my whole heart went into that look. Before today, I wouldn't even have been able to give that look. I was so undone, like I told you before. Since I became Jesus's, it seems like he has given me my whole womanhood back. I've had feelings I never had before. So when you were napping, I asked God if I could be a gift to you for all that you have done for Jenny and me, and because you lost your family. I believe God could nullify any age difference.

"Well, he told me 'No!' too. When I woke up from *my* nap, I think I was subconsciously, or maybe not so subconsciously, irritated that you weren't the right one. I don't know how anyone could be more right than you! Please forgive me. Matt, how can I ever make that up to you?"

"Maggie, what you just said about me more than makes it up to me. Yes, I forgive you." He leaned a little closer. "I really appreciate how you are being so open with your feelings and what is going on inside you. It's as if you were bending over backwards to make up for the first story you told me about Jenny's father. And please forgive me, too, as I was a little miffed at your rejection of my present."

"Of course. I think I had to say all of what I said, that anything less wouldn't have been the whole truth. And to tell the truth, I wish I did have that hair-tie. You were kind to get it for me."

Jenny, sensing the peace that now reigned between the two adults, asserted her presence with a plea to be fed. Maggie was happy to comply. Matt rummaged around in what little moonlight there was, and fetched her another water. And another pink-and-gold ribbon.

As Jenny got started, Matt thought about what had just happened. He knew any romantic involvement wasn't going to happen, but sensed that they both felt God was bringing them together, and there would be some attachment between them. What did God mean when he said, "You are my gift to her, but not in the way you were thinking?" He would wait and see.

"Maggie, I have a question. What was going through your mind earlier, when you finally decided you would be willing to die so Jenny could live?"

"If you had asked me that at the time, I don't think I would have been able to give you a very good answer. There was just something, way down deep, that was telling me it was the right thing to do. Now I realize that that deep-down thing was God letting me know I could trust him, even though I didn't deserve anything good for the life I've lived. And even though I didn't really understand what dying might entail."

"That's wonderful! I'm in awe of your understanding of spiritual things, of the things of God. You know, there are other people who need to know what you are finding out."

"Yes, I can think of lots of people like that. Friends, relatives, fellow teachers, the childcare workers who looked after Jenny."

"I know some folks who need to hear this good news, too. Let's ask God to show himself to them like he showed himself to you. I'd like to start, for a friend of mine, a young businessman named Larry Williams."

They prayed while Maggie nursed Jenny. As they were finishing, Maggie prayed fervently for her brother Charles and his friends Ted and Billy, asking God to give them success in their lives, and especially to show himself to them like he had to her.

"Maggie, I can tell your forgiveness of them is complete, the way you asked God for only good things for them."

"Yes, I wanted to do that ever since I forgave them earlier, but didn't know quite what to say. What you asked God for, for your friend Larry, helped give me the words."

Jenny was finished, and presently gave up the obligatory stomach air.

Maggie was not sure about the next step. "How do you suppose we will be able to change her in the dark?"

"You've done it enough in the daylight with these velvet cloths, so do it the same way, and trust that you got her clean enough. Then check her in the morning."

Matt's mention of trust brought Maggie back to their earlier conversation, about trust. About trusting fathers. About how she had trusted Matt. ... Matt. ... "Matt, I've been thinking. I believe we will be rescued, hopefully soon. Before that happens, I want to talk about my father. But not yet. I still don't want to remember yet."

"Okay." He wondered why she brought it up. "God hasn't told me any of those secrets."

"No. He's been gone a long time. You've been like a father to me. I can see what a father should be, just in the short time we've been together. In some ways, I still need a father. I know God is my father now, but for my whole life, I've longed for that human relationship without realizing it."

She waited briefly for a reply, but Matt was enjoying watching her silhouette in the moonlight, gently swaying to rock Jenny, who also needed a father.

She went on, "I was wondering if you would be my father. I don't know how that would work, and if you didn't want to, I would understand. Maybe I'm being—"

"Oh, Maggie," he interrupted.

Matt realized he was listening, not to a 28-year-old woman, but to a twelve—perhaps thirteen or fourteen—year-old girl. He could tell that the façade of maturity, forced on her by her own intellect, had slipped away completely. He marveled at the working of the Holy Spirit in her innermost being. The false was being pushed away, to be replaced by the true. Earlier, as he had watched Maggie nurse Jenny for the first time, he had sensed the beginning of the dissolving of this veneer.

Something had died in Maggie' emotions when she was twelve, and God had resurrected it as surely as he had healed her body. He wondered if her father had somehow contributed to this death. Was there more in her psyche that needed healing? Yes, she certainly needed a father. Probably a mother, too, from what she had said. Having been forced to grow up on her own, she would need help navigating the throes of puberty and the transition into adulthood. She was already through it physically and intellectually, but not emotionally.

Like the child who walked without crawling—and therefore needed to learn to crawl later—she needed a restart. God, in his mercy, had chosen the North Atlantic Ocean to allow this to happen in isolation.

Matt felt a tremendous rush of responsibility and compassion for her. She trusted him, and so, it seemed, did God. Was this the job he was going to England to find? His fatherly instincts started coming back in full force.

"Yes, I would love to be your father! It would be such an honor. Such a privilege and delight. I feel you're already my daughter in spiritual things, but nothing would please me more than to be your father in physical things as well. How could we make that happen?"

"Maybe we need to make a pronouncement before God and shake hands or something?"

"I think we need to make a vow to each other with God as our witness. You saw how powerful the vow you made was, and vows made for good purposes should be that powerful, too."

They discussed this for several minutes, and decided they should vow to love, honor, support, and respect each other as father and daughter.

As they spoke, Matt thought again about the part of Maggie's emotional development that had gotten stuck at twelve years old. He knew it was due to the vow she had made against herself. It had been only a few hours since she became unstuck. How long would it take her to catch up? "One other thing," he said. "Do you trust me?"

"Yes, with my whole life. Do we need to add that?"

He was searching his brain for a term that would apply to a pre-teen as well as an adult. "Maybe not that word. I'd like you to add something to your vow that shows the accountability you have to God. An earthly reminder that you now answer to your heavenly father. Something indicating the trust you have in me to protect you, to watch over you, to help with that accountability. I'm thinking back to my own Rachel. She would let me know what was going on in her life, not so much to gain my approval, but to make sure she wasn't making a big blunder."

Maggie was thinking about her father and the still-locked door. "None of the words we're using ever applied to my father."

The darkness prevented Matt from seeing her facial expressions, but he could tell by the quiver in her voice that she was close to tears.

"I'm sorry. As your dad, I would never do anything that would cause you pain or anguish. And I certainly would never try to interfere with what the Holy Spirit was doing in your life. That's not my place."

"Then how about simply the word 'trust'? We'll both know what it means."

"Okay. That's where we started, isn't it? Is there anything you'd like me to add to my vow?"

Maggie thought a moment. "Yes, I would like you to add 'cherish' and 'nurture' to your vow. That's what fathers are supposed to do. I know the time for my physical nurturing is passed, but your spiritual nurturing has been so wonderful. And add Jenny, too."

"Yes, of course Jenny. Your becoming my daughter will make Jenny my granddaughter, but there is more to it. Being your father brings me a lot of responsibility, but there is one privilege I look forward to very greatly."

"I give up. What is it?"

"I claim the right to walk you down the aisle one day, when God has brought the right one into your life."

Maggie giggled with delight. The sound of it woke Jenny, who giggled with her and fell back asleep.

"I said that, to say this: until that day, I will be Jenny's father also. That spiritual authority will act as a covering for her, until I transfer it to your new husband."

The negotiations finished, they made the vows before each other and their Lord. Matt went first, standing and raising his right hand as he spoke. Then he took Jenny while Maggie followed his lead and made her vows.

"This has been quite a day for you, Maggie. You died and were born again as God's daughter and Jesus's sister, then as my daughter. We could call today your rebirthday."

"Yes, and we had both put in a full day's work before that."

"I now welcome you as a full-fledged member of the Carven family!"

"Thank you. I'm sorry I never had a chance to meet my new brother and sister."

"I never told you what happened to your brother Todd."

They were both silent for a few minutes. Maggie could tell it was going to be painful for him. "I'd like to hear it if you can tell it."

"They were on a trip to Arizona in their small family car. They had just come over a small hill and were stopped at a light at a T intersection, waiting to turn left. Ahead of them was a guardrail and a ravine on the other side of it. Traffic was moving pretty fast in both directions in front of them. All of a sudden, a drunk driver in a Cadillac came over the hill. It didn't even slow down, but crashed into Todd's car.

"The impact ruptured their gas tank and slammed them into the middle of the intersection, where they were smashed into by a truck. The car immediately burst into flames and went through the guardrail into the ravine. None of them survived.

"The airbag in the Cadillac deployed, and the driver was not even hurt. We found out later he was the son of a diplomat, driving drunk and without a license. He was flown back to his country before charges could be pressed. They would never even tell us what country he was from."

After he finished the story, Matt wept for a long time. He was still holding Jenny, so Maggie reached up to the pile of coffin-liner nappies and ripped one in two. Half for him and half for her.

She could tell he was grieving, but could not sense any bitterness. In a way she could not quite understand, Jenny was being a comfort to him. "I'm so sorry."

Matt heard her, but he was busy saying good-bye, one at a time, to his grandchildren, his children, their spouses, and finally his wife. I'll see you again, he said to each one. He felt God's love enveloping him, comforting him, receiving his family members as he offered them up to the one who had given them to him for a time. The sovereign one, the one who brought him to this time and place to give him a new daughter. And granddaughter.

"Thank you," he finally said. "You were kind to let me grieve. I needed that. And now we still have a job to do."

"Thanks for holding Jenny. My arms were starting to go to sleep. The little boy?"

"Exactly!"

It was beginning to get dark as Dusty Mae Watt passed the hallway for the fifth time, seeing JC at the window at the end, overlooking the city. She understood what he was going through; she herself had lost a long-time friend and colleague when she was a field agent. However, now she had some business with JC Smalley, and it was getting late.

"JC, I didn't know Joel Barth, your friend. I hurt for you, though. I know what it's like. I understand you'll be leaving us soon, and I need to talk to you about it. Please come with me."

She led him back to her office and stopped by a bank of small lockers outside her door. "May I have your cell?"

She locked it in one of the lockers, and motioned him into an office adjoining hers. When they were both inside, she dead-bolted the door from the inside. Alarm bells started going off in JC's head.

She grinned. "Don't be concerned. Your phone on the outside and the deadbolt on the inside are what turns this office into a Top Secret space. I'm told you're fixing to go to Brazil. Congratulations, I think! Phil told me. He said to help you get ready any way we can.

"I'd like to send one of our agents-in-training with you, either Luke or Harper. Have you met Harper? He comes from an Army background, so he may be the better choice. It will be great experience for him. He could learn a lot from y'all. Penny would be appropriate for that environment, too, but I'll find something important for her to do here."

"Thanks. I think I have a very narrow lane, and most of what will happen will be outside that lane. I haven't met Harper yet, but he'll be okay. What did he do in the Army?"

Dusty Mae opened a file on the desk and pulled out a photo. "Harper Avalon was an infantry platoon sergeant and boot camp drill instructor. He got out after twelve years, graduated from the University of Delaware with a criminal justice degree, then came to work for us."

"He will probably already be more prepared for this than I will," JC said. "I assume all the combat will be over when we get called forward, so the biggest issue will be the heat and bugs. How is Harper at recognizing booby traps? Do you have standard training for that?"

They briefly discussed the intelligence and other training the FBI gave their recruits. Their meeting over, Dusty Mae opened the office, gave JC back his phone, and summoned Harper.

Matt gave Jenny back and stood up to look around. There was nothing to see except the moonlight glittering on the water. It felt good to stretch. He and Maggie switched places to give them both new positions.

"Maggie, when the Lord let me know I would be calling an island into existence, I thought it would be cool. However, I know God doesn't do things randomly or without a good reason, just to amuse us. This island is going to be very important for a reason I don't know yet. Maybe lots of reasons. I have no idea how deep the water is here, or how long it might take the bottom of the ocean to come up this high.

"In the dream, I was very specific in the things I called out. I don't remember what they all were, and maybe that part of the dream was just to show I need to be very specific right now. That's why I'm asking you to help me. While Jesus was on the earth, he said he did only what he saw his father do, so we need to ask the spirit of Jesus, the Holy Spirit, to show us what our father is doing. We are not going to make stuff up and trust God to do it. Rather, we are going to let him speak through us to bring into being what he wants."

"Wow! This is going to be incredible! What do you want me to do?"

"First, we ask for wisdom and instruction, you and I. Then we wait to hear and see what God shows us. I'm counting on you to see and hear too. Then we act."

"How long will we wait? I know we'll wait as long as we need to. I'm just wondering how long that might be."

"God's timing is always perfect. Part of what we ask for will be the wisdom to know when and how to do the acting. Are you ready, my daughter?"

Maggie was already filled to overflowing with the joy and the presence of God that Jesus brought her, and the thrill that went through her whole being when Matt called her "daughter" was almost too much. All she could do was nod.

Matt caught the nod in the moonlight. "Okay. I'll start, and if you feel there's anything important to add, then by all means do so."

It was a short prayer. They acknowledged God's sovereignty and his wisdom, thanked him for keeping them safe during all they had been through, recognized that this was his plan and work, and asked for specifics and details so the finished product would meet his desires. Maggie added a heartfelt thanks for bringing Jenny back to her.

While they waited, Matt volunteered to hold Jenny again, and had Maggie stand up and look around.

"How does that vast ocean make you feel?"

"Incredibly small. Matt, if I were that bottle we talked about earlier, I'd feel even smaller."

"If you were that bottle, you would also be incredibly safe out there in the midst of it. But you are that bottle in the care of the spirit of God who will bring you places he wants to bring you, some of which you might balk at. But always trust him. Keep your eyes on him. Feeling small is a very good thing. It makes us realize that we are nothing without him who is everything. For me, it evokes a deep and godly longing to know him better. When we are small, then he is great in us and on our behalf. It is when we know our weakness and smallness that true worship just bubbles up from the most central core of our being."

"The most central core of my being is starting to do that right now."

Matt began to sing. It was a different song this time; it was a love song he had prepared for his wedding with Helene. "Long before the world started, God gave me to you … "

He had sung it as he held his children for the first time after they were born; when they got married, he sang it for their spouses as he welcomed them into the family, and he sang it when he held his grandchildren for the first time. It was a song about them to God, a song of commitment, of protection, of support, of love.

Now he sang it as Maggie and Jenny, whom he was still holding, became part of his family. Then, as before, he started singing the words known only to God, sweet words, gentle words. Before long, he heard another voice join him. Higher in pitch, a little hesitant at first. Matt kept the tempo and melody the same, and soon the other voice gained more confidence. He felt Maggie relax, and in a moment, she was singing in perfect harmony with him. After several more minutes, he slowed down and stopped, and she with him.

Maggie was breathless and excited. "Wow, I did it!"

"It was great, wasn't it? Did you understand any of it? And did you feel any special kind of way?"

"Not a word. I'm not an expert, but it sounded like a real language. I didn't feel anything, except that it was okay to sound strange and foreign."

Matt laughed. "You mean because it sounded like gibberish?"

"Yeah. I would have said that, but it sounds somewhat, um, irreverent."

"What I heard while you sang, and what you told me about it, tells me your experience just now is what is normal. Occasionally the Holy Spirit will let you perceive some of the things he is saying through you, like when I mentioned the sword fight earlier."

"Your singing earlier had a distinctive effect on me. It seemed like you were somehow pulling on me."

"That was one of those times I thought I felt what the Holy Spirit was doing. He was actually the one doing it, calling to your spirit. Many times, I can set my own tempo and rhythm, but that time I was just following his leading."

"Well, it was brilliant!"

"The song I started with, I didn't think I would ever sing it again."

"It was beautiful. It made me cry. I've never heard it before."

"It made me cry, too, as I was writing it. You should hear it with a mandolin and a fiddle." He told her the history of his singing it. "I give Helene the credit for wanting me to sing it for my children. That song was a surprise to her when we got married. She cried at her own wedding!"

"I'm so glad Jenny and I are your children."

"Me too! But now we have work to do."

At NOAA observatory K103, Jacob Strauss slept peacefully through the night. There was no alarm signaling any seismic activity anywhere in the world. The vibrating pens made barely a ripple on their slowly advancing rolls of logarithmic graph paper.

After they rested a few minutes, Matt explained again what he remembered regarding the island dream. Maggie listened carefully, curious about what would happen next. "In my mind," he told her, "I'm seeing and hearing what the Lord is showing me, and I believe he is showing you, too." Matt went on to describe what he saw. "Tell me what you're seeing. Is there anything you think we should add to our list? Anything, no matter how impossible or frivolous it seems?"

Maggie adjusted Jenny in her lap, then put her hands on her temples and closed her eyes. "I'm not sure how to do this. I'm not seeing anything more than what you told me."

"That's okay. There's no secret method or posture. When God communicates with you, it will seem like the most natural thing in the world. Like when he spoke to you earlier."

She relaxed. "Let me think … What about your two dreams? Could there be anything you left out? How about the petunias? Could they have been real petunias, or just representing flowers in general, or maybe plants in general?"

"I don't know. Let's just ask God to interpret that as he brings forth the island. It will be his island, after all."

"Let's ask for some kind of natural bridge over the waterway."

"Okay," Matt said. "That makes sense. And in the hilly corner, a very tall mountain or hill so you can see the whole island."

"Yes, a spot you can see from anywhere on the island. A guidepost, so you always know where you are."

"Maggie, I think we're ready. I want you to do some of the calling up. You're a teammate on God's team, and therefore, you already have what it takes."

"Do you think so, Matt? I wouldn't know what to say or how to say it. I'd rather just watch this time."

"No, absolutely not! I believe it's vitally important you participate in a substantial way. I'll tell you the part I'd like you to play. Okay?"

"Will I feel the electricity too?"

"That was part of the dream, wasn't it, Maggie? There may not be any electricity at all, or any other supernatural thing. There might not even be any evidence that anything is happening. No lightning. No feelings. No awesome displays. It will be enough that we know God wants this island, and he has called on us to call it forth."

"Us? I thought he was just asking you to do it."

"You're my helper, and the part I want you to do, if it doesn't happen, then the whole island will wash away. I'm giving you a very important part. You'll see, your words will have the same force as mine, since it's God's power, not ours."

"Okay, let me know what you want me to do."

He told her, and she responded, "Oh, that seems simple enough."

Matt started. "Father, you have shown us what you are doing in heaven, so we might do that on earth. Let your power come now, to cause the words you have given us to come to pass, for your glory and the glory of your kingdom. In Jesus's name.

"Let now an island appear here in the middle of the sea, twenty-five miles long and five miles wide, coming up smoothly and gently, without causing a tsunami anywhere."

Maggie said, "Let it be high enough out of the water that the high tide will not overflow its boundary, with one side of it perfectly flat for half its distance."

"The other side will have texture, hills and valleys, at one end, with one of the hills tall enough to overlook the whole island. Let a stream of fresh pure water come from the hills, flowing to the other end of the island."

"Let there be a flat ridge extending the length of the island, with a natural bridge over the stream in the middle of the island."

Matt added, "Dirt from the lands will cover the hilly areas, and much of the flat areas."

"The dirt will be full of life. And Father, we don't know what to ask about the petunias. Please do what you have purposed about that."

"Let there be large domed caverns under the water, at least four, at thirty feet, sixty-five feet, one hundred feet, and one that is the appropriate depth. And let there be a natural harbor, a rounded opening in the side of the island, a half mile across to a mile inland."

They finished, and Maggie had some questions. "What's the flat ridge for?"

"It will become a road from one end to the other."

"How about the caverns? You were pretty specific about them."

"There is getting to be more and more evidence that this earth had its environment drastically changed in its past, that the atmosphere was much denser then. Have you heard of hyperbaric chambers?"

"Yes," she said. "I've heard that some hospitals do medical procedures in them because the patients bleed less and heal faster. Near my flat, there's a therapy center, the Brightwell, a charity that treats multiple sclerosis in a barochamber, as they call it."

"The domed caverns would become giant hyperbaric chambers, once they pump the domes full of air from above. They would be used for medicine and all kinds of research. At least, I believe that's what they will be used for."

"What did you mean by 'the appropriate depth'?"

"Only God knows what the original atmospheric pressure was. Nature would be perfectly tuned to that pressure. I suppose he could have told me an exact number, but he didn't. I'm wondering if the 'appropriate depth' is where the medical procedures will be done, with the other depths used for things like post-op recovery or prep. He may want it all for an entirely different purpose, though. Do you know what the long flat part would be for?"

"While I was saying it, I thought of an airfield. That's my guess, Matt. How long do you think it will take before we see what God will do? An island this size will be hard to miss, especially when they come to investigate what happened to our plane. I hope we're close enough to it, that they see us!"

Maggie nursed Jenny again. When she had finished and changed her, Matt cleaned the used makeshift diaper in the ocean. Then he took Jenny, giving Maggie a brief break. Before long, Matt helped Maggie get her back in the sling as drowsiness overtook them all.

Matt woke with a start. Something didn't feel right. There was still no breeze, and not a ripple on the water. The sliver of a moon was still high in the sky, not giving much light, but there was enough to see silhouettes and shadows. It was movement that had wakened him; Maggie had stood up. He watched her make her way to the far end of their lifeboat and hold the baby in a seemingly strange, almost detached way.

"Good-bye, Jenny," she whispered. "I will always love you."

She held her cooing child out from her, to take one last look.

"MAGGIE! Jesus!"

Hearing her name, Maggie turned, suddenly irresolute, confused. Upon hearing the name of Jesus, the spell was broken.

Matt quickly made his way to her, holding on to the coffin handles for stability. "Let me hold her," he said sternly.

The enormity of what she had been about to do overwhelmed her. Meekly, she put Jenny into his waiting arms and burst into tears. Her head sank down and her arms dropped limply to her side. Her silhouette in the moonlight was one of utter dejection. Gone was the joy.

"Come sit," he said. She complied, as if in a trance. "Don't say anything. Just let me speak. I know what happened."

"How could you?" she countered weakly.

She could feel his compassion, for her and for Jenny, as he laid the baby gently in her arms and put a strong arm around her shivering shoulder. She was not cold; the shivering was due to the near-death experience she had just had. Not her death, Jenny's.

He answered her, "I am so sorry. If Jenny had died, her blood would have been on my hands. Kind of like with my Rachel." He paused, gathering his thoughts. "I knew what would happen. I just didn't think it would happen while I was with you. I thought I had time to warn you. I should have known better and told you earlier. Maggie, the first thing I want to tell you, is God's love for you is sure, and nothing will ever grab you out of his hand. But there is one who hates you. Hates everything about you. Wants to steal everything you have, kill you and your loved ones. Destroy you completely."

"The devil." She knew about the devil. "And he almost grabbed Jenny."

Matt could see that Maggie was settling down. "Yes, exactly. The devil would like you to think he is God's equal, that his battle against God is a battle of equals. But he is not. He is a liar and the father of lies."

She had stopped shivering so he relaxed his hold. "But God is still in charge," he said. "Tell me what happened."

"I was holding Jenny. I woke up and a person was standing in front of me, on top of the water. He was glimmering, sparkling very brightly. He looked beautiful, like an angel. He said, 'I am Jesus. I am very pleased with you. You have passed all my tests so far, but there is one more. I gave you Jenny back so you could say good-bye to her, but you must give her back to me. Don't worry, I will keep her safe and give you peace. I will heal your scars completely and give you children in place of Jenny for you to love.

" 'You pulled her out of the water. You must give her back the same way, by pushing her under the water. I am going back to heaven right now, but I'll be watching. Say your good-byes, then give her back.' Then he disappeared.

"I felt sick at what I had to do, but I didn't want to disobey Jesus, who has been so wonderful to me. Oh, what happened? I felt powerless to do anything except what he told me to do. So I said good-bye to Jenny. She had her hand around my finger. She was so trusting and so little. Then you called to me, and when you said the name of Jesus, a cloudiness went out of my mind and I realized something was very, very wrong." It came out all at once, and she ran out of breath.

"Maggie, you have a very sharp mind and an excellent memory. I could give you a long checklist on how to tell if it is the devil, and you'd be able to recite it to me right off. But our fight with the devil is not a battle of wits. If it were, he would most assuredly win, anyway. The devil is a liar. He can tell all kinds of lies. He can take the nastiest, foulest lie and make it appear to be the truth. However, there is one statement that God won't let him make, and that is 'Jesus is Lord.' He cannot say it. When a spirit presents itself to you, either physically or in your mind, you can use that as a test.

"Another thing the devil does is to pander to your desires, especially physical desires. He did that two ways. He said he was pleased that you had passed the tests. When he said that, you let your guard down, because it is a wonderful thing to be told that by Jesus. The other way is that he promised to make you beautiful, by healing your scars completely. Everyone wants to be beautiful, right?"

"Yes. Is that a bad thing?"

"When you met the real Jesus, was he beautiful?"

"Beyond all comparison!"

"And then he showed you his scars? Did that make him less beautiful?"

"No. Really, it made him more beautiful when I found out he had those scars because of me and he wanted me anyway."

"Look at it this way. You had a perception of beauty that you desired, and the devil tried to get you to trade Jenny for that beauty."

The darkness hid the shame written on Maggie's face. "It almost worked. I was willing to trade my whole life for Jenny earlier."

"When Jesus, himself or through his spirit, tells you to do something, he won't make you feel sick about it, or confused. There will be clarity and peace. You're very young in your new spirit. Let me back up a bit. Your spirit is full-grown, but as long as you're in this life, your actions are going to be done by your soul and body working together. Your soul is that part of you that thinks, has emotions, remembers, and decides. Your spirit is that part of you that is joined to God's spirit and talks with him.

"The reason you felt sick was that your own spirit recognized the devil and was reacting against him. But you haven't learned yet in your soul, how to hear what your spirit is saying to you. Don't worry, that will come as you mature."

"God used you to save Jenny. You said earlier we might go our separate ways, Matt. I don't look forward to that at all. What will I do then? My spirit has so much growing up to do."

"As far as Jenny is concerned, remember that children are a gift from the Lord. They are awesome gifts, but they are awesome responsibilities also. Jenny will belong to the Lord one day the same as you do now, and you will help her. You may eventually have other children—I hope you do—and they will be just as special as Jenny.

"The devil is temptation personified. When you're tempted to do something wrong, or right for that matter, learn to listen to your spirit. If you don't have that peace, chances are it's not the right thing to do.

"Find a friend, a woman, who has the same kind of relationship with God that you do. Or a group. Look for someone more mature in spiritual things than you. Just remember that your relationship with God himself is most important, and he will never give you bad advice, even by mistake.

"Finally, rehash daily the gifts God has given you, and thank him for them. When you get back home, write them all down. As amazing as your day has been, there may come a time when you are tempted to give those gifts up, to reject them or renounce them. Remember that God has shown you great things because he wants to use those things in other people's lives. The devil doesn't want that. He will try to steal them from you."

Maggie was silent for a few minutes, trying to absorb everything. "Can we take a few minutes and do that now? I'd like to reminisce about everything, starting when I won the prize and came over to the States."

"That's a great idea, and I'll add to it some things that got me onto your return flight. But first, I need to admit to God that I failed you and ask for his forgiveness and yours."

"And I need to ask forgiveness from God, for not listening for his spirit, and almost giving Jenny away."

Their prayers and discussion took them longer than they thought it would, then sleep came quickly. And with it, Maggie's joy came back.

In the morning, just before dawn, there was the faintest shushing sound, like a sled makes when it goes down a snowy hillside. There was light in the sky, but that edge of the sun peeking first over the eastern horizon had not yet put in its appearance. The sound did not waken the sleepers, nor did the next sound, a rattling like marbles in a metal can. After that, they all three slept through a clanging and banging like all of the silverware falling out of the drawer onto a wooden floor. Then silence. It was not the stillness in their ears that woke them; it was the stillness of their lifeboat. The Good Ship Myrtlewood had run aground!

Maggie opened her eyes first. Jenny was still quiet in the sling, but she opened her eyes and focused on her mum's smiling face. Maggie was sitting on the pad with her back on the upper coffin. Her bum was sore, and she found herself hungry. But wait, what is that? She balanced Jenny between her knees so she could rub her eyes and come back to the reality of unending ocean all around them. "Matt, look!"

Matt sat up, perplexed that the GSM was not shifting in the water with his movements. Ahead of him was the sea, but it appeared they were much higher than it. What they saw all around, between them and the sea and in every direction, was very light-colored and flat. It was impossible to tell if it were liquid or solid. "Wow!" was their simultaneous reaction.

Just then, the first golden rays of the sun washed over them and they got a better look. A solid surface beckoned to them, exciting them, tantalizing them. They turned to each other and burst out laughing. Uproariously. Jenny, startled by the hilarity, cried loudly with fright. Maggie held her close and the fright subsided, but not the crying. "She's hungry. I'll feed her in a minute, but first let's put our feet on solid ground and thank God for rescuing us."

"No, Maggie, wait! Not yet. Besides, I don't think you could feed her in a minute. That would be a world record."

"Well, I could feed her a lot faster than you could!"

The banter was good; it took their minds off their increasingly complaining stomachs. They were both hoping, without mentioning it to the other, that God's showing himself strong for her involved food.

"We need to think this through before we step off our little ship," Matt said. "God has just given us a one-hundred-and-twenty-five-square-mile island. That's bigger than some countries. Let me hold Jenny while you stand up and get some circulation back. While you get started with her, I'll take a quick look around."

Maggie took Jenny back and began to nurse her. She followed Matt's gaze where her field of vision would allow. There were shallow but wide grooves on either side of the pallet leading to the ocean, about fifty meters away. The area in front of them was flat and level, and there was either a sharp slope or sudden drop-off in front of that, which was not obvious from their vantage point. It appeared the pallet on which the coffins were secured was completely resting above the surface of whatever that solid substance was. She watched as Matt stood up and turned to survey behind them.

Suddenly, he whirled around and jumped down onto the pallet, coming to a rest on the pad next to her. He was wild with delight and excitement, gasping for air, and pointing.

Whoa, she thought. "Wow, you're pretty agile for an old man!" Calm down, please, and tell me.

"What?! If you were my daughter I'd, um, …"

"I am your daughter. You'd what?" she demanded.

"I'd wash out your mouth with soap."

"Right, you have soap? You've been holding out on me?"

"You should see—"

"Jenny's not half done yet."

He stifled his excitement, at least for the time being. "Okay, here's what I've been thinking. You're a British citizen, I'm an American. Both countries may try to claim this island as a sovereign territory, you know, being part of the UK or the United States. I'm hoping they will recognize our right to own this island. I don't know how anyone else could claim it. It wasn't even here yesterday.

"They may try to decide by asking who got here first. We were both asleep when that happened, and it may come down to who stepped on the surface first. I propose we step off the pallet simultaneously. After that, I don't think there's anything special to do besides explore."

When he said "explore", Matt got excited again. Then it was time to switch Jenny to the other side.

"Matt, there is something special to do while we wait for Jenny to finish. We still need to thank God for the fulfillment of your dream and worship him for being who he is. Wow, where did that come from?"

"Yes, he is teaching you in your spirit, and that teaching is filling your heart and flowing into your conscious thoughts. As wonderful as it is to sing in the spirit, let your mind, heart, and voice worship in English, too. And some of our deepest worship comes when there are no words at all. 'Worship him for being who he is' is very profound. There are a lot of reasons to worship him. He is our creator and that in itself is also a sufficient reason."

They spent several minutes thanking God for what he brought them through, and for the promises still to be fulfilled. Then Maggie asked, "When you start to sing in the spirit, you almost always start with the same song. Would you teach it to me? It sounds so simple, but so wonderful."

"Sure."

He sang it several times, while she followed along. Then he stopped. She looked at him in surprise.

"I'd like you to start," he said, "now that you know it. You will eventually have your own starting song, or maybe you'll use that one, or maybe no song at all. I do it that way often. You start, and I'll follow. You pick the key and the tempo. Act as if I'm not even here. Sing in English as long as you like, whatever words you want, whatever comes to you.

"Change the melody if you want to, sing in the spirit if you want to and for as long as you like. After we start, when you are singing in English, I'll just hum or be quiet. That way, I won't interrupt you, and I'll join in when you sing in the spirit."

Jenny finished long before Maggie, but she just rested quietly in Maggie's arms, enthralled. Finally, their voices trailed off, and they basked in the silence, each quietly enjoying the closeness of their father.

Directly in front of them, the sun was fully up, with the entire reddish-gold disk above the horizon. "I guess we know which way east is. Look, Maggie! What do you see in the water?"

"The dolphins."

"I didn't think we'd see them again. There must be several dozen."

"C'mon, Matt. I'll bring Jenny and we'll explore the brave new world. I wonder where we are?"

They stood together on the pallet, facing the ocean. Maggie held Jenny in one arm and put her other around Matt's waist. Matt put his hand around her shoulder. They each put out their right foot and stepped forward off the pallet, promptly sinking in the mud up to their knees. Their left feet were still on the pallet. They both lost their balance and started to pitch headlong. Matt twisted them both hard to the left. Maggie ended up on top of him, holding Jenny on top of her.

"I think I'm still pretty agile for such an old man. Or maybe that four-letter word starting with 's'."

"I didn't think you used that word."

"What, 'spry'?"

140

Belly laughs. A little mud wasn't going to ruin their joy.

They had picked the deepest part of the mud to step into. After they sorted themselves out, they made their way to the trough running around the north side of the GSM, where the mud was only about four inches deep. It was quite solid under the surface mud. All around, as far as they could see, it looked like the surface of the mud was covered with large and small potatoes.

"Come around to the back and I'll show you what I got really excited about. You'll never believe it!"

Maggie was learning quickly. "Why are people so surprised when they ask God for something and he does it?"

"Touché!"

They followed the trough around, and there were lined up five identical shiny metal cabinets, connected to each other in a big tangle by a long jumble of wires, belts, and steel cables. The empty one they had examined earlier was still held fast in the cargo net. The trough extended past the farthest cabinet.

"It's as though God made us a path, so we could get to the cabinets without sinking in the mud."

"Hmm," Matt replied. Suddenly, he shouted, "No! It's an anchor! Look, when the island was coming to the surface, it was pushing all the water up. The water had to go somewhere. It rushed to the ocean. It would have swept us back out to sea, but these cabinets acted like an anchor and held us back. The water flowed around the sides of our boat and the cabinets, and washed some of that mud away and piled it up in front of our boat."

"Yes, I still think God made us a path, so we could get to the cabinets without sinking in the mud."

"Well, let's follow this narrow path. It's God's way, you know."

After the empty one, the second cabinet held plastic bags full of empty water bottles, soda cans, snack wrappers, and other trash in small metal bins. "The water bottles were mostly capped, so the cabinet tried to float," Maggie said.

The third cabinet was loaded with trays containing the alternate dinners that the economy passengers had ordered, but never got to enjoy. The meals were well wrapped and mostly intact.

"I will never again complain about how hard it is to unwrap the meals." Matt said. "Let's put Jenny down on this, then you can join me for a most sumptuous feast. Look, there's even plastic knives and forks."

"Don't you want to look in the last ones first?"

"No!"

They said a quick thank-you to God, the source of all their sustenance, then dug in.

"Aah," Maggie said contentedly.

"Aah," Matt replied.

The fourth cabinet contained soggy rolls of paper towels, some cloth towels, a roll of plastic bags, a spray bottle of a popular carpet cleaner, and other miscellaneous cleanup supplies in metal bins.

The fifth cabinet was lying on its back. When they opened it, they found it completely full of sea water. "Nice!" Maggie said. "We can use the water to wash Jenny's makeshift nappies, which I think she'll need soon."

"Yes," Matt replied. "We can use those metal bins, so we don't contaminate the whole cabinet full of water."

"Maggie, it hasn't been twenty-four hours yet."

Maggie remembered the promise. "All during, right?"

"Yes, you remembered. I also owe you a question."

"You do? I hope it's an easy one."

"I said I'd ask you again tomorrow to see if you'd change your answer. Our plane was shot down and destroyed."

"Yes! Yes, yes, yes! Except for the poor people who died."

Maggie had been thinking about the questions earlier. "I have one for you."

"You do? I hope it's an easy one."

"Jenny was born missing a foot."

Matt grinned. "That doesn't count. It wasn't after I whispered in your ear. But I want to see where you're going with this, so I'm going to let it count. And I'm going to say yes, because I'm sure that's the right answer, but you're going to have to explain it to me."

Maggie grinned back. "The teacher becomes the student. Just about everybody in Bristol and Cheltenham knows about Jenny's foot. The doctors, the hospital staff, my mum and of course all her friends, my friends, the teachers at school, and the childcare place. There are x-rays and the birth certificate with her footprints. When we get back, it will be undeniable that something amazing has taken place, and it will be so exciting to tell them all about it."

The sound of thunder in the sky told them a plane, probably military, was approaching. "There's no haze," Maggie observed. "It must be friendly."

Matt couldn't fault her logic. "Yes, it's still 'all during'."

They made their way back to their coffin-boat and were standing on the pallet when the plane screamed overhead. They both waved wildly. The US Air Force fighter jet flew a little farther, then the pilot circled around. He slowed down as much as he could without stalling, and headed straight toward them, waggling his wings as he came. They watched him fly past, speed up, and disappear over the horizon.

Then Maggie remembered something. "Matt, with all the excitement, not the least of which was the food, I almost forgot something important, I think. I had a dream during the night."

"Wow! Tell me about it."

"It was in amazing color. I've never had a dream like this before. So detailed. We were on the GSM, just Jenny and I. You weren't there, and Jenny was a grownup. Suddenly, a great white shark rose up out of the water and threw up. Out came a lot of broken life preservers, a lot of empty water bottles, and a lot of plastic bottles half full of what looked like a brown liquid with gooey solids in them.

"Jenny and I were grabbing what ones we could and throwing them in the open coffin on top, but some were flowing away faster than we could get them. Some of the ones we got, slipped out of our hands and fell back in the sea. When there was nothing left to grab, we looked at the coffin, and light was coming out of it, and singing. We looked in, and it was full of people. Live people!"

Matt thought for a few moments. "Was anything written on the broken life preservers? And were you *you* in the dream, or were you an observer watching you and Jenny from above or some other vantage point?"

"I was me in the dream. I could see Jenny, but I couldn't really see myself, just my hands and arms. But I knew I was there. Yes, there was writing on some of the life preservers, but it was too small for me to be able to read it. Some bottles had writing, too."

Matt spoke from his experience. "Here's what I've found. Whether we think the dream is a spiritual dream or not, that is, one that God gives us, we need to ask him for the interpretation. That's before we try to figure anything out. So, Lord, we ask you in Jesus's name to give Maggie the interpretation of the dream you gave her, because you delight in giving good gifts to your children."

"What do you think it means? I'm new to dreams, but you seem to be an old pro."

"Well, it would be tempting to think your dream was simply a reliving of the shark incident yesterday, except that it was in such vivid color. Therefore, I believe it was God's dream. When God gives a dream, some things are usually constant, meaning you can generally interpret them the same in almost all dreams, but of course there will be exceptions. For example, Jenny being an adult doesn't necessarily mean she is, say, twenty-one years old, but God considers her mature enough in spiritual things to be able to help you in what you are doing.

"I think all the bottles and life preservers are people. Your act of catching them, Maggie, was that you have a great story to tell them. The story that started, perhaps, with your getting an airplane ticket, and it's not finished yet. It seems like there were three different types of people, and because they came out of the shark, they were all dead.

"You and Jenny fished them out of the water, which may mean you were telling them the whole story of what happened to you over the last day or so. Some rejected your story and slipped away, and others listened, but didn't receive what you had to tell them. Some received Jesus when they responded to your story. Those were the ones who came alive and were full of joy. I'm sure there's more, and my thoughts might not be completely correct. We will have to ask God for him to give you more understanding."

Maggie gasped. "Matt! I just thought of something. Close your eyes!"

"And stick out my tongue?"

"No, silly. Remember your dream. What color was the little boy's hair? Do you see it?"

"Yes, it was light, almost white. Why?"

"Now open your eyes and look at the mud. Is it the same color?"

"Yes, exactly! Maggie, you're a genius."

"Help me put the pad between these coffins and I'll lay Jenny on it, then we'll scrape the mud down to the hard bottom we felt. It was only several centimeters in the shallow areas."

They were both getting more and more excited as they talked about this. Soon Jenny was deposited into the makeshift bed where she was still sleeping peacefully. When they stepped down onto the mud on the south side of the pallet, they found that the sun was beginning to dry the surface of the mud, and it was crusting over. The crust was very thin, and it was easy to scrape the mud from the bottom of the trough.

"Only about ten centimeters. Look, Matt!"

The water leaking out of the mud kept pushing fresh mud onto whatever the hard surface was underneath, but finally they scraped it away fast enough to see the jet-black rock under the mud. "It's the boy!" she said.

Maggie took a closer look at "the boy." "It looks like lava, like the lava I send around the class when they're learning about volcanos."

Matt got down on his hands and knees in the mud. "I think it's basalt."

"So we're both right. Why do you think it's basalt and not lava?"

"I picture lava as being rounded and long and flowing, like giant logs. Like pictures I've seen of the Hawaiian lava flows. But as you can see, this island is perfectly flat here, as far and wide as we can see. Why do you think it's lava and not basalt?"

"I didn't say that," Maggie said. "After all my students have felt the lava, I tell them lava is simply molten basalt that has come to the surface."

At 6 a.m. in Chicago, JC Smalley's phone woke him out of a rather pleasant dream. Hoping to sleep in, he had not set his alarm. It was Phil Henry. He was excited, a feeling JC was sure was foreign to him.

"JC, I'm activating the VTC as we speak. Get your VTC controller to light it up there. I'm having Bob McGee and Captain Palova on, too."

"Is it okay for Dusty Mae to join us?"

"Yes, certainly. There is some astounding news. All the field offices will eventually hear it, and there's no reason she shouldn't hear it first."

JC had no phone list, so he called Penny, to have her tell Jackie to crank up the VTC, and let Dusty Mae Watt know.

"Dusty Mae is out of the building on a different issue, but I'll tell her when she gets back, which should be soon. I'm going to join you unless you tell me not to."

He dressed hurriedly and got to the VTC room in time to see Jackie in her bathrobe in the control room. His monitor lit up along with the monitors of the other three. All of the other monitors glowed dimly; they were on, but not getting a feed from the other participants. Captain Palova and Bob

McGee were already visible. Phil's monitor merely showed a vertical white oblong on a dark background.

Captain Palova was speaking. "I believe you should call the others also. They may not be able to make it, but they would be pissed if they found out something from the news, whenever they finally watched, that they could be finding out here."

Bob and Phil agreed, and Phil's assistant started making the calls.

Phil's voice came from the oblong object. "We won't wait for them. In the meantime, what you see in my monitor is a satellite image of the location where AW flight 94 went down yesterday. Captain Palova's Air Force contact had his boys change their normal patrol route to include that site. What we know is that at 11 p.m. Eastern last night, even though there was very little moonlight, we would have seen this and it wasn't there. At 4 a.m., it was already light there and the patrol sent word that not only had an island appeared, but at one end of it was the airplane. Upside down, with parts scattered everywhere. Captain Palova, what else?"

"What they reported is that the forward section of the plane was separated from the fuselage, the bottom of the plane appeared to be shredded, and there were objects present which looked too big to be luggage or cargo. Halfway up the white area, at one edge, were two people who looked like they might be survivors. Before we go any further, is it possible for you to zoom in any more on the island?"

Phil was on the phone with the agency controlling the satellite. "Yes. I wanted to show you the whole island first."

Soon the southern end of the island filled the monitor. A little more zoom put the plane in the center of the picture. It was slightly out of focus and nothing else on the ground could be identified. Phil was still talking on the phone; soon the camera panned north and east. A small brown square appeared, but no details could be seen.

Bob McGee had access to assets that could provide the necessary detail. "It may take a few minutes if they aren't on a higher priority mission. I'll let you know."

While they were waiting, JC asked Captain Palova if the USAF planes had video capability. He guessed they didn't; if they did, they would already be seeing that video.

"They generally have the capability, but this morning, the pilot reported his video was non-operational."

Bob reported the satellite, which was not quite directly overhead of the island, was in the process of retasking to slew its camera to it. Another minute or two should do it.

Captain Palova spoke up. "I just heard from the Air Force. As soon as the patrol aircraft reported the island, they sent a recon aircraft with video and survey capabilities to that area. They should be there soon. Their main job is to do a complete three-dimensional mapping of the island, and they will send us video of whatever we request.

"I also alerted the Marine Corps at Camp Lejeune to deploy their new King Stallion MH-53K heavy lift troop-carrier to that location. They have no idea of their mission yet. All they know at this point, is they have one hour to get that helicopter in the air. It will take at least one refuel on the way, and they will coordinate with the Air Force for that support. I alerted the Air Force that the Marines would be calling them."

JC added, "You may have already thought of these, but I am going to make some recommendations. One, an anti-aircraft battery. The plane was shot down, for some reason, over a very deep part of the ocean. The whole world will soon hear about the island and the plane on it. Whoever destroyed the plane might send more sorties against it.

"Two, an Explosive Ordnance Disposal team. The forward section having separated from the fuselage tells me there was explosive ammunition fired at AW94, and there may be duds present. The EOD team needs to take their chemical detection kits and equipment, since we don't know yet if there is any connection between the chemical threat and this event.

"Three, a coroner and three-hundred-plus body bags."

They were in the middle of a second breakfast, when Maggie looked all around, perplexed. "Matt, I'm suddenly having a powerful thought, that we are being observed by a satellite."

"Okay, let's act on that thought. Let's wave to where you think the satellite is, and raise up Jenny to show her to the satellite. This may sound silly, but our action doesn't cost us anything and may prove to be very profound. You start waving and I'll follow your lead."

Maggie looked somewhat overhead, and slightly to the south. She pointed, then they both waved. After five seconds, Maggie held Jenny up.

Matt said, "Continue to look there about ten seconds, so they can see our faces."

When they had finished and turned away from looking skyward, Matt explained, "If they have the technology to get a good view of our faces, then they should have the technology to compare those faces to the passport photos of everyone on board. They should be able to figure out who we are."

"That assumes my thought was a reality."

"I'm treating it that way. If it was really a God-given thought, we'll eventually get confirmation of it, for your sake."

"For my sake?"

"Yes, so you'll understand how God can communicate with you. I mentioned it didn't cost us anything. If acting on the thought may have had bad consequences, then we should ask for God's peace or his red flag."

While JC was speaking, an image of the island surrounded by ocean filled Bob's monitor. The satellite's camera zoomed in and slewed to the southern end. The airplane came into view. The zoom continued; they could see the shredded underbelly in sharp focus. JC asked Penny to have Jackie move the images to the larger monitor for better viewing.

Bob spoke. "From here it would get a little tricky. In moving laterally, the picture would seem to jump rather than moving smoothly. So instead, I'll have the operator zoom out, move laterally, then zoom back in. We'll look at several objects in the vicinity of the fuselage."

The first object was the cockpit portion of the plane. It was located a short distance from the fuselage. It was lying on its side, severely damaged, and the edge where it had joined to the fuselage was mangled and badly torn and jagged. Cables were stretched out from that edge a little way. The camera zoomed in closer, but nothing inside the cockpit was visible.

In turn, they viewed the tail section, several pieces of luggage and cargo, and what appeared to be a large metallic tank, split wide open in the middle. "This is what I believe Captain Palova was referring to, about the object too large to be luggage or cargo. Phil, did you get the passenger, cargo, and baggage manifests from Air World?"

"Yes, Bob, the cargo is listed by weight and cube. I don't see anything on the list that would match that volume."

"Captain Palova will eventually have folks there to examine that more closely, and it doesn't look like anything there will be changing over the next several hours. Now, what I really want to see are these survivors."

The camera zoomed out and slewed north. When the brown square became visible and centered in the monitor, the camera began to zoom in. They could see the square was made up of brown rectangles side by side, with a series of five shiny squares starting at the brown square and leading toward the interior of the island. The zoom continued, and the image resolved to two people standing at the middle shiny square, which now appeared to be a metal cabinet.

The camera finally reached the limit of its zoom capability; the two could be clearly seen in the monitor. One had shoulder-length brown hair and was wearing a gray top, and appeared to be holding something pink; the other was a dark-haired man wearing a white shirt, and was larger than the first one. They appeared to be concentrating on the contents of the cabinet.

Suddenly, they both looked up into the sky. The smaller figure pointed directly at the camera, and they both started waving! After several seconds, the smaller of the two, who they could tell was female, held up the pink thing she was holding; it was a baby! She brought the baby back down, pushed the hair out of her own face, and they both stared directly toward the camera. After about ten seconds, they both waved and went back to what they were doing at the cabinet.

"Are you kidding me?!" "Holy cow!" "Did you see that?" Everyone was shouting at once, then "What just happened?" Everyone fell silent. The camera was still focused on the pair.

JC tore his eyes away from the screen long enough to realize Dusty Mae was now on, along with one other new attendee he didn't bother to take the time to identify.

Bob McGee was the first to offer a suggestion. "I can think of three possibilities," he said slowly. "Either the satellite came down and hovered about twenty feet above them, or every couple minutes they turn to the sky and wave, or ..." He couldn't bring himself to say it.

JC finished the thought for him. "Or something supernatural is going on. I began to think about that, when the island appeared at exactly the right spot at exactly the right time to bring the plane to the surface. Look at them down there! Both appear unhurt and not anxious about anything. We saw what condition the plane is in. How could they be like that? Walking around, checking things out, not caring about waving anymore. And, I might add, how did they know the exact direction to point and wave? And how could they have gotten that baby out alive?"

Captain Palova had been pondering the images of the two survivors. "It seemed they were staring at us. But since they were still for a while, it gives us the opportunity to identify them, by comparing their images to the passport photos of everyone on the plane. We have the passenger list. Would Air World already have their photos?"

Bob volunteered to contact the right persons to get the identities if Air World had trouble. But Phil, consulting the passenger list as well as the cargo lists, had some more immediate information. "The passenger list notes one passenger boarded with an infant-in-arms. In other words, just one seat for them both. Rachel Trillbey, from the UK, in seat 4A. The annotation shows the infant's name is Jennimore Trillbey. And from the cargo list, if I'm not mistaken, that is a pallet, one of several, with three caskets strapped to it, from the Hardwood Casket Company. Something doesn't look quite right about it, though."

"Hi, this is Dusty Mae Watt, FBI Chicago. Seat 4A is a window seat. Perhaps that's how she got out. I suppose it is also possible that a different woman escaped and the mother died, bless her heart. The picture should confirm it though. Were there any other Trillbeys on the passenger list? And can the camera zoom in on the pallet of caskets? Maybe we can get a better look."

The "better look" revealed a fourth coffin on top of the three strapped down.

After a few minutes, "We have a match!" Bob's monitor went blank briefly, and the mesmerizing effect was broken. Everyone breathed again; they hadn't realized how much they all had been holding it in. Those visible in their monitors, which now included Jon Whitaker, FBI, started to relax and move around after being rigidly unmoving for the past several minutes.

The blank screen was replaced by three sets of two pictures each, the pictures from the satellite next to the nearly-identical passport photos. "Ladies and gentlemen," Bob said dramatically, "may I present Matthew Carven, Gary, Indiana, seat 21E, Rachel Trillbey, Bristol, UK, seat 4A, and her daughter, Jennimore Trillbey. Positive IDs on all three!"

Phil Henry's mind was racing, and he was clicking on all cylinders. "That's wonderful," he started. "Let's not waste time speculating on how they got out. I'm sure they will be glad to tell us in a few hours. We have received calls from all of the others. They are on their way in and should all be in place by around 9 a.m. Eastern. I am having my VTC controller replay all of this as soon as everyone is in place.

"Captain Palova, has your 53K taken off yet? If so, what are they bringing? And how long will it take them to get there?"

"They are still on the ground. Mr. Smalley's suggestions were good. We were already implementing them when he made them. The anti-aircraft section is making their ammunition draw. Camp Lejeune is sending two EOD teams, and they will have explosives with them for possible disposal actions. We do not have a coroner at Lejeune who can go, but a coroner from Bethesda will be flown to Lejeune to make the second lift. We are also sending a small engineer section and an armed infantry platoon. They expect to be off the ground by about 7:30 Eastern. At max cruising speed, it may take them six hours to get there.

"I would like to add at this point, that my higher-ups are considering this support to be a courtesy. Military support to a civilian endeavor of this sort is generally not allowed by Department of Defense regulations. However, we are selling it on the basis of the possible toxic chemical agent threat we received from a source reliable to the CIA. We haven't convinced them yet, but they are very practical senior leaders who will realize that the US will need to do something, and only the military has the tools to do that something.

"I am assuming there will need to be a second lift to get more necessary folks there. We have no capability to bring back three hundred corpses in body bags, and there is no place to land a fixed-wing aircraft. Or to dock a boat, for that matter. And I'm sure Air World will want their plane back at some point. Was there mail on that plane?"

Phil consulted the cargo list. "Nope, no mail. I'm hoping that a foreign military plane firing explosive bullets would help convince your bosses, too.

"These two survivors are also eyewitnesses. The National Transportation Safety Board's Go Team will probably not make our second lift if we have one. We need to decide if we need to request the Marines to send another of their 53Ks before we break up this morning. At any rate, we will need to ask the questions the Go Team would ask, as well as any other pertinent thing.

"As you know, the board's jurisdiction ends when it becomes obvious the crash is based on criminal activity. It then becomes an FBI issue. I may lead that team myself. We know the flight was shot down. The rest of the world doesn't know that yet, and the board may think it has the responsibility. I think they will mostly be interested in the black box. We are too, to find out the last words of the pilot. But the Marine team en route should be able to tell what shot them down."

The group spent the next several minutes discussing what information might be needed from the survivors as well as from the first group to arrive from Camp Lejeune. Phil finally took charge again. "So much of our next actions will be determined by what we find out from the initial reports coming in from the island. If they leave at 7:30, they should be there by 1:30. They should be able to give us an initial assessment immediately, and a fairly thorough, but not complete, report within an hour of arrival.

"Our communication with the senior Marine officer should go through military channels, of course. What would be best is for them to send us a collection of digital files including audio and video, text and still photos."

"The King Stallion will have satellite communication capability and the Internet-style ability to send files," Captain Palova said. "I will find out who the Marine commander on board is, and start dialoguing with him to express our concerns and find out what capability he has to create those files. I'd like to invite you to listen in, to participate, if you have a secure military radio. I'll get you the frequency when I get it."

"Thanks, Louis. Jon Whitaker and I are both located here in DC. We're strictly admin headquarters type of offices without that type of equipment. Dusty Mae, how about you?"

Dusty Mae knew Phil needed only to go downstairs two floors and he could have all the equipment he needed, and so did Jon. Was he just throwing her a bone? No, in this case it would be the whole skeleton! He must really trust her. Or maybe he had JC in mind. "Yes," she said, "we have that radio, and between JC and myself, we will represent the FBI until you get there."

"No, I have something different in mind for JC. He will be taking a trip soon and needs to get ready. It will be just you and your team."

"Roger."

"Now back to the matter at hand." Phil started to become anxious to end this meeting. "By now the world knows about the missing Air World flight. We are the only ones who know it was shot down, and only we know about the island. The rest of the world will find out soon enough, though, and we need to be prepared.

"On that note, we received transcripts from our London contacts, from interviews they had with the Russians who made the previous Chicago-to-London flight, but whose luggage was delayed until flight 94. Without saying any more, we need to find their luggage, so we need to get the luggage list to the Marines. If they cannot receive the whole list electronically, we need to give them the ID tag numbers and descriptions of just the Russians' luggage.

"Once the Marines get there, we will need to provide a satellite view of the area to the press. One in enough detail to show the airplane as well as the fact that there is protection for it there. However, it needs to be zoomed out, slightly out of focus, and enlarged in order to not give away our satellite capability, location, or identity.

"The manifests I got show that this is also a Britannia Airlines flight, as a partnership airline. We need to talk to Air World and BA to find out what they plan to do, now that the plane is out of the water. The fact that one of the survivors—actually two—are British may encourage BA to take some action as well as Air World. My office here will do this. They will need to know as soon as possible about the island. Does anyone object to my letting them know about this right off?"

No one did. They discussed the requirement to send an additional helicopter to the island. No one could justify sending the flight just to bring a coroner; perhaps Air World or Britannia Airlines could get one there? Captain Palova recommended they wait to see if the first contingent needed reinforcements or resupply, then decide. In the end, this was accepted as the appropriate course of action.

"Lastly, we need to meet again as soon as we receive the second report from the Marines. At that meeting we will need to discuss possible motives and identities of the shooters, the Brazilian connection, and our next steps as a group." Phil was bringing the meeting to a close. "Let's plan to meet again at 2:30 Eastern time. If it will be significantly later than that I will call you."

There was a buzzing sound in the headset. JC put it on; it was Phil. "I still feel Brazil is the best place for you to go. I had considered taking you with me to the island, but I think your expertise will be better used down there. I'll take a different agent with me when I figure out who."

"How about Dusty Mae? I know you have plenty to choose from, but I think she has the right experience and she is already involved with all this."

"Okay, I'll think about it. I also have to figure out how to get there."

JC detected a welcome aroma and looked up to see Penny with a tray holding three plates of breakfast. "Wow," he said, "I'm really hungry, but I don't think I could eat all that."

She grinned at him and set one of the plates on the table. "I hope I guessed right."

She took the tray and knocked on the VTC control room door. Jackie opened it, fully dressed.

JC was impressed at Penny's intuition. When she got back, he told her, "You did great!"

He looked at her plate. It was identical to his.

"This is all they serve for breakfast," she said.

It was the middle of the morning, several hours since the aircraft had left the area. A haze similar to the previous day had developed. Matt had tried, unsuccessfully, to cut the strapping holding the other three coffins to their pallet using the plastic knives in the meal packs.

The mud on their clothes had dried, and they were able to brush it off completely. Jenny was content to eat, sleep, be held, and be talked to by a loving mother and grandfather.

When the white mud had crusted over, it supported their weight without them sinking. They walked east to the edge of the island, and found the mud had been washed into the ocean about five feet from the edge, exposing a black strip. Looking over the edge, they saw it dropped straight down about ten feet to the water.

They turned around to go back. Maggie pointed northward. In the distance, a single mountain peak appeared, black against the bright sky. "Look, our guidepost!"

"It looks like it's on the far side of the island, making this the flat side."

"If I were good at maths, I could figure out how far we are from the south end of the island." Maggie taught year fives maths, which didn't include trigonometry.

They trudged back to the Good Ship Myrtlewood and separated the food that might be starting to spoil from the rest.

Maggie appointed herself Chief Food Inspector. "Salads, breads, butter, cheese, and desserts should get us by while we're waiting. The entrees are suspect, along with anything water-soaked."

After chitchatting with Maggie about life in the United States and life in

England, Matt decided it was time for a serious what-happens-next discussion. "When you get back, Maggie, you are going to have quite a story to tell."

"It has been extraordinary, brilliant, wonderful, and I don't know if I'll be able to do it justice."

"Yes, it has been wonderful what God has done for his glory. But not everyone will be happy to hear about it."

"Huh? How could that be? Who would not rejoice with me?"

They were sitting on the edge of the pallet, facing the ocean. Maggie was still for a minute, thinking. "Yes, I can see how that might be true. But it seems like you've been waiting for a chance to talk about this, so please tell me."

"Maggie, I'm impressed and thrilled at how quickly you're learning, catching on, retaining. It took me a long time to be where you are. I had a lot of unlearning to do! But now I want to talk to you about the opposition you can expect when you tell your story, and about the old Maggie."

"The old Maggie? I thought she's dead. I'm the new Maggie, right? You told me that."

"Yes, you're a brand-new person, with a new life given to you by God, and the Holy Spirit is making you more like Jesus all the time. That's his job. That means your old attitudes have to be replaced by new attitudes, old habits by new habits, old thought patterns by new. That's what I mean by the old Maggie. Those old things aren't evident right now because you're in a completely different set of circumstances. God is really pouring it on, for you to experience his wonderfulness, so you can share it with others.

"In the not-too-distant future, you'll be weaning Jenny. You know it will be for her good, but she won't understand. She'll need solid food for proper growth. Later, she'll be able to feed herself, and later still, she'll be able to feed others. This is the way it is in the natural world. It's the same way in the spiritual world. Do you remember your dream? You were feeding others. How did you get from where you are now, to where you were in the dream?"

"I don't know. I feel like I'm still a newborn."

"Exactly. But the old Maggie, that is, the old attitudes, old habits, and old thought patterns, is still very strong. When you get back to Bristol, you'll open the door to your apartment, and if you're not careful, the old Maggie will punch you in the face, throw you on the ground, and try to jump back inside you while you're lying there bleeding. Sorry to be so graphic, but it's the truth.

The old Maggie must decrease, and the new Maggie must increase. This is what the Holy Spirit's work is all about."

Maggie thought briefly. "When I refused your hair-tie, that was the old Maggie, wasn't it?"

"Yes, and when I threw it in the water, that was the old Matt."

"Then it wasn't me?"

"It was the old Maggie trying to take over. But you are responsible if she succeeds. She won't succeed forever, although it may be tough on you for a while. Here's one way you can tell the difference. The old person tries to hide and doesn't want to expose what's inside, for fear of being found lacking, or untruthful, or less than what he or she is trying to portray. The new person wants to show forth the new life the Holy Spirit is producing, and therefore desires to be transparent. Do they use 'transparent' that way in England?"

"That meaning has been coming into popularity in our country. I've known it for a while, but haven't used it much that way. It's a word that's the opposite of itself."

"Uh, what?"

"Eleven letters. Totally visible synonym and antonym."

Matt groaned. Then they both laughed.

"Here's another example. It was the old Maggie who gave me that look last night."

"Wait, Matt. No, like I said, the old Maggie could never have given you that look. She had nothing to give that look with."

"Remember that the old Maggie is not your old body or even your old intellect. It is your old attitudes and ways of doing things. God removed a barrier within you and let your whole femininity come gushing forth. It was a wonderful thing, a real delight! It was God's gift to you. What did you do with that gift?"

She thought for a moment. "I wanted to give it to you. Was that such a bad thing? I know God told me 'No' later, but in my heart, I thought it was the right thing to do."

"You were being very generous, kind, and compassionate, which are good things. Things of the new Maggie. And you didn't look at it as a gift, but as a natural part of you, which it was also." Matt picked up one of the potato-like rocks, felt its roughness, and tossed it back down. "What makes it the old Maggie, is that you discovered this new something in your life and immediately decided to do with it whatever you wanted. Whatever pleased you. Later, you asked God about it, and he told you he had something much better in mind. You'll find his ways are higher than our ways, and you'll learn to ask first, then act, rather than acting first and asking him later."

Matt thought his pupil looked perplexed, so he leaned over, looked her straight in the eye, and said, "You're going to do fine. Trust me on that. I know you've got plenty of questions and perhaps some apprehension. Let's talk about something else, and we can come back to this later. So let's talk about the new Maggie instead."

"Yes, let's do! Things are going to change, aren't they?"

"Almost everything will change. The things that cause you to be the way you are have just changed completely. But don't worry, God is not asking you to give up anything for him. Rather, the Holy Spirit will work the life of Jesus into you, so what was attractive and desirable and fulfilling before, may no longer be that."

"Nothing was very fulfilling before. And even then, it didn't last very long."

Matt went on, "Your tastes may change. The music you listen to, the food you like, the clothes you wear, what you read, your enjoyment of crosswords, your hair style, the art you hang on your wall. Don't try to change anything. Let God do it. He knows you better than you know yourself. You won't even notice the changes as they are occurring. Those around you will, though. One day you'll just realize things are different, for the better. On the other hand, those things I mentioned may not change at all."

Maggie thought for a moment, gathering her hair in a bunch and retying the velvet strip around it. "You know, I didn't like myself very much before."

Matt nodded. "Those things I mentioned are all just externals, symptoms of something going on inside, which is really what God is working on. Your motives and attitudes especially. When you get back to Bristol, you will face the same circumstances as before you left. What will change is how you react to those things that used to bother you. Like when you walk to your school every day and Mrs. Smythe's dog barks at you. Instead of kicking dirt on the dog, you would ask God how you could show love and compassion to Mrs. Smythe, so perhaps something you do would inspire her to want to know him like you know him."

"Ask first, then act?"

"Exactly. There may still be times when you don't like yourself, and that will almost always be when the old Maggie has temporarily gotten the upper hand. But realize God doesn't love you any less when that happens. Just pick yourself up, dust yourself off, apologize if necessary, forgive yourself, and move on. Remember, we don't always learn by doing the right thing, but sometimes by experiencing the consequences of doing the not-right thing."

As they were talking, they got up and unwrapped all the suspect food. They put it into a couple of the metal bins, which they took back to the edge of the island and emptied into the ocean. Back at the GSM, they put all the wrappers and other trash in one of the plastic bags they found. Maggie fished the used diaper out of the top coffin, and they put all the trash into the empty stainless-steel cabinet.

"That's enough to chew on," Matt said, "so let's take a break."

"Okay. We need to name this island. I've been thinking about that. It's God's island, and maybe we can name it that."

"God's Island, like with an apostrophe?" he asked.

"Yes, that's what I was thinking."

"Hmm. I like it. Except that many maps won't be able to put the apostrophe in, like Sana'a and Hawai'i have become Sanaa and Hawaii. That may lead some to think it's an island full of gods, you know, full of idols."

Maggie had another idea. "How about, 'The Boy'?"

Matt chuckled. "I like that, but maybe we can call it that just between ourselves. I don't think anyone else would get it."

"Is there another name that means God we can use instead? I feel if we don't name it, they will just call it by the latitude and longitude or some other silly thing."

"The name Father comes to mind. Father's Island, with or without the apostrophe. Although I think God wouldn't mind if we named it Myrtlewood Island. Let's think about it for a while."

I wonder if I should tell her, Matt mused. He had been thinking about what he saw on the plane during the attack. Not now, he decided. Maybe later.

Their conversation eventually turned to their rescue. "Matt, do you think, once they find us, it will take long to get us back to civilization? We don't know how far we are from anything. There's nowhere for a plane to land yet. This part of The Boy is nice and flat like we asked, but it's covered with this white mud."

They examined the mud a little more closely. It appeared to be wet ashes mixed with crushed sea shells. The potato-like things crushed fairly easily with a metallic sound when Matt smashed two of them together.

"I don't know, Maggie. That plane has been gone for hours. If we were somewhat close to land, we should have seen more planes by now, since someone should be looking for debris on the water. Not only that, but they know there are two survivors, maybe a third. And a brand-new island."

"Eventually, a plane should come. I hope they can drop us some food and an umbrella or two. The airlines may send a scouting plane. Let's scuff up the surface to spell out our names, so that unless the sun is directly overhead, the shadows should tell them who we are. If there were really a satellite, then they would already know."

"Yes," Matt said, "and we should use the names on our tickets."

They carved out their names with block letters about ten feet high. Underneath RACHEL TRILLBEY, Maggie wrote JENNY. "She didn't have a ticket, but of course they knew I had her with me. They will wonder how Jenny survived when none of the others did." With her recollection of all that had transpired with Jenny, her face suddenly filled with tears.

Matt finished the thought for her. "She didn't."

When she could speak again, she continued, "I will have such a story for them!"

"It's funny," she went on, "but if I hadn't been overwhelmed by this joy I feel, I don't think I would have had any tears just now."

"Yes, I could tell. Those were tears of gratitude."

He decided to tell her. "When I got on the plane in Chicago, the business class section, where you were, was full. I've been thinking about this. After I went forward to find an oxygen mask and saw the front end of the plane had been shot off, I noticed a lot of blood up there, and there was an unoccupied window seat which looked like it had been blown apart." He let that sink in briefly. "Your seat."

She nodded, grimacing a little. "God called Jenny and me to go back and visit you. And he arranged that you should have an empty seat next to you. He is amazing! He was already proving himself strong on our behalf. Maybe we could add that to the list?"

"Technically not, however, it is part of our story. There is one thing to add, though, and that is that he provided us the GSM with all those cabinets attached. The one thing that rose out of the plane's cargo hold was something that preserved our lives."

"That reminds me, Matt, you said not everyone will be happy to hear about the brilliant things that happened to me. Who are those, and why?"

"There will be skeptics, even in light of Jenny's foot and the rest of the supernatural things you will be telling them about. There will be folks who refuse to acknowledge God and resent any person who attempts to speak of him. They'll ignore you, mock you, and try to make you irrelevant. There are others who don't believe God cares enough about people to intervene in their lives. There will be those who point to your past, and say, 'Who are you for God to do that for you?' But it is actually the religious people who will be the strongest opposition."

Just then, a second, more conventional-looking plane appeared from behind them. The pilot indicated that he saw them and turned around for another pass. He appeared to be flying out over the water, when they saw the plane abruptly dip down and disappear. Then all was quiet. Maggie and Matt exchanged alarmed glances. After a few seconds, the plane seemed to rise from out of the light-colored mud, unharmed. It flew away from them, toward the north, until it was out of sight. They heard the plane for the next hour or so, and occasionally saw it traversing east to west and back, starting in the north and slowly working its way south.

"Matt, they must have been below the sheer cliff at the edge. I bet they're surveying your new island."

"No. Our new island. If they let us have it, whoever 'they' are, then I say it's half yours. After all, you helped call it up. People own islands all over the world, and I don't see any reason we shouldn't own this one. However, since we're citizens of two different countries, it might be less sticky, legally, if a corporation owned it."

"I don't know anything about that. As far as I'm concerned, you can have my half."

"Nope. And please don't tell anyone that. Keep your options open."

"That was the old Maggie, wasn't it?"

"Yes. The Boy is a gift to us from God. To you and me equally. We don't know the extent of the gift yet, but we need to ask God what we're to do with it. Let's do that now."

They sat together on the GSM and asked for God's favor from whatever countries might claim the island as sovereign territory, his success for whatever his purposes for the island might be, and his wisdom for accomplishing what he called them to do.

"Let's go back to what you were saying," Maggie said when they finished.

"Why would religious people be the strongest opposition? I would think they'd be happy that I'm telling people about God."

"There are preachers and religious folks who, full of religious pride, will say you are a heretic, especially because of what you will say about the baptism in the Holy Spirit. Or, they'll try to nullify your influence and experience, or say women cannot do what you are doing. There are those with religious influence, you know, in leadership positions, who will be extremely jealous because of your joy, your communing with God, and especially the crowds you will be drawing."

"Big crowds? Oh, Matt, I don't know if I'm ready for that!"

"You'll need help, but don't be afraid. God will provide it at just the right time. Just revel in being that little bottle being carried about in the vast ocean!"

About fifteen minutes before the scheduled 1:30 VTC, Penny burst through the door to JC's makeshift office. "I have bad news and good news," she announced excitedly, "and since you didn't specify, I'll give you the bad news first. I thought I would be going with you to Brazil, but I found out it would be Harper. He's a good choice, since he's more used to hot weather." All her words ran together, like it was just one long word. She took a long deep breath and continued, "And here's the good news: I'm going to the island with Phil!"

That took JC by surprise. His jaw dropped open momentarily and his eyes got wide. A big smile replaced the gaping jaws. "Wow! Great! How did you swing that?"

"Phil called Dusty Mae and asked which of the three trainees would be best, and she chose me. I leave in about a half hour to go to the airport. We'll be taking a helicopter from Camp Lejeune, an MH-53K like the one already there."

That makes sense, JC said to himself. Phil wouldn't need a seasoned agent, all he would really need would be an aide, a helper, a recorder. A trainee would be perfect.

"Well, she made a good choice. Congratulations! After all the help you've given me here, I think I'll make out okay. Will you be carrying?"

"Yes, but just in my backpack. For just in case. It's a 9mm Glock I started using when I got here. Do you have any advice before I go?"

"You probably know this already, but take a pocket notebook, and use it. Write down questions for later, observations, details and where the details came from, and especially people's names. Learn to read people, especially your teammates, in this case Phil. He knows you're in training and will have lots of questions, but ask intelligent questions, not ones he would expect you to find out the answers to yourself. There's a fine line between being an eager learner and being a pest. Learn where that line is and don't cross it.

"You'll probably be among only friendlies, but don't let your guard down. Don't *ever* let your guard down! One other thing about this particular case: learn everything about the sea floor there, before you go. Knowing what that white stuff is might come in handy."

"Thanks!"

"Send me a selfie with the survivors, and keep in touch. Let me know how things go. You may be back before I leave. And have a safe trip."

They both heard it at the same time; a helicopter was approaching. It started descending when the pilot saw them. Matt was watching the dried-mud surface as it got closer. "Maggie, quick, get behind the coffins with Jenny! Then get down!"

She ducked down as he ran to the upper coffin and pushed it over the edge. Jenny screamed as a storm of white debris started blowing past them. The down-blast from the helicopter rotors was sending chunks of the drying mud flying in all directions. As the engines started to slow, the debris stopped. They were able to stand up and see the giant helicopter with US Marine Corps markings, parked in a large black circle. The names they had drawn were completely obliterated.

The rotor blades stopped turning, a door opened, and three uniformed figures stepped out. Matt and Maggie, who was carrying Jenny still wrapped in pink and gold velvet, came around the GSM and the trailing metal cabinets. They headed toward the Marines, whom they met halfway. The tallest appeared to be in charge. One carried a camouflaged bag with a bold black cross on the side, and the third carried a rifle pointed at the ground.

Matt spoke first. "Hi, and welcome to our island!"

"Hi, I'm Lieutenant Colonel Paul Washington from the Fourth Battalion,

Second Marine Expeditionary Force at Camp Lejeune. We are the first ones here. Others will follow. Are you Matthew Carven, from Gary, Indiana? And Rachel Trillbey, from Bristol, England? And more importantly, are either of you injured or sick in any way? We have medical help if necessary."

He turned to the medic, who stepped forward, and nodded.

Matt and Maggie turned to each other and laughed, he proudly and she triumphantly. "You heard it exactly right, Maggie!"

Matt turned back to the senior Marine. "Yes, sir, Lieutenant Colonel Washington. I'm Matt Carven. We are all three in good health and uninjured, thanks many times over to God."

"And I'm Maggie Trillbey. This is my daughter Jenny." She proudly held her up for the Marine officer to see. Jenny's anxious crying from the fright of the aircraft landing had subsided.

They showed their passports to LtCol Washington. Matt explained, "This is all we have left. Everything else went down with the plane."

Matt addressed LtCol Washington. "We have a thousand questions, and I'm sure you do too, but I'd like to make a suggestion. This white mud is slushy underneath and crusty on top. If you hurry, you can fly your helicopter in a straight line at a low level and create quite a runway. This side of the island is perfectly flat for much of its length. On the other side of the river, it gets hilly on the north end. We saw what the rotors did to the mud. If you act now, you can make a runway several miles long before the mud dries out completely and hardens."

LtCol Washington gave Matt a peculiar look before responding. "It does sound like a good idea, but we can't do that. The debris would tear up our rotor blades. Your suggestion intrigues me, though, and I'll get back to it in a bit. I have some news for you first. Your plane is on this island, too. On the south end, spread over about a mile-wide circle. There is debris everywhere."

"Wow," Maggie said, "I bet that's why God wanted this island!"

"What?! What are you saying? Wait, let's go sit in the helicopter. It will be more comfortable there. By the way, please call me Paul. All my Marines call me Sir or Lieutenant Colonel, of course, but I'd like to make this as informal for you as possible. There will be enough formality later on. Follow me!"

Matt was eager to show off their lifeboat. "Wait, before we go, let us show you what God provided for us to float on when we first hit the water, and while we were waiting for the island to come up. We named it the Good Ship Myrtlewood, or GSM for short. The coffins are made of myrtle wood. As you can see, there are three coffins strapped to a pallet, and the loose one was on top when we climbed aboard."

The tour took no time at all, including taking pictures, and soon they were seated around a small table in the helicopter.

"This is a King Stallion," Paul said. "Our aircraft wing at Cherry Point has had it less than two months. There might be another en route from Camp Lejeune which could be here in several hours.

"I have a checklist of questions to ask, because you are eyewitnesses as well as survivors. But I can tell there is a whole lot more to your stories than what's on the checklist. That's what I want to hear first. Before I do, I want to make sure you're comfortable. Are you hungry? Do you need to use the head? Uh, the loo? Is there anything you need for your infant, um…"

"Jenny."

"Yes, Jenny. We will be leaving here in about ten minutes for our base camp in the south. Is there anything you need to retrieve from the GSM?"

Maggie answered for them both. "There was some food in the metal cabinets and we've been snacking. We're hungry, but not ravenous. I think we could both use the bathroom but we can wait until after the flight,"—she looked at Matt, who nodded—"and I'll need a bed or something soft for Jenny, along with her outfit and blanket from the top coffin. If you don't have anything for her, we can rip out some more coffin liner, now that you're here. Hopefully, you can cut through the straps on one of the lower coffins. A hot shower would be nice, but we don't have anything to change into."

"I'm afraid it will be fairly primitive while you're on the island, and we don't really have an exit strategy yet," LtCol Washington said.

He spoke to a non-commissioned officer who was standing by; the NCO left with the medic and headed for the GSM.

"Okay! I'm dying to know, why wasn't it a surprise to you that I knew who you were?"

"God spoke to Maggie and told her about the satellite overhead. So we waved and let it see our faces, so they could figure out who we are."

"You heard God speak?"

"It wasn't exactly a voice. I told Matt it was more like a powerful thought. I'm new at all this." Then she added eagerly, "God became my father yesterday, when I gave myself to Jesus and received him as my Lord."

Paul could barely wait for her to finish. "I gave my life to Jesus when I was a teenager. I knew something was up with you. I could see that joy all over you. A radiance not explainable by anything else. And I sense that same spirit in you, Matt.

"I want to hear the whole story. But that can wait until later. First, I want to ask, do you know where you are? When we were coming in, it was obvious to me you hadn't ventured more than thirty feet from your craft, except to go to the water. That's what your footprints told me. So how could you know about the river?"

Matt started off, "We don't know exactly where this island is, but we can tell you it is twenty-five miles from north to south and five miles east to west. In the northwest, there are hills and one mountain you can see from anywhere on the island." He went on to describe the natural harbor, the flat ridge, the stream of fresh water, and the bridge. "Maggie, did I forget anything?"

"It is high enough out of the water that a high tide won't overflow it. Did you want to mention about the caverns?"

"No, they're deep under the water, so they won't be seen. We'll tell about those in the long version of our story."

"But how could you possibly know all that?"

Maggie answered, "It's part of our story, but God told us to call up an island from the bottom of the ocean. The two of us." Then she grinned. "Okay, it was Matt, but I got to participate. We believed we were to be very specific and detailed rather than asking for just any old island. Do you wonder how we got the GSM up on top of it?"

By this time, the NCO and the medic were back and were listening, too, along with the pilots and the guard with the rifle. "Yes," they all said.

"I think we have to go now, but we'll tell you when we tell the long version later, if anyone wants to hear it." Maggie was enjoying keeping them in suspense. "I'll give you a clue, though. We got there first."

The NCO, Staff Sergeant Phelps, showed Maggie the duffel bag full of velvet from one of the lower coffins. He also had both thick pads, which were too big for the duffel bag. "Here's a memento from the casket," he said, producing the tool kit.

It was identical to the other one, except they could see that the slip of paper said "INSP BY SUE S".

Staff Sergeant Phelps, the loadmaster, helped Matt and Maggie get seated in the troop seats where they could look out the window, and gave them headsets set to the channel where they could converse with Paul if they desired. "I'm sorry I don't have a headset for your daughter, but these earplugs should help. It will get really noisy when we take off, until we land." He showed her how to insert them, and brought Maggie some of the velvet from the duffel bag. "Don't hold her up on your shoulder, but lay her on this on your lap. It will dampen out the vibrations better and make it easier for her. I have a daughter, too."

They took off and gained altitude quickly, heading west, toward the opposite edge of the island. When they reached the middle, the pilot leveled off and headed south. Below them, the terrain was just as Matt had described. It appeared the edge was black all the way around the island, and they saw two thick black lines heading north and south on the otherwise white surface. "The road and the river!" Matt exclaimed.

Paul verified the river. "It comes fairly close to where we'll be landing. The perfectly straight one may very well be the flat ridge you mentioned. We'll be on the ground soon, and you'll see I have a number of squads of Marines here, and they'll be busy with different tasks. One is a bomb squad. Before we left to pick you up, they verified that whoever shot you down was using explosive bullets. You must have been terrified! Anyway, we can't go look at the plane before they certify all is clear."

They landed. While the pilots conducted their post-flight checks, all of the other Marines except LtCol Washington departed. They were replaced by other Marines with clipboards.

"Sir," one said, "we have some urgent information, but we should probably be briefing just you." He looked at the pair of civilians, knowing they were the survivors, and continued, "We are guessing you will want to report this immediately, so it might be best if they step outside."

"Yes, that would be best. Get Staff Sergeant Phelps for me."

By the time they got out of the helicopter, SSgt Phelps had appeared. Matt had made another sling for Jenny, so Maggie and Matt took turns holding her. The white mud had been blown away from an even bigger circle than the one where they were picked up. When they got off the flat basalt area, the pale surface crunched underfoot, like the frozen slush left on top of snow the morning after a spring thaw.

"Yes, sir?"

"Staff Sergeant Phelps, please show our visitors around, keeping out of the exclusion area. I'll be a few minutes with the reports." With that, he disappeared back inside.

In Washington DC, Phil Henry kicked off the 2:30 VTC, and lost little time in turning the meeting over to Captain Palova.

"Thanks, Phil. We received the initial report from the Marines on station about an hour ago. They confirmed AW94 was shot down with American thirty-millimeter high-explosive incendiary bullets. The island's surface near the plane is littered with dud rounds, which will have to be disposed of before personnel can approach the aircraft. This is consistent with the last words of the pilot, Captain Merkel. The EOD teams identified the rounds as those which are fired from the American GAU-8 machine gun. They provided a list of sixteen different ammunition lot numbers. We are tracking them down to find out when they were produced and where they were sent.

"For the past few minutes, I have been speaking with Lieutenant Colonel Paul Washington, Marine commander on site, who picked up the survivors and brought them back to their command post near the airplane location. We will have the opportunity to speak with them in a few minutes. My radio here will be connected to the VTC so you will hear both sides of the radio traffic.

"Now for the news we've been waiting for. One of the EOD teams detected nerve agent consistent with sarin gas in the baggage of one of the Russians. The suitcase had been booby-trapped. It appears the triggering device was a very simple non-explosive bellows-and-plunger designed to function when the suitcase was opened. The technical details are being provided to Bob McGee and Jon Whitaker of the FBI WMD Directorate. I say 'consistent with sarin gas' because there are variants, including binary chemical agents, that show up in EOD's test kits as sarin even though not strictly chemically identical, but have the same effect on human bodies."

Captain Palova's monitor switched from his image to the picture of a shiny metallic tank. "The Marines were able to send all kinds of pictures and data. This picture shows one of three similar tanks like the ones we saw earlier. It could not have been aboard the airplane, since nothing like them were on the manifests, and the cargo hold did not appear to be large enough. All three tanks were ruptured quite badly. One possible explanation other than that they are connected to this incident, is that perhaps they were already there on the seafloor.

"I'm turning the meeting back over to Phil. I will let you all know when we have the survivors on the radio."

"Thanks, Louis. When you talk with the survivors, please ask if they suffered any symptoms of nerve agent poisoning, even a little. Also, the WMD nerve agent being on board appears to tie the shooting down of the plane to the goings-on in Brazil. Pedro, I see that you're here. Please get with the ambassador to add this new information to his meeting with his counterpart. Brazil doesn't owe us anything, but their cooperation would sure make our job a lot easier. Ty Harris, if your folks at State would get with the ambassador also, the liaison with your bureau might prove invaluable. Until we find out the motives and agenda of these shooters, we have to assume the worst.

"Just thinking things through into the future, it will be impossible to hide the fact the plane was shot down. Air World Airlines will eventually get their plane back and find the bullet holes, some or most of the bodies will have shrapnel in them, and insurance companies may want photos to support claims. I propose we publicize now, not only that we recovered the plane, but that it was shot down. It may come as a shock to the perpetrators, and they may make a wrong move or otherwise expose themselves. Not the sarin gas yet, though. Does anyone have thoughts on this?"

There was a little discussion among the team members, and in the end, they approved of that course of action.

Just then, Phil announced, "I've just been notified by Captain Palova, that Lieutenant Colonel Washington is being joined by the survivors. Let's listen in, and we'll talk some more afterwards."

Staff Sergeant Phelps appeared to be a year or two younger than Maggie. He was a little taller than she, muscular, and walked with the confidence of a man highly proficient in his business. He had an easy manner about him, one comfortable talking with other people besides just Marines.

"We didn't know what would be here," he said, "so we brought a couple portable toilets. We'll start there with the tour. We had to put them and the mess tent far enough from the helicopter to keep the rotor wash from blowing them away."

There were foot trails already crushed into the dried mud. Odors of canvas and motor oil overpowered the salty ocean smell. As they went, they could see the wreckage of their plane off to the left, inside a large circle of yellow caution tape held in place by the potato-looking rocks, which were scattered everywhere.

The mess tent was a camouflage net tied to heavy objects at each of its corners. Underneath were two vehicles which looked like military dune buggies, and another two which looked like Hummers. There were also makeshift tables and a food locker. The portable toilets were on the other side of the mess tent.

Soon the tour started. "We're about a half mile from the eastern edge of the island," SSgt Phelps said, "and about two miles from the southern edge. Our engineers and one EOD team put that tape out. On the other side of the yellow tape, there are dud explosive shells from the machine guns all around the plane. Mostly on the other side of the plane.

"In case you didn't know, EOD is Explosive Ordnance Disposal, the Marines' bomb squad. They have to dispose of all duds before we can get near the plane. They are going all around the plane, finding the farthest-away dud as they go, and putting the tape there. They are not quite finished. They are also checking the cargo and baggage areas for explosive devices and dud bullets. The baggage is strewn everywhere. One of the EOD teams is making special checks of all those that are outside the cargo hold."

Matt pointed to a group of Marines standing near a vehicle he didn't recognize. "What is that over there?"

"That's an anti-aircraft section. There wasn't enough room to bring the whole battery with all their equipment, with everything else we brought."

"Anti-aircraft? The horse is already out of the barn, isn't it?"

SSgt Phelps laughed. "Soon the whole world will know an island came up under the plane and brought it to the surface. Our mission includes protecting the remains from whoever shot it down, in case the reason they did that was to make the plane disappear forever. We will be able to see and engage them before they get close enough.

"The only other things to show you are the vehicles in the mess tent. The ones that look like dune buggies are called Light Strike Vehicles. The other ones are Joint Light Tactical Vehicles, or JLTVs. It turns out the surface here can support both sets. Our battalion is not scheduled to get our JLTVs until next month, so we had to borrow these from the School of Infantry. If things are quiet, we will give everyone a chance to get proficient in driving the

JLTVs."

Just then a Marine ran up to their guide, and told him the Lieutenant Colonel wanted them back as soon as possible.

Paul was seated by a radio, and there were chairs for Matt and Maggie. He motioned for them to sit, and gave them each a bottle of water. A voice came out of the radio, "Thank you, Lieutenant Colonel Washington. We'd like to speak with the survivors if they are nearby."

"Yes, sir, they are right here. Matt Carven, Maggie Trillbey, and her daughter Jenny."

"Thanks. I am Captain Louis Palova of the US Navy. We have you on speaker to a gathering of folks very high up in our intelligence community. Is that okay?"

Paul kept pressing the push-to-talk button when it was their turn to speak. Matt and Maggie answered in turn. "Yes, sure." "That's fine."

"I'd like to say, first of all, what a tragedy this has been for our country, the UK, and five other countries who lost citizens yesterday. We are thrilled, though, that you three are alive and well. We won't keep you long, but we have some important questions that will help us in our investigation and future actions.

"Before we start, how the heck did you know to wave to our satellite? No sooner did we focus on you than you turned and waved. It was apparent you knew what you were doing. How did you know where it was and that it was watching you?"

Matt gave him the same answer he had given Paul. "God spoke to Maggie and told her."

The radio was silent for a while. Captain Palova said, "That took a moment to sink in! There are ten stunned and incredulous faces here listening to you. For the last four hours, we've been trying to come up with an explanation, but nobody's been able to think of a single plausible one. We'll move on. Please tell us how the three of you managed to get out of the plane. We know Rachel, uh, Maggie and Jenny were by the window in business class and Matt was in the middle of the plane in economy."

Maggie started. "Jenny and I had moved out of first class and were sitting with Matt. Sorry, I keep calling it first class. It was first class on the trip over.

The pilot had given us a warning about some rough flying coming up, and a few minutes later, we were being shot at. All of a sudden, the oxygen bags came down. I was holding Jenny, so Matt put mine on me and he put his on Jenny. He was on the inside so we switched places so he could find a mask.

"We both had our seatbelts off when the plane started crashing into the water. We were thrown all about inside the plane and I lost hold of Jenny. The plane crashed nose first into the water, and the next thing I knew, water came in through the front and blew me out through the tail. God protected me from hitting or being caught on anything inside the plane, and from being torn by the jagged metal as I went through."

Matt continued, starting from what he saw in the front of the plane until he exited the plane like Maggie had.

"What happened to your infant?"

"Like I said, I lost her when we were thrown about. She's three months old, and I had swaddled her in a blanket. We didn't see her at all once we were out of the plane, which sank immediately. We never saw it again until today, except for the tail which had separated and briefly came to the surface. It was obvious she had drowned."

Matt added, "There was nothing at all on the surface but us two. Maggie couldn't swim, and by the time I got her stabilized in the water, the pallet of coffins had floated up and we got on it. Maggie stood on the top, but we couldn't see Jenny anywhere. We didn't see her body again for at least an hour or two."

"Then what happened to Jenny?" Captain Palova was clearly intrigued.

"The Lord appointed a great fish to swallow Jenny, and she was in the stomach of the fish."

Matt would have continued, but Maggie interrupted. "The shark rose up out of the water three or four times as high as the GSM. I was scared out of my wits, but Matt very calmly commanded the fish in Jesus's name to throw up. All kinds of things came out, including Jenny. Her skin looked like it was already starting to be digested. We washed her off and looked her over. The shark hadn't bitten her and she wasn't torn on her way out of the plane. Later on, God brought her back to life."

"That sounds fantastic!"

Matt frowned. He thought he could discern "like a fantasy" rather than "wonderful" when Captain Palova said "fantastic", so he said, "Jenny was born missing a foot. That's well documented at the hospital where she was born. When God brought her back to life, he gave her a new foot."

Maggie opened up the velvet blanket for Paul to see both of Jenny's feet. "See if you can tell which is the new one," she whispered.

He took a foot in each hand and gently massaged them. "No, I can't. They both feel the same."

"What hospital is that?" Captain Palova seemed to be somewhat off-script.

Matt looked at Maggie, who answered, "She was born in the New Horizons Unit at Southmead Hospital in Bristol."

"Thanks."

Paul noticed Matt's furrowed eyebrows. He deduced Matt was starting to get bothered by the questioning. Paul understood what was happening, and without pressing the push-to-talk, he explained that with all the publicity this would get, they wanted all the information they could get to corroborate the story. Matt was not convinced, but didn't say anything more about it.

"Let's move on," Captain Palova finally said, "You said 'GSM'. What is that?"

"Oh," Maggie replied, "our rescue craft had four coffins all made of myrtle wood. We named it the Good Ship Myrtlewood."

"From when you hit the water until now, did you ever feel your muscles tightening up, or have chest tightness, nausea, muscle twitching, abdominal pain, or diarrhea?"

They both said "No," and Matt added, "except for normal reactions to losing Jenny, swallowing too much salt water, and watching those planes come screaming at us and shooting into the water when we were on the GSM."

"They were shooting at you? Tell us about that."

"There was fire on the water," Matt said. "I guess it was fuel from the plane. After we got on our lifeboat, we felt pulled away from the fire even though the breeze was against us. There was a haze all over the water, like a cloud you could see through. Suddenly two planes flew directly overhead and started shooting into the water."

Maggie held Jenny tight, as if to protect her while she relived the experience.

"At first," Matt continued, "we thought they were going to shoot us. Then we thought they were going to shoot the burning spot, but finally realized they were shooting something farther from us than the fire. The shooting made the same noise as when we were on the plane, except much louder. There was an explosion, and black smoke went up. They did that three times. There were three separate explosions. Is that how many you counted, Maggie?"

"Yes. One, and then two close together. As soon as they shot the third time, they flew away and your Air Force planes chased them. We felt that God was watching over us when they didn't see us. I mean, how could they not see us? Then the Air Force came back, and they didn't see us either."

"Well, that explains the black smoke. Now, one last thing. Tell us what you know about the island."

Matt and Maggie started by briefly recounting Matt's two dreams, the calling of it into existence, the specifications, and waking up with it underneath them. They ended by telling of the coming dirt. Matt added, "We know all about the island, we just don't know where it is."

"You are in the middle of the North Atlantic, more than three miles above what is known as the Sohm Abyssal Plain." Captain Palova checked with his team for further questions, but no one had any apropos to their missions. "That's all for us. We will likely call you again with more questions to satisfy our own curiosity later. Do you have any questions for us?"

Maggie did. "Have you called Britannia Airlines, or Air World Airlines, for that matter, about this? If they're going to come to pick us up, I'd like to talk to them first, about clothes and nappies, and I'd like to give Jenny a bath if possible."

So did Matt. "I imagine you may need to use what we told you, to help in your efforts to find out who shot us down and why. That's fine. But the world will want to know our story, and we'd like to be the ones to tell it. Would that be possible? We don't want to impede your investigation in any way, though."

Captain Palova understood their concerns. "We have been in constant communication with both Air World and BA on several different levels, and will continue to do so. We're not sure how long you'll be on the island. It may be several days before we figure that out."

Matt had one more thing. "Maggie and I called this island up from the bottom of the sea, and therefore we consider this our island. Legally, I don't know how that will work out. We would at least like to be the ones who name it. We haven't decided on a name yet, but we are working on it."

Captain Palova laughed. "Yes, I think that will be entirely possible." He and Lieutenant Colonel Washington talked for a few more minutes, then they both signed off.

Phil Henry spoke first after the radio interview with Matt and Maggie. "That is truly an astounding story those two have. Regardless of your views on how things happen in the universe, however, and I'm not doubting their story for a minute, but the fact is, the island is there, and for our purposes, at least at the moment, how it got there is irrelevant."

"As long as it stays above water!" someone interjected.

"Yes, let's hope so. And a couple things before we move on. It seems the Trillbey infant's foot will be a critical part of their story, but they have no way of obtaining and safeguarding the information at the hospital. It may somehow be invaluable to us, also, to protect it. I will get with my British contact to see what their protocols are. The other thing is the dirt. It seems rather far-fetched, but it would sure lend credence to the rest of their story.

"Now let's talk about our next steps and what we can glean from what we know so far. We need to discuss the apparent connection between the nerve agent and the attack on the plane, the identities of the shooters, possible motives, who has MiGs and where they are being kept, the nerve agent and its ingredients, and the Brazil connection, to name a few. Do we have anything else to ask the Marines on station?"

Everybody else was thinking, so JC jumped in. "We need at least one tank brought back for analysis. Two, if possible. If they were used for fuel, we need to find out the capacity so we can calculate fuel, and therefore distance. There may be manufacturing details that could help in identifying the culprits. Have we heard if the Marines need anything else brought there that would justify the second Stallion?"

"I have spoken to Lieutenant Colonel Washington," replied Captain Palova, "and they will need more chow and water in a couple days. The surface soil is not more than six inches deep in most places, which means they can't bury anything or dig latrines. That will require replacing the portable toilets. They can dribble the contents into the ocean, since the chemicals themselves are eco-friendly. All they'd need is the replacement chemicals.

"He was proposing to do all that with a C-130 air drop, but if we're bringing back the tanks, we need to be able to land. Phil, could you check with the airlines to see what their plans are for bringing back the survivors? If they don't have a plan, we can justify bringing them back, too."

Phil just got the transport he needed for himself and Penny, like he had told her, if the second MH-53K were going to be sent. He finished scribbling several notes. "Yes, but the airlines wouldn't be able to land either. Bob, would your team find it easier to examine the tanks at Camp Lejeune or at your place?"

Bob put down his diet soda. "Our place would definitely be easier, but we could send a truck to Lejeune to pick them up if necessary. Washington Dulles would be a shorter flight for the Stallion, but not by much."

Captain Palova was thinking about how much positive press the military would be getting from all this. "I'll check on the logistics with the Marines. We could send the Stallion tomorrow, with a return flight on Monday."

"Ty Harris here. This isn't my bailiwick within the State Department, but I'm going to let the boss know about this, and recommend we get with the British consulate to figure out ownership of the island. I believe the sooner we stake our claim, the better. I'm talking about sovereign territory rather than personal ownership. To my way of thinking, the first two who landed on it, that is, the survivors, should certainly have the right to personal ownership."

After the radio call, Matt spoke privately to Maggie. "I'm a little uneasy about Jenny's hospital records."

"Do you think I was unwise in telling them about her foot?"

"Oh, no, not at all. I told them, too. It's just that if someone wants to deny your daughter was missing a foot, all they would have to do is make those records disappear. Do you think your mother could help if you could get in touch with her? Maybe she could make copies at the hospital or get spare originals."

"I'll try."

"She needs to hide whatever she gets until the whole world knows about Jenny's foot."

The VTC was still in session, and it would last another hour. Most of the discussion centered around possible motives. A whiteboard replaced Phil's image on his screen, which he used to write down suggestions from the group, annotating each with high, medium, or low, depending on plausibility.

Suggested motives ranged from desire for world domination (low) to lunatic renegades (medium) to retribution against someone or something on the plane or the airlines (high). Drug cartels and exterminating the Jews were ruled out fairly quickly, but Phil wrote them down anyway. Bob McGee said he would check with his teams for any activity along those lines. There were a dozen other suggestions all rated low.

Pedro Santos, who had disappeared from his monitor immediately after the interview with the survivors ended, came back on about thirty minutes later. He reported that he had updated the ambassadors of both the US and Brazil. This prompted those delegations to set up a meeting for 9 a.m. the following morning, Sunday. He also said the US Ambassador wanted Bob McGee to attend the meeting if possible, and could bring his assistant, Harvey Hostetler, if desired.

The meeting was just about to wrap up when Phil, who had left shortly after he finished writing on the whiteboard, reappeared in his monitor. "I've just gotten off the phone with Air World," he said. "The official count is two hundred ninety-one bodies. They have hired a fishing trawler with a refrigeration unit capable of holding the bodies, space for their personal effects and baggage, and any cargo worth salvaging. They will be sending a team of insurance adjusters. Any cargo deemed a total loss will be abandoned in place.

"Air World is assuming the plane itself is a total loss. However, they will eventually recover it so their structural engineers can examine it. They are asking that EOD remain onsite, in case any duds are found during their loading operations. They will be sending three coroners, several engineers and photographers, a small squad of workers, and a chaplain. Air World will also invite reps from the six other countries which lost citizens. They will be leaving Boston tomorrow afternoon, and with good weather, will arrive at the island late afternoon or early evening on Monday."

Ty Harris had a suggestion. "Next time you talk to the airlines, have them bring an American flag and a British flag. Have them take pictures of the flags hoisted up on the island. Then have them send all of us copies. Those might come in handy later."

Captain Palova was concerned for the Marines onsite. "In light of all we've discussed, we will need to do a threat analysis to determine how long the Marines need to remain on station."

"Yes," Phil answered. "I'll be getting there tomorrow, and Lieutenant Colonel Washington and I will discuss that with you after I chat with him. We probably won't know exactly, until we find out how long Air World will take. I can bring some flags."

To the entire group, he said, "I will be sending you updates by secure email. I'll be in the air by the time the Brazil meeting starts, so I'm asking Bob to update you on that. We all have tasks we realistically won't be able to start before Monday. With the holiday on Thursday, this will be a very busy three days. I propose we don't schedule the next VTC yet, but wait until we have something substantive to report. We can give status updates by email, and save the VTC for briefings with Q&As and the like."

That was agreeable to everyone, and the meeting was adjourned.

Matt and Maggie heartily agreed to Paul Washington's suggestion of supper. Meals, Ready to Eat, were new to Maggie.

"If you eat the recommended three MREs per day, you'll gain about four pounds per week," Paul told her.

Paul was about an inch taller than Matt and seemed extremely fit. Either he was able to burn off about four thousand calories a day, or he didn't consume the full allotment.

"I have some catching up to do," she said with a chuckle, "and I'm eating for two. By the way, do you have a phone I can use to call Cheltenham, just north of Bristol? I'd like to let my mum know I'm safe."

"There's not a cell tower within a thousand kilometers of here, but I do have a satellite phone you can use. It connects only to our military phone system, so I'll have to type in a code or two to make an off-net call." He looked at his watch. "By the time we eat, it'll probably be after 8 p.m. in Cheltenham. When we get to the Stallion, tell me your mom's number."

They ate and went back to the helicopter. Maggie told him the number, but had a question. "I know there's an investigation going on. Can I tell her we were shot down, and there's an island?"

"Yes. That's one of the discussions I had with Captain Palova's group. They intend to release the news that the plane was shot down but is now on this island. They will publish a satellite photo of the wreckage and this helicopter, which they have already taken. Don't worry, it will be zoomed out and a little blurry. The intent is to try to flush out the group that shot you down. It will be a shock to them, so they may make a misstep."

Paul had to consult his notebook twice before he could punch in the Cheltenham number. When it started to ring, he handed the receiver to Maggie. She had hoped she could speak to her mum in private, but Paul looked like he was going to stay.

"Hi Mum? It's me, Maggie! I'm safe! … Yes, Jenny too! … Already? Well, they didn't know about any survivors … God saved us! It was a real miracle … Yes, a man named Matt. He's such a wonderful man … No, he's in his sixties. He's … Guess what? God healed Jenny's foot! It's brand new! … Yes, I'm sure! … I just know. Matt helped me know … Guess what else? I'm nursing Jenny! … Yes, that was true until yesterday, but God healed them both … Yes, I know that already. Oh, Mum, there's so much more to tell!"

The tears started to flow, so Matt said to Paul, "Maybe we should give her some time." He started for the door with Jenny.

"Yes," Paul said, and followed him out.

A few minutes later, Maggie came out, wiping her eyes and grinning broadly. "She's very happy for Jenny and me. I told her she didn't know the half of it."

"What was it you knew already?" Matt thought he knew, but didn't want to guess out loud.

Maggie was too proud of her new figure to blush. "She said, 'You know, they make nursing brassieres!'"

Charlotte Trillbey put her phone down and cried. Different tears this time. Then she started to laugh. "Maggie's alive! And Jenny too!" And promptly forgot all the other details.

A few minutes later, she remembered. "Maggie's alive! And she needs me!"

She ran to the kitchen and got a plastic bag, then hastened back to the living room and picked up all the used tissues off the floor, along with two empty tissue boxes. She sat at the heavy oak desk and pulled out a manila folder labeled "Jenny", and leafed through pictures, forms, a newspaper birth announcement, more pictures, a copy of an x-ray, and finally what she was looking for, a small business card. There were two phone numbers under the name of Madelyn Jennings; she dialed the first one.

"Good evening, Southmead Hospital, Maternity Section, Nurse's Station. May I help you?"

"Yes, does Nurse Madelyn Jennings still work there? And is she there tonight?"

"Yes, I'm Madelyn Jennings. Is there something I can help you with?"

"You were so helpful to my daughter and me when my daughter delivered about three months ago. You said if I ever needed any more help to give you a call. I'm Charlotte Trillbey, Maggie's mum."

"Oh, I remember her! She had the little girl who was born with a foot missing. Jennifer. We all fell in love with her. No, it was Jennimoore. How are they doing?"

"Oh, they're doing fine. Maggie's out of town and asked me if I could get some information from the records you have on her there. Would that be possible?"

"Yes. If it's important, you could come now. I get off in about two hours and would be glad to help."

"I would be most obliged. I can be there in about forty-five minutes. I'll see you then."

Her next call was to her friend Alma, who had caller ID and answered on the first ring.

"Oh Charlotte, how are you holding up? Is there anything I can do for you tonight? I'd like to bake you a pie. Would you rather have chocolate or peach?"

"I don't need a pie! I just got a call from Maggie. She and Jenny are safe! She needs me to do something for her, so we're going on a trip. Get ready—I'll pick you up in five."

"Your daughter needs you? Good gracious! Of course, I'll come."

There was little for Alma to learn on the trip to Bristol. "Did she tell you how she got out of the plane? The news said they crashed into the ocean from thirty thousand feet."

"No. She didn't give me any of those details. She did sound happy, though."

"Really? When have you ever heard her sound happy? I guess I'd be happy too, if I were in her shoes."

"Not recently. Back before, maybe she was eleven?"

"Where did she call from? Anything else you can tell me?"

"She didn't say where she was. Must have been close to a cell tower, though. And get this, she said God healed Jenny's foot! That's the reason for our trip. She wants to get before and after pictures."

"Another reason to be happy—Jenny's foot. Something she won't have to deal with later. She's never been too good at dealing with things, from what you've told me. And she wouldn't even tell you who the father is. She needs you! Good gracious, again. But I don't get the part where she said God healed Jenny's foot. What do you suppose that's all about?"

"I don't know. All I know is she really loves that baby. It sure tore her up the first day she had to bring her to childcare."

Charlotte quickly outlined her plan to her friend. There might not be many records, and the hospital might not want to part with any of them. Alma thought for a moment, fingered her amethyst brooch for inspiration, shut her eyes tightly, then helped refine some of the details. They arrived at the nurse's station without much fuss, and Nurse Jennings met them with three manila folders.

"One is the official file. It looks like we just threw everything into a folder in March, intending to sort it out later. As you can see, we are not too busy tonight, and I sorted it while I waited for you. The other two are extras of almost everything in the official file. One is pre-delivery and is mostly ultrasounds and doctors' write-ups, and the other has everything to do with her delivery and x-rays of Jennimoore's right leg and ankle.

"You can have them. Look through both sets, the official file and the other two, and if you need me to make copies of something in the official file, let me know. This is all the information we have."

Charlotte decided she needed to take Nurse Jennings into her confidence. She lowered her voice. "Jenny is about to become world-famous. Did you hear the news about the missing Britannia Airlines flight? Well, Maggie and Jenny were on that flight, but they both survived the crash. And listen to this: God healed Jenny's foot! She's got both feet now."

"Wow! That's brilliant! Tell me how this happened."

"Maggie didn't tell me that part, but she's concerned someone will try to disprove that God healed Jenny. I don't know why they'd do that, but she's afraid someone will try to steal Jenny's medical records here. I wanted to get copies of everything, but it looks like what you're giving me is much better than that."

"Don't worry, Mrs. Trillbey. People can't just come in here and look at records, unless they're the police. And I can't approve anyone to take them out of this area."

Charlotte and Alma looked through the files and requested a copy of only one item, a doctor's health certification.

"Thank you very much, Nurse Jennings. You've been so helpful a thousand times over. One last thing—please don't tell anyone we were here or that you gave anything to us."

"Okay. And when Maggie gets back home, please have her bring Jenny in. We would all like to see her new foot."

On the trip back to Cheltenham, Charlotte remembered the man. "She said there was another survivor, Mack. I tried to wheedle more information out of her about him, but she said she wasn't interested. She told me he was older than me. Anyway, when we get back, we need to make two equal packets and we'll each take one. That way, you'll have something in case they make Nurse Jennings talk and I end up getting bumped off. Just hide it out of plain sight."

"Okay. And I'm glad we didn't have to use our plan. I would have felt like a lunatic or a spy, or maybe both."

Paul left the survivors alone in order to take care of business with his men. Matt got two chairs from the helicopter while Maggie found a shady spot next to the Stallion. Matt retrieved the largest piece of coffin liner he could find. They put Jenny in the middle of it on her back, and let her wiggle around on it while they chatted.

"How is your mom? Or is it mum?"

"Mum's the word!" She laughed. "You know, we don't use that word much to mean 'silent'. And for me, it's another word that's the opposite of itself. At least until yesterday."

"Oh?"

"Yes. Chatter, chatter, chatter! How I wished my mum would be quiet sometimes. After I went off to the university, we didn't get along well at all. When we were together, it seemed she found fault with everything about me. It got to be unbearable, so I rarely went to see her. Looking back, she was probably right about nagging me so much. I was pretty miserable. But now, I want her to know Jesus like I know him. I can tell my whole attitude toward her is changing."

"That's wonderful, but be careful."

Maggie leaned forward in her chair. "Be careful?"

"Yes, the old Maggie will try to kick the new Maggie out of the way and take over. It's the old thought patterns that need to be replaced. Your attitude is changing, which is good, but it will be tested immediately. Your mother will doubt that the change is permanent, and she may put you to the test herself. Just love her and share your life with her. Especially the part that started yesterday, even before the crash, but also the things that made you who you became on your way up. Of course, there are things you don't need to share, and you'll know what they are. I expect, when she sees that you are really changed, she will become your friend and greatest supporter. Except for me, of course." He grinned.

"Well, that's as it should be. You're my dad after all!"

"Well, as your dad, let me counsel you: if you blow it and the old Maggie says or does something, be quick to apologize."

"Okay, that may convince her quicker than anything else."

They spent a few minutes quietly enjoying each other's company. Maggie decided to bring up something she had started to wonder about. "Matt, I've been listening to myself talk."

"Yes?"

"I sound so … gushy. Juvenile, like a pre-teen. Like I have no filter when expressing my emotions, especially when I'm telling you how wonderful you are, and have been, to Jenny and me. You must think I'm pathetic!"

"No, not at all! I'm really delighting in your candor. What has happened, and you don't realize it, is that you have become completely unguarded, totally unpretentious, with me. This is wonderful, a gift from God for both of us to enjoy for a time. Something died in your emotions when you were twelve, and God has brought it back to life. Yesterday, the thing that died restarted at twelve years old, and has been hurtling forward since then. You've entrusted me with all your secrets, and you are trying out your newfound emotions on me. You have a lot of catching up to do!"

Matt picked a small piece of shell out of the dried mud with his shoe, and continued. "We have been very intensely personal with each other, and you have deemed me so trustworthy with your entire being that you thought it fitting for me to become your father. Don't worry, you won't behave this way with anyone else, and soon enough, you'll be the right age in everything."

"Thank you for that. I was beginning to think there was something wrong with me."

"Just relax and enjoy what God is doing in you. From my point of view, it's really beautiful."

After a few minutes, Matt started thinking about the dirt. "This looks like a desert, Maggie. I wonder how and when the dirt will come, and how this island will hold up in a storm. I've heard of these massive dust storms in the Middle East. Perhaps that's what God will use, but it will need some rain, too, to stabilize the dirt."

"I think the dirt coming will tie the knot in our story of The Boy. We told the intelligence group about the dirt coming. They must have thought we were completely bonkers in predicting the dirt. But when it comes, Matt, it should prove to them that we were the ones calling the island into existence, because we said it in advance.

"Paul said he wants to hear the whole story. I'd like us to tell it to him and to as many of his men who want to hear it. Matt, if you don't mind, I'd like to tell the whole story, with your help from time to time, especially your dreams and messages from God."

Matt looked at her in amazement. "That's a great idea. Are you up to it?"

"Yes, I believe so. I'm eager to tell how good God has been to me, to us, and wants to be to them. I feel deep down that I will be telling the story a lot when I get back home, so this will be practice for me. I'm a teacher, you know."

"You're going to do wonderfully. Just remember your audience. You'll be speaking to only men."

After a few minutes, Jenny let it be known that she was hungry. Matt got up to prepare another diaper, but Maggie said, "Wait, there's something I want to show you."

She hiked her shirt up all the way under her vest to give Jenny access to dinner. "Look, Matt, at the scars!"

There was the thinnest of lines going across, and the stitch marks had reduced to mere dots. "I noticed it the last time I fed her."

"Nice! Your body waited sixteen years to close itself up. It was waiting for your soul to be healed and the curse to be broken!"

Paul Washington was finished with his chores and joined them. Aside from the EOD teams still toiling away, it was quiet. "We have some time now," he said, "and I'd like to hear the whole story, or as much as you want to tell."

Maggie said, "We'd like to tell it to as many as want to hear. God did some amazing things, and I'm sure your men would benefit from hearing how wonderful he has been to us. Would that be possible?"

"Absolutely! I'll round up everyone who's free. I'll get you two chairs and we can all sit in the tail of the Stallion. There's enough work going on that we'll have to have two groups, though. I sure wouldn't mind hearing it twice, but are you up for it?"

"Oh, yes," Maggie replied, "that would be great."

While Paul was gathering his men, Matt prayed for Maggie, asking God to give her confidence and wisdom, and an open heart and mind to those who would be listening. Paul came back and arranged the area where they would be sitting. "They'll be along in a few minutes. Here's some water. Take as long as you wish."

Their voices preceded them as the men approached. Boisterous and animated language, punctuated by cursing and vulgarity. Lieutenant Colonel Washington, looking somewhat distressed, started to go out to quiet them.

"I know all those words," Maggie let him know, "and more besides. And I used to use them with regularity." She looked at Matt. "But not in front of the children."

He went out anyway, spoke a single word, and there was immediate silence.

There were nine Marines besides the pilots and Lieutenant Colonel Washington, who introduced Matt and Maggie. "Men, these are the survivors of the airplane when it was shot down. Mr. Matt Carven and Ms. Maggie Trillbey. I'll let Ms. Trillbey introduce her daughter. They have quite a story to tell, and I thought you all might be interested. Mr. Carven?"

"Thanks. Please call us Matt and Maggie. I'm going to let Maggie tell most of the story, but I want to let you know why I was even on this flight. Within the past year, my daughter and her family were all killed in a flood on a mission trip to Costa Rica. A month after that, my son and his family were killed in an automobile accident in Arizona. A month later, my wife died of a burst brain aneurysm."

Matt started to choke up, but then went on, "As you can imagine, I was devastated, numb, and pretty much unable to function. Things happened so fast that I couldn't even grieve properly before the next thing came. I was hardly able to hang on, but God was hanging on to me. He provided me some battle buddies who got me up and made me walk. I was feeling pretty useless, without any purpose, until God spoke to my heart and told me he had a job for me to do in England. I immediately got a ticket for that airplane out there, and here I am."

One of the Marines asked, "What was the job?"

"I didn't know then, and I still don't know. I got the distinct impression I would find out when I got there."

Another, whom Matt recognized as the one using the loudest vulgarity, said, "So God told you to get on that plane? He knew it was going to be shot down. What kind of God is that?"

"He's a God I have found to be infinitely trustworthy."

"So he saved you and the woman and the baby. Why didn't he save everybody?"

"He could have, but he didn't. He could have gotten all the people off the plane before it sank. He could have made all the bullets miss or bounce off, he could have made the attacking planes crash upon takeoff, he could have prevented whoever it was from obtaining bullets, and more, but he didn't do any of those things."

"Well, what makes you so special?"

"Nothing. There's nothing at all about me that would make God choose me over anybody else. He does what he wants. Our place is to salute and say, 'Yes, sir!' I have found he has a plan for each of us—for me, for Maggie, for you—that if he told us in advance, would make us want to sit on the sidelines and let it happen to someone else. Do you know you're not here by accident?"

"I didn't want to come. I don't want to be here. My leave got canceled, so I had to come."

"I'm sorry that happened. What is your name?"

"Lance Corporal Wilson."

"Thank you, Lance Corporal Wilson. Now I'd like to turn it over to

Maggie. We didn't know each other before yesterday, and how we met will be in her part of the story. Maggie?"

"Thank you, Matt. As I start, I'd like to introduce my daughter. Jenny is about three months old. When she was born, she was missing a foot. During pregnancy, an amniotic band wrapped around her ankle and basically squeezed off her foot."

Maggie turned Jenny around on her lap, undid the blanket, and showed them both feet. "The other thing you need to know about Jenny is that she did not survive the crash. She drowned. But that is part of our story."

It took about five minutes for the charm of her accent to wear off, about the same amount of time it took them to process the differences in pronunciation. All in all, an even trade.

Maggie handed Jenny to Matt, then started her story at the point of getting the plane ticket in the raffle, intending to show how God was taking care of her and Matt every step of the way. The listeners didn't understand why she left first class to go to economy.

"I didn't really understand it myself. There was a mysterious drawing in my inner being, and I just had to go. It wasn't Matt, because he didn't know I'd be coming back to see him until God told him. He just happened to have an empty seat next to him, and if you look in the plane at my first-class seat, you'll see it's blown apart."

Matt was enjoying Maggie as she told their story, and became aware of another voice. The voice. His voice, speaking directly to Matt's spirit. "It's a delight to listen to your daughter, your pupil."

"Yes, Father," Matt's spirit answered. "I'm in awe of how much you have done in her so quickly."

"And yet, she is about to encounter something for which she is totally unprepared."

Matt was in anguish. "We prayed for wisdom and a heart to love the people. What did I not do?"

"It will take more than wisdom, son."

Matt clearly saw himself tossing the bottle filled with seawater back into the ocean. He heard his words to Maggie again, and realized what was missing. "Father, please show Maggie what you are doing in heaven. Please send your Holy Spirit to reveal himself however he wants to, for your purposes. Let her hear your words and see what you would show her, I ask in Jesus's name."

Maggie had gotten to the part where she had found herself in the water without Jenny, where she panicked and got hysterical. How Matt had told her the promise from God that she would nurse Jenny. How this strange sensation called hope was starting to make itself known.

Lance Corporal Wilson spoke up. "I can see your daughter is healthy. She has both feet. How do I know you're not just making all this up? I don't think God, if there is one, would do that."

The other Marines, sitting cross-legged on the floor of the giant helicopter, became a little fidgety. They noticed their leader maintaining his relaxed attitude, so they settled down.

Maggie was not taken aback. "There is plenty of proof that Jenny was missing a foot. X-rays, ultrasounds, photos taken when she was born. People who have seen her, eyewitnesses. Unfortunately, we don't have those with us. And of course there's a God. He did all these wonderful things for me, and I didn't even know anything about him. The reason I'm telling my story, is to help you believe, too."

"No! I cannot believe!" Lance Corporal Wilson got louder and his hands clenched into fists. "And you claim God speaks to you. Do you expect me to believe that?"

Matt marveled at Maggie's calmness. Lieutenant Colonel Washington looked like he was about to intervene, but Matt quietly held up his hand and lightly shook his head. Let her handle it.

Maggie replied, "Yes, and he is speaking to me right now."

"Is he telling you what a jerk I am?" His voice echoed in the cavernous belly of the helicopter.

"No, he is not mentioning you at all. He is telling me about a woman named Rosilia Burkett, who is dying of brain cancer."

Lance Corporal Wilson suddenly looked stricken. "That's my mother! How did you know about the cancer?" Tears started coming to his eyes.

"Now he is showing me a picture. It's a scene of you, screaming at him. You love your mother, don't you, Juan?"

"Yes, my mother is Rosilia Wilson Burkett. My father died and she remarried. She is all I have. I love her dearly. I'd do anything for her. I asked God to heal her, but he never did. I begged. I pleaded. I prayed to all the saints. She just got worse and worse. Why are you doing this to me? I got the news about her being on her deathbed. I wanted to go see her, but my leave got cancelled. I should have gone AWOL."

"We didn't know!" "If you had only said something!" "Is it too late?" Evidently, no one in his unit knew anything about this; it was a burden he had not shared with anyone.

"Juan," Maggie said gently, "you said you would do anything for her."

"Did God tell you my name was Juan? Yes, I said that and meant it. I did scream at God. He's the only hope she had. He just ignored her. I told him he should take me and let her live. He didn't even listen to me."

"Juan, God is showing me two pictures. In one, there is a pleasant-looking lady wearing a green and brown smock. The side of her head is missing, and mush is dripping from it into a pan. Her eyes are looking in two different directions. In the other, the same lady is there, smiling and looking very alive. God is saying you may choose one of those two pictures, but there is a cost."

"What if I don't pick one?"

"Then the first picture will just happen naturally. By not picking, you have really chosen the first picture. This is an opportunity God is giving you to change pictures."

"How can I know God would do this? What is the cost?"

"This is all about trusting God to do something we are incapable of doing ourselves. The cost is very high, and you can't pay it. But God has a question for you, and before you answer it, I want you to listen to more of my story. Then I'll ask you for your answer. You see, I screamed at God, too, and said the same thing you said."

Juan gulped. "What was that? And what is the question?"

"When I realized Jenny was gone, I got frantic and panicky, and something way down deep inside me screamed at God, that he should have taken me instead. Here's the question: He is saying to you, 'Are you really willing to die so your mother can live?' He asked me the same question about Jenny, and I was in agony about how to answer."

"I just got back from Afghanistan a couple months ago," Lance Corporal Wilson said. "We saw combat there. Every Marine has asked himself that question about his fellow Marines. We always answer 'Yes, we would,' but we always wonder if we would. We hope that in the heat of battle, our instinct would make us do the right thing. But right now, there is no heat of battle. I don't understand how me dying would make my mother live."

"That wasn't the question. It was God's question, not mine, and he is asking, would you be willing to trade places with your mother?"

"That's not fair!"

"No, it's not fair. It's not fair that your mum got cancer. It's not fair that hundreds of people are dead in that airplane out there. It's not fair that Jenny died, and you might think it's certainly not fair that Jenny is alive now. But please listen to the next part of our story."

Maggie paused, giving Juan a chance to speak if he desired. He sat quietly, wiping away tears, so she continued.

"I didn't understand why, but I felt compelled to answer the question that Matt was asking on God's behalf. Like you, Juan, I tried to think of a way out. I wondered, if I traded places with Jenny, maybe I could watch her grow up from heaven. Matt asked me why I thought I'd go there, and I told him I thought everyone went there. But they don't. Hell is real, and some do go there. Deep down, we all realize God's standards are very high and we don't measure up. Adam and Eve blew it, and the whole human race has suffered the consequences ever since. It's part of our very nature to refuse to meet the standards."

She looked over the group of Marines, took a sip of water, and adjusted herself on her chair.

"I can tell you, I didn't measure up for sure. It was torture, trying to decide. In the end, even though my love for Jenny was so strong, that wasn't the reason I said yes, I would trade places with her. Rather, there was something deep within me telling me to just trust God, even though I didn't deserve anything good for the life I'd lived. I didn't really know what that would mean, but once I decided, that was my final answer. I started to cry, even though I knew I made the right choice. When I looked up, Matt was smiling, even gleeful. He said that was so much the right choice. He said, 'This is what God said, "Tell her I did the same for her, and she is worth it!" '

"I said, 'Huh?' and he told me how he, God, died so I might live, even though he's God. How he had to create a human body for himself to live in, to meet all the standards in spite of the temptations, and for that human body to die a horrendous death. And how that death was acceptable to God, to pay the price we couldn't pay. That human body has a name, and I heard some of you saying it on your way here—Jesus.

"He died and was buried, but God raised him from death to show that his death was acceptable as payment. Now it's possible for us to have a new nature, the one Adam and Eve were created with. And because Jesus paid the price for all people, God made him Lord of all creation."

Maggie paused, letting her words sink in. Wow, God, she thought, this is amazing! She glanced over at Matt, who smiled and nodded. She continued, telling of God's desire for people to have that new nature, and of the new relationship God wanted with the people he had created. Of his desire to lead them in fulfilling things rather than destructive things like she had been doing all her life. Of his desire for them to choose life and leave death behind. Of his desire for them to trust him.

The question was still gnawing at Juan. "I would like to see my mother live," he said. "I want to choose that picture. But how would that work?"

Maggie looked over at Matt again, as if to say, "Jump in if you think I need help." Then she answered.

"Juan, it's a matter of trust. Trusting God to do what he said. In order to get this new nature full of life and peace and joy, the old nature must die so the new nature can replace it. This is what Jesus's death enables God to do, to make that trade. Do you trust God?"

"As you've been talking, things have been making more and more sense. And I see in you what you're talking about. The things I said to you didn't get you upset. I want that new nature. It's been getting stronger and stronger as you spoke. But I keep thinking about my mother, too."

"Would you want this new nature even if your mother was not in the condition she's in?"

"Yes, how can I do that?"

Maggie looked around. "Would anyone else like God's forgiveness and new life?"

Several hands went up. One Marine took the opportunity to leave and go outside. Lieutenant Colonel Washington didn't stop him.

Maggie was trying to remember how Matt had put it. "It would be a secret transaction, just between you and God. You would have to die. Don't worry about the death part, though. You will not even notice it. I didn't. But you will surely notice the coming alive part. He will change your life forever!

"First, though, you need to know what your part of the transaction is. You must believe in your innermost being that God raised Jesus from the dead, since that is the evidence that the price is paid. This is not the same as believing it in your mind, since then you would have to have proof of some sort. This kind is believing with no proof. God himself, by his spirit, will provide the proof as you say the words. And you must receive him, Jesus, as the master and ruler of your life, since God made him to be that. If you understand your part and are still willing, then you are ready."

They all were ready.

Maggie continued, "It's a secret transaction, but it starts out in public, with your words. Don't worry, God will help you with the words. He's been calling you, getting you ready for this moment, so talk to God now."

There was a low babble as four sets of words went up to heaven. Then silence. Maggie, Matt, and Paul were watching as joy slowly settled on four faces. All four were smiling when they finally opened their eyes.

Juan Wilson spoke for all of them. "Wow!" Then he added, "I think I know what to do now. God, I choose life for my mother. Please heal her of this cancer. Thank you, Jesus."

Lieutenant Colonel Washington wanted a brief break for his men. "Come with me, Lance Corporal Wilson. Let's go call your mother!"

They all gathered back in the Stallion for Maggie to continue her story. Before she could start, however, Lance Corporal Wilson stood up with a story of his own. "They were trying to get hold of me. They wanted to tell me there was nothing they could do. They had taken her off life support. She went into cardiac arrest twice. Each time, her heart just started beating again. Her vital signs were going down really fast. She had only minutes to live. Suddenly, right before I called, everything became stable. They couldn't believe it. They said it was a miracle. I said, 'I know!' They're keeping her in a coma for now, to see what happens next."

After the cheering and wonder died down, Maggie asked Matt to tell about the dreams and messages he had gotten before they exited the plane. Then she told about the shark bringing Jenny back, God giving her the ability to nurse, Jenny coming alive and her foot being healed, and finally about calling up the island and how it rose up under them.

Lieutenant Colonel Washington also had part of the story to add. "There are so many supernatural things that happened to you two over the last day and a half." Then turning to the group of Marines, he continued, "Here's one I'd like to add. There is a group of military and civilians, very high up in the terrorism investigators in our government, who were in a video meeting to look into this plane being shot down. They were watching the island with a very powerful satellite camera. The satellite was more than two hundred miles above them. As soon as the camera moved to focus on these two, they immediately turned to it and waved!

"The group in Washington DC was stunned into silence for several minutes. But them waving at the satellite allowed their pictures to be taken, and compared to the passport photos of everybody on the plane. When we went to pick them up earlier, I asked them how they knew to wave at the satellite, and do you know what they said?" No one did, so he told them, "Matt said, 'God spoke to Maggie and told her!'

"There's one thing I'd like to ask Matt and Maggie before we finish up," he went on, "and that is about the dirt. You've said several times there will be dirt. Is the dried white mud what you're talking about?"

Matt answered, "No, in the hilly areas, and in a lot of the flat areas, there will be a covering of good old brown dirt up to almost a foot thick. We don't know how that would be possible, or when it would happen. Perhaps God is waiting to bring it, in order to show that this didn't occur by accident, since we are telling of this before it comes.

"You see, I suppose it would be possible to imagine a scenario in which the island suddenly appeared because of natural causes, and Maggie and I got here before everyone else and took a tour of the island before you flew in. But this dirt will be just as supernatural as the rest of our story. God is not finished yet!"

Maggie added, "It won't be just plain sand, either. There will be life in the dirt, things starting to grow right away."

LtCol Washington thanked the two of them. There was a short round of applause from the Marines. Matt gave Jenny back to Maggie, and said, "It looks like we will be around for several days. If anyone has further questions, please come ask us."

In a small parlor in a large city on the other side of the world, two men were discussing their options. The project had not been progressing according to plan.

"Rishaan, I just learned they found the plane."

Rishaan Chabra's teacup clattered back into its saucer. "Ridiculous! They sank the plane in five thousand meters of water. The search boats could not even have gotten there yet. The pilots told Maria there was nothing left on the surface."

"Yes, all that is true. But it seems an island rose over five thousand meters off the bottom and brought everything to the surface. The plane—all its parts—as well as most of the baggage and the three fuel tanks they blew up. The island is over two hundred fifty square kilometers. How could this have happened?"

"I don't know, Dasya. How do you know this?"

Dasya turned on the television. The story was on three of the four news channels. He stopped at the one showing a distant picture of the site, perhaps from an aircraft or satellite zoomed in as close as possible. The front of the plane was separated from the fuselage, which was lying upside-down on the white surface of the island. Four round shiny blobs were scattered nearby. A short distance away, a helicopter sat in the middle of a jet-black circle, barely visible in its camouflage. "Look how well our pilots did."

They sat watching the photograph for a few minutes, thinking. The newscaster was offering all kinds of opinions and conjectures, and little in the way of facts. Finally, Dasya offered an opinion of his own. "Only your God could do this. Unless there is another explanation, our project is doomed. We should abort now while we have that option."

"No, damn it! God directed us to this project! I believe God is simply testing our resolve."

Dasya rubbed his bushy eyebrows with hands as thin as the rest of his frame. "You are the only one who heard that from God. I am just saying what my eyes and mind are telling me."

Rishaan was not ready to give up. "We are still acquiring the materials. The tanks are to be delivered soon. We will see what the world does in the meantime. If we are not discovered, we will take that as a sign. If we are discovered, we can abort. We meet with the others soon, and we will discuss this again then. Dasya, do you still believe in our project?"

At the beginning, there had been a little doubt in Dasya's mind. The more he considered the project, the more that doubt diminished. Dasya was now fully committed to the project, and didn't need God telling him what to do. To Dasya, if there were a God, he was probably far away and very angry. "Oh, yes. Absolutely! It's the only way, really, and we are the ones to do it."

Darkness was descending as Paul took Matt and Maggie aside after the second group of Marines started leaving the Stallion. "I just found out they want to examine those tanks back at Langley, so they'll be sending another Stallion to get them tomorrow, if they are clean enough. There are other things they want, too, like samples of the mud, water from the river, and several pieces of baggage. An FBI team will be aboard to start their investigation here. One of the two Stallions will be leaving Monday morning, and I'm told the three of you will be on it. I will be sending Lance Corporal Wilson back also."

"Wow, that's good news!" Maggie said, hugging Jenny tightly. "It will be good to get back."

"Yes," Matt agreed, "and tomorrow I'd like to make a call or two on your satellite phone, if that would be okay. One business and one personal."

"Sure. Just let me know when."

"Okay. Oh, do you have a Bible with you? I'd like to show Maggie a few things."

Paul reached into his backpack and pulled out a plastic zipper bag with a small camouflaged book in it. "Here's the New Testament, psalms, and proverbs for you, Maggie, courtesy of the Gideons. I always carry some extra ones, for troops who need one. I have four more to give away, too.

"Thank you for sharing your stories with my men, especially the first group. We train our Marines to be the most feared warriors in the world. You might think showing emotion is somehow inconsistent with that, but our fierceness in battle is prompted partly by the fierceness of the loyalty we have for each other. From the day we enlist or are commissioned, until the day we earn the right to be called a Marine, we are taught honor, courage, and commitment. It lasts throughout our careers. Passion, properly directed, is a good thing."

The evening was clear, and the mud had hardened to the extent that the Marines not on duty all elected to sleep under the stars, except for the two pilots. They, along with Matt and Maggie, pitched their camp inside the Stallion. Matt laid out the two coffin pads putting Maggie next to a wall, with a used MRE case between the two, into which Maggie was arranging the velvet coffin liners as a bed for Jenny.

Sleeping arrangements complete, Matt said to Maggie, "Bring Jenny, and let's go look at the stars while you feed her."

"Okay, good. I want to ask you about what went on with the second group of Marines."

They walked a short way from the helicopter. When they were out of earshot, they sat down on the dried ground facing each other. A warm soothing breeze played with them. Maggie distractedly smoothed Jenny's hair, her own hair, and Jenny's velvet covering. Matt knew she was disappointed about something, and even knew what it was, but wanted to wait until she started nursing her daughter and was able to put her thoughts in order. It was warm, like it had been the previous evening. After they had enjoyed the stars for several minutes, Maggie began telling Matt what was bothering her.

"That first group was great! I could tell God was showing me brilliant things, words and pictures and just what to say. And four Marines gave themselves to Jesus. It was so easy. It really felt wonderful. Then the second group came, and everything went just the opposite. They all seemed squirmy, some even bored. They were polite enough, and seemed to appreciate our story, but I felt like I was walking uphill the whole time. I was expecting things to be easier the second time. What happened? I got the distinct feeling I disappointed Jesus somehow."

"I'm glad this happened. I could sense your distress, and you did a good job of not showing it."

Maggie was on the verge of tears. "What? How could you be glad this happened to me?"

"The second time you told the story, it was just as good, if not better, than the first time. So what was the difference, and why was I glad? I was glad that it happened to you while I was around to explain it. The same thing happened to me, where I felt I let the Lord down after pouring my heart into the story I told. Only nobody was there to help me understand. What happened was inevitable, because you have to understand how the story works."

"What do you mean? We have a wonderful story of God's goodness and love, and we were simply telling it."

"Yes, indeed. And why were you telling it?"

"Why was I telling it? We were both telling it."

"Yes, but why? One day, you will be telling the story by yourself. Why?"

Maggie swallowed hard, trying to get rid of the lump forming in her throat. "Oh, I see." She thought for a moment before answering. "Because I want them to know Jesus like I know him."

"Yes, that's right. And when they didn't receive him like you received him, you blamed yourself."

"Yes, I did."

"Do you know what that tells me? Think about it."

She thought about it. "No, what?"

"It tells me that for the first group, you gave yourself the credit."

Maggie opened her mouth to speak, but thought better of it, and waited for Matt to continue.

"Who did all the work in them, to draw them, to call to them as we spoke? To convince their hearts of God's trustworthiness? Of his desire for them?"

"The same one who drew me, who called to me, who received me! Oh, Matt, you never took any of the credit, I realize that now. Oh, Lord, I'm so sorry!"

"Maggie, look at me! I learned this exact same lesson the exact same way. Our job is just to tell the story. The rest is up to him."

"God's Holy Spirit."

"Yes!"

"I feel like such a dunce right now."

"You oughtn't to. That feeling doesn't come from God. I can tell you, he is incredibly proud of you."

"He is? After what I just did?"

"Yes, absolutely! Look, in about a year, Jenny will take her first step or two. You'll be so proud. You'll cheer and congratulate her and call your mom. Then she'll try to take another step and fall right smack down on her butt. How will you think about her then?"

"I get it. I'll still be proud. I'll lift her up, give her a big hug, and help her try again."

"Of course you will. Did you know that's why God lets us be parents, so we'll understand how he is as our father?"

"I'm so glad he chose you to be my dad."

"I'm so glad we added 'nurture' to my vow. Oh, I almost forgot. Just before you finished with the second group, I was thinking about your dream. I think I was mistaken about Jenny."

"Oh?"

"I told you I thought her being an adult meant that she was mature enough in God's sight to be a help in your ministry. I'm beginning to realize that when God healed her foot, that in itself is proving to be a vital part of the story."

"Yes, that will be especially true for the people who saw her missing the foot."

"I'm also getting a clearer picture about the three different types you rescued. Remember, they were all dead. A life preserver is for saving people's lives, so in a spiritual dream it may represent a member of the clergy. The empty bottles may represent people who have never heard anything of God's plan, and the bottles filled with the brown goo may be people that are full of untruths about God's plan.

"The writing may be something that is preventing them from responding like you did, because of a vow they made or a lie they believed or something else. We need to ask God to start working even now, in the hearts of those who will hear our story, when we each tell it and when we tell it together. And to give us the wisdom to tell it however it will best serve those we tell."

Just after midnight, about an hour after Madelyn Jennings went off and Abigail Hammond came on at the Southmead Hospital New Horizons Mother and Baby Unit, a police detective and another man came to the nurse's station of the maternity section.

"Hullo, Constable Morton! What brings you out tonight? Something I can help you with?"

"Evening, Miss Hammond." He showed her his credentials. "I'm here escorting Mr. Smith from Her Majesty's Security Service. I am vouching for him, as he has worked with our department before."

"You didn't have to show me your badge. I've seen you around enough that I know your favorite brand of tea."

Mr. Smith offered his badge as well. Abigail took it and checked his face against the picture, looked at the identifying information, and handed it back.

The night nurse, a plump, middle-aged woman with curly graying hair, was used to visitors and wanted to keep this as short as possible. "Are you here to see a newborn, or is MI-5 making an official visit?"

"I need to see the records on a Jennimore Trillbey, who was born here about three months ago."

Abigail got the file. When she brought it out, she wondered what their interest was.

"Can't say much about it."

Mr. Smith elaborated a little, though, while he was leafing through the contents. "Did you see on the news about the Britannia Airlines flight that crashed into the ocean? Jennimore and her mum were on that flight and survived the crash. The mum is claiming that God protected them and also healed Jennimore's foot. The service is concerned that there is really no other explanation, especially if the foot is whole. They want to prevent someone from trying to discredit the mother, Rachel Trillbey, by eliminating any proof that there was a missing foot. So they sent me to get the records for safekeeping."

"I'm sorry," the nurse replied, "but I cannot approve anyone taking the records from here."

Mr. Smith glared at the woman behind the counter. "Who can approve it? Are they here now?"

"The section chief is over in the main building. Would you like me to call him? He is also a doctor, and he may be in clinic or surgery."

"In clinic? Or surgery? It's after midnight! They don't schedule those things after midnight, now, do they? Yes, call him right now!"

"He's on duty in Emergency this evening. I wish we could schedule emergencies, but we can't." She moved the file from the counter to the desk while she made the call. Yes, he was free. Yes, he knew the rules. Yes, he would be right over.

Mr. Smith explained his purpose to Dr. Patterson, who gave his approval but insisted an inventory of the file be made and kept in the records room.

"Would a list be okay?" Mr. Smith asked. "It looks like those x-rays and ultrasounds won't copy too well."

"Yes, that's the procedure." Nurse Hammond was being very thorough. "We have a form to fill out with the list, the approving official, Dr. Patterson's signature, and your signature as receiving the file. I'll give you a copy. Then we'll put everything in this specially marked medical records envelope and give it to you. I'll need the address where the file will be going and your phone number in case we need access to the records. I'll need to make a photocopy of your badge."

The list was made, the photocopying was done, the file was packaged up, and the form was signed. Constable Morton and Mr. Smith departed and Dr. Patterson went back to the main building, leaving Abigail Hammond alone and wondering what this world was coming to.

Why does everything happen at night, after bedtime, Jacob Strauss asked himself, on duty at K103 in the Gulf of Mexico. He had heard about the plane and the island on the news, and Jimmy had thrown in some more information. He decided to keep track of the weather in the vicinity of the island, which was starting to be called Sohm Island based on its location in the North Atlantic Ocean. He had set his weather-tracking programs to the island's coordinates. This allowed him to track Doppler radar, temperature gradients, and air density. With no weather station on the island, he couldn't track atmospheric pressure, which would have been helpful for hurricane reporting.

At 11 p.m. on Saturday night, June 29, Jacob checked one last time before bed. Strange, there was a storm brewing on the radar, but not over the island. The monitor was programmed to zoom out if an intense storm were discovered in another part of the world. Right then, the southwest portion of the Sahara Desert was centered in the monitor.

Sand storm! This was more exciting than baby-sitting the weather over the island, he thought. He reset the computers to track the storm, and decided to brush up on the NOAA Sand and Dust Storm protocols in the morning, since entry-level personnel did not receive much SDS training. Only three more days here, he reminded himself as he headed to bed.

On Sunday, June 30, at 6 a.m. sharp, the US Marine Corps MH-53K King Stallion lifted off from its pad at Camp Lejeune, North Carolina, for the six-hour ride over the Atlantic. Penny Hasid had taken the FBI courier flight from Chicago to Washington Dulles Airport, which continued to Camp Lejeune after picking up Phil Henry and his gear.

"It's good to see you again, Penny," he said when he met her at Dulles. "Dusty Mae has been telling me good things about you."

"Thanks! At first, I thought she was too hard on us, but now I appreciate it. It was good to see JC again, too. I want to pick your brain, but JC said don't be a pest."

"Pick away, at least for the next hour," he said. "The helicopter will be fairly noisy. I hope you brought something to read."

At Camp Lejeune, Phil and Penny were joined by a coroner, six armed Marines, a number of various-sized crates and boxes, and tanks of diesel fuel strapped to pallets.

Phil was right, Penny thought, even with noise-cancelling headphones, six hours of this is going to be tough.

It was Sunday morning. Matt and Maggie had finished off the MREs they had started the night before, and Maggie had fed Jenny. They were sitting close together in the shade of the mammoth helicopter as the Marines went about their business. Jenny was happily wiggling around and cooing on the two coffin pads they had joined together. Matt opened the Bible Paul had given Maggie the night before, and was explaining what they now held in their hands.

"The Bible is divided into the Old Testament and the New Testament. What Paul gave you is just the New Testament and some of the poetry and wisdom from the Old Testament. The Old and New Testaments together are what God wants you to know about him and his kingdom. It starts at the creation of the world and ends at the end of the world.

"As you read it, God will speak to you, to your spirit and to your mind. It is the primary way the Holy Spirit of God will speak to you, although as you have already found, he will speak to you other ways as well. It's an amazing book, and if there is something you don't understand or need help with, ask God first, then ask others, like me."

"Thanks, Matt. I've been thinking about this a lot since last night, like when I was nursing Jenny before everyone woke up. When my friend in college took me to her Bible group, they would open up to random places and talk about it. Where should I start?"

"Start at the beginning of the New Testament, at the Gospel of Matthew. Just read straight through. If you have a question, either ask right then or wait, because a lot of questions will be answered later on as you read. When we get back, we'll find a bookstore and I'll help you get a good complete

Bible."

Later on, Paul came by to let them know the EOD teams were almost finished. "When they're done," he said, "they will want to blow up a lot of duds. I thought I should get permission from the owners of this island. What say you two?"

Maggie was busy reading and was quite oblivious to Paul's presence, so Matt answered for them both. "Yes, that would be fine. Would it be possible for them to blow them up near the edge? That way, if the explosion causes a big crack in the basalt, we won't be in any danger here."

Paul left with that suggestion. Matt tapped Maggie on the shoulder to get her attention. "I'm taking Jenny for a walk to see the sights," he said, and looked around. It was flat, white, and featureless in every direction except toward the plane, which was still off-limits.

He had an idea for the next morning; if it were clear overnight, he would take Maggie to a spot where they could see the ocean and the sun coming up over the horizon, on their last day on the island. He got Jenny's carry-sling and a strip of pink and gold velvet and headed east. He continued until he could stoop down to Maggie's height and see the ocean above the white of the dried mud, and tied the velvet to one of the ubiquitous potato-rocks.

Maggie was waiting for him when he got back. "I have some questions," she announced.

"Great!" Matt said. "You may have more questions than I have answers, but after one of us changes Jenny, we'll talk!"

They would talk until the sun was overhead, at which point they took a break for lunch, another box of MREs. Halfway through lunch, there was a loud explosion to the southeast.

Kevin Bhatt was a minute or two late, so instead of watching the marquee scroll through all the meetings and dinners, he asked the front desk clerk. "The International Bread Consortium? Yes," the clerk said, "it's in the Hibiscus Room, down that hallway next to the Lotus Ballroom."

Kevin thanked the clerk and headed to the Hibiscus Room. Along the way, he reflected on his part in this project. He was forty-six and the youngest, and most successful by far, of four brothers. Their father had been successful also, dealing in exotic woods from Brazil: bloodwood, cumaru, ipe, pernambuco, tamarind, and tigerwood, which he sold in world markets, most notably New York City.

The brothers had split the business when their father retired and moved back to their native India, but Kevin was the only one of the four who could make it work. He spoke impeccable Hindi, Portuguese, and English, necessary languages in his business. He had bought a large tract of land near the Amazon River from where most of the wood had come. He owned several barges and an ocean-going ship for transport, along with a pier giving access between the Rio Jari and the roads leading back to his plantation.

Although many nations had embargoes on threatened or endangered species like cumaru and tamarind, Kevin had always been able to find a market. But selling wood got to be quite boring over the years. One day a man named Rushil Singh came along and asked him if he would like to add a little spice to his life. And so he became part of the International Bread Consortium. He wasn't quite sure of the ultimate goals of the IBC, but the money was good and they wanted little more than use of his resources, with his oversight.

In the year since joining the IBC, his involvement had increased. He had hired information technologists and set them up in an office near his shipping headquarters in Macapá, and built an open-air hangar on the west side of his plantation. They were rebuilding MiG fighter planes, but Kevin had learned not to ask too many questions.

The catered dinner was about to start; Kevin was the last of a dozen attendees. During the dinner, most of the guests noticed one of the wait staff who seemed more than a little interested in their conversations. The talk among the diners was all about families, bread truck customizing, uniforms, and different types of flour. By the time dessert was served, that server had disappeared and was not seen again. Dasya Khatri asked discreetly about it, and was told the man had had a family emergency and had to depart.

After the dinner was over and they were left alone, Rishaan Chabra called the meeting to order. Patel's Bakery, Wilson's Bakery, Dmitri's Bakery, and Ming's Bakery team leaders reported on progress toward procuring and outfitting bread delivery trucks as well as obtaining warehouse space on the edges of their respective locations. Rishaan was pleased and commended each of the teams, in turn, on their reported progress. Kevin reported the hangar activity was on schedule, and the only glitch in the funds transfer and disbursement was that the IT Survey Specialist had to go direct instead of indirect, and explained why.

Next, Rishaan called for the reports of the Master Baker and Bakery Equipment Designers. As usual, he was using the terms developed several months previously, in case of eavesdropping. The Master Baker reported the new recipe for the ingredients had been proven out, and the ingredients themselves had been placed on order with thirty different sources in thirteen different countries. Delivery was scheduled to be complete in fourteen days. The Bakery Equipment Designers reported the LED prototype arrays for the mixing tanks had already been tested successfully. Enough arrays for all the tanks should soon be delivered to the bakery teams.

"Very good," Rishaan said, as the business portion of the meeting was drawing to a close, "all very good. Of course, we will wait until all supplies and equipment are in place and operational before we make any move. And Kevin, I have a box of materials I need you to take to the Amazon tomorrow."

The discussion turned to the plane which crashed into the Atlantic, and the subsequent discovery of it on the island which mysteriously appeared under it. Jovan Stojanović, the Serbian team leader of Dmitri's Bakery, quietly shut the door to the hallway. Addressing Rishaan, he asked the question on everyone's mind. "We shot that plane down, didn't we?"

Rishaan's plump fingers ran through his slick hair. He was ready to defend the action. "Yes, we did. It was necessary. Damn idiots were involved, and we needed to fix things!"

The response was not "why" as he had been expecting, but "how". As in, how did we know it was the right plane, how did we know where it would be, and how did our planes get there so quickly?

Rishaan, with Dasya's help, explained. "Some of this most of you already know. Some know different parts than others, so I'll explain the whole thing. We realized early on, after we had acquired six MiG fighter planes, that those would not work well enough for delivery. We had designed the tanks so we could load them and use them on the MiGs, and during testing, we found we could use them as external fuel tanks.

"Several of the MiGs we got were armed with machine guns. We didn't need them, but since we were offered thirty thousand rounds of American ammunition for a good price, we decided maybe we might need the MiGs for self-defense. These were parked at our operational base. As you know, we had recruited several MiG-qualified pilots who stayed where the MiGs were, because that was the best place for them in case we needed them.

"There was an apprentice baker on staff who was in a position to do a live test using the latest recipe. A Russian man and his wife were selected. A device was inserted into their baggage on their trip to the USA, designed to function upon opening their baggage. The test was to check effectiveness, time delay before onset of symptoms, and dissipation. We had another apprentice baker observing them on their trip, but the pair never opened that piece of luggage, and boarded their flight in Minneapolis en route back to Russia. We were notified immediately. We realized our project would fail completely if they got back to Saint Petersburg safely.

"We thought we had only two hours, but we were tracking their flight details and found that their baggage was delayed because of a tight schedule. That gave us an additional three hours. That was enough time to arm and fuel the two MiGs and get them in the general location of the Air World plane. The MiGs don't have their own radar, so we had logged on to the air traffic control radar and we relayed its location to the pilots. The plane almost got away since the pilots weren't completely sure it was the right one, but then they got confirmation and finished the job."

Zhao Zhang Li, the Chinese team leader, thanked them for the excellent explanation, and everyone agreed. However, she wondered what would happen now that this island appeared under the plane.

"Rishaan thinks of this simply as a test of our resolve," Dasya offered. "All the equipment and ingredients are ordered and on their way. We shouldn't have to delay delivery at all."

Bob McGee set down his diet soda as he opened the classified email.
CLASSIFICATION: SECRET
FROM:       PEDRO A. SANTOS
TO:         VTC TASK FORCE
DTG:        10:00 AM 30 JUNE 2019 (30JUN19 1400Z)
SUBJECT:    MEETING SUMMARY, BRAZIL/US AMBASSADORS

1. Subject meeting took place 9:00 to 9:45 a.m. this date. Attendee list is available upon request.

2. Purpose of meeting: to discuss the situation in and around Macapá and

the Rio Jari, to determine necessity for action, to delineate responsibilities and limitations of American military and civilian agencies, and to determine appropriate publicity.

3. Accomplishments/Decisions:

a. Brazilian military forces and Agência Brasileira de Inteligência (ABIN) will conduct police action with advice and support of American military and civilian agencies. Overall task force leader will be Brazilian Army Major Antonio Silva. The US will provide explosive ordnance disposal (EOD) support to Brazilian Army EOD unit involved.

b. Brazilian agencies will hold and question all personnel detained. If citizens from the US, Brazil, or other countries are detained, and it is determined no crime was committed, those personnel will be released, otherwise they will be tried in accordance with Brazilian law. All property involved will be held by Brazilian agencies until final disposition is determined. Requests for extradition will follow normal protocols.

c. Neither US nor Brazilian press will cover. Appropriate notifications will be made per embassy protocols.

4. Action Items:

a. ABIN will provide operations location, transportation, and medical support to American personnel, and equipment as necessary. ABIN will be responsible for all detainees. Brazilian Army will provide command and control. Brazilian Army will provide one EOD team and disposal materials.

b. US will provide one EOD team. US will provide operational advice and expertise.

c. Brazil and US will share all intelligence gained.

5. Reports Due: N/A.

CLASSIFICATION: SECRET
CLASSIFICATION EXEMPT FROM STANDARD DECLASSIFICATION SCHEDULE

Dasya Khatri was a condensed-matter physicist and father of four sons. He had done his doctoral work at Leipzig University in Germany, where he defended his thesis on the effects of cosmic dust so well that he had an immediate job offer from that university. He had turned them down, however, to return to his native India to work in industry. He had dreamed since his youth of doing something with his life to benefit all of mankind. The company he worked for allowed him the luxury of doing research toward that end—on his own time, of course—as long as he accomplished all his assigned research, operations, and development tasks.

As he progressed into middle age, his idealism slowly turned to pessimism, brought on by incessant changes to government regulations. These were, at the heart of them, prompted by a desire for India to be world-class in many scientific fields. However, due to excessive bureaucracy, usually compounded by corruption, these rules most often had the opposite effect. He had joined the Federation of Indian Scientists soon after returning to his home country, for the purpose of networking with like-minded scientists. It was at an FIS meeting that he met Rishaan Chabra.

Rishaan Chabra was a chemical engineer by trade and considered a master by his profession. He had several patents for products and processes, mostly dealing with environmental research. He had never married. He blamed his determination to never be disappointed romantically again on the death from cancer of his childhood sweetheart, Prisha Bakshi, after they had graduated from the university. He tended somewhat toward mysticism, and his strange ideas were dismissed by his colleagues as generally harmless, or at least non-threatening.

He was currently the president of the FIS, the youngest ever to be elected to that position. India's reputation as the world's most polluted country disheartened him, and he recognized that the government's policies allowed much wealth to be generated at the expense of clean air. This problem, which seemed to him to be manifested all over the world, was worst in his own country.

Rushil Singh was what Rishaan thought of as a "general scientist," that is, a person without a PhD after his name. He was very gregarious, but uncharacteristically reticent concerning his own history and abilities. Dasya thought he joined the FIS to make contacts to find employment. Like

Rishaan, he was taken with his outgoing nature and ready solutions to just about any problem. They could see he didn't have a political bone in his body, and was not swayed by promises of wealth or reputation.

The three became fast friends and had many discussions about the future of India and the obstacles that threatened its standing in the world of science.

"What would you do," Rushil had asked the other two one day, "if you could eliminate all the pollution in the Ganges River by the sacrifice of just a few people?"

Rishaan wondered where this was going. "There are probably a hundred dead bodies thrown in the Ganges every day. There are hundreds of sewage entry points on the Ganges. What few people are you talking about sacrificing? How many is a few?"

Dasya had a different take. "It's really just about money and education. Graves and crematoriums for the bodies and sewage treatment plants should fix all that. But who would pay for it all?"

"That wasn't my question. If you could eliminate the pollution by sacrificing a few people, would you do it, knowing how many people would live as a result?"

Rishaan and Dasya agreed, yes, they would. Sacrificing a few to save many seemed like a good deal. The question had evolved over the course of the next six months, and so had the definition of "a few."

The evening's dinner and IBC meeting were now over, and everyone had left except Rishaan, Dasya, and Rushil. Dasya wondered out loud about the server who had seemed to be spying on them during the dinner.

"He was mine," Rishaan said. "At the last meeting, I thought there were some who were a little careless with their words. I asked him to see if he could detect any purpose of our group other than baking. Just before dessert, he gave me the thumbs-up signal I was hoping for."

Rishaan, who had led the meeting, was not happy about what had gone on. "I'm glad the money got transferred and distributed, but why the hell did Jackson use her real damn IP address? Did we put so much pressure on her to get this done that she got careless?"

Dasya tried to get his friend calmed down. "You heard what Kevin said. The US bank security system demanded a real IP address, and she thought it would be no big deal since the total time on station would be less than thirty seconds. She logged in to both banks, intercepted the money, received the money, sent the money, deleted the account, and logged out within nineteen seconds. That was remarkable because there were thirteen accounts the money was transferred to. She said that was no riskier than trying to find and co-opt a legitimate IP address somewhere in California, where if some user typed something during the transactions, the money might have been lost."

Rishaan had lost patience with Kevin Bhatt and had already decided what to do when the meeting was over. "It was sloppy," he said. "What do we have in the Amazon? Anything we can't afford to lose? We just need to watch and wait for a while. Are they still sending us a code every morning?"

Rushil was acting as go-between. "Yes, and I'll get with Kevin before he leaves tomorrow and tell him no shipments in or out, except for food and bug spray, for what, fourteen days?"

"Yes, that's about right, except that he needs to get the tank out and send it to California. We're short there, one spare tank." Rishaan turned to Dasya. "Why did you tell them the MiGs already had the guns installed?"

"The less they know about Kevin's operation, the better. They think he's just the money guy. Not only that, the delivery teams don't know it was your pilot friend who stole those extra parts."

"Why would that be an issue?"

"In case something happened to one of the teams."

Rushil smiled, a self-satisfied smirk. But the other two didn't notice.

At noon on Sunday, Eastern Daylight Time, the second Stallion arrived on the island. The dried mud was hard enough to withstand the rotor wash of the heavy helicopter as it came in. Only a small amount of loose debris was thrown into the air. It parked about fifty meters from the first Stallion, on the other side of it from the mess tent. Phil Henry did not wait for the blades to completely stop, and LtCol Washington was waiting for him as he came down the steps.

The introductions were quick. Phil and Penny Hasid, who had parked herself just off Phil's hip, notebook in hand and camera at the ready, introduced themselves to the Marine leader and his NCOs. They immediately got to work, comparing notes and photos. The Marines started to offload the second Stallion, which they nicknamed "King Two", in preparation for loading two of the tanks and other items.

Phil's stomach was telling him it was lunchtime. "What time is it here?"

"Just after fourteen hundred hours," LtCol Washington said. "Officially, we are two hours behind Zulu time and two hours ahead of Eastern Daylight Time. Let's set up shop in the other Stallion. We'll have chow, and then, since EOD is finished, we'll take a tour of the plane."

Matt and Maggie stayed at King One when the other helicopter landed. "It's not about us anymore," he had told her. "We need to make sure we don't get in the way, and they'll be discussing things they won't invite us to hear. I'm sure they'll take care of us, but truthfully, from this point on, we're just excess baggage."

Maggie and Matt played with Jenny and chatted under the mess tent while Phil and Penny had a working lunch with LtCol Washington and the EOD teams. The sun was directly overhead, and there was otherwise no shade. At three o'clock, SSgt Phelps let them know the FBI team wanted to meet them, so they followed him back to King One.

"We're getting ready to look at the plane," LtCol Washington said after the introductions were finished. "After that, Phil wants to see your life raft, and you're invited to come along and say good-bye to it. We have enough drivers trained up on our new vehicles, so we'll take the two larger ones. When we come back, we'll take you all to see the river. I'm afraid that part might not be very exciting."

"This evening, over supper," Phil said, "Penny and I would like to sit down with the two of you. We have some questions for you, and perhaps some answers."

They all walked over to the plane, approaching it from the rear. The yellow caution tape had been removed, and what was left of the baggage and cargo was arranged in small, orderly piles in thirty or forty spots. One spot held a pallet with two mangled coffins attached and one missing between the two. Jagged, twisted metal threatened to pierce anyone approaching too close to the plane.

"Look where we came out!" Maggie pointed to spiky, razor-sharp metal which seemed to enfold the tail opening like arms, holding back debris from making its escape. They could not see into the fuselage.

At the front of the plane, a short ladder afforded access to the interior, which LtCol Washington had put off-limits. Since the aircraft was upside-down, it appeared that all of the seats were hanging from the ceiling. The nose of the doomed Dreamliner had been ripped off at row one, which was still attached to the cockpit. All of the row-two seats and some of the row-three seats were missing.

The EOD team chief, Gunnery Sergeant Sims, explained that the missing seats, all occupied, were located further back in the fuselage. "It looks like the seats were torn from the floor by the force of the water coming through as it slowed the plane down. Ms. Trillbey, after I heard your story last night, I came back to see where your seat was. Come over here and look."

Matt took Jenny while GySgt Sims climbed onto the ceiling of the aircraft. Maggie stood below while he pointed to what was left of her seat. "You would never have felt the water," he said. "You would already have been dead from the explosions."

"Sometimes God protects us and never tells us about it," Maggie said, "but God has been showing me all the ways he has protected me since even before I got on the plane. I'm in awe of how and why he chose to protect me, because I didn't deserve any of it."

LtCol Washington directed the group away from the cockpit section and toward the tail cone. "The EOD team didn't find the black box when they were looking for duds, but maybe they didn't know exactly what to look for."

"We need to take it back with us," Phil said, "so I got a quick lesson from Air World where to find it. From what I see, it should still be inside the rear of the plane, and it won't be black, but bright red or orange. There should actually be two devices."

"We got all the way to the rear, to where the light was coming in, during our dud sweep," GySgt Sims said. "I remember seeing them there, but damaged. We'll pull the back end open and we should be able to get them out."

The tour was soon over, and the group headed back to King One. Matt looked to the north and pointed. "Look, everyone!" There, just barely ascending above the horizon, a lone black peak proudly stood guard over the island.

Back at King One, Penny brought Phil his satellite phone and he started punching in numbers. "Matt and Maggie," he said, "Air World asked me to have you talk to them about your return. This will be Abby Cameron. You'll be getting back to Dulles between eleven and noon tomorrow."

Abby wanted their cell phone numbers and carriers and approximate arrival time. "Upon your arrival, you will be met by representatives from Air World Airlines and Britannia Airlines," she said, "and there will most likely be media coverage. Don't worry, we'll take good care of you."

On their way to the GSM, Penny explained about the potato-like rocks. "They're called manganese nodules. It looks like you have millions on this island. The rocks are about a quarter manganese and varying amounts of nickel, cobalt, and copper, and trace amounts of a lot of other metals. Depending on the percentages, they're worth anywhere from three thousand to thirty thousand dollars per metric ton."

She sounded like an encyclopedia, and Matt the businessman was impressed. He immediately thought about his friend Larry Williams, how this would be perfect for him.

At the GSM, Phil was amazed at the pallet raft with the coffins attached. "This was all that floated to the surface, once the plane sank?" he asked. "These steel cabinets stayed together, even though they were not connected by a single cable, and didn't try to tip the raft over? This is incredible!"

"Do you see how the last cabinet acted as an anchor?" Maggie asked. "It kept us from being washed over the edge as the island broke the surface."

"Let me show you what else the shark brought us besides Jenny," Matt said as he opened the coffin which had been on top. He pulled out the half life preserver and several of the plastic bottles. "I haven't seen these caps in a long time, maybe twenty years or more. For some reason the shark couldn't expel them. When she threw them up, they must have been in the front part of her stomach."

Phil was more interested in the life preserver. "Penny, when we get back, I want you to find out what ship this is. Probably US Navy. Find out what you can about why this life preserver might have been in the ocean. Let me know, and Matt if he's interested."

"I'd like to know too," Maggie said, feeling left out.

Phil turned to Matt. "If you had just found this floating in the water, it would have been covered with a layer of green algae and other scum that you wouldn't have been able to get off. How big was the shark?"

"I estimate there was about fifteen feet of it out of the water, and we saw only the belly the first time it surfaced, so I couldn't tell you if the rear fin was out of the water or not. The second time, when it threw up, maybe about eight feet was showing."

Penny was taking pictures of everything and listening at the same time.

"You must have been terrified!"

"I was," Maggie said. "I wanted to hide in the coffin. But Matt very calmly just pointed at the shark and commanded it in Jesus's name to throw up. That's when we got Jenny's body back."

GySgt Sims had volunteered to be one of the JLTV drivers. "How did you know to do that, Matt?"

"God showed me," Matt said, "just like he showed Maggie about the satellite overhead. In my case, after the shark disappeared the first time, I saw a scene play out like a YouTube video. It was very vivid and in detail. I watched the shark come out of the water and I watched myself commanding it. So when it did indeed come out of the water, I knew just what to do and say. We had no idea right then that the shark would throw up Jenny's body. After that, we never saw the shark again."

"Before we go back," Penny said, "I'd like to get a picture of you two, Maggie and Matt, sitting on the coffins, just by yourselves."

"It was great of Staff Sergeant Phelps to volunteer to take care of Jenny if she woke up before we got back," Maggie said, "but it would have been nice to get a picture with her, too."

After Penny took that photo, Matt reached into the coffin, which had been put back on top, and grabbed a couple leftover velvet cloths. He wrapped them around some of the water bottles. Maggie held the simulated baby for a few more pictures.

It was time for supper when they got back to the base camp. The EOD team had located and removed the black box assemblies and packaged them for the trip back. The Marines had loaded one of the large tanks onto King Two, and were preparing to load the other prior to nightfall.

Phil, Penny, Matt, and Maggie found some boxes to sit on in a quiet area near King Two while the Marines all ate their chow at the mess tent. Maggie put Jenny on some velvet cloths and let her wiggle around while they ate and talked.

"I have started to believe in miracles," Phil said. "There's no explanation for why you're sitting here, other than that a miracle happened."

"Yes," Matt said. "We've started a list, and between us we count at least twenty miracles, plus other manifestations of God's mercy and care for us."

"Please tell us," Penny said.

Matt and Maggie started with the loss of Matt's family and Maggie's winning the trip in the raffle. When they came to the part in the story where

Maggie received Jesus as Lord and became God's child, Phil interrupted.

"When I was ten, between fourth and fifth grade, my sister and I went to vacation Bible school and gave our hearts to the Lord, too. Our family moved that October, and I never pursued it after that. I always kept religion at arm's length. Not that I disliked it, but I guess I was just watching, looking for a real reason to embrace it. There seems to be too much phoniness. In my profession, I have to be a tough guy, and I've learned to never take things at face value. I will say, though, that I've always been tender toward stories where God is merciful to those in need of it. Like you two."

"Is that why you were so interested in the life preserver?" Matt asked.

"Yes. I am by nature a skeptic, and by trade an investigator. But everything about your story checks out."

Matt and Maggie continued their story up to the arrival of the second King Stallion. Maggie felt comfortable relating about her trauma as a twelve-year-old, her forgiving those who did that to her, being completely healed, and being able to start nursing when Jenny was three months old.

As they finished, Matt asked, "Those symptoms Captain Palova asked us about, what were they an indication of? He seemed pretty specific."

"Right now," Phil said, "there is an ongoing investigation into who shot your airplane down and why. I hope you realize, both of you, that some of what we are about to tell you, if it got out, could hamper the investigation or allow the perpetrators to escape. Or, heaven forbid, set you up as a target for them."

Matt and Maggie both expressed their understanding and cooperation with the investigation.

"Some things the world already knows or will know shortly. We don't mind you confirming you were shot down, or anything else you tell us. Things we tell you, however, we are asking you to keep to yourselves, like the symptoms you asked about. Those are symptoms of nerve gas poisoning. I won't say any more about that, since it appears you were not exposed to any nerve gas.

"For some reason, someone was willing to kill three hundred people to accomplish his or her purposes. There is one thing I would ask everyone on board, but obviously only you two can answer. Is there any way you could have been the target?"

"I teach year fives in Bristol," Maggie said. "I've never had a problem with any of the parents, and the oldest of my former students would be fifteen or sixteen. No one knew I was on that flight except my mum and my cousin in Macon."

"I retired about eight months ago, after the death of my wife," Matt said, "and while I was still working, I traveled a lot, but my job was mostly administrative. No, I can't imagine I'd be a target."

"Thanks. Have you ever been on a frozen lake and heard the ice crack?" Neither Matt nor Maggie had.

"I have," Penny said, pausing from her note-taking task. "It makes a most unusual and unforgettable sound. It's hard to describe, a sharp crack and a dull boom at the same time."

Phil showed them a copy of a report which had a lot of names and agencies blacked out. It detailed the findings of a NOAA representative as reported by one of his own agents. "It appears this exact location was experiencing these cracking sounds for years. We don't know when they started. NOAA didn't start monitoring the Atlantic until around 2005."

"Wow!" Matt said, after reading through the report. "Exactly every eight years a set of three, exactly eight days apart."

"I would have told you about this anyway, since those sounds took place here, but it leads to an important question which could help the investigation. These sounds didn't happen randomly, but precisely on a schedule. There's an orderliness to it that defies chance."

"God knew the plane would be shot down right here," Maggie said.

"Yes," Phil answered, "but why did he need an island? Why did he need the plane to surface? And I don't mean to sound callous, but why did he need two survivors?"

"He could have done it with one," Maggie said, "as long as it was Matt. I was lost and clueless. I couldn't even swim. God saved me from the plane in order to save me from hell."

"I understand that. Our question is, when you were sensing the things God was having you do, did you get any idea of the purpose for any of it?"

"No," Matt said. "We discussed this even before we spoke the words to cause the island to come up. We believed God had purposes for the island we knew nothing of. At the time, we realized that was a secret he was not telling us. We didn't know the plane would be on the island. It just never occurred to us. In fact, we weren't even sure that *we* would end up on the island."

"Okay," Phil said. "We'll have to go where the physical evidence leads us, then." He glanced at Penny, who was busy taking notes, then back at Maggie. "You mentioned dirt. I'm telling the skeptic in me that if you were making this up, you never would have promised dirt. Tell us about that."

"There's not much to tell," Matt said. "It will be a wow for us just like for the rest of the world. We don't know how God will do it, just that he will do it. We don't know when, and we don't know where the dirt will come from."

"There's no need for dirt," Maggie said, "unless people were going to be here to enjoy things growing on this island. When we called it up, we called for the dirt to be full of life. Things of beauty, flowers, maybe even petunias."

"Things will have to grow fast," Phil said. "With no roots to hold the soil together, the dirt and this dried mud will wash off into the ocean."

Paul Washington joined them, carrying a metal box with a pink and gold strip tied around the handle. "This is for you, Maggie. Matt told me you're a fourth-grade teacher, so I had my engineers put together a memento of your time here."

"Thank you, and your men too," she said.

Inside the box, she found three large zipper bags full of the now-dried white mud, six various-sized chunks of basalt, eight manganese nodules ranging in size from five to twenty centimeters, and two full water bottles.

Maggie was delighted. "Wow! Now I can do show-and-tell along with my students."

"There's one set for Jenny when she's older," Paul said, "and we gave you enough so you can give Matt a set if you want to. The bottles are full of water from the river. We are sending some water back to be tested, so don't open those until we send you the results."

After Paul left, Matt asked Penny for some of the photos she had taken. "Email us pictures of the three of us on the GSM, and one of the coffin end plate showing the details of the Hardwood Casket Company. Maggie and I need to write them a nice thank-you for letting us use their coffins."

"And one showing just the two of us," Maggie said. "The before-and-after photos of God bringing Jenny back to life!"

Phil wanted to address one more issue before their meeting ended. "I'll be here tomorrow when the insurance adjusters and airline reps come. Unfortunately, we can't look through personal items before the bodies are taken out, and you'll be gone by the time that happens. We expect the cargo will be determined to be a total loss, which the insurance companies may abandon in place.

"The airline will attempt to retrieve all personal belongings and luggage not damaged by fire or the exploding bullets, and try to deliver what is identifiable and practical to the next of kin. Most likely, that will only be what is on their person, under the seats, or in the overhead bins."

"If the GSM coffins are a total loss," Matt said, "then they belong to the insurance company. In that case, would you ask if Maggie and I could take ownership? The pallet and coffins wouldn't need to be moved. They can stay right where they are."

"Sure," Phil said, "Penny or I will have to escort the insurance adjusters, so I'll ask. What do you want them for?"

"One day we'll come back," Matt said, "and build a museum around them."

Kevin Bhatt was waiting at Indira Gandhi International Airport in Delhi for his flight to São Luis, Brazil. He had been seated less than three minutes when a young man wearing sunglasses and a turban plopped his backpack on the floor and sat next to him.

"Hello, I see you're flying to São Luis, as I am," he said. "Then I'm catching the short hop to Macapá."

"Do you live in Macapá?" Kevin asked.

"No, Jaipur, just southwest of here. I'm going on a scouting expedition in the state of Amapa for my father. I'm to meet a guide in Macapá."

"Have you been to Macapá before?" Kevin asked. "Where will you stay?"

"The guide told me I should have no problem finding a hotel."

"I am from Macapá," Kevin said. "I can recommend a few places."

"Wonderful! I am Manan Ganguly. Please tell me about Macapá. Do you know anything of the Amazon rainforests in that area?"

"I am Kevin Bhatt. I've spent about half my life near the Amazon and the rainforests. In fact, my business takes me there frequently. What sort of scouting expedition is it?"

"My father is a hunter. He has a large exhibition hall for a trophy case. He has one of every kind of monkey in India, and many from South America, but not many from the Amazon. So I'm to set up hunting parties, and he will come during the fall."

"The rainforest monkeys are small and hard to find. He will need a good guide and lots of patience."

Manan adjusted his sunglasses. "My father will have both. He knows that's the only way to catch monkeys. There are several varieties of spider monkeys he wants to start with, and he won't consider the trip a success unless he goes home with a black-bearded saki."

Kevin knew that a good many Brazilian monkeys were threatened or endangered, but that was the guide's responsibility. "Good luck getting them out of the country. By the way, I have several days' worth of errands when I get back, but I'll be in the office on Thursday. If you're still in Macapá, call me and I'll take you to dinner at my favorite restaurant." He gave Manan his business card.

"Thanks, I'm looking forward to it. I don't fly back here until Friday."

It was still dark when Jenny started to cry. Maggie picked her up, checked her makeshift nappy, and nursed her. As she was finishing, she woke Matt per his request from the night before. They quietly exited King One and headed east, where there was the faintest glow on the horizon. The sky was completely clear.

As they walked, Maggie said, "This is awesome. I've never seen the sky this bright. The stars seem like they're alive!"

"The heavens declare the glory of God," Matt replied. "It's easy to see why some civilizations worshiped them. Now we worship their creator. Just a little farther to go."

They reached the rock with the cloth tie. "This will be a special sunrise," Matt said.

"Yes, our last one on the island. In a very small way, I will be sad to leave. Our two days here have been extraordinary, absolutely brilliant."

"When I met you, Maggie, you were in some ways still a child of twelve. Since then, you have died, come very much alive, and are now an adult, a full-fledged woman in every sense of the word. And I'm thrilled that God chose me to be your dad."

It had been growing lighter. Suddenly, a bright green flash appeared briefly on the horizon as the first edge of the sun broke over it.

Maggie was momentarily speechless. "Wow!"

"I've never seen that either, just read about it. I was hoping it would be clear enough this morning for it to appear. We need to go back soon and eat breakfast, since we'll be leaving in about an hour and a half, but let's sit and enjoy the sunrise. There's a couple more things I want to talk about before we get back to civilization."

"There's one I want to talk about too, Matt. It's what I promised you on the GSM."

"Let's pray first. We need to ask God for wisdom concerning the island, safety for the trip back, and courage for what lies ahead. We should start by worshipping God, in English and in the spirit. I'll start, and you join in when you feel comfortable."

"That would be right away!"

They worshiped and prayed. As they were finishing, Matt said, "Lord, help me be an adequate father to Maggie and Jenny."

"Maggie, last night when I was thinking about my other daughter Rachel, I realized there was something very important missing from our father-daughter relationship."

"Yours and mine?"

"Yes."

"But what could that be? You've been so wonderful and patient with me, helping me to live and grow up and know Jesus!"

"You don't know it because I think you've never experienced it. It's a very important part of a father's job to show his kids affection. I gave a lot of that to Todd and Rachel."

Matt noticed Maggie starting to tear up, her lower lip quivering. "With Rachel," he said, "even when she was an adult, we'd be sitting on the couch, and I'd put my arm around her. She'd just sort of melt. She'd relax, lay her head on my shoulder, and just be happy. Amy and Jack would see this, and jump on my lap, wanting some of the love, too.

"With you and me, I think it has to be a little different. It would be awkward for me to hold you like I did Rachel. I know we've set boundaries for ourselves, and it would be tempting to relax those boundaries for the sake of my showing you the affection you so richly deserve and sorely need. I would like to figure out a way to show it that would honor each other and God as well."

Maggie just nodded, and burst into tears. "I'm starting to remember," she said between loud sobs.

"Let me hold Jenny," Matt said gently. Jenny had started crying along with her mother, but relaxed and became quiet as Matt held her close.

Maggie closed her eyes and shuddered, weeping. Matt watched as she struggled, sometimes crying out in anguish, sometimes giving looks of shock and fear and abject helplessness, sometimes rigidly holding in her breath as if in expectation of a horror, pressing her palms against the middle of her chest. At last, she relaxed and wiped her eyes on her shirt sleeves.

"Come here and sit by me," Matt said.

Maggie complied, and he put his arm around her shoulder and held her tight. "I know what I said earlier, but right now you need a hug from a loving father."

"Thank you." The tears were still flowing.

Matt held her until the tears subsided, then relaxed and waited for her to speak.

"I didn't know there was that much to remember. I don't know if there's more, but I'll tell you some of it. I know I need to forgive him, and I'm hoping you can help."

"Yes, by God's grace I will."

"We may have been on holiday. I don't remember. I was four or five and it was summer. We were in a house not our own, and not on the ground floor. I was playing with my favorite doll, made from an old sock, with button eyes. I wanted to show my father. Maybe I was being a pest, but suddenly, he picked me up by my wrist, and took my doll in the other hand. He opened the door onto a balcony and lifted me up over the railing, still holding my wrist.

"The street was far below. He looked back and forth from me to my doll, as if deciding on one or the other, and suddenly threw my doll away. He never said a word. I remember we looked at each other—he looked mean and grumpy—and finally he brought me back inside. I ran to my mum and cried, but she didn't know what to do.

"He was always poking me in the chest if I got too close. Right here, in the center, where it hurts the most. I learned to not cry, but he would laugh. I don't remember him ever doing that to Charles. Sometimes he would grab my hair and pull my head back, then stroke my chin. I was terrified he would hurt me."

"Oh, Maggie! Wow, you were really brave, both enduring it and telling me about it. You said he died when you were fifteen?"

"Yes, he did, but he quit poking me and pulling my hair when I was ten, after 9/11 in New York. I don't know what made him quit, maybe my mum, or maybe he realized life was short."

"I can see those memories would be very painful to carry around."

"It was like they were locked in a secret room, secret from me that is. Your telling me about Rachel smashed the door wide open."

"How can I help you forgive him?"

"I don't know. I know I have to, and I am going to say the words like I did with Charles and his friends. I think I need something to get the words started."

"Okay." Matt held Jenny up and gave her a good look. He cradled her in his arms and kissed her.

"Maggie," he said to Jenny, "you are so beautiful! So little, but so full of promise! I am so glad you've finally come. You are my pride and joy! I'm really lucky to have you as my daughter." He kissed her some more. "You are great and wonderful. I'm sorry I didn't treat you with the honor and respect you deserve. I'm so sorry I ever did anything to hurt you. I don't deserve your forgiveness. How can I ever make it up to you?" More kisses. "I'm —"

"Stop!" Maggie was laughing through her tears. "You can't."

Matt looked at Maggie, back at Jenny, and at Maggie again.

"Thanks," she said, wiping her eyes once more. "I needed that. I needed to hear every one of those words. It's what my father should have said. And I could tell you weren't just playing, but you really meant each one of them."

"Yes, and I've already sung the song for you. I meant every one of those words, too."

"Okay, I'm ready now."

Like she had done for Charles and Ted and Billy, she forgave Adam Trillbey. Soon the secret room was completely empty.

The sun was slowly rising. Soon they had to turn away from it. "We still have a few minutes," Matt said.

"I can be in student mode for a few minutes, then it will be time for snack."

Matt was getting hungry, too, and promised to keep it as short as possible. He handed the baby back to Maggie as they sat facing west, toward the Stallions and the wreckage of the Dreamliner.

"Maggie, why do you think God chose you for this? Maybe I should ask it this way, why do you think you were the one God chose?"

"Well, I heard you tell the Marines there was nothing about you that would make God want to choose you over anyone else. So I would say that's true for me also. Probably more, since you belonged to him already, but I had nothing going for me."

"But that would be exactly the reason God would choose you. I had nothing going for me, either. There are two reasons God chose you, Maggie Trillbey, out of all seven billion people in the world. One purpose was for you, and one purpose was for himself. The purpose for himself was for you to tell others about him and his love for them, all the wonderful things he's done for you, and how you came to be his eternally. He will use your words to speak to them, to draw them to himself."

"He has been doing that already. He said he has a great work for me, but everything has seemed so easy. I know you've told me things I could expect when I get back home, but he has promised to be with me forever. Doesn't that mean things will work out fine?"

In the distance, they could make out movement at the giant helicopters as the Marines started their day with an exercise formation.

"Yes, Maggie, things will work out fine. What does that mean, though, 'work out fine?' I don't want you to ever be misled into thinking your life, now that you belong to him, will be a bed of roses. Jesus didn't have it easy during his life on earth, and neither will you. As long as you keep your eyes on him, however, it will be very rewarding and you'll be full of joy. Do you know what the 'rewarding' part will be?"

"I can think of several things. Does it have to do with God's purpose for me, the other reason you mentioned?"

"Yes, very good. God chose you for this, to know him. He has that desire for everyone else, too, but right now I want to talk about just you. He has shown you his wonderfulness, filled you with such joy you feel like you'll burst, and spoken to you personally on several occasions. That's great, but there's more, infinitely more. He has indeed promised to be with you forever. Do you understand what that means?"

"I think so. Well, no, I really don't. I think I'm still that infant."

"Let me give you three examples. Let's say you are driving your car and start to cross a snowy bridge. There is a car in the opposite lane slowly coming toward you. All of a sudden, a Mercedes pulls out from behind him and tries to pass. He hits a patch of bare ice and starts to spin, and hits the guardrail. In an instant, you remember God's promise to be with you forever, so you relax. In the first example, the Mercedes bounces off the guardrail and misses you completely. God was with you, right?"

"Yes. He protected me from the accident."

"In the next example, the Mercedes also bounces off. It hits your car so hard it flips you over the guardrail and your car lands on its roof on the road below, killing you instantly. Just as instantly, you are in his presence forever. In which of these two examples do you get to know God better as a result?"

"In the second one, definitely. In the first one, he was protecting me, but I didn't get to know him better."

"Exactly. God said he would show you wonderful things as you kept your eyes on him. The wonderful things for you will always have to do with knowing him more. The wonderful things for others—the miracles, the healings, the wisdom—will be for them to know him, or know him better. He may show you how to ask for those things for others. Let me warn you, there may be a temptation to ask God for something more than your basic needs, that benefits you in a worldly, extravagant way. If you do, you may get it, and claim it shows God's favor toward you. I tell you, that thing will drive a wedge between you and God."

"I hope I always remember that. I don't want anything to ever separate me from God's love."

"Nothing will ever separate you from his love. What it would separate you from, is fellowship with him. He will always draw you back to himself, though. Remember that knowing him more will be the key."

"I wish I had a pencil and a notebook. Matt, how will I ever remember all these things?"

"Maggie, everything I told you is already written in the Bible Paul gave you. Anyway, in the third example, the Mercedes crashes into the driver's side door, breaking your leg in four places. Broken ribs puncture your lung and spleen, and you suffer a concussion and a broken jaw. You're in the hospital three months and rehab three more months. You're in pain for over a year."

Maggie didn't know what to think. After a few minutes, she asked, "Could that really happen?"

"Yes. Things worse than that have happened to people who love God with all their hearts. After it was over, they say they wouldn't trade the experience for anything in the world, because God was with them and revealed himself to them in the midst of all their pain. That pain and misery brought them closer to God than they ever could have imagined."

Something about the intensity of Matt's examples made Maggie consider what she knew of his recent history. "That happened to you, didn't it?"

"I would gladly have traded the loss of my family for what I just described." Matt started to tear up. "I was in agony, but God held me close. When you became my sister, and then my daughter, the comfort and joy that brought me made me realize how much God loves us both. That comfort allowed me to grieve like I needed to, and in the joy of holding Jenny and helping you, I realized how God can make all things new, and it is the eternal things that matter. All the things of this life, the good as well as the bad, are of little lasting importance."

"I want to know God better, but I don't think I could wish for that."

"As many people as there are in the world, God has that many ways of making himself known. I don't wish that for you, either, but if it happens, remember God will be with you, and will hold you up, the whole time."

At 8 a.m. Monday, an aircraft identifying itself as National Intercontinental Airlines departed Dulles International Airport en route to Macapá, Brazil. Harvey Hostetler and his team had been anticipating Pedro Santos' email, but it still took a full day to gather the right personnel and equipment. JC Smalley and Harper Avalon had spent the night at the FBI headquarters, studying all the material they could find on Macapá and its environs.

It would be a ten-hour flight, and they would arrive in broad daylight. They would rely on their tourist garb, nondescript local transportation, and the size of the city to keep their mission a secret.

At 11:30 a.m., the King Stallion settled onto the pad at Dulles International Airport. The flight had gone smoothly enough, although Jenny had fussed about the earplugs. They eventually took them out, and Matt traded his noise-canceling headset for her earplugs. The inflight refueling was interesting to watch through the windshield, and it caused only a small amount of extra turbulence.

As soon as the blades stopped turning, the cargo hatch opened. They were met by a pair of workmen wearing nametags that identified them as working for Ace Movers, the company hired to move the items to the CIA headquarters at Langley. Matt and Maggie said good-bye to Lance Corporal Wilson, who set to work with the loadmaster and the other Marines to load the cargo into the Ace truck. A representative of the National Transportation Safety Board took the black box pieces away for analysis.

Three individuals with the appropriate nametags were waiting to speak with Matt and Maggie: John Henderson from Air World Airlines, Betty Glyncoat from Britannia Airlines, and David Clark from the State Department.

After introductions, Mr. Clark told them a meeting was scheduled for them in the morning. "My British counterpart and I, among others, would like to meet with you to discuss the new island. If it meets with your approval, at 9 a.m. my driver will pick you up at your hotel. Mr. Henderson here has told me where you're spending the night. The meeting will be at the State Department building across the river. Will that be all right?"

After receiving two affirmatives, Mr. David Clark departed.

"Technically, you never left the US," John Henderson assured them, "so there's no need to go through customs. However, your survival has been announced to the whole world, so the press and many well-wishers want to welcome you back to civilization. They know you're coming here, but they don't know when. I'm sure there are folks already waiting out front for your arrival. I would like to propose we tell them that 3 p.m. will be your arrival time.

"That will give you time to get some clothes and baby things, freshen up at your hotel, rest a little, make some phone calls. Then we'll come back at three o'clock. So you will actually be arriving at three like we will tell them. Betty and I will be your escorts for the rest of the afternoon, until we drop you off at your hotel later. Will that be okay?"

"Yes," Maggie replied, "that would be wonderful!"

Matt agreed, but had one thing to make clear at the outset. "I echo Maggie's sentiments. It is wonderful what you're doing for us, but there is no way that what happened to the flight could possibly be your responsibility. I don't know what Maggie's feelings on this are, but as far as I'm concerned, you really don't owe us anything. I am extremely grateful for all this. It is more than I could ask for. On the other hand, please don't think I'm refusing your generosity. It's really great and I thank you."

Maggie nodded her concurrence as John led them to the Air World

Airlines van parked a short distance away.

"It's really refreshing to hear you say that," Betty Glyncoat said. "No, we are not trying to obviate a lawsuit. The two airlines got together and decided it would be highly appropriate for us to help you get your feet back on the ground, so to speak. And, to be frank, this will be good PR for us."

They had reached the van and John started off. "Our first stop will be Buy Buy Baby," Betty told them, "where they have volunteered to trade a stroller with baby carrier snap-in, nursing and baby-care paraphernalia, and three outfits for Jenny, for five minutes of photos. Then to Macy's for clothes. Jeans are fine, but you'll also need something nice for your visit to the State Department tomorrow. You'll need some luggage too. Don't worry, I have a company credit card and we get good discounts! Then to Walmart for whatever personal hygiene items you need."

She reached into a bag and handed them each a box. "Replacement cell phones. Maggie, the model you told Abby, they don't make that one anymore or even have any left, so we got you an upgrade. The phones are paid for; they have your phone numbers in them already, and your carriers have already added them to your accounts, so you can use them. You just need to stop in to one of their offices with photo IDs to complete the transfers."

Maggie's tears had started when she heard the words "baby carrier" and they hadn't stopped. "Do you have a tissue?" she asked. "All I have is this wad of velvet coffin liners."

They made their stops and were headed to the Canopy Hotel. Betty wasn't finished. She gave an envelope to Matt, and asked Maggie, "We'd like to give you some spending money for your couple days here, and if you have anything left over, you can take that home. Would you rather have US dollars or pounds sterling?"

Matt looked in his envelope. "Get it in pounds. We can share mine, and you can pay me back when we get to London."

"One more thing," Betty said. "We still owe you both a flight to London. You have the hotel two nights. You can fly out on Wednesday, the third of July, or a different day of your choosing. We know you didn't book together, so you don't have to go back together. And you don't have to fly from Dulles."

Matt and Maggie looked at each other. "Can we get back to you on that?" Maggie asked.

John answered, "Sure. Most of the BA flights from the States will be partnered with Air World, so I'll be handling those. Business class of course. If you don't fly from here on Wednesday, then I'll need a couple of days' notice."

Matt had one more request. "Do you think you could find me a copy of the flight magazine? I was in the middle of something I would like to finish."

Both John and Betty assured him they would try.

They were at the hotel. "I'll pick you up at 2:30. Just meet us here," John said.

They loaded everything in the stroller, and Matt took Jenny in the baby carrier. At the front desk, they showed their passports to the clerk. "Yes, I have your rooms ready. Mr. Carven, I see you are a Diamond honors member. Thank you for your loyalty."

"Yes, I like the Hilton chain. Are our rooms adjoining, or maybe across the hall?"

"I can get you connecting rooms."

Matt looked at Maggie. "Sure," she said. "I may need help with Jenny."

Rishaan Chabra's phone rang part way between "Oh, Prisha, we're almost there!" and "That stupid damn island!". He had been going back and forth between the two, and was working himself into a lather. His neck veins started bulging out and his face got darker and darker. The phone broke in, and Rishaan was sidetracked from his tirade.

"I just wanted to let you know," said the soft female voice at the other end, "that only Kapoor made it back. Kashyap was lost on the trip."

Pranay Kashyap, Rishaan's friend since the university, had recently taken an early retirement from the Indian Air Force. The IAF had considered him somewhat of a liability for destroying too many airplanes. The first one, a MiG-23, ran out of fuel over the Indian Ocean, and he had parachuted to safety. The other two MiGs on the training mission made it back to the training base on fumes, and his training unit took the blame.

Several years later, on a training mission over West Bengal, he made a mayday call to the control tower where he was supposed to land. He advised them the right wing had frozen in position, there was a fire in the cockpit, and he was ejecting. He landed the MiG-23 at the abandoned Dudhkundi Airfield, parked it in a deserted hangar, and waited for Rishaan to pick him up and bring him to a desert area nearby. He waited there—his uniform torn, his ejection seat functioned, and his parachute deployed—for his unit to find him and pick him up. Of course, the crashed MiG was never found.

Because of his experience with surviving crashes, the IAF had Squadron Leader Kashyap participate in the investigations of two IAF A-10 fighter plane crashes prior to his discharge. In both cases, the armed aircraft were destroyed, but the pilots all ejected and were safe. Whatever was salvageable from the A-10s was retrieved, including the GAU-8 gun systems, which had only minor damage. The ammunition drums for the two gun systems were somehow lost to the inventory, and no one had ever missed them. Rishaan and Pranay had boxed them up and labeled them "Combine Parts". Kevin Bhatt had taken them to Brazil very early in his relationship with Rishaan.

"Maria, why did you wait so long to tell me?"

"I felt like if I rushed, Kapoor would not tell me everything. I waited, and I got the whole story."

"Which is what?"

"Kashyap jettisoned both fuel tanks. Kapoor didn't know if it was an accident, or if they were both empty. He said he realized Kashyap did not have enough fuel to make it back here, so about ten minutes after the US Air Force broke off the chase, he shot down the MiG Kashyap was in, and ensured there was no survivor. He said that was the only way to ensure Kashyap couldn't give away your secrets."

Rishaan muttered under his breath while he considered his options. The project didn't need MiGs, or pilots, any longer, and using them for anything else would be sheer lunacy. Pranay was his friend, and the other pilot had killed him.

"Maria, execute Plan B, and let me know when complete. I'll send you money one more time—let me know how much—then you can close the account."

Five minutes later, Maria made another phone call. Rushil Singh answered the phone.

"Chabra wants to execute Plan B," Maria said. "Is that good?"

"What is Plan B? I don't know of a Plan B."

"Eliminate the pilots, but one is already dead, abandon the planes and ammo, and scatter. I will tidy things up here, pay off the workers, and disappear like the rest."

Rushil thought for a moment. It was obvious that Rishaan was burning his bridges behind him. This was a bridge that needed burning, however. It was just as obvious that Rishaan was becoming unhinged. He thought about Maria; he might need her services again sometime.

"Yes," he said, "that's good. Let me know how much you need. I'll find you if I need you."

At 1:30 p.m., the remains of two steel tanks rested on pallets in a laboratory in the third basement of an undisclosed building in McLean, Virginia. Nearby, a Pelican case, double-wrapped in plastic bags, lay by the entrance to a "clean room", hermetically sealed when the door is shut.

Jeff Peterson, leader of the CIA's hastily-assembled team to investigate the shooting down of AW flight 94, was discussing the Pelican case with two men partially dressed in chemical-protective rubber suits. "Here's what we learned from the Marine EOD team. I spoke with Gunnery Sergeant Sims on the radio this morning to clarify their initial report. They had found the suitcase out of the cargo hold and separate from other baggage and cargo, which was scattered all over.

"They said the suitcase looked like it had been hit by the high explosive incendiary ammunition, crushed by the water pressure, filled with seawater, and expanded when it came to the surface. Sometime during that time, the device inside functioned.

"The device itself never got water in it that they could tell, but its two parts had separated when they found it. Once they ascertained that it had no explosive components, they tested the two liquids inside, one a bright green liquid and the other a clear oil. Neither responded to their test strips. They accidently tested both liquids with the same test strip, and it immediately turned bright yellow, indicating nerve agent. As they watched, the test strip slowly faded. The yellow disappeared completely in about a minute. This was puzzling to them, as the yellow should not have faded at all."

One of the suited men asked, "Could they establish the cause? What was their conclusion?"

"They weren't sure, Tom, but they think there was something in the test strip that caused the two liquids to join together to form the agent. The agent was so short-lived that it disappeared quickly. You have better testing equipment, so you should be able to tell exactly what was going on. They isolated the liquids into vials, and included some of the test strips."

Tom and his partner finished suiting up. They brought the double-wrapped Pelican case into the clean room, and Jeff shut the door behind them. The clean room was a state-of-the-art lab for analyzing and disposing of chemical and biological warfare agents. It featured a sealed analysis chamber referred to as the "fume hood", which was connected to an incineration chamber, various filters, and an electrostatic scrubber guaranteed to release only pure air at the end.

Jeff and the fourth man in the lab, Tony Barlowe, turned their attention to the tanks. Both tanks had multiple gaping holes from the explosive bullets. There was a dividing wall about two thirds of the way back from what appeared to be the front. One tank had the front part blown open; in the other tank it was the rear.

"They said the third one had the front ruptured," Jeff said, "and they wanted us to have one of each."

Part of Tony's expertise was aircraft systems. He looked over the two tanks carefully. "It looks like whoever designed these tanks knew what they were doing. I wouldn't say they were necessarily experts, but the tanks are aerodynamically shaped, and the piping to drain the fuel from them looks just like the fill and drain lines in a MiG external fuel pod." He pointed to the interior dividing wall. "It's safe to say that fuel wasn't the originally intended payload, otherwise it wouldn't need this partition."

"Tony, how many of these do you think you could get on a MiG-23 or 27?"

"The MiG-27 comes in different variations. The MiG-27K is also known as the MiG-23. NATO calls it the Flogger. Size-wise, only one of these tanks would fit under each wing. Weight-wise, I'm going to guess the plane couldn't get off the ground with two of these plus the internal tank full of fuel, without some sort of external assistance."

Together, Jeff and Tony examined the tanks more carefully. The top of the tank was thickened—the strongback, Tony called it—with a connector to attach it to the aircraft wing.

Internally, the tank had tubes, wires, cables, junction boxes, and clear tubes containing LED arrays. There was a faint smell of jet fuel.

Externally, there was a weld line the circumference of the tank, corresponding to the interior partition. There were numerous access plates bolted closed on the top and bottom. They unbolted one of the bottom-side access covers and discovered a cylinder containing a motor-driven impeller.

"Wow!" Tony said, as he traced the interior visually. "It looks to me like this whole setup is to mix two liquids together." He looked closer. "It's quite an ingenious method to ensure mixing regardless of percentage of fill. I don't know what the LEDs would be for, though."

"Maybe to provide illumination during maintenance?"

"Looks like if we open the top access plates, we could get one of the LED tubes out."

This was easier said than done, but they finally got one out. Jeff found a battery charger, and they hooked it up to the array. Nothing appeared to happen other than a faint hum.

"Perhaps it was broken when the tank was blown up," Tony said.

"I'll have the electronics guys look it over. I wish we had an intact tank. We need to find out how much each side holds; that ratio might be important somehow. We could get a good approximation by making some basic measurements. Did you see any markings or embossings that might indicate who built these?"

"No, but I wasn't looking for that," Tony said. "Let's check both tanks."

Jeff looked at the outside of the tanks while Tony looked at the insides. At the top of the second tank, something didn't look right. "Tony, look at this connector. It looks partly crushed and this lip is broken off."

Tony looked. "Yes, I can see the tank broke loose from the MiG. If it had been jettisoned normally, this fitting would be intact. Look at the other tank. The fitting should be undamaged. When the 6-30 fires, the vibration could get so bad that it might do this. That vibration has been known to destroy the MiG's landing lights and cause the canopy to fly off."

"Really? I thought they said it was an American GAU-8 that fired the rounds. The report said the pilot recognized that the sound was not a 6-30, but something different. I listened to the recording and the pilot said he thought it was a 'g–'. The duds they found on the island were what the GAU-8 fired."

"I can explain that," Tony said. "The Russians build their weapon systems so they can fire our ammo but we can't fire theirs. It's sneaky of them. When the gun fires, it's the propellant burning and the projectile coming out of the barrel that makes the sound, not simply the machine gun barrel itself. Thus, the pilot associated the sound with the gun he was familiar with."

"Would it be possible to mount the GAU-8 on a MiG?"

"No, not at all. The GAU-8 and the Air Force A-10 were built for each other. It's not a simple matter of mounting a machine gun on one platform or another. The GAU-8 recoil is much stronger than the 6-30. The MiG couldn't handle it."

"Since there were three of these tanks on the island and two planes capable of carrying only two tanks each, one of the MiGs left the scene without any tank," Jeff said. "Perhaps he didn't make it back to where he came from. We need to contact the Marines and find out the condition of the fitting on the third tank."

Jeff called Tom in the clean room and found out all the items were sealed under the fume hood and analysis would start in earnest shortly. Tom and his team of chemists and chemical engineers would work all afternoon and through the night, with additional crew members coming on in the evening, but couldn't estimate how long the analysis might take.

Jeff sent Bob McGee a brief initial report summarizing his discussion with Tony and the progress of the chemists.

"Wow, that was refreshing!" Maggie said, as they got ready to go downstairs.

"Yes," Matt replied, "I didn't know which I needed more, to take a shower or brush my teeth."

Maggie grinned. "Do you want me to tell you?"

"No! And I really do have soap this time, young lady!"

"Don't you dare, you'll wake the baby!" She giggled.

Matt looked over at Jenny in the baby carrier, who was waving her arms and cooing.

"That reminds me, Maggie, what do children call their grandfathers in England?"

"Mostly, Pappy. But I've been thinking about that too, and I'd like Jenny to call you Grampa, the American grandfather. I'd like to save Pappy for the other one, assuming he's British."

"Perfect!"

While waiting for John to pick them up, they discussed what might happen at the airport. They didn't know, so they asked God for wisdom and understanding.

"Let's not mention her foot unless someone asks," Matt said. "If they ask, that means there's proof, or at least knowledge, of her missing foot. If not, I'm still concerned about the safety of her medical records."

"Okay. You know, though, her new foot is proof she died. Anyway, I'll hold Jenny as we enter, but I hope you won't mind holding her if she gets fidgety. You have such a calming way with her."

"Oh, absolutely! Especially if they start asking the pretty British woman all the questions."

At the airport, John was very much in charge, protecting them from the onslaught of the press. He explained they were exhausted from their ordeal, and limited the questions to about fifteen minutes. Matt and Maggie explained briefly about their escape from the plane and finding the myrtlewood coffins, explaining how God protected them at every turn.

Maggie related that Jenny had not escaped but drowned, and that God had brought her back to life. And yes, they would be willing to tell their complete story to as many as wanted to attend, after they had a chance to rest. John agreed to arrange a press conference for the next day at noon, with the location to be announced later.

At 5 p.m., the trawler arrived. They threw lines from the front and rear to the Marines, who tied them to the JLTVs a good distance from the edge of the island. There would be a Marine guarding the vehicles continually; if it looked like the vehicles would be pulled into the water, the guard would untie the lines to protect the vehicles.

LtCol Washington led Phil Henry, Penny Hasid, and the group from the trawler to the mess tent. After the introductions, he took charge of the meeting.

"We will start with a safety brief from my EOD Team Leader, Gunnery Sergeant Sims. Listen carefully. Anyone who cannot follow the instructions will be hazardous to himself and others, and will find himself or herself back on the trawler for the duration. After that, we will discuss the game plan Mr. Henry and I developed for the next few days' activities. I expect we didn't think of everything, so we will modify and fine-tune as necessary. As soon as that is done, we'll take a quick tour and get right down to business. We have about four hours of daylight left today, so let's get started. Gunnery Sergeant

Sims, the floor is yours."

After fifteen minutes, the gathering broke up into teams.

Four hours later, at 9 p.m. local time, no one noticed when National Intercontinental Airlines flight 102 touched down at Macapá - Alberto Alcolumbre International Airport. It parked at the terminal. A number of tourists deplaned and processed through customs. They picked up their luggage and were met by their tour guide, who led them to a bus advertising Amazon River and Rainforest Tours in Portuguese, English, and Mandarin. After a brief ride through the city, the bus pulled inside a warehouse on Pedro Lazarino Avenue.

A few minutes after they left the airport, a delivery truck pulled up to the rear of the plane. When the cargo hatch opened, a man got out of the passenger side of the truck, introduced himself to the crew inside the plane as Major Silva, and directed the transfer of several large wooden crates and smaller metal canisters to the delivery truck.

When the passengers got out of the tour bus in the warehouse, they found the delivery truck waiting for them.

Kevin Bhatt looked at the clock over the service counter as he came through the gate in Macapá. Ten thirty. Good, he said to no one but himself, if I can get rid of the pest, I can get something to eat, check the mail, and get to bed at a decent hour. He regretted ever saying hello; the man was a nosy chatterbox. If he never heard another monkey story that would be too soon. And why so many questions about where he lived? Wasn't he going to start out at the Equatorial Hotel at his suggestion? Grrr!

"Good night, Kevin," said the pest. "See you soon."

"Good night, Manan, sleep well."

He stopped by the office at his warehouse on his way home. It would be empty, he knew, but he would check his workers' schedules to see whom he would be taking up the river tomorrow. He tidied up in anticipation of Manan's visit later in the week—why did I ever invite him—and checked the mail for anything urgent. He didn't bother trying to cover up the wood tickets; Manan had weaseled out of him all about his export business.

During the half-mile walk to his house, it occurred to Kevin to wonder why it appeared that Manan already knew he was from Macapá, when they first met.

It was after 9 p.m. when Matt and Maggie got back to the hotel. John and Betty had taken them to dinner with executives from both airlines, who wanted to meet them and hear their stories for themselves. The survivors had been happy to oblige, as well as answer all their questions.

Matt joined Maggie in her room as she was getting Jenny ready for bed, which turned out to be a drawer from the dresser lined with bath towels. "We can ask them to bring you a crib if you'd like," he said.

"Right, but this is how Jenny has slept since she came home from the hospital. I don't want her to get too used to the luxury at such a young age."

Matt laughed. "We have some serious things to discuss before tomorrow."

"And some not so serious things too, Matt. Do you know what was the most delightful thing that happened to me today?"

"That we made it back here in one piece?"

"No."

"That we got all those nice things from the airlines?"

"No."

"Then I give up. What?"

"It was when you said, 'You can pay me back when we get to London.' I get you for a little while longer! I was afraid we'd be parting company here."

"Aww, that's sweet. That's one of the things we need to talk about. You have come so far, but I think I need to spend some more time with you to get you ready for what's ahead when you get back to Bristol. Do you have to be there by a certain date? I'd love to bring you to Indiana to meet my group of friends."

"I don't need to be back before school starts at the end of August. When I get back, I'll have bills to pay and I'll have to replace the contents of my purse. Maybe my mum can help out."

"We also need to come up with a name for the island. They said it was in the middle of the Sohm Abyssal Plain, so one possibility would be simply

'Sohm Island'. I don't like it, but it may get named that unless we have our own idea. How about 'Petunia Island'?"

Maggie laughed. "How about 'The Island Where The Wreck Emerged'?"

"I think the airlines will go get their plane before a lot of time passes, and there won't be anything to see."

"I wasn't talking about the airplane, I was talking about *me*!"

"Oh, Maggie! Wow, that's really great. It's too long, though. I think you should turn our story into a book and call it that. It would be awesome."

"Maybe I will, but you'll have to help. What else do we need to discuss?"

"Just what will happen in the meeting tomorrow. I don't know what their plans are, but I do know this: if they ask us to decide anything, we need to excuse ourselves and talk in private. Paul showed me on a map where the island is. He said it could be a significant military location, and the island itself should be very valuable. Do you have any thoughts on this?"

"Do you think we should have a lawyer?" Maggie asked.

"That's a good point. I know someone who would help us. Someone I trust. Before I go, let's thank God for all he's done and ask for his wisdom for tomorrow."

"And worship him for who he is."

It was evening on July 1. Jacob Strauss had almost finished packing after his week-long tour of duty on K103, in preparation for the 8 a.m. arrival of his transport back to solid ground. For the fifteenth time that day, he hunkered down in front of the computer screens monitoring the sand and dust storm which had originated in the Sahara Desert three nights earlier.

The NOAA SDS handbook was rather skimpy of information, so he had gotten a much better understanding from the Internet. He had first noticed the storm about twenty-four hours after it had started forming, and now the leading edge of the storm was heading west-north-west over the Atlantic Ocean.

Jacob had expected that the storm would have produced a pattern like a hurricane, like a frisbee moving across the land. However, the storm, which had started in western Niger, was still in western Niger, and now covered the northern part of Burkina Faso, southern Mali, and Senegal. He zoomed in for a closer look, and was able to discern individual swirling dust clouds across the whole length of the storm.

"Egads!" he said, loud enough for Jimmy Branson to hear.

Jimmy came into the lab and looked over Jacob's shoulder at the forty-six-inch monitor. "Wow!" he said, "too bad you're leaving tomorrow. You're going to miss all the fun."

"You can have it. I'm on vacation for a week, and I'll have all the fun I want. I might even send you some pictures."

"When does your replacement get here?"

"No replacement. No more interns for about three more months. You'll be gone before the next recruits start their training. I'll take one more look tomorrow morning before I shut this down and lock it up."

"Nah, don't do that. I want to continue to watch this, to see where it ends up."

"Why do you care? It will lose all its energy and just dump all the dust into the ocean somewhere."

Jimmy showed Jacob what he was holding, two pages from an email whose header he had cut off. "This is the transcript my boss sent out earlier, of an interview from Saturday with two survivors of the plane that was shot down and ended up on Sohm Island. They're claiming the island is going to be covered with dirt."

Jacob read the transcript. "Look," he said, pointing to the second page, "they said God had told them to call up the island, and part of the instruction was to have dirt cover the island."

"When did they do that?"

"Friday night."

"And when did the storm start?"

"Friday night!"

"That's why I care."

104

At six o'clock Tuesday morning, Tony Barlowe joined Jeff Peterson in the CIA lab. They looked like twins in their white lab coats. Jeff said, "I just got off the phone with Tom. He's back in the clean room after getting a couple hours of sleep next door. They've analyzed the two liquids and found them to be variants of what we are already using for binary nerve agent. He said the problem is that they can't get the two liquids to combine to form the agent.

"They tried agitation, heating, different catalysts, and pressure, but nothing has worked. They worked out the chemical structure of both liquids, and can tell where on the two molecules they should join together, but they just won't join."

Tony started to get excited. "I think I know the answer! Look at my hands." He held them out for Jeff to see.

"Red," Jeff replied. "They look like you spent too much time in the tanning booth."

"Yes! Exactly! Yesterday afternoon, trying to get the LED strip to work. It worked! It burned my hands. Quick, call the electronics guys. We need to find out the wavelength of the LED light. It has to be ultraviolet light for it to give me the sunburn. That's why we couldn't see any light. Maybe that's what joined the chemicals together."

Jeff called their electronics chief at home, explained the situation, then added, "We also need to find out what power these LEDs require. When you come, bring some gear so they can plug it in when we give it to Tom."

He called Tom in the clean room and told them to take a break for a while. "Come on out and we can compare notes."

While they were waiting for the electronics crew, Jeff showed Tony and Tom his calculations on the volume of the tanks. "A rough estimate of the total volume is a little over two hundred cubic feet, or a little less than sixteen hundred gallons, divided by the partition into one hundred and twenty-three cubic feet and seventy-seven cubic feet."

Tom was looking over Jeff's notes, and now it was his turn to get excited as he completed a quick mental calculation. "That's precisely the same ratio of the volumes of the two liquids we've been analyzing!"

Jeff looked at the other two, then at the tank. He shuddered and said, "Sixteen hundred gallons of nerve agent. Times two tanks. Times two MiGs. We don't know how many tanks and how many MiGs they might have. We don't even know who 'they' are!"

"Time is not working in our favor," Tom said, "so our first step is to provide a basis to extend electrical power to the LEDs. The exact wavelength is quite irrelevant if it successfully excites the two chemicals to coalesce. They can make an exact determination of the wavelength later. Tony, see if there's another undamaged and fully functional LED strip for your testing."

Jeff said, "At the same time, we need to query every chemical manufacturer worldwide, to find out who is making these chemicals and who's buying them. I'd better call Bob."

Jeff hung up from his phone call to Bob McGee about the same time as the electronics experts arrived, Ken Stokley and his assistant. While they were setting up their equipment, Jeff told Tom and Tony, "Bob said he would start working on the chemical producers, because it's obvious someone is making the nerve agent. However, at this point, there is no concrete evidence linking the tanks to the liquids. They just happened to be on the island at the same time. This is important because if they want just a small amount of the liquids, we may never find the manufacturer, and they may be making it themselves."

"True," Tom said, "and as soon as we are provided an LED array giving the appropriate output, we would be able to verify the efficacy of the protocols we have developed. If utilization of the LEDs results in the conjoining of the two liquids, that would be presumptive evidence of the link between the tanks and the liquids."

"What I can't understand," Tony said, "if this tank would be used to disperse the agent, I assume as an aerosol or a gas, how would they use a MiG to do it? They might have to be too high over their target for it to be effective, and the exhaust from the MiG might burn up all of the nerve agent as it flies through it."

Ken Stokley brought over one of the LED tubes with a cord attached. "There are one hundred LEDs per strip, and each one takes one watt of electric power. That's pretty strong for as small as they are. They should get that much out of the MiG electrical system, though. It will take us a little while to get the wavelengths. The tube surrounding the LED strip is plastic. When you set it up in the clean room, bear in mind that ultraviolet light gets blocked by glass, rather than passing through it."

After Tom took the tube into the clean room, Jeff asked Ken, "Did you find any markings that might show where it came from?"

"No, the only things on there were the plus and minus signs for the connectors and a number printed with a white paint pen. We think it's a serial number because the two we've seen so far are different, '016' and '039'. We'll check the other two tubes, also."

The other tubes were '006' and '018'.

CLASSIFICATION: SECRET
FROM:          ROBERT R. MCGEE
TO:            VTC TASK FORCE
DTG:           7:00 AM 2 JULY 2019 (02JUL19 1100Z)
SUBJECT:       PRELIMINARY REPORT OF ISLAND OBJECTS INVESTIGATION

1. CIA Lab received two metal tanks and one packaged baggage from
unnamed North Atlantic island '35.2N 52.2W' at 1 p.m. 1 July 2019.

2. Metal tanks.

   a. Tanks were aerodynamically-shaped, with fittings to attach to MiG-27
wing stores. Volume approximately two hundred cubic feet. Internal
dividing wall separated front thirty-eight percent from rear sixty-two
percent, with flaps to allow transit of liquids between front and rear. LED
arrays illuminated both sections. Complete physical description is available
upon request.

   b. One identical tank was left on the island.

   c. Of the three tanks, two appear to have been torn loose from the MiGs,
perhaps during the firing of the machine guns.

   d. Initial indications are that the tanks most recently contained jet fuel.

3. Baggage.

   a. Suitcase contained device to function upon opening. Suitcase was
crushed by water pressure. Device was also crushed but did not leak.

   b. Device contained two chemicals identified as binary nerve agent
constituents. These chemicals are different than any known binary pairs.
Analysis is continuing to determine method of joining.

c. We have initiated worldwide search for possible constituent manufacturers.

CLASSIFICATION: SECRET
CLASSIFICATION EXEMPT FROM STANDARD DECLASSIFICATION SCHEDULE

Maggie and Jenny joined Matt in the rooftop restaurant for breakfast. "Wow!" Matt said. "I didn't realize what a good-looking daughter I was getting."

Maggie blushed and giggled. "I give all the credit to Macy's."

During breakfast they discussed the island's name again. "I went downstairs to the business center this morning, Maggie, and pulled up a map of the world on the Internet. A lot of larger islands don't have the word 'island' in their name."

"Like Australia?"

"Haha! So I was thinking, how about 'Emergent'? It refers to you, of course, and to the plane, but also to the island itself."

On the brief trip to the State Department, Maggie related the conversation she had just had with her mum. "She has a key to my flat, and she said she would get my mail and check the due dates of any bills that might come in. There shouldn't be many. I told her it might be a week before I get back and she was okay with that. I think we should call John Henderson and tell him not to book us on tomorrow's flight. I told her I missed her. She wants to meet you."

"Maggie, are you trying to, uh…"

"Well, I have thought how nice it would be for my father to be married to my mother, but no, absolutely not. It was all her idea."

Mr. David Clark met them at the main entrance to the Truman Building, and led them to a small meeting room next to the Benjamin Franklin Room. He introduced them to his counterpart, Mr. Nigel Barnett, representing the British Foreign Secretary. Matt and Maggie also met representatives of the British Ambassador to the US, the American Ambassador to the UK, British and American militaries, several lawyers representing both countries, and finally Captain Louis Palova of the US Navy.

"We talked to you on the radio," Matt said to him.

"Yes, I'm not here in an official capacity, but I wanted to meet you both. I'd like to speak with you after the meeting. I have something for you that I think you'll find useful this afternoon."

Mr. Clark ushered them all to a large U-shaped table filling the other end of the room. It was set with name plates, and at each name plate was a microphone, napkins, note pad with State Department pens, and a glass of ice water. The Americans were on one side of the U and the Brits were on the other. Matt and Maggie found their names at the head of the table, with Mr. Clark and Mr. Barnett to their sides. Maggie parked the stroller between her and Matt so she could keep an eye on Jenny. Everyone sat except Mr. Clark, who presided over the meeting from the open end of the U.

"Welcome, Mr. Carven and Ms. Trillbey. This has been quite a sensational and traumatic five days for the world, since last Friday. We mourn the 291 people who lost their lives, but we rejoice that you were spared. We have set aside some time at the beginning of this meeting, for you to tell us what you want to about your part in all this. Before you do, though, I want to explain that the main purpose of this get-together is to figure out what to do with this island that popped up in the middle of the North Atlantic. Most of us have heard your interview at the airport yesterday, but we are willing to hear those things again as well as everything else that has happened to you both since you left Chicago."

Matt and Maggie had the audience captivated for the next twenty minutes as they recounted the wonderful things God did for them, starting even before the plane trip. It was a very condensed version, and concentrated mostly on how they escaped the plane and how they called the island into existence, starting with the dreams Matt had, the specific things they called for, and ending with them waking up with the island underneath them. They answered several questions, some about Jenny's drowning and coming alive again, as well as about the dirt. The dirt always seemed to generate questions, so they had developed a stock answer, marvelous in its simplicity: "We don't know when the dirt is coming."

Mr. Barnett, on Maggie's right, brandished a remote control. "I can help with that."

He pressed a few buttons, and soon a projector somewhere above him lit up a screen which was descending from the ceiling behind Mr. Clark. "The BBC World Weather Service is reporting a massive sand and dust storm," he said, "heading west from Africa on a track normally followed by hurricanes."

He switched from television to Internet, and found the weather service. "It evidently originated in the Sahara Desert sometime last Friday evening."

They watched the display for several minutes, and learned that a high-pressure system west of the Canary Islands would probably force the storm to the north where it would not threaten the east coast of America. Viewers were advised to check back from time to time for the latest updates.

"Of course, this doesn't prove anything yet, but it certainly gives credence to your story," Mr. Barnett concluded.

Mr. Clark resumed control of the meeting. "Okay, everyone, let's get down to business. Mr. Carven and Ms. Trillbey, the US State Department and the UK Foreign Secretary's Office, together with the military departments of both countries, have been in heavy discussions yesterday and this morning about this island. We need to act quickly before another country beats us to it. We, that is, our two countries, have a proposal which will meet our needs and we feel will be attractive to you. Before we tell you what it is, we have to ask, which of you actually reached the island first?"

Matt responded for them both. "We anticipated this. We were asleep when the Good Ship Myrtlewood, as we called our little vessel, was lifted up by the island. So after we woke up, we stepped off the pallet together, touched the surface together, and fell into the mud together."

"Then here is what we propose," Mr. Clark said. "Mr. Barnett, please correct me if need be. Both the US and the UK would claim the island as a joint sovereign territory, with a line between the two sectors to be decided later. Both countries recognize your right to ownership, with the stipulation that if either of you ceases to be the owner, either through death or sale or gift or abandonment, then ownership reverts to the other and it would be the sole sovereign territory of that owner's country.

"Further, both countries recognize the military importance of the island, and would desire to purchase or rent areas of the island for this purpose. They initially propose to build an airfield, a small seaport, and radio transmission relay towers on the tall peak, with a fuel farm and other structures."

Matt asked, "What do you need from us right now?"

"Just your general agreement, then our legal teams will prepare the documents. We expect you will want your own lawyers to review them before you or we sign anything. We also need to name the island. Without your input, it will simply become Sohm Island, since it is in the middle of the Sohm

Abyssal Plain. But we would like to give you the opportunity to name it."

"Could you excuse us for a few minutes? Maggie and I would like to discuss this in private before we give you an answer."

Mr. Clark called a brief recess and Matt and Maggie strolled Jenny out into the main hallway.

After a quick prayer, Matt said, "What do you think, Maggie?"

"Sounds good to me. We need to find out if they expect us to live there to maintain ownership. I didn't like the sound of that word 'abandonment'. I like that they are willing to let your lawyer look at it, and I like 'Emergent' as the name."

"I agree with you completely. Especially about letting our lawyers look at it first, before we sign anything. It takes the pressure off. I'd like to stipulate that commercial flights and boats be able to use their facilities. Even though the island might be a three-mile column of basalt, we should demand mineral rights and full access to the underwater caverns when they're found. I'd rather do a rental than purchase. I don't expect we'd get rich, but it would make it easier for all if they ever decide to abandon it themselves. Oh, and it would be fun to have our own zip code."

"And postal code. Maybe part of the rent could be the permission to use their facilities, and cell tower if they have one."

They were about to go back into the meeting, when a thin, rather short man approached. He looked to Matt like he needed some quantity time in the sun and fresh air, and he walked with a slight limp. "Hello," he said, "Matt Carven and Maggie Trillbey? I'm Bob McGee. I'm one of the ones who watched you wave to our satellite. Do you have a few minutes?"

"We're about to go back into a meeting right now," Matt answered. "Do you know Captain Palova?"

"Yes, we watched you two together."

"Come on in," Matt said. "He's sitting in the back. He said he wanted to have a word with us after the meeting. Won't you join us then?"

"That will work out great."

They rejoined the group inside and explained their desires and thoughts. They got clarification on abandonment; they would not have to live on the island to maintain ownership.

"What you've said all sounds doable," Mr. Clark said. "We will have our team check into the legality of what you've asked for, and we can negotiate the rent later. You said 'Emergent', did you mean 'Emergent Island' or simply

'Emergent'?"

Maggie spoke up, "We meant simply 'Emergent'. Would that be a problem for navigation or maps?"

"I don't think so. I just wanted to clarify. Do you have anything else, or does anyone else here have anything else?"

No one did. Mr. Clark said, "I have one more photo I'd like to show you as we close."

He clicked the remote. The island appeared, showing the American and British flags hoisted side-by-side, with Matt and Maggie in front, facing the flags of their respective countries. The US Marine Corps members were saluting the American flag, and the rest of the people were standing at attention facing both flags.

After a brief round of applause, Mr. Clark adjourned the meeting with the request that Matt and Maggie would provide him with their lawyers' names and email addresses. He told them that by the end of the day, the two countries would issue a statement to the world that Emergent was now a joint territory of the US and UK.

After the meeting was over, Captain Palova and Bob McGee approached Matt and Maggie. Captain Palova gave a manila envelope to Maggie, saying, "You probably thought I was being nosy asking where your daughter was born. I'm sure some of the rest thought I might want to discredit your story by making her records disappear, but to tell you the truth, your story made me start to question the things I believe, and I wanted to see for myself what Matt had said."

Maggie opened the envelope to find x-rays and photos of Jenny, taken after she was born with a foot missing. She was not sure how to feel about this apparent invasion of privacy. "Thank you. How did you get these?" was all she could muster.

Matt quietly took a step backwards. Maggie looked up and saw him mouthing, "Ask first!"

She got it, the admonishment to be the new Maggie and let God's love shine through. She brightened and looked to Captain Palova with a smile.

He responded, "They borrowed the medical records and scanned these at high resolution, then emailed them to me. They are just copies. I see they spelled Jennimore's name wrong."

"Yes, the 'they' is the passport office and not the hospital. It's really Jennimoore. The passport is missing the second O. If it had been spelled correctly on the passport, I never would have believed that Matt's message for me really came from God. That misspelling is what gave me hope after Jenny drowned."

"You're giving me a lot to think about. If there's anything I can do for you while you both are in town, please let me know. Good luck with your interviews later! Now let me introduce you to Bob McGee."

"We've already met," Bob said. "I'll be just a few minutes, and you can stick around if you want to, Louis."

Captain Palova wanted to hear what was on Bob's mind. The room had cleared out, so they sat at a table.

"In my intelligence job at the agency, I deal with facts. Speculations, rumors, and opinions are useless to me," Bob said. "The security of our nation depends on the accuracy of the data we give out, so I need all the help I can get. It's not simply facts I need from you, though, it's understanding as well. I saw you both wave to our satellite, and you claimed God told you it was there. Then an island appeared, and you stated God told you that, too. I am going to assume everything you told us is true, because I have no other explanation. I am putting my personal thoughts on all this on hold for the time being, because what I personally believe is irrelevant."

Matt interrupted. "No, it's not irrelevant. Look at this as an opportunity to change what you believe based on seeing what God is showing you."

"Okay. Anyway, the island is there, and the airplane is on it, as well as other things that were on the plane. My teams have examined what was brought back, and without getting into details you shouldn't know, life on earth as we know it is being threatened. If that island hadn't brought that plane to the surface, we would never know it until it was too late. Even now it may be too late, and that is why I've come."

"If God hadn't brought Maggie back to see me, we'd both still be strapped into our seat belts at the bottom of the ocean."

"Here's what I need to know and understand. I have to tell you I feel really awkward and funny asking this. And please don't breathe a word of this conversation to anyone, otherwise the results may be disastrous. Not to you—this is not a threat—but to the whole world."

"Okay," Matt said, "you have our word. Right, Maggie?"

"Yes, definitely."

"When God spoke to you about the island, either in words or dreams or feelings, did he give the slightest explanation of why he wanted it? There have been natural catastrophes and man-made disasters which have killed millions upon millions where God didn't step in and prevent it. I sense quite an urgency to find out who is behind this. If you can shed any light at all it may point us in the right direction."

"Matt and I discussed this before we called up the island and after, and we had no idea why. We didn't even know the plane was on the island until the Marines came and picked us up."

"I don't remember any part of either dream that I didn't tell Maggie," Matt said. "We asked God for wisdom in calling up the island, so it would meet his desires, but neither of us got any answers like that."

"Thank you," Bob said. "We will continue our pursuit, but I thought it would be wise to check with you as part of that pursuit. If you think of anything that might help, it would be best to call Captain Palova."

"Before you go," Matt said, "may we pray for you and ask God to let you be successful?"

Bob said yes, so Matt and Maggie asked God to give him peace, clarity of mind, and the answers he was looking for.

Matt looked at Maggie as the two men departed. "Whew!" he said.

"Whew is right!" she replied. "Almost the same question Phil Henry had."

"We need to put this out of our minds for now. We don't need to have any of this affect our interview later."

Mr. Clark's driver was waiting to take them back. At Matt's request, he took them to Franklin Square instead of their hotel. "It's a surprise," he told Maggie on the way over.

CLASSIFICATION: SECRET
FROM:     BERNARD C. MANTILE
TO:       VTC TASK FORCE
DTG:      10:30 AM 2 JULY 2019 (02JUL19 1430Z)
SUBJECT:  REPORT OF MONETARY TRACKING

1. Background:

a. In May 2019, an individual set up a savings account at Bakersfield

Savings Bank (BSB), Bakersfield, California.

b. On 21 June 2019, the account was accessed at 1:03 a.m. through IP address 191.6.118.145.

c. $232M was transferred in and immediately transferred out to thirteen separate accounts outside BSB. The account was then deleted.

d. Treasury was notified 24 June 2019.

2. Our investigation revealed the following:

a. Account was set up by a college student who said he and friends were cooperating with federal Treasury agent's investigation by opening accounts with cash at BSB and giving the account numbers to the agent. After thirty days they would be able to close the account and keep the cash, if everything were in order. Student did not know the account had been deleted.

b. There was nothing illegal about the transfers into or out of BSB.

c. BSB would have raised no concerns if the account had not been deleted. The deletion caused an audit flag error of fifty dollars, the amount of the initial deposit.

d. The deletion of the account erased all transactions for the account. However, those transactions still existed within BSB's transfer registry. On 27 June 2019 we asked BSB to determine where the funds were transferred from.

e. On 24 June 2019, Treasury logged on to the Worldwide Bank Registry (WBR) in Amsterdam, to which all banks report transactions of over one million euros. For most banks, including BSB, this is done automatically at the conclusion of the transfer. The WBR entries for 8:03 a.m. UTC showed transfers to thirteen accounts worldwide: Brazil (one), India (four), Italy (one), Serbia (one), US (two), Unknown (four). The registry total for the thirteen transfers was $232M.

f. There was no record in the WBR of the transfer to BSB.

g. On 1 July 2019, BSB reported it had tracked the transfer from a bank in Allahabad, India, but there was no associated account number.

h. Another US agency with contacts in India discovered the funds disappeared from the account of Mr. Hem Laghari just after 2:30 p.m., 21 June 2019, in Allahabad. He was in the process of transferring eighteen billion rupees to the account of India Quality Air. Further investigation revealed that at that time, an unknown individual was in the process of opening an account at the bank, using the IP address shown in paragraph 1b above.

3. Banks and account numbers referenced in paragraph 2e above will be provided to those proving need-to-know.

CLASSIFICATION: SECRET
CLASSIFICATION EXEMPT FROM STANDARD DECLASSIFICATION SCHEDULE

"A jewelry shop?" Maggie asked, after they had walked a couple blocks from where their ride dropped them off.

"I looked up this place on the Internet this morning. I thought we'd have enough time before the press conference."

When they arrived, Matt reached into his pocket and pulled out the ring. "My granddaughter just inherited this ring and we're wondering what you can tell us about it," he said to the man behind the counter, who was wearing a nametag that said Pete. Underneath, in small letters, it read Master Jeweler.

Pete took the ring, winked at Maggie, and said, "It's nice to inherit things, ain't it?"

Maggie laughed, a good hearty hoot. She looked at her "grandfather" Matt and mouthed, "Ask first!"

She pretended not to see Matt mouth back, "Soap."

She turned back to Pete, gestured to Jenny, and told him, "She's a little young to appreciate it just yet."

Pete sprayed a cleaning solution on the ring, rinsed it, dried it off with a cloth, and looked at it with his loupe, which he had pulled down off his forehead. He looked at it some more with a double-lens magnifying glass. He turned around and yelled to someone in the back of the store, "Hey Gino! C'mere! I want ya to see something."

While Gino was coming, Pete said, "Two emeralds, mebbe a half carat each. The ruby in the center is mebbe a carat. Hafta measure to be sure. Good color in the stones, worth probly ten grand total. But that ain't what makes it so valuable. It's the ring itself. Lookit how it shimmers."

By this time Gino had arrived and inspected the ring. "We saw one just like this years ago. It was sapphires that time." Then to Maggie, he asked, "Where did you get this?"

Maggie wanted to say, "Jenny swallowed it when she was dead," but Matt said, "It was in the belly of a shark for some time, we just don't know how long."

Gino went back to the rear of the shop to the office, and Pete handed them the magnifying glass. "Lookit the surface of the gold."

They took turns. "It looks like it has a texture to it." "It looks almost 3-D."

"Yes. The shark's stomach acid leached away the copper outa the gold. The longer it's in the stomach, the more copper is gone, and the more it seems to shimmer, 'cause the light it just bounces around inside the surface of the gold. We've tried to duplicate it with different acids but we ain't never been able to. How big was the shark?"

Matt estimated based on how much of it they had seen. "It was a twenty-foot great white."

Gino came back with a photo of the sapphire ring. "Twenty years ago. The photo doesn't do it justice. It was caught on something plastic in a great white shark belly and wasn't able to pass through." Attached to the photo was an appraisal sheet explaining the circumstances of its condition. "I don't know exactly how much it would be worth, but if you left it with us a few days, we could get you a fairly accurate estimate."

"No thanks," Maggie said. "This is all my daughter inherited from my father and we'll let her decide when she's old enough."

After a phone call, John Henderson picked them up at the corner of 14th and H Streets. They had gotten a quick bite to eat at Grist Mill. While Maggie fed Jenny, they had discussed the upcoming press interview. "I guess now that you have Jenny's photos, you can talk about her foot," Matt had said.

"Yes, and we can show them the proof."

Betty was not with John. Instead, he introduced Wayne Smith, a talk show host from a local television station. "Wayne will be the interviewer, and he will tell you how the interview will be set up on our way over. Betty will join us there. Go ahead, Wayne."

"Hi, Matt, Maggie. Will it be all right if I call you that?" After he got the affirmatives, he continued, "The first thirty minutes will be aired live on several national and cable networks and the BBC. So we have to start right at twelve o'clock sharp, and we need to be in our places by 11:55. Three segments of eight minutes of interviews and two minutes of commercials. We're not real strict on time. That is, we won't cut to a commercial while you're in the middle of a sentence.

"After that, are you up for an hour or so of recorded free-play where you talk about whatever happened for however long you want, and answer some more questions? That will be more about what you were feeling, what was going on in your minds when the plane was going down, things like that. During the live part, are there any questions you want or don't want asked? I have a list of questions. Look it over and tell me what you think."

He handed them the list and they looked it over together. Maggie answered first. "After the live show, we will be yours for as long as you like as long as Jenny doesn't get too fussy. I would like to hold her because of her foot, which we haven't talked about in the interviews so far. I think your viewers would be really interested in knowing what happened from the time the pilot told us to get ready until we ended up in the ocean. We could do a whole eight-minute segment on that alone.

"I don't have any questions to add other than what you have, and the list looks like a lot more than thirty minutes. By the way, which BBC station will be airing the show? I want to call my mum and tell her to watch."

Wayne didn't know, but they could check when they got there.

Matt said, "Please don't ask these questions about romantic involvement. There was none, and I think the questions would just be a distraction."

Wayne made a mental note to put them on the spot, if there were a good opportunity.

CLASSIFICATION: SECRET
FROM:        ROBERT R. MCGEE

TO:       VTC TASK FORCE
DTG:      6:30 PM 2 JULY 2019 (02JUL19 2230Z)
SUBJECT:  SUPPLEMENTARY REPORT OF CHEMICAL AGENT
INVESTIGATION

1. Reference email, Robert R. McGee, 02JUL19 1100Z, Subj: Preliminary
Report of Island Objects Investigation.

2. Characteristics of the binary agents:

   a. Chemical structure available upon request.

   b. The two binary constituents join readily when illumined by wavelength
357 nanometers. Volatility: resulting agent diffuses rapidly in air.

   c. Agent is stable in the absence of oxygen. It decomposes rapidly when
exposed to air, with half-life approximately eleven minutes. Decomposition
in the molecule does not occur at the point of joining. The residue after
decomposition will not rejoin and is not toxic.

   d. Agent subject to eight thousand psi (approximate pressure at fifty-four
hundred meters sea depth) decomposes into original binary constituents.

3. Lab has been able to reproduce constituents.

4. Worldwide search for producers of the chemicals has been refined to
suppliers and producers of these constituents.

5. Investigation and analysis are ongoing.

CLASSIFICATION: SECRET
CLASSIFICATION EXEMPT FROM STANDARD DECLASSIFICATION SCHEDULE

It was beginning to get dark on the Amazon River as Kevin Bhatt approached
Macapá. Only about a half hour until the barge reached his warehouse. He
had been thinking about his dinner date with Manan Ganguly ever since they

turned off the Rio Jari and headed east toward the ocean.

Something didn't seem right, and dread settled over his thoughts. What did he know about the son of the monkey hunter? One, he had known Kevin was from Macapá. Two, he was incessantly asking questions about his home. Is it in a secure neighborhood? Are the houses close to each other? Kevin had to admit, though, that he had let it slip that he was rather well off, so those questions might have seemed natural to ask if one were from Jaipur. On the other hand, one had to be well-to-do himself, if his father could afford his own ape museum.

Couple that with recent events with the IBC. Three, Rishaan had lashed out at him about the money. What was the big deal about that? He was glad Dasya was there, or else he might have come back to Brazil with a black eye or worse. Four, why did they send a broken plane? Please keep this at your place, and we'll send the parts when we can. At least the money came to his account and he could afford to pay the workers. Five, why the drawer full of health brochures? He didn't need those here.

When he got to five, he realized he was dead meat. Specifically, lamb. As in, sacrificial lamb, and Manan Ganguly was to be the butcher.

He had his pilot drop him off at a pier off the Rua do Araxá. "I'm going to have a few at the Bier Haus, and then walk home. Have the men unload the tank at the warehouse. I'll see you tomorrow."

When the barge was out of sight, he texted Manan. "Out of town errand lasting until Sat. Sorry I'll miss you Thurs. Let me know next time you're in town."

Kevin waited at the Bier Haus until he got the reply from Manan, "Yes. OK. Probably late Sept." He turned off his phone, removed the battery, and started off in the opposite direction from his house, toward the home of an old friend who owed him a favor.

Rishaan closed his eyes, and a dreamy expression covered his face. "Prisha was on her deathbed. It was so quick. Her family was there, and my parents." He wiped away a tear. "We were so right for each other. When my parents met her, they agreed, and started making the arrangement with her family." Another tear. "It was the pollution that caused the cancer, from the smokestacks and vehicles in Allahabad. She would die within the hour. She looked so peaceful, so calm. She said she got a visit during the night, and now she was one with God. She asked me to do what I could, to help end the pollution."

Dasya had never heard this story. "She was one with God? Who visited her? Did she explain that at all?"

"I was so distraught. I wasn't thinking, I was just staring into her beautiful face. She was talking, but I didn't hear her words, just her voice. Such a soft, sweet voice. Then she stopped briefly, and I focused on her words again. That's when she said she was one with God. She smiled at me, and then went into the coma."

Rishaan leapt to his feet, the reverie abruptly broken. "So when she spoke,"—he turned and looked Dasya straight in the eye—"it was God speaking!"

"That was almost twenty years ago," Dasya reminded him. "And soon, very soon, we will fulfill your promise to her."

Rishaan started pacing. "The bastards will pay. And the others will pay. The whole bloody mess of them! Like the sardines in the plane."

"There were three sardines that escaped. Did you see the interview on TV last night?"

"No, and I don't care about them. It was the plane we needed to get. And now the bloody plane is, is … THERE!"

"You should have seen the interview, Rishaan. A man and a woman. The woman, mostly. They claimed they called up the island from the bottom of the ocean so the plane would be exposed." Dasya added the last part to try to explain to himself the serendipitous raising of the aircraft out of the sea.

"WHAT?! I hate them!"

"They said God told them to call up the island."

"NO! That can't be!" Rishaan hurled his tea cup across the room, shattering the glass in a picture frame holding a photo of his mother. "They don't know anything. If our project fails, it will be their fault. If we don't succeed, I will kill them! I will kill them both! Just like I killed … "

"Like you killed who?"

Rishaan sat down slowly. He didn't understand how his friend could be so calm about things. Nothing seemed to be going according to plan. First, it was Luka. Then it was Bhatt and his idiot hacker. There might not be any consequence to that, however. Time would tell. As for Bhatt, he brought it on himself. Maybe Dasya just didn't know.

"Luka. Luka Stanković. He threatened me."

"Luka? Are you kidding me? He is the creator of our recipe, our solution. Without him we have nothing! You and he worked together on this to perfect it. Tell me you're just joking."

"No. He was a fool. About ten days ago he came to me complaining that the recipe was a mistake. The liquid was too strong, he said. Idiot, I told him, how can it be too strong? Dead is dead! He said something about the pollution being a problem. I exploded on him and didn't want to hear any more. Of course the pollution is a problem. That's the problem we're going to fix!

"He said we had to quit before it was too late. The chicken-hearted wimp. 'No,' I said, 'we are too close. The materials are all ordered.' He told me if I didn't stop now, he would tell the team leaders himself. I forced myself to appear calm, and told him I would think about it. So he went home."

"I guess he didn't tell the team leaders. Nobody mentioned him when we had our meeting."

"No. I went to visit him after supper, with my pistol in my pocket. I told him I had thought it over, and God said to go forward with the plan. I shot him in the chest, and when he fell on the floor, I shot him twice in the head."

Dasya didn't even blink. "What did you do with the body? Did you just leave him there?"

"No. He had his motorbike parked in the living room. I dressed him in his pajamas and motorcycle jacket, put him upright on his bike, propped it against his stove, and tied his hands to broomsticks to keep them up in the air. I took all his papers and notes.

"I came back about two in the morning and rigor mortis had set in. I put his helmet on him, got on the bike, and tied his hands around my waist to keep him upright. I drove him to the New Yamuna Bridge, on the motorcycle lane, and it was quite deserted. When I got to the middle of the bridge, I threw him over. I said 'Good riddance, coward!' Prisha would have been proud."

Dasya suddenly had a bad feeling about this whole adventure. Rishaan was becoming quite irrational, and the chemical expert, Luka, had wanted to back out. Too late for what, he wondered. As much as he had been convinced their project would work, now it seemed like the bottom was about to fall out. He needed an exit plan. "Does Rushil know what happened?"

"Yes. Rushil went to visit Luka, saw the blood and searched for him. He couldn't find him, so he confronted me about it. I told him Luka wanted all the glory for himself and attacked me. I was only defending myself. I don't think Rushil believed me, but he can't prove otherwise. He hasn't said or done anything about it since."

Or so he thought.

JC Smalley had been showing Harper Avalon, the FBI trainee, an improvised trip-wire detector when the alert sounded on his phone. It was midday on Wednesday. "Ah, the end of radio silence," he said to the group assembled in the second-floor room of a warehouse at the end of Pedro Lazarino Avenue. Besides the two FBI representatives, the group consisted of a US Navy EOD team, a Brazilian Army EOD team, several translators, a Brazilian policeman from the state of Amapá, and several members of the Brazilian Intelligence Agency, the ABIN.

This was the signal they had been waiting for. The signal that the hackers' lair at the eastern end of Dos Caramuru Avenue overlooking the Amazon had been taken. The signal that the Rio Jari hideout had been captured. They quickly loaded up their gear, and headed to the police bus waiting to take them the half kilometer to their first destination.

On the short trip to the workplace of the hackers, JC stood up and reiterated the plan to the group. "Remember, EOD goes in first and finds and safes any booby traps. After ABIN goes in and does their work, photographing and policing up documents and equipment, the rest of us go in. Do not touch anything until ABIN gives us the okay."

He waited until the translator finished and the Brazilians nodded their heads. He continued, "Those of us going to the other site need to work quickly, not conducting any in-depth analysis. Then Carlos of the ABIN, the two EOD teams, Harper, and I will take the police helicopter to the other site while the rest analyze this location and bring everything back to the warehouse to the tables in the red area. The green area will be used for the other site."

When they arrived, they found the rooms abandoned except for an ABIN agent, who informed them the terrified suspects had already been removed to ABIN HQ for questioning. In addition to the small office with radios and computers, there was a comfortable-looking living area and kitchen strewn with personal items, clothing, and food.

"Take a quick look around. Does anything look missing?" JC asked Harper.

After the quick look around, he replied, "Luggage. I don't see any luggage. And everything is in English. Nothing is in Portuguese."

"Yes, good. They would have luggage if they're not from around here. If the rest don't find it here, it must be somewhere else that would need to be found and searched. Perhaps with more personnel there also. The other thing I noticed is that everyone seems to have their own personal space, but there are only two beds. We were told there were three people, one female. Perhaps one is a local."

They were finally at thirty thousand feet again, on a hop to Chicago. Maggie was by the window, reading the New American Standard Bible Matt had bought her before they left, Matt was on the aisle, and Jenny in her new baby carrier was in the middle. Noticing that Matt had the flight magazine open to the crossword puzzle, Maggie said, "It's too bad they forgot about the Air World flight magazine. I guess you'll never find out about the fishing net."

"No, but I've moved on. If you ever see it in another puzzle tell me. Oh, and I thought you handled Wayne Smith's question perfectly."

"You mean 'Did you think you owed Matt anything special for saving you?'? It was crude how he asked it, and he knew it. If I had gotten angry or flustered, our whole story would have been sidetracked. I remembered what someone very famous once told me, someone very dear, 'Ask first, then act.' So I was doing that even before he finished the question. Besides, I knew Mum was watching, and I wanted her to see the new me."

"And God sure answered, didn't he, Maggie? 'God used Matt to save my life not once but three times, and yes, I owe God something very special. My whole life!' He was speechless for a moment, giving you an opportunity to tell the world how you gave yourself to the Lord. Anyway, tomorrow is Independence Day, and for the last thirty-seven years, I have taken my children and or grandchildren to see the fireworks. I'm so glad this year will be no exception."

He looked over at Maggie, who had leaned back into her seat. He had never seen anyone with such a look of contentment. "I have another surprise for you," he said, "when we get to Gary."

"I like surprises. What is it?"

"Swim lessons."

She looked around for something to hit him with. "Just kidding!" he said, "but if I told you, it wouldn't be a surprise."

"I changed my mind. I don't like surprises anymore."

"The week we're in Gary, you'll be staying with some friends of mine a few blocks away. Gert and Harry Somerset. Their grandchildren come to visit often, and they have everything you'll need to care for Jenny. Baby bathtub, crib, you name it. That's not the surprise, though. Harry and their son-in-law Bill will be gone on business together the whole time you're there, and their daughter Lisa is bringing her kids Madeline, who is three, and Danielle, who is eight months old. I called Harry to ask them to watch our interview, and called Gert back last night to ask if you could stay. Gert and Lisa are both eager to meet you."

"I don't know if I like this arrangement."

"Do you still trust me?"

"Yes. Is this where that part of my vow kicks in?"

"Absolutely! And next week about this time, you'll give me an A-plus in the nurture, love, and support categories. Do you have any misgivings?"

"No, since they're your friends, but tell me about them."

"You'll like them. They are like family. Lisa is a little older than you, and she was best friends with Rachel growing up. Gert and Lisa are both bottles of water adrift in the ocean."

"In that case, I'm looking forward to it!"

After twenty minutes the helicopter team had left. As they flew to the Rio Jari site, JC thought about the events since the ambassador had reported the result of his negotiations with his Brazilian counterpart. His day at home had been somber, and he had told Nicki about Joel Barth. He hated snakes, and not knowing what the Brazilian environment would be like, he had bought a pair of leather pants and heavy-duty boots. The trip south had been uneventful, and he had enjoyed the chemistry between Harper and himself.

Harper Avalon had decided he wanted to make his career in the FBI not too long after his Army promotion to sergeant. He was physically fit, but not ostentatiously so, courtesy of eleven years, ten months, and three days in the infantry. He was intelligent without being bookish, and sociable without being dramatic. He had been married, once, but the marriage had succumbed to long deployments and a wife who had a career of her own.

Harper had thought he had found an adequate replacement at the university, but that didn't work out, either. He applied to the FBI when he got out of the Army, but they pointed to his lack of education as evidence that he wouldn't be a good fit. They suggested biochemistry, pre-law, or criminal justice; he chose the path of least resistance. He made the Dean's List every semester in criminal justice and graduated with honors.

For JC, the waiting was the worst part; it always was.

He thought about the briefing they had received late on Monday, when they first got there, from the team leader, Harvey Hostetler. He had told them they knew who owned the hackers' hideout, a Mr. Kevin Bhatt, an Indian citizen. They were also aware of the other properties owned by him, including an office building, river barges, a merchant ship, a parcel of property a hundred twenty miles to the southwest, and several warehouses full of lumber products including brazilwood, brazilian teak, and brazilian rosewood. Those woods were on the endangered lists, and almost all countries on earth had made their import illegal. The parcel of property was where the radio signals had originated.

If there were the least connection between Kevin Bhatt and the downed aircraft, he would be detained for extensive questioning, and the ABIN would hammer on the illegal wood shipments in the hope of his giving up information on whatever the connection was. That's the way he would do it too, thought JC. Harper agreed, and wondered if the Brazilian interrogation techniques would be as effective as the Americans'. "They're working together," JC had told him.

Harvey met them as soon as the helicopter landed in a small clearing. He brought the team to the edge of a large open-air work pavilion with a camouflage-painted roof. It was hot, but there was a slight breeze, and on the way there, it seemed to JC they were walking in a woods rather than a jungle. He did not in the least regret wearing the snake chaps, however.

JC looked over the work area, which had a dirt floor littered with soaked-in oil spills, metal debris, plastic sheets covered with dried blue and black spray paint, and other garbage. It looked to be at least an acre under the metal roof. On one side were living quarters, a series of huts with window air conditioners and what appeared to be a communal bathroom with showers. Nearby, a larger hut had a thick cable leading to an antenna outside the pavilion roof. Probably an office. There were workbenches and tables scattered throughout, and in the very middle of the area, a MiG was sitting with one wing supported by jack stands and the other wing was missing.

What really got their attention were two groups of men. The larger group was eating chow. All were wearing camouflage; some wore military uniforms which neither JC nor Harper recognized. They assumed they were either the Brazilian Special Forces that were to be part of the mission, or police; others wore American military clothing with no markings.

All were armed, mostly with rifles. Some had holstered hand guns; others had what Harper recognized as tasers. A few from this group were separate from the main body, and were at the alert with weapons drawn.

Harvey said, "I think we got them all. We searched the huts, office, and generator pit and haven't seen anyone else, but just in case, we are ready. We also have a few lookouts for anyone approaching."

The smaller group was flat on their bellies, with hands cuffed behind their backs and feet spread apart. Most were wearing jeans or khakis or shorts, tee shirts, and leather work boots. There were fifteen altogether, including one covered with a tarp off to the side. A plastic bag at each man's head contained his pocket contents, mostly passports, wallets, keys, and cell phones.

Harvey conferred with one of the uniformed men, a Brazilian Army officer, Major Antonio Silva. The two of them directed the EOD teams to start searching the whole area for booby traps. "There was nobody who had any chemical protective gear on them, and we didn't find any such gear anywhere, when we were conducting our clearing of the buildings," he told them, "but if you come to anything closed or suspicious, we'll assume there's nerve agent present and go to our safe spot until you give us the all-clear."

Harvey and Major Silva assigned sectors to the two EOD teams. They began their sweeps, the US team at the aircraft, and the Brazilians at the office. Armed soldiers stood guard over the captured men while the searches were completed, which took about an hour.

While the EOD teams were busy, Harvey briefed the newcomers, JC, Harper, Carlos, and the police helicopter pilots, on the seizure of the compound. "We took them completely by surprise. They had three armed guards milling about under the pavilion, and when we came charging in, one tried to raise his weapon to shoot at us." He indicated the body covered by the tarp. "When he went down, nobody else so much as moved. There was one on the radio in the office, trying to warn the hackers at the other end, but there was no one at the other end." He laughed. "We got them at the same time. Then we sent you the signal."

JC introduced himself and Harper. "Harvey, you may not remember me, but I met you electronically during the VTC last Friday. I'm JC Smalley, currently on assignment to the FBI, and this is Harper Avalon from the Chicago FBI Field Office."

The three of them shook hands. "I'm pleased to meet you in person, JC, and you too, Harper. Once we get EOD clearance, please look around. We're good at taking things down, but only so-so when it's time to amass data, and we appreciate your input and expertise. My team is pretty good at doing analysis and making conclusions, but it's those intermediate steps we could use your help with. We have photographers for this site. We'll use Mr. Bhatt's trucks over there to bring everything to the Jari for transport on Mr. Bhatt's barge."

Harper asked if the Dos Caramuru group could be more than just hackers. Harvey thought he knew where he was going with that, but asked, "What do you mean?"

"Well, they send coded messages here, and get requests for supplies and equipment. Either they take care of those or are working with someone else who does. That would be either Bhatt or whoever is sending the MiGs here. Or someone else. Have you been able to tap their emails? If so, are they in the same code? The addressees have to be in plain text; do those help?"

"How would you like to come work for us?" he said, grinning. Harper took that as a compliment.

Harvey went on, "That was good. They don't send emails, though. All they do is log onto a certain email account, open a draft email which is already there, attach or download a file, save the draft, then log out. Nothing ever gets sent. We've been able to open the files, but they're encrypted using an unknown algorithm. There are no other emails in the accounts, and they change email accounts about every week. We've been surveilling them. They never go out, but every other day or so someone comes to visit. Flunkies from the warehouse, mostly, bringing food, and twice it was Bhatt."

"How long have they been there?"

"I'm not sure. The ABIN team onsite might be able to figure that out.

We've known about them about two weeks, since the money transfer in California. It took us several days to find them. Our electronic surveillance has been about two weeks, onsite about ten days. Listen, I have to go talk to Major Silva about getting the prisoners back to Macapá, which we'll do after dark. EOD should be finished soon. Go ahead and start looking around."

JC asked for a list of the prisoners, annotated with which country issued their passports, or where they were from in Brazil if they had no passport. He also suggested all the cell phones be switched off mute, with someone writing down the calling or texting party when the phones alerted.

"Harvey," JC said, "let's assume Bhatt is guilty as charged. He may be a recipient of some of that money Barry Mantile sent us the email about. Perhaps the ABIN would visit his bank and find out if there were money deposited and when."

"Okay, I'll add that to their list."

Neither EOD team found any booby traps or toxic chemicals. They declared the area clear. JC and Harper went to the MiG.

"Let's see if we can tell if it is one of the MiGs that shot down the Air World flight," JC said. "What do you know about foreign aircraft, or US military aircraft, for that matter?"

"Not much. It's been just book learning since I started."

"Well, you've come to the right place. I spent my Air Force career as an intelligence officer."

JC spent the next twenty minutes giving Harper the rudimentaries of aircraft design in general, MiG construction, how bombs and other ordnance are attached and released, and explosive components in the cockpit.

"Climb up inside," JC finally said. He followed Harper up the ladder, and stood on it outside the plane while Harper sat in the pilot's seat. He pointed out the different dials and controls, then said, "What do you see of interest in here?"

"There's a briefcase; it looks like EOD has already opened it. There are a few papers in it but not many. There's something hanging down under the seat, but it seems like it's stuck. It won't pull out."

"Don't touch it! That's the handle that functions the ejection seat."

Harper grinned. "I knew that. Also, when I got up here, I saw that the ejection seat safing pin was installed."

JC was impressed. "How'd you know about that?"

"I watch a lot of movies."

Together they looked over the rest of the cockpit, and saw nothing else of value. They had even looked for, and found, some hidden compartments between the pilot's seat and the outside skin of the aircraft. There was a workbench near the MiG covered with hand tools, welding fittings, a welder's hood, an open maintenance manual, gloves, and a cell phone. JC had Harper note which page of the manual was open.

"What do you notice that's strange, out of place, or missing?" JC asked Harper as they finished making their way around the compound.

"We didn't find the wing. There doesn't seem to be a pilot, at least not one wearing a flight suit. I didn't see any chemical protective gear or store of ammunition, security is really lax, and everything is in English. There's only one plane, so I think this wasn't one of the shooters. Besides, there's no machine gun attached."

"That's a good start. Yes, it was interesting that the filing cabinet had no lock on it. We'll examine the contents more thoroughly back in Macapá. We need to bag the drawers individually to keep them dry on the barge trip back. You probably noticed the plane has no external markings. I didn't see any stencils, so I assume the markings will be applied elsewhere or it won't have any. There was no data plate or other identifying information anywhere. There are a lot of countries which have bought MiGs, but I don't know of any which paint the top black and the bottom light blue. No wing and no pilot means the plane didn't fly here nor will it fly out, hence the barge. That was part of Harvey's brief last Friday.

"Where is the truck and trailer to move this to the barge? Perhaps they are part of the lumber operation. Harvey and the ABIN may want to take a look around to see if there are any other roads close by. I agree with you that the MiG was not one of the MiGs that shot down the Air World flight."

JC and Harper briefly conferred with Harvey and Major Silva on the way back to the MiG. Yes, they had seen the truck and trailer on their way in; EOD had already cleared it and found the keys inside.

CLASSIFICATION: SECRET
FROM:      ROBERT R. MCGEE
TO:          VTC TASK FORCE
DTG:        3:00 PM 3 JULY 2019 (03JUL19 1900Z)

SUBJECT:    SUPPLEMENTARY REPORT OF CHEMICAL AGENT
INVESTIGATION

1. Reference email, Robert R. McGee, 02JUL19 2230Z, subject as above.

2. After contacting twelve American chemical producers, three were found
which recently produced the chemicals identified as Part A and Part B of
the agents discussed in reference. Two produced Part A and the other, Part
B. None of the three produced both.

3. Our agents visited all three, who cooperated fully.

   a. All three received a solicitation in response to answering a query in the
Commerce Business Daily. The solicitation for Part A was for an herbicide,
Part B was for an insecticide, allegedly for agricultural purposes. We
obtained a copy of both solicitations.

   b. Contracts had been let for one thousand gallons of Part A from each
producer and six hundred fifty gallons of Part B. Delivery location for all
three producers is a warehouse in Bakersfield, California. Schedule called
for incremental deliveries with final delivery no later than 12 July 2019. One
producer had already shipped five hundred gallons of Part A. The Part B
producer has a partial delivery scheduled for 5 July 2019.

4. Ongoing Actions.

   a. Our agency is conducting a worldwide search for producers of Parts A
and B using the chemical names shown in the two solicitations obtained.

   b. A search warrant is being pursued by the FBI WMD Directorate, who
will execute a search of the warehouse and will question all employees there.
Surveillance of the warehouse has been initiated.

CLASSIFICATION: SECRET
DECLASSIFICATION SCHEDULED 3 JULY 2031. EXEMPT FROM FREEDOM
OF INFORMATION ACT REQUEST PRIOR TO 3 JULY 2031.

On Thursday at 5 p.m., Dasya arrived at Rishaan's house to find him cursing loudly at his television. He turned it off when he heard Dasya at the door, and said, "It's 9:30 a.m. in Brazil, and I haven't gotten the code." The "code" was a coded text message letting Rishaan know everything was copacetic in Macapá.

"Is that what you called me about earlier?" Dasya asked. "Could they be a little late?"

"They've never been this late before. They know they have until 7:30."

Dasya sat on a stool. "You knew this was going to happen, didn't you?"

"Yes. I should never have brought Bhatt on board. Rushil was stuck on him, though, and it would have been hard to say no. He was an idiot, but I didn't see it at the time. Where he found Jackson I never could figure out."

"She seemed competent enough at the time," Dasya said, "but got careless. At least she got the pilots to the plane on time."

"We don't need them anymore. They are a complete liability now that we have the money. It's only a matter of time before they get put away."

"What about our operations base there? Our hideaway? Where will we go to wait this whole thing out? Isn't that why we got Kevin to begin with?"

"We can stay here in Allahabad. We'll just pick a day with favorable winds. Who would suspect us of poisoning our own city?"

"Kevin will know. He doesn't seem like the kind who would keep our secrets once the heat is on him."

"No! He will never tell on us. I am certain of that."

Dasya had been impressed with Rishaan's calmness once he stopped his rant at the television. He had something to discuss that might jeopardize that, but it needed to be said. First, though, he wanted to find out why Rishaan was so confident about Kevin Bhatt. "Why are you so sure?"

"I took steps."

"Do you mean that box of brochures you sent back with him?"

"No, that was just to throw them off the trail when they caught him."

"Rushil? Something with Rushil?"

Rishaan shrugged his shoulders.

It was Rushil that Dasya wanted to talk about, so he abandoned his pursuit of Kevin. "Speaking of Rushil," he said, "I've been thinking about him. Do you realize we are where we are completely because of him?"

"Yes, and we must congratulate ourselves on finding such a worthy friend."

That was not the direction Dasya anticipated. "Who was it who convinced us that killing a lot of people was justified by maybe or maybe not ending pollution in the world and slowing down global warming?"

"It's just a few, and you believe it too, don't you?"

"Yes, I don't doubt it for a second," Dasya replied. "The question is, will our project work? And who was it that convinced you that Prisha wanted you to undertake this project?"

"It didn't take much convincing. I heard her say it myself."

"How did it happen that people from all over the world came to you and volunteered to help you on a project they didn't really understand, but were quite enthusiastic once they found out how a few deaths would help clean up the earth?"

"That was quite fortuitous, I admit."

"Who was it that introduced you to Luka? I never did ask how you knew him."

"I saw him several times at the Federation meetings. As president, I like to meet all the new scientists. He happened to be talking to Rushil when I came up to him, so Rushil introduced us."

Dasya realized he hadn't put a dent in Rishaan's admiration of Rushil. He wanted to exit gracefully without setting him off, but also wanted to protect his friend from himself. After complimenting Rishaan on the amazing design of the mixing tanks, and discussing how the project would be completed soon, he stood up to leave.

"The reason I came over tonight," he said, "was to tell you since there is a week or so before the excitement starts, that I'm taking Ananya and the boys on a holiday, before the summer gets too far gone. We haven't been on holiday since Raj started school."

"Where are you going?"

"Delhi. They have beautiful gardens and parks, and Ananya has never been to the zoo there. We'll be gone about four days."

But he was really planning the trip for Goa.

Soon after dark, the seven-and-a-half-hour trip back to Macapá had commenced and was completed without incident. It was decided to leave the MiG on site with a guard and retrieve it in the morning or wait until the following evening. The prisoners, including the threesome taken earlier, had spent the rest of the night sequestered in ABIN custody, and the next day were taken to an undisclosed location where they would eventually tell all they knew.

The Americans had changed into tourist garb and checked in at a local hotel. Harvey had initially gone with the ABIN personnel. He joined JC and Harper about lunchtime. He looked like a warrior returning from battle: exhausted but jubilant.

"Happy Independence Day! Sleep well?" he asked over a cup of strong black coffee.

"Yes," Harper answered, "and as soon as we finish breakfast we are going over to the warehouse."

"Before that, let me tell you some news. We, that is, the local police, raided Mr. Bhatt's warehouses and office. We didn't find Bhatt at his warehouse on the Rua Beira Rio as we had hoped, nor at his home. The ABIN has been watching his house and businesses since mid-morning on Tuesday, but he hasn't appeared. They found his passport in his house, so we know it was stamped on Monday evening at São Luis.

"The ABIN has his house, office, and boats under constant surveillance, and they'll stop him at the border if he tries to leave the country. They'll eventually catch him. There is something I'd like you to see before you look at the rest of the stuff at the warehouse. My escort will be here in five minutes to pick us up."

JC wondered what had been found out from the prisoners so far. Harvey told them he would get them a list of the prisoners with what information they gleaned from their pockets. "They haven't started the interviews yet," Harvey said. "We should know in a day or so who will talk and how much."

The warehouse looked more like a sawmill. There was a drying kiln at one end, with stacks of planks labeled with type of wood, date of cut, processing methods, dimensions, and destinations. At the other end were piles of unprocessed logs. In the middle were milling machines, band saws, material handling equipment, a small office, and a large object covered with a tarp. It was to that object that Harvey led them. "Go ahead, uncover it."

When Harper pulled off the cover, he and JC gasped. A steel tank, like the ones on the island! "We got the photos and rough dimensions the Marines sent back," said Harvey, "and it's a match to the tanks we saw from the satellite. I believe this ties Bhatt to the aircraft attack."

JC pointed out to Harper the strongback for attaching the tank under the aircraft wings, and reminded him of the MiG he had seen the previous day. "Remember the feet I showed you, that push the bomb away from the aircraft? If this proves to be an external fuel tank, when it was empty of fuel, they would jettison it so it wouldn't be a drag on them. Harvey, I hope this goes back to DC with you. This one is intact, so when we get the exact capacity, we can determine how many extra miles the MiGs could fly. Let's see if we can find a measuring tape to get a rough estimate of volume."

"Yes, it will probably beat you back. We will fly it out tonight. It will probably take you until tomorrow to examine the documents and things at the other warehouse."

They found a ten-meter tape, and measured the tank to be 4.5 meters long by 1.2 meters in diameter.

"This was quite a find!" JC said. "Thanks for showing us. Harper, are you ready?"

Harvey dropped them off at the warehouse on Pedro Lazarino Avenue. "I'm going to sleep for a few hours, then I'll come over and we'll chat."

In the three hours since Dasya left, Rishaan had wondered at his words about Rushil. Especially his comment about Prisha. He had had many one-sided conversations with his beloved since her death. "She would want you to do this," Rushil had told him.

After that, for half a year, he had told Prisha, "I'll do this for you." Every time, she had smiled at him, then faded away.

At about 8 p.m., he sat at his laptop and logged in at the FIS website. The Federation of Indian Scientists kept all their records on a server in the cloud, with many records behind a password-protected firewall. The public side of the firewall contained abstracts, event applications, meeting notes, and several user forums, which Rishaan never accessed.

He logged on to the restricted side and opened up the record of Rushil

Singh's application to the FIS. Under Education, Rushil had claimed a Master's degree in chemical engineering from a university in Australia. Frowning, Rishaan tried to remember any conversation he had ever had with Rushil where chemical engineering had come up. None.

An online search of Australia's universities failed to list the university Rushil had claimed had awarded him the chemical engineering degree.

At 9 p.m., Rishaan paid a visit to Rushil. "I'm concerned about how our project is going."

"My friend," Rushil answered, "if you hadn't shot down the airplane, everything would be fine. As it is, it should still work."

Rishaan thought he detected some smugness in the reply.

Changing the subject, he said, "There was no code today from Brazil."

"Why is that my problem? You were preparing for that even before Bhatt left the meeting. Now where will you hide, until this all blows over, so to speak?"

"I thought we were in this together. We've been planning this for months!"

"Brazil is out now, isn't it? You need to find yourselves a new lair, you and Dasya."

He is trying to separate from us, Rishaan thought. Why? "We will stay put and wait for a favorable breeze. How about you?"

"I will be taken care of. Well taken care of. Your problem is not about the project, is it? It's about the island that brought the plane up."

The anger started to bubble at the mention of the plane. He struggled to maintain control. As always, thoughts of Prisha calmed him down. But just a little. "I hate them. They are dead meat! Especially that woman. Why didn't the pilots see them?"

"They couldn't have made the island come up, but even if they had, so what? Rishaan, you need to get hold of yourself. Focus on the project. There's not much left for us to do. Work on your speeches while we wait."

"A week or so until the deliveries are complete. Then Prisha will be avenged! The air will be clean and the world will change their ways. Prisha would be so proud of our work. That British woman is nothing, a dead dog. That man, too."

"Prisha, Prisha, Prisha! Oh, please! Prisha's dead and she can't help you. Stay focused on the task at hand or that woman will be your undoing."

At first, Rishaan thought "that woman" was the British woman, then realized Rushil meant Prisha. Thoughts of her kept him from apoplexy at this disrespect, or else he would have become violent. Instead, he mumbled to himself words unintelligible to Rushil, excused himself, and headed home.

It was on the way home that Rishaan remembered Rushil's words, "I will be taken care of." What did that mean? He had seemed smug, even arrogant, instead of the mild-mannered friend he had appeared to be for the past year. He realized Rushil had successfully changed the subject after saying, "Well taken care of," by immediately making him angry about the plane. It was almost as if Rushil had a hidden agenda and wouldn't need him or Dasya much longer. He thought back to Dasya's comments about Rushil, and regretted not giving him credit for knowing anything. Only ten days to go, he told himself and Prisha.

It was about noon Thursday on Emergent, when the last body bag was loaded onto the trawler. The steel tank had been hoisted on board by the trawler's crane, as was most everything else that could be loaded on pallets. Almost all of the items from the cargo list were declared a total loss. A small squad of workers, assisted by the Marines, consolidated these items near the plane while the rest of the workers conducted the main effort of moving the two hundred ninety-one bodies to the trawler.

The airlines decided to assess the condition of the baggage after its return to Boston rather than disposing of non-returnable belongings on the island, to prevent personal items from floating away and being washed up on a beach somewhere.

The announcement of the approaching storm brought a sense of urgency to the operations. Every hour, the weather reports were received and analyzed, followed by a stowage status report to determine the need to accelerate the loading of the trawler. Each hour, the analysis confirmed they had set the right pace at the outset, and would be able to depart in plenty of time.

Phil was in frequent contact with Bob McGee, exchanging technical data on the tank and airplane damage and updates on the course of the investigation on the mainland and in Brazil. They agreed to meet early Saturday morning after JC Smalley returned from Macapá.

At 1 p.m., the trawler headed south, rounded the southern end of Emergent, and headed to Boston.

JC and Harper were opening the last bagged-up drawer from the Rio Jari compound. "What's that smell?" Harper was closer and smelled it first.

"Curry," JC said when he had gotten closer. "Funny, we didn't smell it with the other drawers, and I don't remember it at the compound, either in this drawer or in the huts."

"Maybe closing it up in a bag allowed the vapors to accumulate. Let's leave it open, go look at something else, then come back and see if the smell is still there."

"Good idea, Harper. Let's go see what was on the page that the maintenance manual was opened to."

Harper found the page number he had written down and turned there. "Preparation for JATO Attachment," he read. "What's a JATO?"

"That stands for 'Jet Assist Take Off'. Basically, it's a rocket motor they attach to a plane to help get it off the ground, because either the runway is too short or the plane is too heavy. MiGs don't need much of a runway, but if they had two of those tanks filled with fuel, they might need the extra help. Look, there's a grease smudge on this page, so it probably wasn't opened to here merely at random."

"Let's see what else this book has to offer." Harper started to flip through the pages.

"No, start at the front and turn to each page. Page one should tell us who published this and when, then we'll look for grease marks and handwritten notes on each page. First, though, dangle it by its spine, and we'll see if it tries to open to any specific pages."

He lifted the manual and gently shook it to loosen its pages. The pages separated in quite a few places, and Harper tore strips from a page in his notebook to mark each one. Then they started their exam from page one, where they found it was downloaded from the Internet. The pages Harper marked did not tell them any more than that normal maintenance was conducted. When they got to page 184, however, there was a small piece of paper that had gotten stuck to the page. On it were written in a single column, "Zeljava, Mostar, Dudhkundi, Bagdad, Hangzhou."

"Here's an assignment for you, Harper. When we get back to the hotel, find out what these mean, and if possible, what they all have in common. Let's go back now and check on that last drawer."

That last drawer had no remaining odor. It was full of manila file folders, with dividers between sets of folders. The first set had folders labeled Medtronic, Thermo Fisher Scientific, HCA Healthcare, Fresenius, Becton Dickenson, Stryker, Essilor Luxottica, Boston Scientific, Baxter International, and Labcorp. The second set were McKesson Corp, United Health Group, CVS Health, Ameri Source Bergen, Cardinal Health, Express Scripts Holdings, Anthem, and Kaiser Permanente. The third set were Johnson & Johnson, Novartis, Roche, Pfizer, Sanofi, Merck & Co, Mankind Pharma Limited, and GlaxoSmithKline.

The folders were filled with prospectuses, earnings statements, major office locations, and major clients. Most of the information appeared to have been downloaded from the Internet, and many of the pages had penciled annotations. The last set of folders was labeled US, UK, Canada, France, Germany, Hong Kong, Australia, and Japan, but all the folders were empty.

"Wow! Harper, do you recognize these names?"

"Not all of them, but it looks like the Who's Who of the healthcare world. There's something odd, though, that I can't put my finger on."

"My exact thought. We need to think about this carefully."

Harvey came in just then, carrying a sheaf of papers. "You know what's crazy? All fifteen at the compound and the two hackers are Americans, and all but the two hackers are ex-military. Why'd they have to come here? It seems it would have been a lot easier to do what they were doing at some airport overseas. It turns out there were only two hackers. The third person at this end was a translator. We, uh, they checked the customs stamps and all seventeen came to Brazil within two days of each other at the end of May."

JC and Harper quickly brought Harvey up to date on what they found.

Harvey had a theory. "Perhaps whoever these folks are working for will use the nerve agent somehow to either extort the healthcare systems or to bankrupt them. I don't get the MiGs, though. Who'd they get them from, and the ammunition? Why'd they use an American gun system when there's already a gun system on the MiGs?"

"I can answer that one," JC said, "When the MiG fires a 6-30, the vibration and recoil might tear the aircraft apart. So a different gun system would be preferable. The Russians are famous for making their aircraft and

271

weapon systems compatible with foreign weapons and ammunition while keeping us from being able to use their stuff. In other words, I think, but I'm not positive, they can put a GAU-8 in a MiG but we can't put a 6-30 in an Air Force A-10 without severe modifications. That mix of lot numbers the Marines gave us might lead to whoever sold them the ammunition. My question is, why do all the healthcare brochures smell like curry?"

"And why are those brochures even here?" Harper added. "It doesn't fit with the other three drawers. One drawer had first aid supplies and lots of bug spray, with a couple pair of used heavy-duty gloves on top. One drawer had records of all the barge movements, supply requests and receipts, and maintenance records of Bhatt's forestry equipment. The last drawer had a money box with a couple hundred reais in small bills and coins, about fifty dollars worth.

"I'm just thinking, I wonder if the gloves were in the fourth drawer all along, and were thrown into the other drawer to make room for the healthcare brochures. Maybe recently, since the curry smell hasn't had time to completely disappear. Perhaps the records came from a place where curry is common and would not be noticed. Bhatt is from India, right?"

The more they talked, the more they began to realize this place might be a decoy or a false trail. Harvey informed them the other MiG wing was not in any of the buildings or barges they searched. "Perhaps this place was set up to be expendable from the very beginning," he said, "a place to sacrifice if necessary, when it had served its purpose.

"There were no heavy hitters among the Rio Jari folks. We checked their passports against their military records and they were all mechanics, electricians, military police, and a few other military occupational specialties, and only a few had been out of the USA before this. In short, this is not an important place. Perhaps the hackers were put here because the leaders would know they would eventually be traced to here and not where the important things were happening."

"Harper could be right," JC said. "Whoever is behind this could be trying to lead us on a wild goose chase, perhaps to point us in the wrong direction. Did you check Bhatt's passport, to see where he was last and for how long? Oh, and has Bob heard from Rudy recently?"

Harvey checked his sheaf of papers. "He got stamped into India last Friday evening, and arrived at São Luis Monday. With the time difference and a full day of travel, he was there only two days. Doesn't look like a visit home. I don't know about Rudy."

"Would it be possible to check his flight coming back here, to see what kind of baggage he might have had?"

"Good idea. I'll have ABIN look into that."

"In the meantime, we should take the healthcare threat at face value until proven otherwise. Harper and I will spend some time going through the files anyway. You never know what might turn up."

Harvey left with his driver after coordinating a pickup time with JC and Harper.

After the departure of the trawler from Emergent, it took four hours to load and board the Stallion, King One. This had included eating chow, collecting pocketfuls of manganese nodules as souvenirs, and completing driving tests for Marines who had not yet demonstrated their proficiency in operating their new vehicles.

LtCol Washington had allowed the loading operation to proceed at a much more leisurely pace than when they left Camp Lejeune, not only because of the strenuous work the Marines had done over the past five days, but to allow the in-flight-refuel aircraft time to meet them at their rendezvous point.

It was now 5 p.m. on Emergent, and it would be over two months before another human being set foot on the island.

At just after 3 p.m., Tom Faraday, in the clean room at the CIA lab, called Jeff Peterson, who had set up a temporary office on the first floor of the building. "Jeff, I have some good news and some bad news."

"Okay?"

"The good news is we discovered the bad news, which I'll tell you about in person."

It must be serious, Jeff thought, for him to drop his sesquipedalian affectations.

On his way down the stairs, he texted Bob McGee, "There's bad news. I'll call you."

"We had an unanticipated deflagration cessation in the incinerator," Tom said. "The reason eludes us. The overarching emergency control mechanism terminated the process immediately, but the incinerator filled with effluvia from the fire. We did a manual scrubbing starting at the outflow, at the precipitator, checking for the agent prior to each decontamination step. That's the protocol. Everything was clean until we got to the first filter."

The fire went out, and smoke happened, Jeff told himself.

"If you recall," Tom continued, "the agent decomposes quickly in air. We supply extra oxygen to the incinerator, so it should all have disappeared even more expeditiously. But when we examined the residue at the first filter, it was still there. A half hour later, the agent had lost none of the efficacy it had exhibited at the filter. We isolated it from its environment and have been ascertaining its propensity for neurologic interdiction ever since."

Jeff looked at his watch. It was half past three. "What time was the flame-out?"

"About 9:30 this morning. To make a long story short, the agent attached itself to the ash in the smoke and the oxygen no longer could disintegrate it. Nor could moisture in the air. The agent would release from its host when in water but would need unbound oxygen to destroy it."

Tom always became even more incomprehensible when excited, Jeff knew, so he tried to calm him down. "Whoa! What host are you talking about? Please tell me all this in plain English."

"Sorry! This is a nerve agent, which acts by preventing muscles from relaxing once they tighten." Tom started at the beginning, to force himself to put everything in layman's terms. "You breathe it in, it releases in your lungs, and your heart pumps it from your lungs back to your heart, then to other parts of your body, where it attacks the nerves.

"When the nerve agent is by itself, it quickly disintegrates in the presence of oxygen. However, we found that the nerve agent readily attached to the smoke particles, which protected it from being destroyed by the oxygen. Once it got wet, like when it's in the lungs, it would release from the ash. We wondered what other micro-particles would make it behave this way, so we explored different substances and they all worked the same. We tried wood smoke, smoke from burning oil, aerosols like spray paint, and dust like you'd find in a dust storm. In every case, we would have to burn it to destroy it."

"How long do you think it could last?"

"I don't know, Jeff. Several months or more if it were kept dry."

"That would be disastrous if the agent were released in a dusty or polluted area."

"Yes, then it might get into the upper atmosphere and affect the whole world. Not just humans, either. Any animals that have muscles."

Jeff shuddered at the thought of these chemicals in the hands of terrorists. "Do you have more to do here or are you satisfied?"

"Nothing else to do except clean up."

"Help me write this up. Then you can go. I'm not going to send it to everyone yet, but at least Bob needs to know."

At 5:30 p.m., Bob McGee got the report and shuddered too, as he had done earlier when Jeff called him. As did Jon Whitaker, FBI WMD Directorate, Captain Palova, US Navy, and later, Phil Henry, FBI National Security Branch.

After an hour and a half of looking through brochures and other literature, JC could tell Harper was beginning to get a little restless. "Welcome to real detective work!"

"Yeah, I know. The notations I'm seeing aren't making much sense. Mostly just numbers in random places. I'm looking for a pattern but I'm not seeing any."

Five minutes later, about three quarters of the way through the third set of file folders, JC found the remains of a pad of paper. "Get me a pencil, Harper. There was something written on the sheet above this that was torn off."

Harper came back with a big fat carpenter's pencil. "The widest one I could find."

"I'll let you do the honors," JC told him, "Really lightly, just barely touching the paper. But you probably knew that already."

"Yes, I saw it in the movies!"

Slowly, words appeared on the paper, all the way down to the bottom. When he finished, Harper read them off to JC, who wrote them down. "Gwalior, Allahabad, Raipur, Ludhiana, Kanpur, Khanna, Xingtai, Baoding, Hengshui, Tangshan, Tetovo, Skopje, Naples, Tirana, Turin, Bakersfield, Long Beach, Visalia, Hanford, Madera."

"I wonder if it means anything, and if so, what? While you're working on your short list, Harper, I'll take a look at this one."

"Sure. Just out of curiosity, what folder was that in?"

JC had the folder open in front of him. "Mankind Pharma Limited. An Indian company. What's interesting is these downloads are dated in May 2019, about a month ago, whereas all the others are at least a year old."

"I noticed the ones I've checked are all a year old, also."

They went back to their searching, not finding anything of any intelligence interest, in spite of their piles of notes. Presently, Harvey came back and they all went to dinner at the hotel. Over dinner, they showed Harvey the lists, but he could offer no immediate help. "I'm clueless," he said, "but we have folks back home who might be able to help."

Several hours before the fireworks were to start, Matt answered his doorbell to find six women of various ages crowding around his porch. Gert holding Madeline's hand, Lisa strolling Danielle, and Maggie strolling Jenny. His eyes lit up with delight as he ushered them in.

Maggie couldn't wait. "I give you an A-plus already, only because they don't have a grade higher than that!"

"Wow, you two must have really hit it off! Tell me, why do I get such a good score so soon?"

"She's like my twin. You knew that already, didn't you?"

"I was delighted when I heard she would be here. There's a lot you can learn from her you could never get from me."

"Yes, that's happening already. Especially with Jenny."

"How's our Jenny liking the Midwest?"

"Fine, but I need to change her. Do you have any old rags, a zipper bag, and a pair of scissors? Oh, wait, I think I brought a nappy."

"Gert," Matt said, "could you show Maggie the bathroom, and help her? I want to talk to Lisa a minute."

When they had gone, he said, "Lisa, Maggie's facing a crucial test when she gets home, her mom. She has no idea how to relate well with her. Before last Friday, they were always at odds. You don't have to teach her, just be a good example. She is very observant and catches on quick. Don't let her know I told you, so in case she wants to know what we talked about, she likes petunias, crosswords, and Moon Pies."

"Okay, I got it."

"How is Bill these days?"

They were talking about her husband Bill, when Maggie and Gert came back. After Matt gave them a quick tour of the house and his garden, they walked back to the house. He chatted with Gert. Maggie and Lisa lagged behind, carrying their infants.

"Are you disappointed," Lisa asked Maggie, "that Matt doesn't have any petunias in his garden?"

"To tell the truth, I'm glad he doesn't have any."

"Oh?"

"No petunias makes his petunia dream more believable. If he had petunias in the garden, he might have thought he was simply dreaming about his garden. I don't need any more proof his dreams were from God, but somebody else might."

They had a bite to eat. As they were walking to the park to see the fireworks, Matt said to Maggie, "Bob McGee called me this morning. I wondered why he was working on the holiday, but I sensed a greater urgency in his voice than we heard on Tuesday. Something's up, something soon. He didn't say what, but he did tell me they got the river water test results back, and guess what they found?"

"I don't have to guess. They found pure drinking water."

"Yep. He said we could bottle it and sell it." He kicked a soccer ball back to a group of boys who had accidently sent it bouncing off Jenny's stroller. "I also got an email from Mr. Clark at the State Department. He attached a copy of the draft he sent our lawyer. I'd like you to read it. Do you want me to forward it to you or print you a copy?"

"Oh, Matt," she replied, "I'm a school teacher. What do I know about such things? Just do what you think is best. You're a businessman. I trust you."

"Maggie, you're not doing this for just you! Think of it this way. You're doing it for all of England. You keep telling me you're not interested in The Boy. You'd like me to just have the whole thing. If you had your way, you'd let me have your share."

"Yes, that's true."

"Then The Boy would become a completely American territory. But you and Jenny are my only living descendants. You and whatever family you have will inherit the whole island one day. I want you to have a say in how this all works out."

Maggie sighed; her new life was becoming complicated. "Okay. Print me out a copy."

"You can pick it up when you come tomorrow. I'll send it to you too." He noticed her droopy eyelids. "You seem tired. I bet you stayed up all night telling Gert and Lisa our story."

She perked up and smiled. "Yes, it was great. We didn't get to bed until two. Then up for a five o'clock feeding."

"One other thing. Larry Williams is coming Saturday afternoon. I want you to meet him."

"*The* Larry Williams? Of course. I feel like I know him already, with all that you've said about him."

"Please bring your sampler from Emergent. I want him to see what's there. What time can you come?"

"If it's okay, Lisa and I will see you for breakfast. Gert already told us she'd love to watch Madeline, the three-year-old, whenever Lisa and I go out. I think she had shopping in mind, but I'd like to spend as much time with you as you'll let me. I have one other thing, too. You're still coming with me back to England, right?"

"I've been asking God about that, Maggie. I'd love to go, but I haven't gotten an answer from the Lord yet. I don't know if his job was you, or if there is something else."

"I still have this envelope full of money you promised me you'd help me spend."

"Ah, yes. There is that!"

And so it stood.

It was 9 p.m. on the East Coast. As the US Marine Corps heavy-lift MH-53K King Stallion helicopter settled onto the tarmac at Camp Lejeune, North Carolina, a small band struck up the Marine Corps Song, and several hundred family members and other well-wishers cheered, waved, and held up welcome-home banners.

In the background, the base Sergeant Major turned to the base commander. "Sir, the best part of any deployment is when you come home!"

"I'm glad we did this for them," he replied. "They earned it. Did you see the paper this morning? The story's been all over the news for the past week, and not a single mention of our Marines. Now that they're back, we can make sure they get the press they deserve."

When Lieutenant Colonel Paul Washington alighted from the aircraft, he looked around at the crowd and spotted Lance Corporal Juan Wilson. LCpl Wilson caught his eye, and gave a quick salute and a thumbs-up, grinning broadly.

After all the Marines had deplaned, a man and woman in civilian clothes came out and edged away from the crowd to a waiting sedan bearing official government license plates. When the crowd had dispersed and the Marines started unloading the helicopter, the car drove to the rear of the aircraft. Phil and Penny retrieved their belongings and were taken by the waiting FBI courier flight to Dulles International Airport.

The next morning, JC and Harper scheduled their flight to Washington, DC, then returned to the warehouse to complete their study of the items from the two locations. They took a break halfway through to discuss their Internet searches from the previous evening.

"My list had six cities in India," JC began, "then four cities in eastern China, five cities in eastern Europe, and five cities in California. Some big, some small. Some had multiple locations, like Naples could be in Italy but also in three different states in the US. Madera could be in Portugal but also in California or Pennsylvania. There are two Raipurs in India. So I assumed they were grouped logically, but didn't really see any connections. I suppose it could be another wild goose chase, but I'm more inclined to think this list got put in by accident. How about your list?"

"I started off assuming they misspelled Baghdad. Bad assumption. I googled Dudhkundi, and there's only one of them in the whole world. It's an abandoned airfield in India. Here's where it starts to get exciting, based on what you told me about your list. When I looked up Bagdad the way they had it spelled, I found it was an abandoned airfield in California. Zeljava and Mostar have abandoned airfields in eastern Europe, and Hangzhou is an abandoned airfield in eastern China. There is a new Hangzhou Airport, but the old one is still there."

"Wow, places to hide MiGs!"

"But for what?"

They finished their analysis, wrote a list of pertinent findings for Harvey, and developed a set of questions that needed to be asked of the prisoners. Harvey's driver picked them up and brought them to the hotel where they retrieved their belongings, then headed to the airport.

At 7 a.m. on July 5, two vans and two unmarked police cars met in the police headquarters vehicle yard in Bakersfield, California. Jon Whitaker, FBI WMD Directorate, addressed the group as they made final plans. "Surveillance reports no traffic has entered the parking lot yet. My personnel will enter and apprehend all persons in the warehouse. Wilson's Bakery is a cover for the terror cell you were briefed on this morning.

"We will make our move as soon as the first workers arrive. We expect we will be able to take them by surprise and avoid a shootout. Officer McArty's team will control the parking lot. There is only one way in and out. Officer McArty, as you pointed out earlier, vehicles entering the parking lot will not see any of the action until they have pulled in.

"There is a chemical delivery scheduled for today. The drivers will most likely not have a clue what they're hauling, but until proven otherwise, they are accessories. The trailer will have a Department of Transportation placard identifying the contents as a combustible insecticide. It must not be allowed to enter the warehouse."

"Will you be wearing chem suits?" Officer McArty asked.

"No, Sean. What they have inside is inert until it's mixed with the component coming later. If the surveillance team reports them entering the building suited or masked, however, we will also suit up just to be on the safe side. Once we give the all-clear, your team will process all personnel while my team sweeps the building."

There was about a two-hour wait. At 8:55 a.m., the call came from the surveillance team that three vehicles had pulled into the parking lot, and three white males not wearing suits or masks had entered the warehouse.

"Here we go!" Jon Whitaker said. "Sean, call your backup and have them ready to come on our alert."

It took the teams less than five minutes to arrive at the warehouse. The two vans pulled into the parking lot while the police cars loitered near its entrance. The vans pulled to the end, swung around, and stopped just short of the entry door. All agents rushed out of the vans. The first agent getting to the door twisted the knob, and when it opened, the entry team carried in the battering ram and dropped it on the floor. Jon Whitaker shouted, "FBI! Everybody freeze!"

Everybody froze. The FBI team quickly rounded up the three in the warehouse. The one in the office was fumbling with his phone, but one of the agents, Paul Ramirez, grabbed it out of his hand before he could lock the screen. Jon called Sean McArty on the radio and gave him the all-clear.

In all, the police team apprehended five more workers as they entered the parking lot. The eight were read their rights, and seven of the eight were loaded into the vans brought by the police backup. The eighth, Michael Walker, the man in the office who appeared to be in charge, declined the invitation to give a guided tour and tell what he knew of the operation there, so he joined his comrades, and they were all brought to the jail.

The agent with Walker's phone immediately changed the automatic screen lock time to Never and opened up the recent calls list. "Jon," he said, when he brought the phone out to where the other agents were starting to look through the warehouse bay, "he must have been on the phone with a Rishaan Chabra when we busted in here. Look, Chabra called him at nine o'clock and was on for one minute."

"Make a list of his entire recent call list, Paul. Note those that are foreign, and see what you can find out about them from his contact list."

"I've already started that list. In the last twenty-four hours, he's talked to Chabra only once but to a Rushil Singh three times. Same country code and area code. Do you know those names?"

"No, but perhaps Bob does. I'm going to do a video tour with him now, to show him what's here. I'll ask him."

The warehouse bay was mostly empty. A delivery truck bearing the name and logo of Wilson's bakery was in the center of the bay. All the doors were open, and several agents were taking pictures.

"Look, Jon," agent Kimberly Hall said, "it's a dually. A heavy duty one at that. Why would they need that to deliver bread and cake?"

"See if the floor is beefed up, Kim. And what is that frame in there?"

"Perhaps it will hold that steel tank by the loading door. It looks to be the same size."

Jon called Bob McGee on a video chat and showed him the warehouse.

Besides the truck and steel tank, there was a plastic five-hundred-gallon tank labeled "SYRUP", a ten-ton forklift, and a chain-driven hoist with a capacity rating of five tons.

"Is the front cab separate," Bob asked, "or does it connect with the rear?"

"It is separate. The driver would have to get out of the truck and open the rear doors to get any bread."

"That's odd. Delivery trucks usually have access right from the driver's seat. Did you see the photos of the steel tanks they brought back from the island?"

"No."

"I'll send you one. You should be able to open the top of the one there and see the insides. Take pictures of that and send it to me with the others. Show me the office now."

The office was rather plain. There was a desk, filing cabinets, several tables, and four maps on the walls.

"What's on the maps?" Bob asked. "It looks like maybe their sales routes or clientele."

"One is a map of central California. There's a route drawn from Madera through Hanford, back-and-forth with Visalia, on to Bakersfield, and finally Long Beach. The other three are city maps of Sacramento, San Francisco, and Los Angeles, with several routes highlighted in each going from north to south. I'll send you pictures of those, too, along with a scan of all the documents in the office."

"Thanks, Jon. If this is a legitimate bakery, there may be another Wilson's Bakery somewhere, with flour, sugar and ovens. Find it, and check them out. I'll see what we have on those names you gave me. Send me everything you can get from the phone. Contacts, emails, pictures, where he's been on the Internet, everything. Make that first priority."

"Roger. I understand you have a meeting with Phil first thing tomorrow. I'll try to have everything to you by then."

Officer McArty was still there, waiting for instructions. "When that other delivery gets here," Jon said, "have him take his load to your vehicle yard or other suitable place. Whatever you do, don't let it be stored here. It's relatively harmless, but don't open the tank."

"How about the eight apprehendees?"

"As soon as the other shipment gets here, it will be intent to produce a weapon of mass destruction. Will that be enough?"

128

Jimmy Branson did not know a lot about weather, but Jacob Strauss had given him a rudimentary understanding of Sand and Dust Storms before the helicopter carried him back to civilization. At 11:30 a.m., he was watching from his station in the Gulf of Mexico as the outer band of the SDS reached Emergent. To the north, a high-pressure cold front sweeping south from the arctic regions caused the storm to stall over the island, dropping thousands of tons of western African farmland, wastelands, and desert as the winds died down.

The warm moisture the storm had picked up from the ocean during its trek north mixed with the icy arctic air to create a massive hailstorm pummeling the island. It would be three days before the tail of the SDS caught up with the leading edge. What was left of it would wander northwest toward Nova Scotia, finally petering out about four hundred miles offshore.

129

Just before midnight, Rishaan Chabra locked his wallet and keys in his desk, locked his house, and walked to the bus depot.

When he had gotten up that morning, he was still in a funk from the night before. Something deep within him was telling him that Dasya was right, that the appearance of the plane on that damned island spelled doom to the project. Fear had replaced the anger he felt toward Rushil by the time he finished breakfast, but his rage was intensifying toward the airplane survivors.

He couldn't imagine what Rushil's ulterior motive might be. He was beginning to realize that perhaps he was merely a pawn instead of the king which Rushil had spent a whole year building him up to be. No, that was impossible. God had put him on this mission and he would see it through. It was his mission, not Rushil's, and all the plans, chemicals, and processes he had developed with the dead coward needed to be hidden, so Rushil would never find them if he were going to try to commandeer the project.

It had taken him until after lunch to gather and wrap all the important papers in oilcloth and to bury them in the yard, deep under his trash receptacle. When he finished, the brick base for the trash receptacle looked like it been there, undisturbed, for years.

He spent the rest of the afternoon fretting, pacing, and outlining several speeches he would give to the world as the project developed.

At 9 p.m., he decided to call one of the team leaders to check on progress, if for no other reason than to calm his nerves. Wilson's Bakery in Bakersfield should be open; the team leaders in Gwalior and Xingtai would be in bed and all Tetovo would be eating supper. He waited the half hour until 9 a.m. in Bakersfield and dialed Mike Walker.

"Hello, Rishaan," Mike said, "you called at a good time. We all just got here. The mixing bowl arrived yesterday, and we're expecting the spare on Tuesday."

"Good. Call me when you get it. Are the ingredients for the latest recipe on schedule?"

"As far as I know. We got five hundred gallons of syrup in a tank so far. A smaller barrel of canola oil is on the way as we speak."

Rishaan was about to answer when there was a commotion at the other end, followed by a clanging noise.

"Gotta go! Call you back," Mike said.

Before Mike was able to press the End Call button, Rishaan heard in the background, "FBI! Everybody freeze!"

A black cloud began to hover over Rishaan. His heart sank, but the rest of his body filled with adrenaline. He understood exactly what had happened in Bakersfield. It wouldn't take them ten minutes to break into Mike's phone and get the numbers for him, Dasya, Rushil, and all the team leaders.

He had deduced two things: one, he would have at least two hours to get out of Allahabad, and two, they didn't know he had heard them storming Wilson's Bakery.

By eleven thirty he had finished filling his backpack with the contents of his emergency box, which included a million rupees in cash and a forged passport Rushil had gotten him early on, for just in case. That, along with his laptop, a change of clothes, some toiletries, and some snacks for along the way, would be enough.

The laptop went in last. Every half hour or so during the day, Rishaan had googled a picture of Maggie Trillbey, with or without Matt Carven, and cursed them with all that was in him. She was the darling of all England for surviving the plane crash, but to him she was the ruin of all his plans to be the hero of the world and the savior of the planet. Prisha, and therefore God, would be pleased for him to be the avenger of the atmosphere by eliminating her from among the living.

Before he got to the bus depot, he discarded the gun he had used to kill Luka Stanković in a trash can outside the store where he bought bananas every day.

He paid cash for a ticket to the Delhi Airport and soon was on his way. He didn't know where he would ultimately end up, but his share of the money from Hem Laghari should last him quite a while. Even Rushil didn't know he had been able to move it to an account untraceable to his name.

Halfway to the airport, he decided he would call Dasya in the morning. Depending on his schedule, he might even be able to see him at the airport, since he would be on holiday near there. Then he would discard his phone.

At the Indira Gandhi International Airport, Mr. Nimit Malhotra purchased a ticket with cash for the next available flight to Zagreb, Croatia.

The fishing trawler carrying the remains of the passengers of Air World Airlines flight 94 had managed to stay about two hours ahead of the storm for the first twelve hours. After that, it was out of danger as it departed from the storm's path. On Friday, at 3:30 p.m., it steamed into Boston Harbor and up to its pier. Waiting for it was a long line of ambulances, a delivery truck bearing the name Ace Movers, and several cargo trucks from Air World Airlines.

It would be several days before the trawler was completely unloaded. The Ace Movers truck was given priority, and soon the steel tank from Emergent was on its way to the CIA lab in McLean, Virginia.

As soon as the raid was over, FBI agents Jon Whitaker, Paul Ramirez, Kim Hall, and Mark Hayes had set up shop in the warehouse office, bringing in several crates of equipment from one of their vans. They quickly discovered that there was another Wilson's Bakery in Bakersfield, and Mark was dispatched to find any connection with the warehouse.

Paul started photographing, copying, and scanning every item and document in the bay and office. Occasionally, he would take a break to upload everything from his phone and laptop to their data repository in DC. He sent a text to Bob McGee to give him access instructions. Kim made a list of all the data she could find on Mike Walker's phone.

Jon was looking over Kim's shoulder as she wrote down the recent calls list. He copied the overseas phone numbers, and immediately started an Internet search of the callers, starting with Rishaan Chabra. There were dozens of hits, mostly from Indian scientific websites.

One site got his attention, the annual convention of the Federation of Indian Scientists, held in New Delhi in February 2019. He clicked on the site and was rewarded with the headline, "Keynote address: India's Contribution to Global Warming, by Rishaan Chabra, President, FIS." He clicked the link for a transcript, selected English, and downloaded the report. It was a short read.

Jon called Paul, who came into the office with a handful of files. "Look at this," Jon said. "A list of the seven worst polluting cities in India, with a detailed list of their pollution: Gwalior, Allahabad, Raipur, Delhi, Ludhiana, Kanpur, and Khanna. Did you run across any list like this in any of the files?"

"I think so," Paul said. "I wasn't trying to process anything yet, just accumulate everything. That list looks familiar, though. Give me a minute." He thumbed through several file folders already out on a table and selected one labeled "International Bread Consortium."

"Here it is. It's mostly handwritten notes. The first appears to be from a meeting in April. There are the cities, except Delhi is missing."

In pencil, about halfway down the page, was the following list:

1. India – Ranbir – Patel – Ludhiana, Khanna, Gwalior, Kanpur, Allahabad, Raipur

2. Serbia – Jovan – Dmitri – Tetovo, Skopje, Naples, Tirana, Turin

3. USA – me – Wilson – Madera, Visalia, Hanford, Bakersfield, Long Beach

4. China – Zhang Li – Ming – Baoding, Hengshui, Xingtai, Tangshan

Jon checked Kim's list of foreign phone numbers. "Look," he told Paul, "Ranbir Varma from India, Jovan Stojanović from Serbia, and Zhou Zhang Li from China."

Paul pointed to the map above them. "The USA list matches the cities on what we thought was a route map," he said.

"It is a route map! But not for cake delivery."

About that time, Mark came back from the other Wilson's Bakery. "I questioned them pretty thoroughly, and I'm convinced there is no connection."

"Someone needs to wipe out these other locations," Jon said as he dialed Bob McGee.

Bob answered on the first ring. "I got your access key and I've been looking through what you sent. You wouldn't have called so soon unless there's something bigger."

Jon told him about Rishaan Chabra's FIS convention speech. "It was a word-for-word transcript, not a copy of a prepared speech. It started off with data and pollution sources, but quickly degenerated into a rant, complete with doomsday predictions and seeming threats to certain cities."

He read off the lists from the penciled notes.

"This is grim," Bob said. "Let me have the phone number list. We have friends in Europe and India, so that should go quickly. China will be delicate, but that should end as soon as we tell them the details. Let me know as soon as that other shipment arrives. Are there any other name lists?"

"Under that list I just read off," Jon said, "there is this line: 'R. C. – project lead; R. S. – advisor; D. K. – advisor; K. B. – financial.' There are two other meetings, but no new names. The meeting at the end of June mentions the airplane and deliveries of baking supplies. The last sheet had details about a visit from Rishaan Chabra on March 12, where he stayed, where they took him to dinner, et cetera, but no other names."

"See if you can find the solicitations and responses. That should lead to the other suppliers."

"Oh, one other name might be important. Rushil Singh, from India, made several phone calls here over the last few days."

Mark came back in as soon as Jon hung up with Bob. "Where are the keys to that delivery van?" he asked. "I'd like to open everything up."

"There's a bunch of keys in the desk," Jon said. "See what they all open."

Mark looked in the drawer. "There's a truck in the bay and none outside, but there are two different sets of Chevy truck keys," he said. "Let's keep an eye out for a second truck."

"Rushil Singh, from India, is the next name," Kim said. "Called five times in the last four days."

"There are whole files with his name everywhere," Paul said, pulling several files together on the table.

In the files were detailed technical drawings of the steel tank and the LED array they found inside earlier. There were also blueprints for the steel frame in the back of the delivery van as well as specifications for strengthening the undercarriage. There was a list of personal protective equipment to be purchased. Street maps of various California cities including Los Angeles, San Diego, San Jose, Sacramento, Fresno, and the five cities from the list. A rental agreement for a one-vehicle space at a private garage on Main Street.

"It looks like Singh was Chabra's right-hand man," Jon said, "the one nailing down the details and doing all the communicating."

"Does it say what space he was renting at Mac's Long Term Parking?" Mark asked Paul.

"Yes, bay three. I'll take you there."

A minute after Paul got back, Mark drove up in a Wilson's Bakery delivery truck identical to the one already in the bay. Inside was a second steel tank mounted on a frame matching the one in the first truck.

Mark said out loud what the other three were thinking. "Why do you suppose they needed to park this in a garage and not here?"

"I don't know," Jon said. "What was the date of the rental agreement?"

Paul turned back to that page. "March 10, two days before their visitor arrived."

Around 2 p.m., they finished their work. The other chemical shipment had come at noon. There was one last call from Bob McGee before they posted a guard and left the building.

"We have three or four analysts going through what you sent," Bob said. "Our counterparts are already taking action. The phone numbers may lead to their operations locations quicker than trying to track down the chemical deliveries."

"Two other things before we're done here," Jon said. "There was a personnel roster for this location, and we caught everyone on the list. In a safe, we found a box of a hundred atropine injectors. What are those for, an antidote for bee stings?"

"No, those would be strictly for nerve agent poisoning. Those bastards knew what they would be making!"

The phone rang just after 3 p.m. on Saturday, at the Central Bureau of Investigation Headquarters in New Delhi, India.

"This is not Rishaan Chabra, and I would like to report a murder."

"This is Deputy Deshpande, please wait a second." He gestured wildly to the other man in the room to pick up the phone to listen, then punched the record button.

"Yes, Mr. not Rishaan Chabra," Deshpande said for the recording, "where did you get our number?"

"It was online. Look, I know what you're doing. This is a prepaid phone. In sixty seconds, I will crush it under my foot, and you can find it in a trash can if you know what city to look in. Do you want my information or not?"

"Yes. Tell me about the murder."

"Mr. Rushil Singh shot Mr. Luka Stanković to death at Mr. Stankovic's home about ten days ago. Luka lived at —" Here the caller gave an address in Allahabad. "I know both Singh and Stanković. I saw Singh throw his body on his motorbike, Luka's motorbike, and ride off with it."

"Do you know where he took the body?"

"No, I was scared. I heard the shots and ran toward the house when I saw it."

"How did you happen to be there?"

"I might or might not be a neighbor."

"Why did you wait so long to call?"

"When he came back—he wasn't gone too long—he threatened to kill me if I squealed. It's been weighing on me, and I finally decided I ought to do the right thing."

"Where can we find Mr. Singh?"

An address came back from the caller.

"Do you know why he killed him?"

"I'm sorry, time's up." Click.

Somewhere in western India, Dasya Khatri found a trash can, then rejoined his family. He hated that he had to tie Rishaan's name to the murder, but he figured the authorities would be astute enough to realize if Rishaan were really the murderer, he wouldn't have called and used his own name in denial. And even if they weren't astute enough for that, he hoped they would use the facts he presented to arrest Rushil. Dasya never did trust him, in spite of Rushil's enthusiasm for the project. Hopefully, when they asked Rishaan about it, he would have the good sense to act puzzled and deny everything.

In New Delhi, Deshpande turned to the other man, who was removing his headphones. "You don't know Hindi, do you, Chuck?" he said.

"No, but I could tell he was calm and purposeful, whatever he was saying."

Deshpande sent the recording through a translation program and handed the page to Chuck, who consulted the printout they had both been studying when the phone had rung.

"Rishaan Chabra. Rushil Singh. Luka Stanković. This is like a gift from heaven."

Fifteen minutes later, a squad of police found the bloodstained floor and motorcycle seat. After two radio calls, a phone call, and fifteen more minutes, Rushil Singh was handcuffed and sitting in the back of a police car, loudly protesting his innocence.

The police chief in Allahabad called Deputy Superintendent of Police Deshpande to report the capture.

"He is wanted as part of an international terrorism group," Deshpande told him. "We believe he may be a spy, and therefore he may have some tool with him to help him escape. I'll send someone over for his phone, and we need to search his house. Keep him in isolation if that would make it easier."

"That was clever," Chuck said after he hung up. "You just took away all his rights, and they won't even tell anyone he's there. I wish we could do that in the States."

Bob McGee had called the meeting for 7 a.m. on Saturday at the CIA lab, but Phil and JC had come early so they started at 6:30. JC brought his notes from his Brazil trip and Phil brought his from Emergent and the operation in Bakersfield. Penny, Harper, and Jeff Peterson got there at seven.

"Perfect timing!" Phil told his interns. "We just reached a dead end about the money. Barry's folks tracked the transfer to an account in Bakersfield, which was owned by a woman with Alzheimer's. She has four living children and a dozen grands. Turns out one of the grandkids is Michael Walker, so we didn't need to follow the money to find him. Not really a dead end. Just a trail we don't need to follow."

JC wanted to start with the MiGs. "I added the two steel external tanks to the internal fuel capacity to get a reasonable estimate of about forty-seven hundred miles for how far they could have flown. That would include the half-hour loiter they did while in the vicinity of flight 94. So they had to have been based less than twenty-one hundred miles from the island. They were heading due south toward Macapá, but that's over three thousand miles, and there's no place there to land a MiG discreetly. So where did they come from?"

"Didn't you find a list of abandoned airfields?" Bob asked. "Harvey mentioned that."

JC handed him the list, which he read out loud. "There's nowhere on this list for them to land. I'll send word out to check them," he said, "with a requested deadline of tomorrow morning. I've already greased the skids with all the locations yesterday, when I told them about the nerve agent terror cells. Especially the one in China."

Penny was looking up abandoned airfields on the Internet. "There are several in Cuba," she said. "Could that have been one of Kevin Bhatt's stops when he shipped his wood?"

"Harvey is still down there accumulating Bhatt's records," Bob said. "I'll have him check. We'll table that for now and try to figure it out later. Let's move on to the device in the luggage."

He handed a collection of photos to each person. "It's a rather ingenious device. Tom took these pictures as he was disassembling the suitcase it was in. There's no metal and no explosives in it. There was a glass sphere inside nested rubber cups holding the nerve gas as a liquid under pressure. As the luggage was opened, a plastic cable would cause the glass to break, releasing the liquid, which energetically became a gas. The rubber was simply to protect the glass sphere. At the bottom of the ocean, the pressure caused the glass to be crushed, but it also divided the nerve gas into its component liquid parts."

"That's probably why the plane was shot down," Phil said. "They realized the device never functioned and it might have been possible to trace it back, via the binary components, to their supplier, and thus to them. It sounds like a long shot, but I can't think of any other reason to shoot it down."

They discussed the shooting briefly. Harper asked for clarification on the weapon which shot the American explosive bullets.

"Tony Barlowe told me all about that," Jeff said. "It's the bullets that made it sound like the American gun system, rather than the gun barrels themselves. They couldn't mount the GAU-8 in a MiG."

"Ah, I was wondering about that," JC said.

"At this point," Phil said, "it doesn't really matter. We may eventually find the planes and we'll know. The Brazilian intelligence folks will be asking what modifications were made to the planes down there."

"It's probably too early," JC said, "but have they found out anything from the Brazilian prisoners, other than that they're all Americans?"

"Yes, it's too early," Bob said, "but you gave us some good intel. The cities on your list match the cities on the list in Bakersfield. That, together with the IP address and the steel tank, definitely ties Brazil to this whole puzzle. Speaking of what we found in Bakersfield, Jeff and I did some research into this Rishaan Chabra. At the Federation of Indian Scientists website, we found not only his rant at the FIS convention last year, but other possible solutions he had proposed for the pollution problems in his country."

"Every time," Jeff added, "the Indian government had turned a deaf ear to his pleas for help. In his articles, he didn't blame the government so much as the industries that made fortunes by ignoring the pollution. It was only in the past year that he really started becoming concerned with global warming, blaming it on all the pollution in India."

"Here's the other thing we found out about Chabra," Bob said. "In Barry's email, he mentioned Hem Laghari and a transfer of money gone awry. He was trying to transfer money to a company called India Quality Air. Laghari owns several companies causing massive unchecked pollution, and India Quality Air is a figurehead company owned by Rishaan Chabra."

"So here's a company which exists in name only receiving funds from a major polluter," JC said. "Sounds like maybe some extortion going on?"

"Could it be," Penny asked, "that Chabra would wipe out those cities to stop the pollution? Stop the pollution by killing the polluters?"

"Why the other countries, then?" Phil asked.

"To stop global warming over the whole planet," Jeff said. "The nerve gas would be virtually undetectable, right? Who would ever suspect a bread delivery truck?"

It was mid-morning on Saturday. Maggie and Lisa had strolled their infants early in the morning to Matt's house and had made breakfast. Gert had brought Madeline, and left with her before it was time to wash the dishes. Matt had parked Maggie in the study looking over the legal papers concerning Emergent, and he and Lisa were in the kitchen cleaning up.

Matt pulled a credit card out of his pocket. He handed it to Lisa and said, "Maggie's a different size now, and will need all new tops before she starts school. See how much room she has left in her suitcase and take her shopping. On me."

"Wow! You're taking this daddy thing seriously. She has you wrapped around her little finger!"

"Yes, and I'm loving it. You know I would do the same for Rachel. Besides, she has some catching up to do."

"I know, Matt. Twenty-eight years' worth. You should hear her speak of you. Like you've been her real father all her life. I can tell she loves you like I love Dad."

"It's amazing to see how God is working in her. It's been hardly more than a week, and she is acting like she's been a follower of Jesus her whole life."

"Yes, and I've seen she is so willing," Lisa said. "She told me that before she met you, her life was going exactly nowhere. She understands why you won't take any of the credit, but she's glad—ecstatic—that God drew her to you. She gave you a score of one hundred on pulling helpless and hopeless losers out of the ocean, being their eyes and ears, and letting God use you for him to heal them and fill them with a passion to live for him."

"Wow, that was quite a mouthful!"

"She made me say it three times before we got here this morning."

Matt laughed. "Does she speak of her mom?"

"Yes, and she can hardly wait to get back. I told her, 'Just let her hold you.' She's afraid she might be a little prickly. I told her to simply relax. They have a lot of lost time to make up."

"I might be like the third wheel if I go back with her. They need some alone time, just the two of them."

"If you went back together, the pluses for her would far outweigh the minuses."

"I've already decided that, but let me tell her."

Presently, Maggie came back from the study. "I think it will work, including your pencil notes. For rent you put, 'Larry input.' What does that mean?"

"Larry Williams has an interesting passion, which you'll find out about when he gets here. Did you bring the box from Paul?"

"Yes, it's in Jenny's stroller."

"Emergent has probably millions of dollars' worth of those manganese nodules. I'd like to make him a deal to harvest all that he can. He's a businessman, and this would give him a project to fulfill a dream he's had for many years. I think he could be wildly successful on just my half of the island, but if you agreed, he could work the whole island, and you and I would split any profits."

"Oh, Matt! You know, Wayne Smith was kind of right. I feel like I do owe you something special, but not in the way he was trying to imply. When I talk to God about what's ahead, I get the impression his plans for me don't involve a lot of money. Yes, he can work my half too. We can talk about the money later, but I want you to have my half. What does this have to do with rent?"

"If rent were in money, it would come in too slowly to be of any help to Larry. I was thinking of them transporting things there instead of giving us cash. It would cost them very little and would be an enormous help."

"Okay, whatever you think is best."

"I got an email from Penny yesterday, but didn't see that she included you," Matt said. "It was about the life preserver. It was on the USS Oklahoma City when the ship was decommissioned in 1979. The Coast Guard picked it up and designated it as 'CG-5'."

"I got a separate email from her. She wanted to tell me things she didn't want to tell you, things that happened to her growing up. She said the ship was destroyed as a target in 1999, so the shark may have eaten it twenty years ago. That's a long time!"

Larry Williams arrived at two thirty, and after the introductions, he, Matt, and Maggie gathered around the kitchen table, while Lisa looked after Danielle and Jenny. They got right down to business.

"My father played football in college, and in the pros for six years," Larry said. "American football. In college, he was one of the first African-Americans in his sports fraternity, Theta Sigma Omega.

"My dad made a lot of money as a pro, but spent it as soon as he got it. In a game in Seattle, he got a head and neck injury, and that was the end of his career. He never recovered from the injury and died when I was ten. We were broke. My mom had to find a job. My dad had wanted to put money away for us for college, but he never seemed to be able to. If it weren't for my aunt, neither my sister nor I would have had a chance. She went to nursing school. I was able to get a business degree, and I got a job in the same company as Matt. Our paths crossed many times.

"There are too many kids of pro athletes whose dads or moms have no idea how to manage their money. Then they get injured or aren't good enough anymore, and they end up broke. The kids really suffer, like I did, and I want to help them. I'd like to be able to find them, see what they're good at or interested in, and mentor them and maybe help them financially. The goal wouldn't necessarily be college, but in setting them up to be a success."

"When I told you I had an idea that might help you," Matt said, "you may not have known that Maggie and I were on that plane that was shot down last Friday, but God saved us."

"Yes, I did. I watched the interviews. When I watched you, Maggie, I almost cried because God was so good to you. When you mentioned some land on the phone, were you talking about the island? Tell me all about that, and any other part of the story you want to."

Matt and Maggie started with them meeting each other on the plane, and finished with the US and UK sharing Emergent, with them as the owners. They were quite detailed about the island. Maggie showed him her samples. She checked on Jenny several times, but Lisa had everything under control.

Matt explained his idea about the island. "It should be quite lucrative to harvest the nodules. The biggest issue I see is getting people, materials, and equipment to and from the island. It would require all kinds of different skills, from building housing to running heavy equipment to agricultural and even tourist activities, and of course the administration of it all.

"Maggie and I would give you access to the whole island. By the time you get there, a good portion may be completely covered by dirt. It may take different equipment to get the nodules out. But even if it doesn't, it should be many years' worth of mentoring the youths you are so passionate about."

"How about the transportation of things?" Larry asked. "It would have to be fairly continuous."

"The military of both England and the States want to build facilities there, and have an airfield and port. We would get to use them. I checked with the naval officer that we met when we were at the State Department, and he said the ships bringing the military construction materials could bring our things also, as long as they were in conex containers. Look at this legal document our lawyer got from Mr. Clark. They will pay us rent when we collectively agree on how much."

"This sounds wonderful. I've been wanting to put to good use all these business experiences I've been blessed with, and it looks like the challenge and opportunity I've been waiting for. I know it's Saturday, but I'll make some calls, get some quick advice, do some calculations, and finally present it to the boss."

"Phyllis?"

"Absolutely! She's my biggest fan. Been so twenty years in September. I'll get you a tentative yes or no as far as being doable, at least by me, in maybe an hour. Whooee—this will be great! Okay if I use your kitchen table for an office for the next hour?"

While they were waiting for Larry, they joined Lisa in the playroom. They played with the babies and chatted about the island, especially the dirt, until Larry came back and announced that he and Phyllis would give it a go. He would call Matt on Monday or Tuesday to give him a final answer and an estimate on the conexes.

"Great!" Matt said. "I didn't want to mention this before you decided, but I don't need any of the profit from the venture. Whatever my share would be, I want to invest it back into your work there."

"And so do I," Maggie said.

Larry left after supper, which was delivered by Matt's favorite pizzeria.

"I called Charles yesterday," Maggie said when things quieted down. "It was good to hear his voice. He said he watched our interview on Tuesday. He sounded happy. He said he had a surprise when I get back. I wonder if I'm to be an aunt again."

"I don't think that's it," Lisa said. "From what you told me of your mom, she would have told you that already herself."

"Yes, you're probably right. It's really hard for Mum to keep a secret."

"Maggie, I'd like to meet your mom," Matt said. "Would Wednesday be too soon?"

CLASSIFICATION: SECRET
FROM:       ROBERT R. MCGEE
TO:         VTC TASK FORCE
DTG:        10:00 AM 7 JULY 2019 (07JUL19 1400Z)
SUBJECT:    REPORT OF ABANDONED AIRFIELD INVESTIGATION

1. Background: On 6 July 2019, this office learned of possible MiG storage at various national and international airports no longer in use for aviation purposes, as listed below. Personnel associated with this office visited each site.

2. Airports and status.

  a. Zeljava Airbase, Croatia. Search revealed underground tunnels and hangars. Abandoned planes were found, but none were MiG class.

  b. Mostar, Bosnia. An abandoned underground military air base is located near the current Mostar Airport. Numerous hangars branch off the main tunnel. Some are open and the rest are closed by steel doors, some of which are locked. Behind one locked door was a MiG-23 which appeared to be Bosnian War vintage. This aircraft was in a poor state of maintenance, with flat tires, missing parts, and animal residue. Most exposed steel parts showed extensive rusting. There was no armament and no engine.

  c. Dudhkundi Airfield, Banka Bhur Kunda, West Bengal, India. Main hangar building has one large maintenance bay closed by locked steel bay doors. A MiG-23 is parked behind the doors. Aircraft appears fully operational but unarmed. Aircraft identifying markings have been provided to the Indian Defence Intelligence Agency.

  d. Bagdad Intermediate Field, Bagdad, CA. One small hangar at the end of the runway was empty.

  e. Hangzhou Jianqio Airport, China. Our contact reports no aircraft of interest. New airport is too close to the old airport to hide activity there.

3. Further actions: N/A.

CLASSIFICATION: SECRET
CLASSIFICATION EXEMPT FROM STANDARD DECLASSIFICATION SCHEDULE

It was Monday, July 8. Kevin Bhatt had just finished his noonday meal at the house of his old friend, Marcos. It was Marcos whose daughter Kevin had rescued from the snake; it was Marcos who kept him informed about the goings-on in town, especially of the take-over of his business by the police; and it was Marcos who knew how to keep a secret. He had just returned from his daily bike ride through the city.

"My friend, the waterfront has been quiet the last few days. I can't tell you if anyone is watching, Kevin, but I can tell you the same trash has been in front of your warehouse door since Saturday."

Kevin knew all about vehicle surveillance; he had watched all of the *Godfather* movies several times. "How about vehicles?" he asked. "Anything suspicious, parked, or slowly moving?"

"I always go past there too early for much traffic. I didn't notice anything unusual, my good friend, even when I rode on the back street. The doorman at the hotel across the street might be a clue. He is the same one who has been there for years. If he's not opening the door, we'd wave or say hello, and I think I'd know if he acted nervous."

"I need to go there, Marcos. They probably trashed the place and took all my files, but I'm hoping they didn't find my cash. I hid it pretty well. I'm sure they're watching my house, so I won't even think of going there."

"You're welcome to stay here as long as you like."

Kevin had decided he was probably wrong about Manan Ganguly, and his itch to get on with his life had overcome the excessive caution after his trip back from his plantation. Paranoia, he had concluded. Manan was probably back in Jaipur reporting the hunting trip plans to his father. "Thanks, but I need to get back to India. If there's a problem with my business, it will die down after a while. There's not a lot of excitement here about rare wood. If I make money, the city makes money."

"I'd be pleased if you took my car."

"No, it's only an hour from here on foot, and the walk will be good for me. I won't have that much to carry, but I'll need a backpack, if you have one."

"Camila has one. She would love for you to use it."

Equipped with a backpack and a sun hat, Kevin headed toward the river.

Across the street from the warehouse, several windows were open on the third floor of the hotel. This was not unusual, even for the second week in July, because the hotel was home chiefly to seasonal migrant workers, and rooms needed to be aired out quite often.

Two windows on opposite ends of the hotel, however, were open for a different purpose. At the north end, a man checked every five minutes or so to see if the trash he had put in front of the warehouse door had moved. He knew there was only one door besides the cargo doors on the east side of the warehouse, and they were locked from the inside.

At the south end, Carlos Souza and José Pinta of the Agência Brasileira de Inteligência were on the day shift, watching for any sign of Kevin Bhatt. They had memorized his picture and vital statistics, and were in frequent contact with the ABIN stakeout team watching his residence.

At five minutes before two, Carlos and José received a text from the surveillance group leader that Bhatt's phone had just been turned on; it was less than one hundred meters from the warehouse location. They donned their service vests and checked their sidearms.

At two o'clock, the watchers in both windows observed the man for whom they were waiting, unlock the warehouse door and step inside.

The man at the north end immediately left his room and went downstairs.

At the south end, Carlos immediately called his superior to report the arrival, and was told to proceed cautiously and arrest the man. Help would be on the way in minutes. Carlos and José went downstairs and across the street. The door to the warehouse was open, so they cautiously entered.

A few minutes earlier, Kevin had let himself in and walked quietly toward his office. Not a sound. Entering, he knelt on the floor and pulled up the edge of the shabby carpet in front of the filing cabinets. Alerted by a footstep behind him, he turned to see Manan Ganguly bearing down on him with a heavy iron bar. He tried to rise, but Manan struck him in the head, and Kevin went down, unconscious.

Carlos and José were walking toward the center of the warehouse, guns drawn, when they heard a crack followed closely by a thud. Then another crack.

"That's a bone breaking," José said quietly to Carlos, and they rushed toward the sound. When they got to the office, they saw that a man with a heavy iron bar had laid the unconscious Kevin Bhatt flat on the floor and had broken his lower right leg. He was preparing to break the lower left leg when he heard the two ABIN agents charge into the office, so he took a step forward to crush his skull instead.

"Stop!" Carlos shouted.

Manan lifted the bar and took another step forward at the same time. Carlos and José both fired, hitting him in the right shoulder and lower back. The impact of the bullets pitched Manan headfirst into a filing cabinet.

Kevin Bhatt would be in a coma for three days, in a fog for a week after that, and in jail for the rest of his life.

The plane from Chicago landed without incident at Heathrow International Airport at 7:30 a.m. on Wednesday the tenth. As they passed through the jet bridge and into the concourse, Matt and Maggie were surprised by a small crowd of their fellow travelers and a BBC camera crew. A man with a microphone and a Britannia Airlines badge raised his hand and everyone cheered and clapped as the cameras started rolling. "Welcome home!" the man said to Maggie as he handed her a dozen red and white roses. "I see your new American friend is with you. Welcome to England!" he said to Matt.

"It's good to be back." Maggie was holding Jenny, who was crying from all the excitement. "We had a good flight this time."

She comforted Jenny and noticed the cameras were still recording. "God was kind to us. I can't wait to see my family. I'm glad to be alive, and I pray that God would comfort those who lost loved ones. Thank you all."

They were enjoying the festive atmosphere. As they pushed the stroller along, Matt said, "That must be why the airline crew wanted us to wait, so they could set things up."

After processing through customs, they collected their luggage and exited the controlled area. As soon as they passed through the doors, they saw a pleasant-looking middle-aged brunette waving. Maggie grabbed her handbag from the stroller. "There's Mum! Bring Jenny."

"Wait," Matt said.

"I remember!" Maggie said, turning toward him, and mouthed the words, "Ask first."

"Go! I'll bring Jenny." He hoped she remembered his other words, reminding her of the old Maggie and what she would try to do when she got home.

After introducing Matt to her mother Charlotte, Maggie couldn't wait to show off Jenny's new foot. "See what God did! And there's more. I'll wait until we get home. I don't want to be interrupted every three minutes by the train whistle."

Maggie and her mum passed Jenny back and forth repeatedly on the hour-long ride to Bristol, chatting non-stop. Matt looked out the window from the seat behind them and gloried in the fields and forests, the towns and rivers, all drenched by the morning sun. His body was telling him it was the middle of the night, but he was enjoying the sights too much to notice. It had been years since he was last in England. He had never been to Bristol.

A taxi brought them from the train station to Maggie's flat near Ashley Down. Along the way, she pointed out her school, now deserted for the summer. When they reached her flat, they saw their way was blocked by several bouquets of cut flowers, welcome home signs, and two foil balloons placed there by well-wishers. When they got close, they saw the door was covered by sticky notes, mostly begging for a phone call. "You are so loved!" Matt said.

When Maggie opened the door, she was greeted by a strong smell of bleach. She took a step backwards and looked at Matt, who smelled it too. Ask first, ask first, ask first, she kept telling herself. "Wow, Mum! You cleaned my flat while I was gone. Thanks!"

"You're welcome, but let's open your windows and let some fresh air in." Charlotte dashed into the kitchen, the loo, and finally, the bedroom to get the needed ventilation.

"Well played, Maggie!" Matt said.

When Charlotte had heard Matt would be coming, she had borrowed two cots, one for Maggie's room and the other for the living room. The only other furniture in the living room was a chair, coffee table, and floor lamp. "I never had more than one visitor at a time and we mostly sat in the kitchen," Maggie said.

"It's been a long time since we ate," she went on. "I need to feed Jenny, and probably change her. Then let's walk over to Tinto Lounge for an early lunch, and when we come back, Mum, we'll tell you our story."

Matt and Charlotte engaged in small talk in the kitchen while Maggie began to nurse Jenny. It was all Charlotte could do not to go right into the living room to watch the new and wonderful sight. Matt finally noticed; he grinned and said, "Go ahead!"

All alone in the kitchen, Matt heard the squeals of delight and the giggling.

"Maggie! Cover yourself up."

"It's okay, Mum, Matt's seen the before and the after. Look at me now! I told you there was more. I wanted you to see how God healed me, too."

At Tinto Lounge, Matt picked up a tourist map. When he and Maggie were out of earshot of her mother, he said, "Your mom is such a delight. I see you've been warm and relaxed with her so far, so tomorrow morning after breakfast, I'm going for a walk. I won't be back until after four or so. It will be the day with your mom I promised you. You will do wonderfully."

"Where will you go? What do you know about Bristol?"

He showed her the map. "I'm starting at the aquarium, the Brunel exhibitions, the art museum, then maybe the zoo or the Clifton Bridge. Call if you need more time, and maybe I'll go find the blue glass factory."

"That must be an old map. I don't think the blue glass factory is still open. And, thank you. You're right, we both need this so desperately. And look both ways before you cross the street. Remember that we don't drive on the wrong side of the road over here."

"Maggie, I have two questions about what you're going to tell your mom."

"I think I know. The vow and cutting myself, and about me becoming your daughter."

"Yes, exactly. What are your thoughts?"

"I should have told her when I was twelve. I couldn't then, but I can now. I owe her that, and it will be in keeping with our new relationship. Including my forgiving Charles. About being your daughter, I don't know what I should do."

"Do you still treasure that?"

"Oh, yes! Every single part of it. I don't ever want to give that up."

"I feel the same way. Maybe it's best to save that part for tomorrow, after she sees how changed you are. You could drop little hints along the way, so it's not like a bomb going off when you tell her."

They spent the rest of the day telling Charlotte about their experiences, including Maggie's two weeks in Macon, Georgia.

The next afternoon, Matt returned from his walk to find two puffy-eyed but deliriously happy women and a wastebasket full of used tissues.

"Matt," Charlotte said, "with all that Maggie told me about you, I can't think of anyone else I'd rather have to walk her down the aisle."

"Mum!" Maggie started laughing. "Matt, guess who gave herself to Jesus this afternoon?"

"I have a new sister?"

"Yes!" Maggie said. "Mum! She's going to call her friend in Cheltenham. Oh, that reminds me, I got two phone calls this afternoon. A fellow teacher wants to bring some friends over to hear our story tomorrow afternoon. I told her yes, but she'd have to bring chairs.

"The other call was from a Bristol talk radio station. They want to record me giving our story next Thursday in Cheltenham at the Doubletree Hotel. I told him yes, too. I grew up in Cheltenham, so I know a lot of people there. He said he picked the Doubletree because it can hold four hundred people. They'll call again on the fifteenth or sixteenth with the details."

"Wonderful! If the teachers are all ladies tomorrow, I think you'd be able to tell them things that they would be uncomfortable hearing if I were there. Maybe I'll plan another walk, just in case."

"After your meeting tomorrow," Charlotte said, "let's go to Cheltenham. I have much more room and a full fridge."

The next afternoon, as Matt had anticipated, nine women came, three from Maggie's school and six she didn't recognize. Her friend introduced them as teachers from other schools in Bristol. Charlotte served tea while Maggie introduced Matt and Jenny. Matt took his leave, explaining he had gotten a text from a business partner, and had a lot of emails to catch up on.

For the next several hours, Maggie told her story of the previous two weeks. One of her fellow teachers, whom Maggie had always thought of as a little odd, grinned knowingly at different points, smiling with delight as Maggie related how she had received Jesus into her life.

As Maggie was finishing up, one of the teachers wept as she explained that her daughter had cut herself on several occasions. "Would you speak to her? We don't know why she does it or what we should do."

"Yes, I would be glad to. How old is she?"

"She's sixteen, and started cutting herself when she was thirteen. She's visiting relatives in Scotland and will be back in a few weeks."

"I hope I can help her. I'll give you my phone number after we're finished."

The meeting over, they packed up Charlotte's Mini Cooper and the four of them headed to Cheltenham.

Matt said, "The text I mentioned was from Larry Williams. He apologized for not getting back with me by Tuesday like he promised, but there was more to consider. We traded emails a couple times. He thinks ten conexes a year for eight years, then two a year after that, to the island and back, would be about right, as long as he could dock a cargo ship there every so often. He wants to visit the island, though, before he makes any firm commitments."

"Those boys are going to get so much good experience," Maggie said.

"Larry went on to say that they would stockpile the nodules rather than try to ship them out in the conexes. It would be more work that way, which was perfect for his purposes. And get this, he said it would be more realistic from a business standpoint if they had to make payments to the owner of the property they were working, so he will send us money whether we want it or not."

"What is all this about?" Charlotte asked.

"Didn't Maggie tell you we are each half-owner of a one-hundred-and-twenty-five-square-mile island?"

"If she did, it went right over my head!"

Maggie and Matt took the rest of the trip to describe Emergent, its assets, and Larry's passion to help certain disadvantaged young men.

Charlotte went to bed at her usual time, but Matt and Maggie were still beset by jet lag and chatted in the kitchen.

"Tell me about your mom yesterday," Matt said as they started a midnight snack.

"I completely blew it not too long after you left. I don't even remember what started it, I think something about Jenny. She fussed at me about something, and I fussed back more. Then it was her turn. It felt so strange. Suddenly, I realized what I was doing. I stopped, put my hand over my mouth, and remembered your warning that this might happen. I apologized and told her how sorry I was. That took her completely by surprise. To her, that was such a foreign thing for me to do. We hugged and made up.

"Later, she fussed at me again, but I just loved her. When she saw the apology was genuine, she asked me where this amazing change came from. I told her, and a little later she said she wanted that change, too."

"That's wonderful. Do you see how God is using you? It fills you with joy, doesn't it, Maggie?"

"That first joy just kind of disappeared. I woke up one morning and it was gone, and I didn't even notice. You're right, though. There's a deeper joy seeing God bless others. When they receive Jesus as their Lord, are filled with his Holy Spirit, and come to know God as Father, there is such a joy in that."

"That's a reward, all by itself."

"Yes, and speaking of rewards, Matt, I still want to do something special for you. Something to honor you as my father."

"I've been thinking about that. I also want to honor you as my daughter. Here's what I'd like us to do. Let's each take our story and write it down in detail, including what we were thinking and feeling, especially things happening before we met each other, things which contributed to us ending up on the GSM. Then send it to each other."

"That's a wonderful idea! We can give Jenny a copy when she's old enough."

"And it will help you when you write the book."

"Matt, I got a letter from Louis Moore while I was gone."

"Jenny's daddy."

"I haven't heard from him for nine months. He started off telling me what a fool he had been, a selfish obnoxious twit."

"That's kind of how you described him. When was it posted?"

"About the time I flew over to visit Clarice. He asked how I was doing, and about the baby girl. He doesn't even know her name. He wants to tell me about something brilliant that happened to him."

"What do you think?"

"He sounded rather upbeat. I believe he wants to see Jenny, and I'd like him to. I want to tell him our story, and of course, show him her new foot."

"Just to be on the safe side, Maggie, have your mother there when he comes to visit. Does she know he is Jenny's father?"

"No. I absolutely refused to tell her, and it has never come up since. Do you think I should tell her now?"

"No, Maggie, not yet. Don't let Louis tell her either. That will let her form an unbiased opinion of him. If she knew, who knows what she would try when she meets him. Wait until later."

The next morning, Maggie took her mother's car after breakfast and went to visit Charles at his home. "Aren't you going with her?" Charlotte asked.

"No," Matt said. "This is something she has to do by herself. Charles told her Ted and Billy would be there this morning. I want to meet your son, but it will have to be another time."

"There has been such a brilliant change in Maggie. She said you wouldn't take any of the credit, but she also said if you hadn't been there, she would be at the bottom of the ocean and Jenny would still be in the shark."

"God put me in the right place at the right time. I don't know what she was like before, but it was God who did that brilliant change. I do know a little. She told me about Charles."

"Yes, she told me. At the time, I suspected Charles had something to do with it. He never would admit anything, though. Maggie was so convincing at pretending she didn't remember. We were always on our tiptoes around it. I think Adam, my husband, blamed himself somehow. When he died in the mine, it wasn't like him to be so careless. There were witnesses who said, no, it wasn't a suicide, but he had gotten so lax in everything leading up to it. Maggie might have told you how hard he was on her. I could never figure out why."

"He's gone now," Matt said, "but I believe God has healed all her memories. The things that caused so much pain in her don't hurt anymore."

About that time, the object of their discussion entered Charles' house. After warmly greeting Sylvia and the kids, Maggie went with Charles to the study where two other men were seated. She noticed all three had open Bibles at their places at the table. Charles offered her the fourth seat.

"Wow," she said after she sat down. "I hardly recognized you both. It's been a long time."

They all looked a little nervous. "We have something we want to talk to you about," Charles said.

Maggie could tell by looking at them what it was. "Before you do," she said, "I have a confession to make. For over sixteen years, I've been telling everyone that I didn't remember what happened to me on my twelfth birthday. But this whole time it's been a lie. There's never been a time I didn't blame you three for everything that happened to me."

She paused a moment to let that sink in. There were tears starting to form in four sets of eyes. "I blamed you for what I did to myself. I hated you all, and I was secretly plotting my revenge for when the right time came. But something happened two weeks ago yesterday. Everything changed. I met Jesus face to face, and he loves all four of us too much to allow this to fester any longer. I gave myself to him, and gave up any right I felt I had to do you harm. I forgave you completely, and I've been praying for you ever since."

"What did Jesus say to you?" Ted asked.

"I'll tell you in a little bit. I want to tell you everything he said. But he didn't say anything about you. He didn't say anything about what I did to myself. He didn't even say anything about the curse I had put myself under. That all came later."

Maggie reached into her handbag and pulled out a small satchel of tissues. She passed them around. "We all need one. Now, what was it you wanted to talk to me about?"

"We all wanted to tell you how sorry we are for what we did to you," Charles said. "It was terrible what we did. We were going to tell you, not knowing you knew the whole time. We have no excuses, and there's nothing we can say that can make it any less bad. Since we became followers of Jesus Christ, we have been asking God how we can make it up to you."

"You can't make it up to me, ever. I know that, because we can never make it up to God. He forgave me, and so I absolutely and voluntarily have forgiven you three. But you can do this. Stand up."

They all stood up, and she hugged each one, looking into their faces and saying, "By God's grace, I forgive you totally." After more tears and more hugs, the restoration was complete.

She learned that Ted had given his life to Jesus about a month earlier at a Fellowship of Christian Athletes rally in Manchester and had immediately told Charles, who did likewise the day before she left to visit her cousin Clarice. Billy said he had the strangest urge during the evening of June 28, so he called Ted, whom he hadn't seen in months. Ted told him all about that urge, and Billy had given himself to the Lord that morning.

"The very time Matt and I were praying for you in the middle of the ocean!" Maggie said.

She told them about being with Jesus at the time she received him and he received her. It was exhilarating to retell it, and they were all quiet for a few moments.

"You said you cursed yourself?" Ted asked.

"Yes," Maggie said. "I made a vow because of what you all did to me, and that's why I cut myself. But Matt helped me break the vow, the curse, by God's power, after I became Jesus's. God healed Jenny and me at the same time, and he did another miracle in me so I could start nursing her."

"We watched your interview," Charles said. "It's on YouTube, so we watched it several times. You did great! We couldn't wait to tell you about us."

"Was that the surprise you told me about?"

"Yes. We were anxious and excited to tell you about our faith, and that spurred us on to confess what we did to you."

"Have you told Mum about belonging to Jesus yet?"

"No, not yet. I'm not sure what she'd say."

She decided to let her mother tell Charles about her newfound faith. "Give her a call, Charles. Let her know. She'd love to hear from you. Now I need to get back to Mum's. No telling what she'll try to feed Jenny, who's probably hungry and complaining about it."

"Promise you'll come back and tell us the whole story?"

"No, you come to Mum's and meet Matt. You'll love him! Come tomorrow. Come early, we have a lot of catching up to do. Besides, Mum has a surprise for you."

"Okay. I'll see you tomorrow."

Matt was waiting for Maggie on the front porch, rocking Jenny, when he heard the voice. "She's ready." He heard the voice again. "I still have a job for you."

On Monday, July 15, Phil Henry reconvened the VTC. All of the original participants were present, but JC Smalley was attending from a location in Phil's building instead of the Chicago FBI Field Office.

"Ten days ago," Phil said, "Jon Whitaker of our WMD Directorate and his team took down the California element of the International Bread Consortium. We discovered this group because of the fine work of Bob McGee's team of chemical and electrical engineers and his international investigative teams."

"I'd like to add," Bob said, "that we wouldn't have been able to do any of that if that island hadn't appeared, giving us the plane back. Without that, we might have that nerve gas swirling around in our atmosphere for years."

"From the evidence we found in Bakersfield," Phil said, "we were able to track down three other cells in eastern Europe, India, and China, as well as the headquarters cell of the mastermind of all this in Allahabad, India. Bob's folks passed along the information to the appropriate agencies, and those other three cells were taken down without incident. We were also able to connect the cell in Brazil to the IBC, although we haven't determined why they were there. Barry, would you comment on the money?"

Barry Mantile, Treasury Department, addressed the group. "In my email, I reported thirteen accounts received the two hundred thirty-two million dollars. Only six of those accounts were discovered when the six cells were captured. Over two hundred million dollars remains unaccounted for."

"The mastermind, an Indian scientist named Rishaan Chabra, remains at large," Phil said. "Interpol and every intelligence agency in the free world have been notified, as well as all countries within a thousand miles of India. Based on all of the evidence so far, his plan was to use the nerve gas his cells would produce to annihilate twenty of the most polluted cities in the world. He would then threaten the rest of the world, in order to stop the pollution that was causing global warming. We have no idea what would motivate a person to plan this, or to think this would be effective."

Kirby Drinkard of the National Counterterrorism Center was concerned for the future. "Could there be sleeper cells that might also try to use the same chemical agents?" she asked.

"We don't think so," Bob said. "Over the past week, we've been getting reports from the other locations. The production of the binary chemicals at the sources matches the deliveries at the cells. In other words, there were no other delivery locations. We have instructed all the major chemical companies to be on the lookout for orders of these chemicals, and to notify us or their own national intelligence services.

"The documents obtained from these cells mention the other cells, but none mention a cell we have not captured. On the other hand, we have not discovered any technical documents at the Allahabad site on the chemical structure or production processes. That data is still out there somewhere. Chabra may have taken it with him when he escaped from Allahabad."

Phil was ready to end the meeting. "We have been in contact with the other locations. They continue to question the cell members, as we are doing here also. They all report that the chemicals they captured are being neutralized and destroyed. I don't see a need to meet again by VTC. All that remains is to capture Chabra and see what he will tell us. I'll keep you all informed by email of anything significant. Or you'll hear it on the news."

Rishaan Chabra checked his watch. Two p.m., right on schedule. He had arrived at the Temple Meads train station a short time earlier and was getting a bite at Starbucks, his haunt of choice since leaving Allahabad. His bus to the Cheltenham Coach Station would leave in thirty minutes. While he waited, he contemplated his flight from India.

He had thought about calling Dasya, but his flight left Delhi too early. In Zagreb, he had paid cash for a train ticket to Ljubljana, Slovenia, where he converted his million rupees into ten thousand euros, using ten different currency kiosks to avoid being seen with so much money. He bought a European rail pass and slowly made his way west, sometimes sleeping on the train and sometimes finding a cheap hotel. The black cloud, which had started haunting him in Allahabad, accompanied him relentlessly and was accusing him mercilessly.

He ate a lot of meals at different Starbucks cafes, not because he liked the food or coffee but because they had free Internet. He frequently went to news sites, especially American ones, to learn the fate of Wilson's Bakery. Nothing was ever reported. In trying to find out about his team in Bakersfield, he had to endure many newscasts about the investigation into the shooting down of Air World Airlines flight 94, and an endless replaying of the interviews with the survivors. There had been no mention of Prisha, ever.

He spent the night of July 9 in a hotel in Vienna. In the morning, the BBC London News Desk announced the arrival, complete with fanfare and many well-wishers, of the woman from Bristol and her baby girl who had survived the plane crash. One of their own. The news clip showed them coming through the airport arrival gate with much cheering in the background.

As Rishaan changed the channel, an airline representative was presenting her with a bouquet of roses, with a clap on the back to her traveling companion. He found a German-speaking shopping channel and turned the volume up to overcome the lingering sounds of England in his ear. He wanted to throw up.

He continued, though, to find that woman on the Internet. To Rishaan, she had become the symbol of his failure. His failure to slow the advance of global warming, as well as his failure to fulfill his promise to the only one who had ever mattered to him. Prisha Bakshi. He was the one, and he had failed. There was only one way to make it right, and he would, for Prisha, when the opportunity came his way.

His determination took him in a new direction, Amsterdam, the city where anything goes. In Amsterdam, as he was googling her yet again, a radio station in Bristol posted a headline on their website announcing that Maggie Trillbey would be sharing her story in Cheltenham, the town where she had grown up, time and place to be announced soon. He had bookmarked that website.

The next day, July 16, he wandered around the not-so-well-traveled areas of the city until he found a firearms shop. He looked at the displays of pistols, and overheard a customer conversing with the shopkeeper.

"I'd like to buy that Glock 17," the customer said.

"Do you have a license?"

"Not yet. I didn't think I needed one until I actually wanted to shoot it."

"What do you know about firearms? I could get in trouble if I sold a gun to someone who didn't know what they were doing."

"My father taught me. I will be shooting with him at a range in Zwanenburg."

"Okay. If you can completely disassemble and reassemble this gun, I will sell it to you. You have ten minutes."

It took him only eight minutes, and the sale was made.

Rishaan pointed to the Ruger he was considering. "How much for that and fifty rounds of ammunition?"

The shopkeeper named a price that Rishaan decided was a little high.

"Thanks. If that's the best price I can find, I'll come back."

"If you come back, I'll give you the ammunition free."

Rishaan went back to his hotel, found a YouTube video of the "Field-stripping and Re-assembly of the Ruger 9mm Security 9", watched it fifteen times, and returned to the gun shop.

"Back, I see," the shopkeeper said. "Didn't find a better deal, did you?"

"No, not with the bullets thrown in."

"Do you know about pistol shooting?"

"I learned on a Glock 17, but I would like to try the Ruger."

The shopkeeper was still being careful. "What's the number one rule in firearms safety?"

"Don't point it at someone if you don't intend to shoot her."

It just slipped out; Rishaan didn't even realize he had said "her". But the shopkeeper guffawed loudly and put a box of fifty bullets and two empty magazines on the counter.

"It's different than the Glock in that it has a manual safety lever." The shopkeeper showed Rishaan how to disengage the safety, how to release the magazine, and how to push out the pin to start the disassembly process. The money changed hands, and Rishaan left the store with his purchases in a plain brown paper bag.

Back at the hotel, Rishaan watched another YouTube video on how to actually shoot the Ruger. He went out to the river after that, to shoot five rounds into a sandbank, just for practice.

The next morning, the radio station website announced that Maggie Trillbey's talk would start at 6:30 p.m. on the following day, July 18, at the Doubletree Hotel on the A435 Highway.

The pistol, two full magazines, and the other fifteen rounds were now in Rishaan's backpack. The bus was in the station and would leave in a few minutes. Rishaan got on the bus, and that same black cloud got on with him.

Maggie arrived at the Doubletree Hotel at 6 p.m., with her mother, Jenny, and Matt. Charlotte chose a seat at the end of the back row, so she could mind Jenny's stroller. Maggie found the host for the evening's meeting at the front of the room, fussing over the placement of chairs, cameras, sound equipment, and a large presentation monitor.

"Hullo," he said. "Take a look around and see if this will work for you. The radio station doesn't usually fret about cameras, but this is special tonight. I'll load your photos onto the monitor and show you how to use the remote."

Maggie was satisfied with the setup and handed him her memory stick. After she introduced Matt, she asked, "How do you plan to conduct the program?"

"Do you feel comfortable standing on this platform? If so, everyone should be able to see you. There are four hundred seats, so you'll need a lapel mic or else they won't hear you very well in the back. I'll have three chairs, one for me, one for you, and one for Matt. At half past the hour, I'll introduce you and you can begin. It was nice of you to indulge us all. Thank you."

"I appreciate the chair," Matt said, "but this is Maggie's show. After she introduces me and has me tell my brief part, I'll go to the back with her mom. I'll come back up when it's time for questions. I know it's really Maggie they came to see. This is her hometown and she's a hero to them all."

The room was beginning to fill up. "Yes, I can stand on the platform," Maggie said. "I may move around a bit. I'm a teacher, so I'm used to standing and talking. I'll call on Matt to bring Jenny forward when it's time to show her foot."

At half past six, the room had filled and the host began the program, introducing Maggie and dimming the lights slightly.

She started by introducing Matt and having him tell the audience what he had whispered to her shortly after they met on the plane, how God had promised he would show himself strong for her. After he left the platform, she started her story at the point where she had gotten on the plane in Chicago.

After about a half hour, she had gotten just past the part where the shark had thrown up Jenny, where Matt had explained that God had a plan to rescue mankind. Suddenly the side door flew open and a man wearing dark slacks and a worn light-colored Nehru jacket burst through. He ran to the front and stopped directly in front of Maggie.

She watched as the man pulled a large pistol out of his waistband. As he pointed it at her chest, her mind flashed back for a split second to the images she saw when Matt told her of Jesus being with her forever. The car on the icy bridge, as it careened off the guardrail, missing her completely; as it hit her, putting her in the hospital with broken bones and internal injuries; and as it pushed her over the guardrail into the waiting arms of heaven.

Her words to Lance Corporal Juan Wilson echoed in her mind, when she had described the images God showed her for him. "You may choose one," she had told him.

"Whichever!" her spirit responded to her Lord, who would be with her forever. Then, as his finger pressed the trigger, she was alone again with Matt on their little boat, when she looked up into his smiling face as he was saying, "Maggie, that was so much the right answer!"

JC Smalley was still in Washington, DC. Harper and Penny had gone back to Chicago. Phil Henry had wanted JC to stay close to FBI headquarters until there was some resolution about Rishaan Chabra's location and status. JC had found he lacked a significant job there, so he had invited Nicki to come and they had spent several days in the museums.

In the middle of the day on July 18, Phil had called him to a meeting at Bob McGee's CIA office, so Nicki had gone off shopping.

"Something isn't adding up," Bob said, "and when I mentioned it to Phil, he said the same thing. You're a fresh mind, so to speak, so you may see something we're missing."

"Bob, have you heard anything from Rudy?" JC asked.

"Yes. It's strange, in the same way that it was strange before. He was feeding me little bits, as if he weren't supposed to be telling me. But he doesn't go off on his own, and we both know that. I think it's just a ploy. On the fourteenth, he said he was going to give me an equation, which was 'Rishaan Chabra equals Nimit Malhotra.' I passed that to our man in New Delhi. Yesterday, Chuck called me back and said a Nimit Malhotra had flown from the Indira Gandhi Airport to Zagreb, Croatia, on the sixth, the day they got Singh and the day Chabra escaped Allahabad."

"Tell me about all these maps. Phil told me about the maps Jon Whitaker found in Bakersfield, but I understand you got similar maps from India and Italy. Did China send you anything?"

"Yes, they were so happy to get the info they gave us a copy of all their findings. We haven't gotten much translated, but they sent us maps. We translated anything having to do with them."

They spread out all the maps on a table, grouped by cell. The groups were similar; there was the main delivery route for the targeted cities, city maps of those and up to a half dozen additional cities, and a map of the garage location in the city where the warehouse was located, showing where an additional delivery truck was being stored.

"These cells had other similarities, too," Bob said. "A visit from Chabra in early March, somewhat lax document and phone security, and all seemed to spring up around the same time, about last December. We're getting some results back from the questioning, too. All the prisoners are isolated from each other. They all refused to talk about anything, but in every case, after five days, they started to talk. They started admitting their association with Chabra, especially when confronted with the documents."

JC didn't know much about interrogations. "Is that normal?"

"No, some are tougher than others and hold out longer. It's almost as if they're all following the same instructions."

"It seems obvious to me that Luka Stanković is involved," Phil said. "Has he disappeared too, or has his name come up?"

"Nothing positive about him. When Chuck called yesterday, he mentioned a strange phone call alleging Stanković was dead. They arrested Rushil Singh, but there is no body and no proof. They are trying to track this down. And his papers still haven't surfaced. Chabra was a chemical engineer. It's likely he and Stanković worked together on this upgrade to the chemicals."

"Let's go back to the maps," JC said. "Something is bothering me about them. I'm thinking out loud here. Why have a map to the spare vehicle? Why not simply park it in the warehouse parking lot? Or in the warehouse itself? Maybe they were trying to hide it from someone, and perhaps someone else was going to pick it up. But who?"

"Why would they do that, JC?" Phil asked.

"I don't know. Do any of the documents show Singh ever coming to visit? He's the right-hand man, so wouldn't you think he'd come here from time to time?"

"It doesn't appear he ever left India," Phil had said. "At least to come to California."

They all sat quietly for a few minutes, thinking.

JC was considering the two main players. A role reversal? Suddenly, he stood up and smacked his palm into his forehead. "DUH!"

"What?" the other two said at once.

"What if Singh were not the right-hand man?"

"Okay," Bob said. "Where are you going with this?"

"Suppose he was the mastermind behind Chabra. Suppose Singh works for the same entity Rudy works for. Suppose Singh doesn't care a whit about global warming. Suppose it was Chabra they were trying to hide the extra vehicle from. Suppose those maps are extra cities not known to Chabra that the extra vehicles, tanks, and chemical agent were going to visit.

"Suppose the Russians saw a fool wanting to end global warming by any means possible and sent Singh there to egg him on. Suppose Singh brought

Stanković with him. Suppose Stanković told his handlers about the agent binding with the pollution to become long-lasting."

"Of course!" Bob said. "They lost him, and the chemicals were bought anyway. Instead of just wiping out some cities in a few polluting countries, now Russia itself would be threatened. I see it now. All Rudy's communications with us have been to point us toward Chabra and away from them. The prisoners may have been told that if they gave up the information about Chabra, the true perpetrators might never come to light."

"For what purpose?" Phil asked.

"Ten major cities in the US. Ten major cities in China. Ten major cities in Europe," JC said. "The world in chaos except for one place. Russia. All their major opposition would be unable to stand against them, because they wouldn't really be sure what happened. Except now Russia is just as vulnerable as the rest of the world."

"So what do we do now?" Phil asked. "The threat has pretty well been neutralized this time, but they may try it again somewhere else."

"Not with that formula," JC said. "They know what would happen in their own country if they used it anywhere in the world. What I'm curious about, is why didn't they simply take out these cells themselves?"

"Because the plane was shot down, and then it surfaced," Bob said. "Once that happened, they had to let it play out. Otherwise, when we found out the details and the suppliers, those cells would be gone. They wouldn't have a Rishaan Chabra and global warming to point the finger at. I imagine they had a Plan B to take out the cells if we didn't figure it out in time."

Bob started writing a few notes. "The first step is to let them know we're onto them. I'm going to accuse them through Rudy. Based on his response, I'll then ask why we shouldn't tell the whole world. First, though, I need to get this to my boss for his okay."

Bob came back in five minutes. He looked at his watch. "It's about three. I got the okay from the boss. We worked out the language, and I contacted Rudy. I'll meet him in the usual spot in a few minutes."

Bob showed Phil and JC the note he was holding. It said, "We know what you're trying to do."

The man squeezed the trigger as hard as he could, but nothing happened. "I hate you!" he had shrieked, but in his fury, he had missed the step of moving the manual safety lever to the armed position. Trembling with rage, he attempted to flip the safety lever, but managed only to depress the button that released the magazine, which thumped softly onto the carpet floor.

By this time the onlookers were starting to recover from their temporary paralysis. An off-duty bobby realized there was still a live bullet in the chamber. He rushed forward. A man and a woman on the front row darted in front of Maggie to shield her. Maggie gently pushed them aside, and stood exposed to her attacker.

Suddenly, the man threw the gun down and fell to his knees, wailing loudly.

Three men near the front, realizing the danger was past, forced him to the floor, face down on the carpet. The man offered no resistance, but kept wailing mournfully, softer now. Several 9-9-9 calls went out simultaneously.

The bobby who had retrieved the gun and magazine came over to Maggie. "Are you all right?"

Maggie, shaken, nodded. "Do you know this man?" he asked her.

Maggie was breathing deeply, perhaps too deeply, as the bobby reached her. He grabbed her by the elbow to steady her until she could stand on her own. Then she relaxed.

"I need to sit down," she said. "No, I've not seen him before. I could tell by looking at him, though, that he saw something just now."

"I just got back from India where I was in security for the Diplomatic Corps. Do you know what he is saying?"

"No, but he does look Indian. I don't know any of the Indian languages. He seems to know English, though.

"Yes, he does. It is Hindi. He is basically saying, 'I'm sorry, Prisha.' Apologizing all different ways."

About that time the police arrived. The host of the meeting filled them in on what happened, and they pulled Rishaan to his feet and handcuffed him. They were about to drag him away, when Maggie rushed over and said, "No! Wait!"

The host said, "Inspector, this is Maggie Trillbey, the woman this man tried to shoot."

"Before you take him away," Maggie said, "I want to talk to him. Have him sit in that chair."

She got down on one knee, even with the man's face, which he had buried in his hands. "Look at me," she said. "What did you see?"

The man looked up and tried to point behind her, but the handcuffs restricted his arms. He burst into tears.

Bob was back quickly. "I gave him the message," he told Phil and JC. "He just played dumb. So I said, 'India, Serbia, United States, China.' He said, 'Yeah, so what?' I said, 'We can let this play out in the world, but there is no need to scare everybody, especially in your own country.' He knew exactly what I meant, about the pollution carrying the nerve agent to Russia, so he said, 'What do you want from us?' I told him we knew Rishaan Chabra wasn't the mastermind, even though he might think he is. I also told him we would never let this happen again. I told him we wanted some acknowledgement."

"Since we stopped it before anything happened," Phil said, "it would be really hard to tie them to anything. What did Rudy say?"

"He said he would think about it. Then right before I left, he told me they knew Stanković was dead even before he told me about him over three weeks ago."

Maggie waited, and the man's tears quickly subsided.

"I wanted to kill you," he said calmly, "but my gun wouldn't work. You were right there, and suddenly I saw the most beautiful human being I have ever seen in my life. Light was coming out of him. He looked to his side, and I saw Prisha holding his hand. She looked more beautiful than I ever saw her before. So pure. So innocent. So trusting as she looked at him. I heard her say, 'Jesus, can he come too?' He said 'Yes' and turned back to me." There were fresh tears at the remembrance. "He reached out his hand to me and beckoned. 'Come' he said."

Maggie looked at him straight in the eyes and asked, "Who was the man?"

"It was Jesus. I know it was. He looked at me with such longing, such acceptance, such … majesty. As soon as he said 'Come', I knew who he was, and what I had done."

Maggie looked around. Not a soul had moved except Matt, who had given Jenny to Charlotte. He had raced to the front and was now standing behind the man. She realized her lapel mic was still hot; the whole audience heard what was happening in the front. She stood up and motioned for everyone to sit, then knelt again by the man. She knew the whole evening was being recorded, and she wanted the audience to hear what the man said.

"What do you mean?" she asked. "Who are you? What did you do?"

"I am Rishaan Chabra. I am the one responsible for your airplane being shot down."

He shuddered at the sound of his own voice admitting to the deaths of almost three hundred people. There were gasps from the audience, but nobody said anything or moved.

The inspector turned to one of the constables and whispered, "He's the one they're looking for all over Europe. Call the station and have them call MI-5 and MI-6."

"As horrible as that was, there is more," Rishaan said. "It should have happened already, but it is waiting for me to give the signal."

Rishaan gave Maggie a good look. "You are looking at me the same as Jesus when I saw him. You are the one who called up the island with your friend. You ruined all my plans, and that's why I was going to kill you. But my plans were all wrong, I know that now. I just don't understand why you don't hate me. Jesus said 'Come', but now he's gone. I don't know what I should do."

"No, he's still here," she said. "You just can't see him right now." She turned to the inspector. "Can we have a few minutes before you take him away?"

The inspector nodded, so she said to Rishaan, "I will tell you what to do. It is what I did, and it was what Prisha did also."

She stood up and addressed the whole audience. "God is able to take the most rotten of circumstances and make good come out of them. This man will never be able to adequately pay for what he has done. We all know, deep within ourselves, that God's standards are so high that none of us can ever meet them. Whether you did what this man did or stole tuppence worth of gum, all are guilty in God's sight. None of us can ever pay the cost for our sinfulness. But God loves us so much that he decided to pay it himself."

From there, Maggie outlined God's plan, and at the end, hands went up all throughout the audience, including Rishaan's. As she did with the Marines, she explained their part in the transaction with God, then let them receive Jesus in their own words.

When the murmur of voices had died down, Maggie nodded to the inspector, who escorted Rishaan Chabra out of the building. One of the constables stayed to get the names of all those volunteering to be witnesses.

The host of the meeting agreed to secure the room for the following night, since it would be hard for everyone to continue after what had just happened.

"Please come back tomorrow," Maggie said to the crowd, "especially those who received Jesus tonight."

After the last volunteer witness had departed, the constable turned his attention to Maggie. "You will have to come to the station to press charges. It shouldn't take too long, since we got all the information we need from some of the people here tonight."

Maggie wasn't sure she wanted to press charges. She looked at Matt, who nodded. "I know your heart," he said. "You want to forgive him. It's right to forgive him, but it's also right to press the charges. If you don't press charges, he may go free and continue to menace society. If he has truly given himself to the Lord, he will know that he has to take what is coming to him."

"I was going to ask about that," the constable said. "Is it possible he made all that up because he knew he was about to be caught?"

"That might be true in some cases," Matt said, "but not in this case. I know he was telling the truth."

"How can you be so sure?" the constable asked.

"I saw Prisha, too."

Bob, Phil, and JC were still meeting at 5 p.m. when Bob's phone rang.

"Bob, this is Chuck. We just got word from Allahabad that Rushil Singh is dead in the prison."

"I'm putting you on speaker here. When did this happen?"

"Best they could tell, within the last half hour, about 2 a.m. here. They found him on the floor, unresponsive. No heartbeat, no visible wounds, no odd smells. They just took him in for an autopsy."

"Was he in isolation?"

"No, they didn't have that there. He didn't have a cellmate, though. There are people in and out all the time, even at two in the morning. They have to sign in and show identification, and they are checking those names."

"Who knew he was there? Anyone?"

"No one as far as we know. Turns out they didn't even have him listed with his real name, at our suggestion."

"Okay, thanks. Let us know what the autopsy finds." They hung up.

"The autopsy won't find anything," Bob said.

"It was Rudy, then," Phil said.

Just then a messenger came in and handed two notes to Bob. "Sir, we got these at the same time," he said.

"The first one's from Rudy," Bob said. "It says, 'Singh recruited all six team leaders.' "

"Six?" Phil said in alarm.

"No, can't be," JC said, "We know better than that. He's just admitting what we already know and trying to lead us on another wild goose chase. Bhatt was the fifth cell, and we would have known about a sixth. Not only that, Singh couldn't have recruited the team leaders. He was the man on the ground in Allahabad, with Chabra and Stankovic. What this tells me is that this is the end of the trail and they won't give us any more information. What's the other note?"

The messenger was still standing where he was when he first came in. Bob gave him a look, but the messenger didn't budge, so Bob read the note out loud, "Rishaan Chabra is in custody in Cheltenham, UK, for the attempted murder of Rachel Trillbey."

JC immediately said, "We need to go there. Quick! Before he ends up like Singh."

Bob turned to the courier, who said, "The plane will be ready in twenty. I heard the boss giving those orders at the same time he sent me here. I'll call the plane, and by the time you get there, there will be three overnight packs and six meals waiting for you."

JC sent Nicki a text from the police car bringing them to Dulles International Airport.

Bob McGee, Phil Henry, and JC Smalley arrived in England at three thirty Friday morning after a six-and-a-half-hour flight. The prisoner was being held at the jail in Cheltenham, and Phil's MI-6 contact, Frankie Ross, picked them up at the nearby Gloucestershire Airport. Bob already knew Frankie, and they introduced JC.

"We questioned him for about an hour," Frankie said as they drove to the jail. "He was most cooperative and admitted everything. Witnesses say he was filled with rage when he came barging into the hotel, but he's been like a lamb since the local police took him into custody."

"How is Ms. Trillbey?" Bob asked. "We both met her back in the States. Was she injured or killed?"

"No. He never got a shot off. They said she was quite a trooper. Shaken a bit, but wanted to finish speaking to the audience."

They reached the jail, which was heavily guarded, as Phil had requested in-flight. Rishaan Chabra was already in an interrogation room. As they observed him through the one-way window, they saw a man relaxed and quiet. "He's gotten about four hours sleep," Frankie said. "We wanted to see if his story changed after he had a chance to think about it, but so far it hasn't.

"My impression is he would respond well if the four or five of us, including my colleague from MI-5, sat and questioned him. If I'm wrong, we can change our tactics. The UK had some deaths on the plane, but it was your plane and mostly your citizens. We'll follow your lead, and we plan to question him more later."

The MI-5 agent elected to watch the proceedings from the observation window to avoid crowding the room. He would relay questions to Frankie via her earpiece.

Since this was international, it was CIA responsibility, and Bob was the lead for the Americans. He introduced his party of three.

"Rishaan Chabra, we are not here to question you about your actions yesterday evening. We are here to question you about the shooting down of Air World Airlines flight 94 and your plan to spread nerve gas in cities in India, China, eastern Europe, and the US. We know about Luka Stanković and Kevin Bhatt, and eighteen billion rupees."

"I will help you any way I can," Rishaan said. "I will tell you everything I know."

"Before we start asking the questions, I want to know why. Why are you so willing to tell us everything? You were working on this for a long time. Why the sudden change?"

"I tried to kill the woman, Maggie Trillbey. I wanted to kill the man, too, but mostly the woman. I hated them both, because they ruined my plans. I was going to wait until their meeting was over and I could escape afterwards, but something came over me, and I lost my mind. I tried to shoot her, but I forgot about the safety lever. Suddenly, I saw Jesus, and Prisha was at his side. He beckoned to me. 'Come' he said. As soon as he said that, I knew what I had done was very, very wrong."

"Who is Prisha?"

"I loved Prisha, and she loved me. But she died of cancer caused by the pollution. As she lay dying in the hospital, someone must have told her about Jesus and she gave her life to him. When I saw her right before she died, she tried to tell me, but all I heard her say was that she was one with God. She asked me to do something about all the pollution. So I spent my career trying."

"So Jesus said 'Come' and that's why you're cooperating?"

"I didn't know what to do until Ms. Trillbey explained God's plan to me and the whole audience."

"What was the plan?"

Rishaan's tears started to flow. Frankie listened to the voice in her earpiece, and said to Bob, "They recorded her entire talk. You can watch the whole thing."

"Yes, please get me a copy." Then to Rishaan, Bob said, "What happened next?"

"I saw Jesus again. He looked very stern. I wanted to hide, but there was nowhere to go. I was very ashamed. He said, 'There is a very high price to be paid for what you did.' In an instant of time, I saw every single one of the people I had killed. I could see what I deserved. It was hideous. Then he looked at me again, and his expression had changed to the one I saw the first time. He said, 'But I have paid it for you.' He lifted my face up, and I knew what I had to do. I'm doing it for him."

"Start at the very beginning and tell me about this nerve gas plan. Were you trying to avenge Prisha's death?"

"No. We were doing it to save the whole planet from global warming. We thought of it as sacrificing a few to save many."

"Who is 'we'?"

"My colleague Dasya Khatri and a scientist we met at a conference, Rushil Singh. We discussed it for months. India was so polluted, and the government couldn't do anything about it."

"Where did you get the nerve gas idea from?"

"A chemical engineer from Serbia, Stanković, who had moved to India, joined our group. He said there was an insecticide they had developed in Serbia. He thought he could convert it to a very lethal gas by getting it to join with another chemical, but he was having trouble with the joining. I helped him. We worked out the details, and found we could make it join by using certain ultraviolet light. Once it joined, it effervesced rapidly. The two parts were fairly inexpensive, and did not become lethal until joined together."

"How did you know it would work on people?"

"We tried it on small animals, then on large pigs. It was very quick. Later, we threw the animals in the Ganges. We wanted to do one more test, on humans."

"The Russian couple."

"Yes. Rushil volunteered to set it up. 'Foolproof', he said. But it didn't work. The couple never opened their luggage. What was supposed to happen was, when they are in their hotel room, they open the luggage and the device functions, and they succumb before they can notify anyone. The gas dissipates and neutralizes before the bodies are found."

"Who built the device that was going to kill the couple? It was fairly ingenious and wouldn't be noticed by an X-ray."

"I don't know anything about the device. I thought it would just be part of Rushil's arrangements. He said he would take care of it."

"Do you know how it got into their luggage? Weren't you afraid it would be noticed by the baggage security agents?"

"I don't know many of the details. I believe it was put in at their start point in Russia. Rushil said they tore the overseas tag so it would come off during handling, and when it got to London, they would think it was domestic baggage so it wouldn't be checked again."

"Is Stanković still in India?"

Rishaan briefly held his head in his hands, realizing how thoroughly he had plummeted from the noble he had considered himself. Then his courage returned, and with it a determination to own up to all his actions. "No, I killed him. He came to me and said there was a problem with the formula. I thought he was being a coward. He threatened to tell the team leaders, so I shot him and threw him in the Ganges, too, where we threw the pigs."

"All the team leaders, as well as the teams, are now in custody. What was the problem with the formula?"

"I didn't let him get that far. As far as I knew, the formula was perfect."

"Where in India were you doing all this?"

"Khushro Bagh Prayagraj. Everyone calls it Allahabad. We all lived there. Dasya, Rushil, Luka, and I."

"You and he must have written down the ingredients and processes for the final formula and any trials. Where are those?"

"Rushil started acting strange toward the end. I thought he might be planning to take over the project, as we called it. When I killed Luka, I took all his papers, added mine to his, and buried them all under my garbage receptacle. I didn't want Rushil to get them."

"We need to get them. What is your address there, and the others you named?"

Rishaan told them, and Bob stepped out for a moment while everyone else took a break. Phil said to JC, while they were outside the interrogation room, "He is being amazingly calm and precise about all these details. He doesn't seem proud of what he's done, but he isn't denying anything, either."

"Yes," JC said, "it's like he is saying the answers for someone else."

After his call to Chuck in New Delhi, Bob continued the questioning.

"I appreciate your cooperation," he said. "I guess you know things won't go well for you."

"I expect as much."

"We know the passenger plane had the booby-trapped suitcase aboard. Why did you shoot it down?"

"It was really Rushil's idea, but I'm the one who gave the order, and I grieve that I did that. Rushil had someone in Minnesota watching the couple, but when the luggage was put on the flight back to Russia, that lookout lost track of it. He called us and we panicked. We thought that if the device functioned after they landed, it would jeopardize the whole project. We should have known they couldn't trace the device to us, and our project would be well underway before they figured out what happened. We believed, too, that the plane would never be found once it sank in the Atlantic Ocean.

"We had gotten a Russian MiG by faking a training accident with the Indian Air Force, and we thought we could use MiGs to disperse the gas. So we got those steel tanks built and we ordered two for each MiG. Rushil had contacts who got us more MiGs because the Russians were changing models and they were looking to get rid of the old ones. When we found out the MiGs wouldn't work, we switched the project to delivery vans, but kept the MiGs at abandoned airfields in different parts of the world near our project sites."

"Where did the MiGs fly from, the ones that shot the plane down?"

"There's an unused airfield in Cuba called Nicaro Airfield. My good friend Pranay Kashyap and his associate Rohan Kapoor were MiG pilots. They flew them and helped design the tanks. When we found out about the luggage, I called Pranay. They calculated if they filled both tanks with fuel, and with the internal capacity, they should be able to reach the flight corridors between Chicago and London, and return safely. They started filling the tanks while we got our contact in Brazil to tap into online systems to find the flight information."

Phil wanted to reach across the table and strangle him immediately, but realized that that would be the end of the interrogation.

Bob asked Rishaan if the pilots were still there, and Rishaan recounted the conversations he had had with Maria at Nicaro Airfield. "So both pilots are dead," he said.

"Why did you send the planes to Brazil? What did you want with that?"

"We planned to run the project from Brazil, from a safe location near the Amazon. Rushil recruited Kevin Bhatt, an Indian citizen who lived in Brazil shipping all kinds of wood to markets in New York and other places. We paid him well, and had him build us an operations area we could use. We hired aviation mechanics and other people to keep that place active. Bhatt had a boat for shipping the wood, and he also did a lot of business in Cuba, agricultural products and such. He would visit Cuba to get a plane on his way back from the States.

"The Cubans wouldn't let the Americans into the country, and we wanted Bhatt to have some investment in our project. But he became careless, and thus a liability. I sent my cousin's son down there to take care of him."

"You might be interested to know Bhatt is still alive and Manan Ganguly is in jail there for attempted murder. You said you paid Bhatt well. We know about the eighteen billion rupees you got from Hem Laghari. How did that transfer take place? Why was it necessary to steal your own money and how did you do that?"

"We knew Mr. Laghari was very influential," Rishaan said. "We didn't know what would happen to us if he changed his mind. He was responsible for a lot of pollution, so this was basically extortion. If the money disappeared before we got it, then he couldn't come after us. Rushil told me Jackson, who worked for Bhatt in Brazil, had done this before, but on a smaller scale. She had logged in to both the bank in the US and the bank in India at the same time.

"Rushil was on the phone to Jackson when I had the appointment to transfer the money. He watched me through a window and when I scratched my head, he told Jackson and she swiped the money. The bank official couldn't believe what happened, and Laghari was furious. I acted bewildered, but he refused to give up any more money."

Bob consulted his notes, and noticed that Phil had added several questions. He glanced at Phil and nodded, then continued, "Bhatt had a computer expert besides Jackson working for him. Did they know the MiGs were to shoot down the plane?"

"Yes. There were two hackers and a translator, who was there only to help them with the locals. I doubt they would have told him their business. They sent me a coded message every day to let me know they were still functional."

"Where did you get the American thirty-millimeter ammunition?"

"We got a good price from a vendor. I don't remember who he was, but the information may be on my laptop. If you give me some paper, I'll write down all the passwords. One of the passwords opens a document I keep the rest of the passwords in. We got the ammunition drums from several Air Force training accidents of American A-10 fighters. They assembled them to the MiGs in Brazil as one of their tasks. All the ammunition was kept at Nicaro."

"You had teams ready to exterminate cities in China, India, Italy, Macedonia, Albania, and the US. Where did you get these teams from?"

"They all came to me based on online publications and speeches I had done. They all volunteered to help out on anything we needed to have done. They all told me how they hated all the pollution in their countries. I had Rushil look into their qualifications and ideologies. He didn't accept everyone, but only those who showed promise. One of the requirements was that they speak English. It made the meetings and other communications go much smoother. We also didn't have to deal with translators, whose loyalty and discretion can sometimes be suspect."

"Tell me about the name, International Bread Consortium."

"When we decided on delivery trucks for the dispensing of the gas, we wanted to have a theme that wouldn't raise any suspicions. All cities have bakeries, so we had our trucks painted to be bakery trucks. We had several meetings in public places, so we adopted the name so we could have our meetings on the marquee. That way, people not connected with us wouldn't be interested in coming."

"You relied on Rushil Singh for almost everything."

"He took care of a lot of the details I didn't have time for. He seemed to be a good assistant."

"Did you ever think he might have outside help in what he did?"

"No, not really. Now that I think about it, he must have had a contact in Russia for inserting the device in the luggage."

"What did he do for a living in Allahabad?"

"I'm not sure. He told me he worked for the university."

"Was there anything that ever gave you the impression he wasn't who he said he was?"

"Not until the last night before I left India. I found out he had falsified the application to the Federation of Indian Scientists, the group I was president of when I met him. Dasya didn't trust him, though, especially the last few weeks. I should have listened to him."

"One last question from me. What were you planning to do after you shot Maggie Trillbey and Matt Carven?"

"I was going to disappear. I got plenty of money from Hem Laghari that is completely untraceable. The account information is on my laptop, along with all the other accounts. I know I will probably disappear anyway, because of what I've done, but I am prepared to take what's coming to me."

Bob, Phil, and JC exited the interrogation room, leaving the British authorities to continue the questioning. "He doesn't have a clue about the Russians," Phil said.

Bob checked his phone. A half hour after he had called Chuck, he had gotten a reply text, "Khatri is ours." Shortly after that, he had gotten a second text from Chuck, "Papers are ours."

"Let's get a little sleep," Bob said, "and then invite Maggie Trillbey and Matt Carven for breakfast somewhere, and tell them what we can. Without their involvement, we'd all be dead. Not only that, if Chabra hadn't decided to kill them, we never would have caught him."

"What will happen to Rishaan Chabra?" Maggie asked over a splendid breakfast at the Doubletree.

The American intelligence agents had been telling Matt and Maggie what they could about the events of the past three weeks. "All indications are that he will be extradited back to India to stand trial," Bob said. "There was an Indian couple on the plane, and there will be other charges. I wish we could tell you both more, but rules are rules."

"You both have an amazing story!" JC said. "They told me on the flight over. I'm glad for you, and I'm glad for the whole world."

"Yes," Bob said, "they promised me a DVD of your meeting last night. I want to see what you said that turned that raging murderer into a calm and peaceful human being. He knows he's facing the death penalty in India, but isn't even fighting it."

"You should all come back tonight and hear the rest of our story," Maggie said.

"And I can tell you," Matt said, "that Maggie's story is just beginning."

"We'd like to," Phil said, nodding to Frankie Ross, who was waiting to take them to the airport, "but we're heading back. We're finished here, and there is a lot that's broken that still needs to be put back together. The world is waiting for us to tell them what happened. Please send us a DVD of tonight's program."

"I will," Maggie said.

"After tonight," Matt said after the others had left, "I'll be going back to Gary."

"I'm sad to see you go, but I know we'll see each other again. God told me I'm ready."

"Yes, you are. He told me that, too. He also said I haven't done the job yet."

"Do you know what it is?"

"No, Maggie. All I really know is that it's here in England somewhere. I think it may involve you. I hope so, and I don't think it involves Charlotte,

# JOSEPH V. WEBERS

but I might be wrong on both counts. Even though it may not involve you, I will never stop being your father! I hope I get to enjoy watching Jenny grow up."

The next morning, Charlotte drove them all back to Bristol. Matt had arranged a flight for the next day, and Maggie announced she and Jenny would accompany him to London to see him off. After lunch, she took them all to see her classroom at the primary school, as well as the childcare facility she passed every day on her way.

After Maggie fed Jenny and put her down for a nap, she and Matt went to Tinto Lounge to reminisce and start saying their good-byes.

"I've been thinking about the time when we first met on the plane," Matt said. "I had lost my whole family. It happened so fast I didn't have time to grieve properly between one tragedy and the next. But God showed himself strong for me, like he did for you."

"It seems like so long ago," she said. "So much has happened since then."

"I want to tell you something," Matt said.

"Oh, what's that?"

"I was a wreck, and you found me."

"No, Matt, it was God who brought me to you!"

"If God hadn't brought you, Maggie, I might have been miserable the rest of my life."

They were quiet for a moment. All over England, petunias were in full bloom. "Trade places with me," she said.

"Okay."

The swap was made. "I want to tell you something," Maggie said.

"Oh, what's that?"

"I was a wreck, and you found me."

330

## EPILOGUE

The Chicago airport was crowded, which was typical for the day after Christmas. When Maggie had called him, she sounded more bubbly than she had lately. "I found a man," she had said, "and I want you to meet him." The sparkle in her voice told him this wasn't just some random man. She was bringing him to her father for his approval and blessing.

The five months had passed quickly. They traded the journals they had agreed to write, and both were amazed at each other's feelings and recollections. After Matt had gotten home, shortly after Rishaan Chabra's arrest, they video-chatted almost daily, and as the months passed, their chats declined to weekly. Maggie almost always included Jenny in the chats. Matt was thrilled at her growth and development. She always recognized him, and lately, she would point at him and laugh when he first came on.

Lisa would not be visiting her parents, Harry and Gert Somerset, at Christmastime, so he had borrowed all the baby things he needed, and set them up in Rachel's room. The young man would get Todd's room. The weather in Gary during their three-day stay would not be conducive to outdoor activities, which was just fine with Matt.

The public address system announced their flight, and the passengers were coming through the exit doors. She had told him they would be flying coach, so he expected there would be a lot of travelers coming through before he saw her. Finally, there she was, pushing the stroller while her companion pulled two rolling carry-ons. He was a little shorter than Matt with a medium build, short dark hair, and a thin mustache. Is he the one, Lord? Matt opened his mouth to ask, but he heard the "Yes!" even before the words were formed on his lips.

They made their way to where Matt was waiting. Jenny saw him, pointed, and said, "Gumpa!" Matt gave them a hug and they kissed each other on the cheek.

Maggie was totally beaming. "Matt, I want you to meet Louis Moore, Jenny's dad. Lou, this is Matthew Carven."

His mouth dropped open in surprise. Laughing, she reached up and pushed his lower jaw closed.

They shook hands. Matt noticed Lou's confident grip. Jenny reached out for Matt, so he took her. He squeezed her and kissed her and made her giggle.

"Don't ask now," Maggie said. "We'll tell you on the way to Gary." They piled the carry-ons into the stroller, which Lou pushed on their way to baggage claim and to Matt's mini-van.

"I didn't tell you at first, because there was nothing much to tell. Later, I decided it would be fun to surprise you. We started seeing each other soon after you left," Maggie said, as soon as they left the airport traffic behind. "It was easy to be with him, and we have a lot in common. He adores Jenny, and she is comfortable with him."

"About a month after Jenny was born," Lou said, "I remembered about her and her foot. I didn't understand why, but I began to feel sick about how I had treated Maggie. About that time, a real longing developed, but it wasn't for Maggie or even Jenny. To make a long story short, it was God pulling on my heart. I had moved from London to Birmingham, and there was an older man at the construction management company I worked for, who told me about Jesus. When I gave myself to Jesus, all that longing was replaced by a peace I had never felt before."

"Maggie, how did your mom react when you told her about Lou?"

"Mum realized when they first met she was a kindred spirit with Lou. They got along great! When I finally told her, she didn't know what to say. The next time Lou came over, she hugged him and cried all over him."

All the way to Gary, they talked about how their relationship had blossomed. He lived about a half hour north of Cheltenham, so Maggie had spent most of the rest of the summer with her mum, who was very willing to watch Jenny while she and Lou spent time together. They talked about their jobs and careers. They prayed together and read the Bible together.

"Have you found groups of other followers of Jesus," Matt asked, "in Bristol and Birmingham?"

"Yes," Maggie said, "we have each found a church which has believers like us. In both cases, it is a smaller group within the church that really follows Jesus. I've told our story twice at mine and once at Lou's."

"Maggie told me about the baptism of the Holy Spirit," Lou said. "I had never heard of it, but she told me about her and your experiences, and we found it in a lot of places in the Bible, so I finally asked Jesus to baptize me, and he did."

They arrived at Matt's house, and after showers and supper, Maggie took Jenny upstairs to put her to bed. "Jenny's schedule is all messed up because of the six-hour time difference. We all slept some on the plane, so we should be okay for a little while. I think we'll get over the jet lag about the same day we go back."

While Maggie was feeding Jenny, Lou said to Matt, "I'd like to talk to you about your daughter."

"She told you all about that?"

"Yes, and I spent some time on the Internet finding out about American customs. I am asking your permission to ask her to marry me."

"You are both old enough so you don't have to ask."

"Yes, I know. We prayed about it together and we even fasted one day. I believe it honors you and her both. What she told me about you has given me the greatest respect for you, and we both want your blessing. I know I owe her this, being Jenny's father, but we look at this as your confirmation that we're not making a huge mistake."

"After Jesus, I love Maggie and Jenny more than anyone else in the whole world. Do you know what that means?"

"I believe so," Lou said. "I know I would be committing to her entire well-being, and Jenny too, above my own, whatever it takes. I just don't know what all that might be. She told me about your song. She didn't remember the words, but she said it's beautiful. I'd like to hear it one day."

"Tell me what you know of how the Lord will use Maggie to tell the world about him, and his plans for her and Jenny, and how you will support her in that."

"God blessed her with absolutely brilliant experiences while she was with you. She talks to groups at least weekly, many times to teens that have harmed themselves like she did. She helped a daughter of one of my coworkers. I know God will use her to bring many to himself. I will never have that kind of ministry, but I know it's my job to protect her in what she's doing."

"Do you know what it would mean to be her covering before God?"

"No, I never heard of that."

"It's not something you do, it's something you are. It's your position as head of the household. God made you strong to protect her—body, soul, and spirit. It is God's plan for a family. The mother and father each have a very important, but different, role. Picture holding a steel umbrella over a petunia plant during a hailstorm. You're that umbrella, protecting your family from all the attacks of the world and the devil. Without your covering, Maggie and Jenny would be very vulnerable. I'll teach you both more about it while you're here."

"Yes, I'd like that, and I know Maggie would, too."

"Maggie is utterly different than she was a year ago. Totally new."

"Yes, Matt, and so am I. The old me would not have the slightest desire or ability to care for her and love her like she needs and deserves, and Jenny too."

"Yes, you have my blessing," Matt said. "You both have my blessing. It would be such a pleasure and honor to sing my song again, and hopefully again sometime after that, if grandchildren come along."

"Thank you. You'll walk her down the aisle?"

"Yes, but only if she tells you yes! Her, and Jenny too. It will be a package deal. Are you ready?"

"Absolutely! If you don't mind, I'd like you to witness my proposing to her."

"It would be my delight."

After a few minutes, Maggie came down from the bedroom. "I'm sorry. I fell asleep after feeding Jenny. Did I miss anything?"

"We were just talking," Matt said. "We have time to worship our creator now, if you both would like."

They did. Matt started, and soon a beautiful three-fold harmony of praise and worship ascended to the throne on high.

The next morning, over breakfast, Maggie asked about Larry Williams. "You haven't told me much, which is fine with me," she said, "but I'm curious, and Lou knows very little."

Matt told Lou about the project, and updated Maggie on the latest. "The US Navy Seabees are in charge of the military part. They are getting help from the Brits, and they've already started working on a runway. Larry and I deal with them strictly through our lawyers. He is using the same lawyers as you and I. The conex arrangement was a stroke of genius. They said it could be flexible up to fifteen per year. The shipments will start in April, and he will ship materials to build a solar farm and houses, which will require a lot of drilling into the rock. Nodule collecting will come in the next phase.

"Larry has been there twice. The airlines let him accompany them on a ship they sent to retrieve the plane and cargo. It wasn't large enough, so they sent a bigger one. He brought samples back the first time and they told him about fifteen thousand dollars per ton. Based on that, he got some backers willing to invest in the boys."

"You're one of the backers, aren't you?" Maggie said.

"Yes, I had some money I could lend him. The company would pay it all back when they became self-sustaining. He's calling his company, 'The Found Boys', a play on Peter Pan's Lost Boys, and envisions it will eventually include young women. There will be an onsite foreman with his or her spouse, dorms set up for housing, and lots of hard work and many life skills learned. Folks would rotate off after some months or years.

"They would eventually run out of rocks to harvest and buildings to build, but there's a second source of work. He had the dirt covering tested along with the dried mud. When the two are mixed, it becomes very fertile. He sent me a picture of a piece of earthmoving equipment designed to mix the two layers while picking out the nodules. He is really excited.

"On the first trip, he brought a dune buggy and traveled all over the island. Weeds completely covered everywhere there was dirt, but they were all blooming. Toward the north end, there was a thick layer of the dirt all around the natural harbor, which I took the liberty of naming Rachel Bay, after my two daughters. I hope you don't mind." Matt looked at her fondly.

"Aww, that's sweet! How about the caverns?" Maggie asked.

"Remember the paper I had you sign?"

"About that treasure-seeking outfit? I didn't know what it was all about, but I signed it anyway. What was that?"

"They came to me in July when I first got back. They thought there might have been sunken ships, with or without treasure, that The Boy may have brought up with him. They had a submersible, so in return for searching for the caverns, you and I told them whatever they found on Emergent they could keep. I thought the caverns would most likely have been formed the same way the harbor was formed, by lava flowing away, so I told them the depths. I had them start looking in Rachel Bay. That's where they found all four, within a half-mile stretch of coastline. They never did find any treasure or a ship.

"When Larry went there the second time, he took several jars of petunia seeds, and scattered them everywhere. I'm hoping you'll go with me there on June 28 next year, the island's anniversary, and we'll see how they did. Anyway, they got the plane completely off the island, but I named that end Plane's End. I named the river, too, Abba River, after the Hebrew word for Daddy. All the names are similar. 'Emergent feature, nine letters.' They'll have three choices."

Maggie was counting on her fingers. "I'd like to name a feature."

"Sure, what?"

I'd like to name the mountain you can see from anywhere on the island, Matt's Peak. Four choices."

"Done!"

"And yes, I'd like to go there with you. That would be so cool."

"Larry said maybe the island can become a sanctuary for endangered animals after it was properly cultivated. Herbivores, of course. He is planning to have divers explore the caverns, and if they are like what we called for, he will invite medical types, botanical researchers, and the Institute for Creation Research to come and investigate their use. The Found Boys will also build gardens and parks, and he has other ideas, too."

"How about the post office?"

"That will be near Rachel Bay along with the rest of the center of activities. His plan is to move the GSM there and make it a combined museum and international post office. It turns out the harbor is very calm even when the ocean is rough. I told Larry he needs to teach the boys how to fish and boat and have fun."

"Speaking of international," Maggie said, "I guess you heard about the man who shot down our plane?"

"Rishaan Chabra? Yes, I read in the news that India executed him and some others for that."

"I wrote him and we traded letters several times. He told me what a changed man he became after giving himself to Jesus. So humble, and so acknowledging of his guilt. He told me he was not afraid of his upcoming execution. He said he was occupying his time by writing letters to every family he hurt, asking their forgiveness, and telling them about his new faith in Jesus Christ."

Breakfast was over. "The dishes can wait," Matt said. "I have a present for you."

Jenny had been crawling around and now wanted up on Gumpa's lap. He picked her up and got a box from the closet. "Merry Christmas!" he said.

In the box was a miniature pallet with three tiny coffins strapped to it, and a fourth coffin on top. Maggie undid the clasp, and all three coffins opened together. "It's a jewelry box! It's myrtle wood. It's beautiful! Look, the interior is pink velvet."

Matt brought out a second box. "For Jenny. An identical one. The top coffins open, too. Look inside Jenny's."

"The ring! Where did you get these?"

"The ring is just paste. I'll give you the real one to take back with you. Have it appraised and insured and put it in a safe place. The Hardwood Casket Company got our letters and invited me to see them in Oregon. I gave them pictures of us on the GSM that we got from Penny, and they agreed to make these. Turns out they already make the miniatures for promotional purposes. I met Steve S and Sue S there. They're a married couple. Nice folks."

"And I have something for you," Maggie said. "I've been carrying it around. I knew I'd see you again, and I wanted to give it to you in person."

She reached in her handbag and pulled out a slip of paper, on which was written:

"Fishing net? he asked. / God sent him for my dead soul. / Dragseine is the word."

Matt read it out loud and laughed. "Drag seine. The crossword answer! A haiku no less."

He looked at Maggie. Tears were forming in her eyes as she said, "The middle line is the most important part."

"Now it's my turn," Lou said.

Jenny, ever the wiggle-worm, had gotten off Matt's lap, so he picked her up again.

"Maggie, there's something I want to ask you," he said, reaching in his pocket and getting down on one knee. "Rachel Margaret Trillbey, love of my heart and delight of my soul, will you agree to be my wife? Will you marry me?"

"Yes! Yes, yes, yes!"

The discussion for the rest of the morning was about wedding plans. Matt told them, "You're both sure, right? If so, there's no reason to wait. Get married as soon as you can find a spot on Maggie's church's calendar. That's my advice!"

"Yes, let's do!" Maggie said, and Lou agreed.

"I'm calling Mum right now," she said, "then I'll call the church and find out how soon we can have it. Then Lou and I can pick a date."

Half an hour later, they settled on March 7. Maggie's mother and Lou's parents were ecstatic, and Charlotte's friend Alma agreed to help however she could.

The next evening, Matt held a reception at his house for his friends so they could congratulate the engaged couple. He saw Harry and Gert Somerset in an earnest conversation with Lou and Maggie, and the next morning, he found out what it was about. Their church service started out with them getting baptized.

"They told us they didn't have any opportunities at their own churches," Harry explained later.

The next two months were a whirlwind of activity. Details were worked out, dresses were bought, invitations were sent. Decorations, organist, flowers, photographer, wedding party, and reception were all arranged. The honeymoon was postponed until summer, when school would be out. There was only one snag.

"Charles' daughter is going to be the flower girl, and it turns out she's allergic to roses," Charlotte lamented. "I'll figure something out, though."

As Matt walked Maggie and Jenny down the aisle, he saw what Charlotte's solution was.

Petunias, of course.

Long be - fore the world started, God gave me to you. As our

God is your shel - ter, so I shall be too. I will

e're lift you up, your good al - ways my goal, and I'll

trea - sure your joy and your pain in my soul.

2. Long before the world started, God gave you to me,
You're a gift I shall cherish 'til eternity.
The delight of my soul, you have captured my heart,
And so nothing but death shall e'er cleave us apart.

God is my all in all, and he has chosen you, to show me his love.

God is your all in all, and he has chosen me, to show you his love.

3. Now we're partners for life as He made us to be,
And His Spirit will lead us in blest harmony.
In His kingdom we'll work to lead others to Him,
In His mercy and grace may we never grow dim!

4. When we stand before God at the end of all time,
We'll see Jesus our Lord in His beauty sublime.
We'll be glad that we're His and our union is too,
He'll say "Well done good servant" to me and to you.

God is my all in all,  and he has chosen you,  to show me his love.
God is your all in all,  and he has chosen  me, to show you his love.

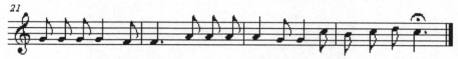

God is our all in  all,  and he has chosen us,  to show forth his love.

# ABOUT THE AUTHOR

Joseph V. Webers earned a BS in Physics from the University of Delaware, and an MS in Quality Systems Management from the National Graduate School. He retired from the US Army after serving over 40 years as a soldier and civilian, in the fields of weapons (including weapons of mass destruction), Explosive Ordnance Disposal, ammunition, and firing range safety.

In various positions during his career, he had the opportunity to make the flight to London's Heathrow Airport using several different carriers and flying from several different US airports. He regrets never having had the opportunity to fly on a Boeing 787 Dreamliner, however.

Joseph wrote this book while living in Williamsburg, VA, with his wife Betsy. He enjoys gardening, crosswords, and traveling to visit his children and grandchildren. He is a member of the Chesapeake Bay Writers, a chapter of the Virginia Writers Club.

# AFTERWARD

This is really a love story. For obvious reasons, I couldn't identify it as such, or else some readers might have been disappointed when it didn't turn out to be a romance. The love between Matt and Maggie spoke of a deeper and more fulfilling relationship than a mere romance could ever produce. However, that's not actually the love about which I attempted to write. In my incomplete and rough-edged way, I tried to present the love God has for his children: how he pursues us, draws us to himself, and showers us with his wonderfulness.

If you took the journey with Maggie, please let me know. I'd love to hear your story and help you take the next steps. Go to the *The Wreck Emerged* website and send me your comments from the Contact page at https://josephvwebers.com/contact, or you can get there with the following QR code:

If you've have finished *The Wreck Emerged* and want to join the conversation, express an opinion, share a story, or ask a question, the QR code on the next page points to https://josephvwebers.com/mmjblog. It is not linked at the home page since I didn't want to advertise it to those who haven't finished the book yet. There are just too many spoilers there! You'll need a password; it's "mrj131" without the quotation marks.

The mmjblog page is still in its infancy, a work in progress. There were some fairly heavy topics discussed in the story, like forgiveness and breaking vows you may have made which are holding you back somehow, and I may pursue these further. Maggie has expressed an interest in blogging about her experiences, especially if they are helpful to anyone going through what she went through. She will have to work that into her schedule filled with speaking engagements, teaching year fives, and raising a two-year-old. I think she and Lou may be getting ready to have another. I'd also like to discuss some technical details of things I mentioned, like the sand and dust storms and the underwater caverns. I'm not an expert, but I can point you to different sites to help your understanding.

Did you enjoy Matt's wedding song? If you'd like to use it, please get in touch with me through the contact link above. I have a special request.

Made in the USA
Monee, IL
05 September 2021

76429121R00208